To M[...],

A great guy,
especially for a
Yankee. Enjoy!

Very Truly,

Tudor

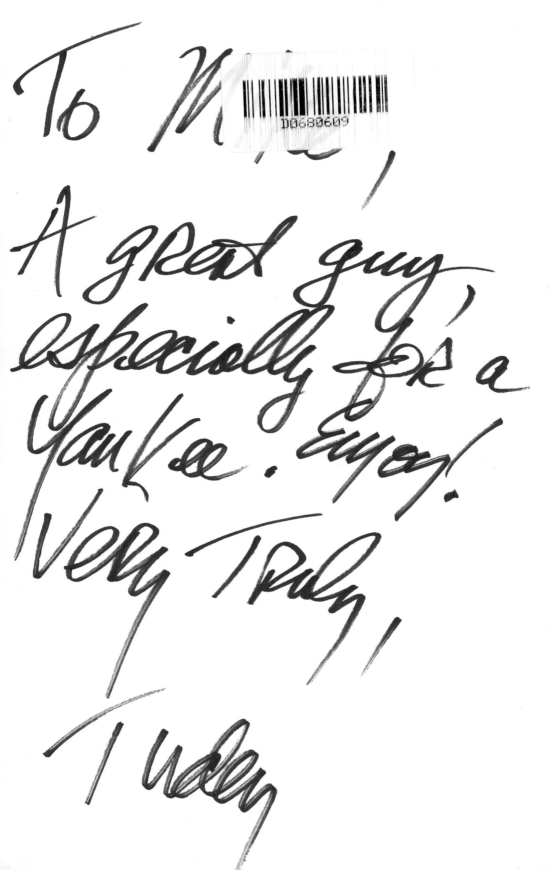

Very Truly, Tudey

An Austin Anthology

BY

WILLIAM "TUDEY" TETEN

To the memory of my parents,
Robert P. and Catherine N. Teten,
for encouraging me to take
the road less traveled,
and to my dearest Deborah,
who has made all the difference

Table of Contents

Acknowledgements

A writer is a mosaic of his experiences. Some of the tiles shine brightly, others are more subdued. What holds them together is often unseen and unappreciated by readers—the mortar. This is a list of people whose contributions to this book have been invaluable; they are my mortar. It is a privilege to bring them from the background.

My parents, Robert P. and Catherine N. Teten, for spending the last half of their lives trying to raise me the correct way. My patient brother, Paul Teten, who shoulders that burden in their absence.

Molly and Bart Stephens, the publisher of the *West Austin News,* for giving me unlimited newsprint to grow as a writer. Somewhere in America there is a denuded forest with Bart's name on it.

Martha Moore, artiste extraordinaire, who came up with the title and Peter Barbour for supplying the sub-title.

Curt Johnson and Melissa Jones who always answered the phone cheerfully and helped lift my spirits.

Dr. George Willeford, Jr., Bishop John McCarthy, and Patrick J. (Rick) Calhoun, very good writers who provided advice when it was solicited. Their unsolicited comments were even more beneficial.

Longtime friends John Burns, Jr., and Jack Gray, Jr. Writers are like boxers; sometimes we bruise and bleed more easily than we should. These "cut men" were always in my corner, ready to apply the salve. They also make me laugh, which is often the best liniment.

Nannie Mae Strong, for more than four decades of friendship and guidance.

My cousin Jim Scott, for allowing me to publish "Death of a Bluebonnet," with the hope it will help others.

TTBC (Tudey Teten Birthday Club)—Susan and Terry Parker, Kristen and Jimmy Holland, and Missy and Jeff "El Jefe" Gray for all those Friday nights at El Arroyo.

Dianne and Gene Schoch, lifelong friends to Deborah and fairy godparents to our children. Thankfully, some of the sprinkles from their pixie dust landed on me.

My publishing consultant, Kathleen Davis Niendorff, who knows writers. She made this seemingly daunting effort much easier with her patience and understanding. More importantly, she helped "peel the onion."

Jenna McEachern, my "Harper Lee." Like that author and the mortar, Jenna was content to remain in the background. Simply put, I could not have finished this book without her.

My children, Amy, William, and Laura. If this effort makes them proud of dear old dad, then this book will have been worth all the effort. They make me beam with pride every day; all three are much better persons than I was at their respective ages. Much of the goodness they carry around emanates from the same wellspring: their mother.

While playing Little League baseball in May 1964, I was occupying third base at Knebel Field and became distracted by a group of fifth grade girls walking up to the nearby concession stand. I asked the third baseman, "Who's the girl in the middle?" Every man remembers the first time his eyes rested on his future wife. That initial thrill of seeing her has not dissipated in 42 years; I relive it daily. Her physical attractiveness is surpassed only by her inner beauty, which radiates from her heart. She is the female counterpart to my father: the kindest, gentlest, and most decent woman I have ever known. Deborah has shared her wellspring of goodness with me for nearly four decades, and if the heartfelt stories in this book move you, she deserves much of credit. The words are not hers, only the goodness. Shine on brightly, dear.

KINDRED

The Original Tudey

The first day of every school year was the same. My teachers would say, "That is not a real name. In my classroom you will be called Bill." My retort, "But it's the masculine spelling of Tootie," didn't help my case. My conspiratorial classmates secretly kept the name alive, more out of defiance than affection for me. It was important to retain the nickname to honor my namesake and great-uncle, William Martin "Tudey" Thornton, who was as unique as his moniker.

At the beginning of the Civil War, John Thornton, educated at the University of Virginia, had returned to enlist with his brother William in the Texas 8th Cavalry, the legendary Terry's Texas Rangers. After the war, "The Colonel" was a correspondent for THE GALVESTON NEWS, and John eventually moved to Austin in 1875 to become the first full-time Capitol correspondent for the newspaper that later became THE DALLAS MORNING NEWS. He married Mary Martin in 1876, and they named one of their sons William, after Thornton's brother who had been killed in the war. The boarding house residents called the baby "Cutie," but his tongue or ears garbled the word and he responded with "Tudey." Fewer than a dozen of his friends ever called him by the name on his birth certificate.

In April of 1898, Col. Thornton passed away while Tudey was attending the University of Texas. One month later, Tudey left the Kappa Sigma fraternity house and replaced his father as the Capitol correspondent for THE DALLAS MORNING NEWS, a post he held for 51 years. He knew and was known by more southwestern politicians than any other man of his generation. His incredible memory and "undeviating integrity in the performance of his duties" (Nov. 2, 1949 editorial, AUSTIN AMERICAN-STATESMAN) allowed him unique access to certain events. One of his more famous moments was telling Texans that FDR would be the party's presidential nominee at the contentious 1932 Democratic National Convention. The Texas delegation was considered the pivotal vote in the nomination.

In the early 1920s, the circus would set up near what is now Auditorium Shores, and Thornton's pre-school-aged niece would blow the whistle under the Big Top to start the circus. Why? Tudey was tight with the circus clowns. Maybe it was because "convivial and animated Thornton was of slightly below medium height, of which he made personal jest. He loved small gatherings and lively conversation with politics, hunting and fishing as the main topics, as well as serious discussion" (DALLAS MORNING NEWS, Nov. 1, 1949). A person who spent his days around men that found humor at their constituents' expense, Tudey chose to spend some evenings around men whose sole job was to make their constituents laugh. The clowns and Tudey took their respective crafts seriously, but not themselves. This incongruous group would sit on stools outside the Big Top sipping lemonade and drinking beers and talking for hours, tossing out opinions and spinning stories as if their dialogue were flying trapeze artists.

Tudey died in 1949 at his apartment at the Normandie Arms, a hundred yards from the Statehouse. The following day the flag at the Capitol flew at half-staff and later a portrait was hung in the Senate chambers making him only the second reporter in Texas history so honored. Known as "The Senator from The Dallas News" he was "my ideal of a newspaper reporter. Tudey Thornton was as nearly 100 per cent accurate as a human could be," said Senator A.M. Aikin of Paris, who was still there 20 years later when I worked as an assistant sergeant-at-arms in the Senate. Governor Allan Shivers said, "Tudey Thornton contributed as much to good government in Texas, with his factual and fearless reporting, as any man I have ever known. His fatherly, if sometimes pointed advice, helped many a young legislator get his bearings at the Statehouse. I was one of them, and I will always be grateful for his help. He was a dear friend whose influence will always be felt."

At his funeral service many of Texas' most influential and powerful citizens were in attendance, including former Governor Dan Moody, who was a pallbearer. Seated in a row near the back of St. Mary's Cathedral was a group of men who went unrecognized by the rest of the congregation—devoid of their greasepaint, brightly-colored wigs, and rubber noses. They were not important men in Texas, but they had been important to the little man in a bow tie, who had felt the same way about them. The original Tudey was a rare and gentle man, one who could make a President laugh and whose passing caused clowns to cry.

Remembrance of Times Past

In the spring of 2002, I was supposed to write a Mother's Day story for the *West Austin News* but kept delaying the task, even though I knew what needed to be written and had mentally outlined the story. It was the one time putting off my mother turned out beneficial for everyone. In mid-December, we had celebrated my birthday at her home; she was visibly in pain, which was unusual for her, and later that night I wrote, "Changing Lives for Generations," an homage to Marywood, the home for unwed mothers, and her. It was published three weeks later, and I realized how serendipitous my procrastination had been. The day the article went to print we were in Dr. John Costanzi's office getting the bad news: Mother had terminal cancer. During the next few days she received numerous phone calls and cards from friends about the article, which were a source of comfort and support.

In February, she drove herself to the hair salon. Two days later she went into the hospital; it was Valentine's Day. The following weekend we took her home for the last time on a beautiful Saturday morning. On Monday her health and the weather took a turn for the worse. In the brief time we were absent she told her friend Nannie Mae Strong, "I want Paul and Tudey and my rosary . . . I'm ready to go." She had not given up: Catherine had led a long, productive life and was giving herself to God, so strong was her faith. This incredible strength and courage sustained the rest of us during the hours ahead. At the suggestion of the wonderful Hospice nurses, we contacted "retired" Bishop John McCarthy that night about summoning a priest. The sleet had begun in earnest with the roads becoming more treacherous by the minute; yet against our protestations he chose to traverse the steep hill of Balcones Drive and was soon at the door. In her bedroom lit only by a single lamp he administered the Last Sacrament and anointed her with Holy Water. Upon finishing Bishop McCarthy leaned over, kissed her forehead, and whispered, "Pray for us, Catherine." These two brave warriors, dearest friends to the end, had revealed to us so much about the sanctity and value of life and how bright our existence truly is when we are given the commitment of time by those we love.

Late that night at her bedside I felt blessed she was being granted The Perfect Death. In this world of sudden and shocking separations, violent endings, and lives stolen away all too soon, hers was a long, full, and rich journey. A voyage that came to a mercifully quick ending devoid of pain and blessed with the opportunity to say goodbye to her loved ones as they surrounded her bed.

While she slipped away, memories of our shared past came vividly to my mind. During spring break in 1993, she had joined us on a cruise. On one island stop she rented a car and driver, and we toured the island. When we got to a deserted beach the females went to a cluster of hut shops while William and I took in the beach scenery. Soon he was staring beyond me and his eyes widened. A portly, 70-year-old man walked by, his full mane of white hair offset by a tan so deep he appeared to have been dipped in bronze; he was buck-naked. William tried to warn the female cohort, but he was too late. A woman who had been trying on a full-body wrap had removed it directly in front of them, revealing her entire body. Standing next to her was my 6-year-old daughter Laura. Mom burst into laughter and later said, "I would love to be a fly on the wall in her class when the teacher asks, 'What did you do for spring break, Laura?'"

Our plan was to meet her for drinks before dinner, but during the first two days all of us were otherwise occupied aboard ship except William, who kept the commitment. After that we manufactured reasons for not joining them: it became their special time. Each evening at the cocktail hour my mother sat at a table in the bar with perfectly coiffed hair, dressed in an understated suit. Seated next to her was William with his pageboy haircut, wearing penny loafers, tan slacks, white shirt, clip-on tie, and blue blazer. She would have "a vodka and water with a twist" and William "a Roy Rogers with extra cherries, please." They would while away the hour content to be in each other's company and discuss the events of the day, along with whatever secret and perpetual confidences are shared between a 76-year-old woman and her 8-year-old grandson.

That made for a "Whooper Day," a term derived from my brother's duck lease, the Hasselmann's Bay Club. Hasselmann's is ostensibly a hunting camp but in fact is much more. A place for friends and family to gather for gourmet meals from scratch, fine wines, fellowship . . . and the occasional hunt. On Thanksgiving weekend in 2002, we joined friends and my brother Paul's family after the 20-minute boat ride. The formation of this modern-day Avalon began a long time ago when a windrow of oyster shell slowly acquired vegetation, eventually spreading into a five-acre island a pebble's toss from the western end of Matagorda Island. Paul had secreted an enormous antenna and small television aboard and the following morning we enjoyed A&M vs. Texas, Hasselmann's style. Under a magnificent blue sky and 70-degree weather we lounged around the enormous deck and cheered on the Horns. During the game thoughts came to mind of another day spent there at the confluence of the Espiritu Santo and San Antonio bays.

It was December 28, 2001, an afternoon of similar weather. William and I sat in the blind watching pink-tinted roseate spoonbills, white and brown pelicans, terns, gulls, and a dozen other species of shorebirds and waders. After an hour we put the guns at rest and stood to stretch. Turning around and peering through our camouflage we saw them: long, spindly legs not much wider than a spider's that led up to large, white-feathered wings tucked against substantial white trunks that narrowed to graceful swan-like necks flowing into black heads with notable red caps. Mates for life, there stood a pair of whooping cranes. Safely placed between them was their juvenile chick, with few of the distinctive light-brown splotchings of immature cranes. They were but 50 yards away. For 30 minutes we watched as they foraged for snakes and wild fruit amidst the elbowbush on the marshland until they were no longer visible. Experiencing this was special, but sharing this marvel with a loved one elevated it to that highest of all days—a Whooper Day—magical moments filled with wonderment that weave in and out of our lives forming a tapestry of support that, combined with our faith, helps sustain us through life's journey.

Around 10:30 that night, the teenagers grabbed their poles and tackle boxes and trudged off to fish. I joined the group and sat on the long wooden bench with Margaret Works and my niece Annie and watched the boys repeatedly cast into the thin "cut" that separated Hasselmann's from Matagorda Island. The temperature was 65 degrees with no wind as they waded back and forth in search of a bite, illuminated by a stand of lights onshore. The fishing was boring, and soon the girls departed. Within minutes the tiny black portable radio on the fish-cutting table announced a change in the evening.

The Texas football team—hopelessly behind Washington in the Holiday Bowl—began to mount a comeback. On cue, first one speckled trout and then another took the bait offered by William and his cousins, Bobby and John. With each successive hooked fish and Texas touchdown the boys yelled, rooting for each other and the Horns. In the distance, the tiny strand of multi-colored lights from Seadrift failed to lighten the cloudless, jet-black sky so that thousands of stars could be seen twinkling and winking approval. Beneath a moon two slivers shy of full, we listened as the Texas team completed their improbable comeback around midnight. The boys were laughing, teasing, and joking with each other while they cast. Bobby yelled to his brother, "John, buddy! You aren't going to keep that fish, are you? It's so tiny!" To which William defended, "It's bigger than any you've caught." And I wondered if they knew how fortunate they were to be immersed in an evening so perfect. Bidding goodnight to the culmination of that Whooper Day, I departed, leaving them free to discuss the events of the day, along with whatever secret and perpetual confidences are shared between two brothers and their cousin, alone underneath a brilliant moon with the fish biting and not a care in the world.

With our recent Thanksgiving visit winding down, Bill Seerden served his incredible gumbo for brunch and everyone waddled to the deck to enjoy another perfect day. I regretted not seeing the whoopers this trip, knowing that they are territorial and were probably somewhere close by. A few minutes later Virginia, my brother Paul's wife, was the first to spot them in flight, 200 yards away and closing. As they approached the complex of buildings they did not veer away but made straight for us, flying only a hundred feet above the water. Bright white, with wing spans over eight feet they glided gracefully above us, their distinctive black-tipped wings slowly moving up and down. Everyone stood and watched them pass overhead; the regulars said it was the first time whoopers had ever been observed this close to camp.

My eyes followed them until they melded into the horizon and disappeared. The symmetry of life and the glorious nature of serendipity moved me as I remembered it was November 30. Exactly four years before, nearly to the hour I had stood at the bedside of my mother-in-law, Polly Thorne, as my Deborah and her sisters Sally and Peggy sat on their mother's bed as she "slipped the surly bonds of earth."

Right now my mother is no doubt honoring the request of Bishop McCarthy: she is praying for each of us to make our time count and create our own Whooper Days—those magical and serendipitous moments that happen to us not in solitude but visit us only when we bestow upon our loved ones and friends the gift of our time. Such days serve a dual purpose: enriching our lives while we experience them and offering comfort and support to loved ones after our time here is past.

Old Rebel

I was 10 years old and needed a new bike. My parents said, "No," before I could explain. The silver fenders were scarred and dented from years of smashing objects intent on harming me; the rusty frame was unsafe and most of the weather-beaten red paint had chipped and fallen off long ago onto empty streets and forest trails; and the tires had been punctured so many times they displayed more patches than an Eagle Scout at a Jamboree.

Old Rebel, my once-trusty transportation, was old and dying the slow, painful death that no bike should have to endure. My brother agreed with me; he was 12 and had a more mature view of the world. "Listen up," he explained, one steamy June afternoon, "you got that bike from Santa, right?" "Yeah." "Well, Christmas is six months away. Which means, if you don't get a new one until you're 12, like I did, you have to keep that bike alive for another year and a half . . . or kill it."

I was stunned by this logic. Questions popped into my mind. Murder a bicycle? Would it hasten the arrival of my dream bike, the big black five-speed Schwinn with metal side baskets?

We staged the "accident" that afternoon. We were at Fort Clark, a converted old army post in West Texas 30 miles from Del Rio that had been turned into a rustic summer resort. It was famous for two things: the movie *The Alamo* was filmed nearby and Fort Clark Springs, which poured out millions of gallons of water a day, more than anyone but Noah had seen. This water was so clean you could bottle and sell it. It flowed into a huge pool about 40 yards wide and a hundred yards long in some spots, with all sorts of weird concrete angles. From there it flowed into Las Moras Creek, but most of the water went through some big pipes to who-knows-where.

One of those pipes was our target. My brother and I stood at the top of the hill. To our left, the road snaked down to the pool; to our right, a grassy stretch and steps down to the pool. Straight ahead, about 80 yards below us, was the pipe. It rested in a man-made ditch protected by a low concrete wall that rose about six inches above the grass on either side. The 200 or so parents and kids around the pool area couldn't see us very well; there were too many trees. I was the lookout. No cars coming or going, nobody on the steps to the pool. I gave him the signal and my brother sped off down the hill.

Now, the plan was for him to get going real fast, aim Old Rebel at that big pipe valve that stuck up in the air a few feet above the concrete wall and jump off at the last second. The bike would get smashed, and he would tell my parents that he lost control, that "It was an accident." As he sped down the hill I felt The Chill. I swirled around and my eyes locked with Mother's. Call it ESP, Mother's Intuition, or Bad Luck. She had picked that moment to drive down to the pool and check on us. I was a dead man.

But it was not too late to save my brother. I yelled at him to stop but he was Superman, a blur streaking down the hill so fast all he could hear was the wind rushing by his ears. He jumped off the bike and it hit the pipe right on the valve stem. Bullseye. Old Rebel didn't shatter into small bits of metal and spew upward toward the sky like I thought it would, but the water did. The bike lay in a heap of twisted death as that pipe started shooting up a million gallons of clear, clean water in a West Texas imitation of Old Faithful. The famous geyser stopped itself; the pipe didn't. The valve stem was broken off, and the people at the pool started yelling and screaming and carrying on so much you would have thought there was a surplus of fire, not water. The springs got capped for a few hours, the pool got drained, and my backside received attention until my eyes gushed like that pipe, but not in that order.

I also learned that crime does pay, if you are willing to walk everywhere for six months. I got the black bike for Christmas. But my parents knew the real punishment was not getting spanked or having to walk for months. It was getting that cold, sleek, but impersonal bike. Old Rebel had been my friend; this new, nameless bike was merely a mode of transportation. I asked my dad why that was and he said, "Because you are growing up." He could tell I was still puzzled. "Most bikes take you places where you want to go, but that bike took you where you needed to go. Places you had to explore for yourself."

That made sense in a way, as I looked back on my years with Old Rebel and all that I had experienced as he steered me safely through the streets of excitement and danger and carried me along the paths to happiness and sadness and all the learning posts in between. But I felt sorry for myself for growing up and guilty for destroying a bike that never meant me any harm.

Had I doomed my old bike to be tossed into a field of junk? Forever to rest beside the twisted, mangled remains of dead cars that rusted quietly amidst overgrown weeds? In a forlorn battleground where rats and snakes played a deadly game of hide and seek? Or, had some dad with magical fix-it powers seen the potential in Old Rebel and replaced his patchy tires, worked off the rust, straightened out and repainted his bent frame, and then smoothed out the fender dents?

Right now that man's son was riding atop the re-born Rebel, traveling down roads that only unfold before the imagination of a young boy on his bike. Before him lay the trails that could lead to special places, where the spirits of tough cowboys and brave Indians are forever replaying their famous battles. Where life-size G. I. Joes fight injustice and always win. Where passwords and secret clubs are created and to those elusive, mystical spots where rainbows end. A familiar noise enters my ears. It doesn't come from the tires charging down one of these roads, but from the heart of that two-wheeled chariot, filled again with its life-blood: the hopes and dreams of a little boy. The sound is Old Rebel's heart racing and singing with joy because he is once again transporting an eager passenger through a time and into a world that young boys briefly visit but never forget.

The Alamo

During filming of the 1960 movie near Brackettville, Texas, director/producer/actor John Wayne didn't socialize very much. He was too busy putting out fires literally—the production offices burned to the ground—and figuratively—budget overruns made it the most expensive cinematic endeavor ever, up to that time. Most of the other male cast members played fun-loving, partying, rowdy men who liked to drink. They made great efforts to remain "in character" when not on the set. Ma Crosby's in Cuidad Acuña and Moderno's in Piedras Negras were frequent haunts, but they were 30 and 60 miles away, respectively. When a group of weekend vacationers rolled into the rustic resort of Fort Clark, the cast smelled a party at House #20.

Two troubadours

The weekenders visited the set and invited the cast over. That night the actors turned out to be accomplished flirts, telling the hostesses they "looked like movie stars." The ladies realized the men had spent months in the hot sun without female companionship, exhibiting the same behavior as convicts on Devil's Island, but the women enjoyed the attention nevertheless. Laurence Harvey, who played Colonel Travis in the movie, was later mentioned as the biggest flirt of all. Leading the charge of revelers were Seagoville-native Chill Wills ("Beekeeper") and Ken Curtis ("Capt. Dickinson"). Wills had been the bass singer in a quartet before launching a successful solo career. Curtis had starred in a dozen singing cowboy movies before **The Alamo**. He was intelligent, unlike his later role on **Gunsmoke** as Festus Haggen, a man whose IQ made Gomer Pyle look like a Rhodes Scholar. Curtis' singing resume was stellar; he had replaced Francis Albert Sinatra in the Tommy Dorsey Band and later joined the Sons of the Pioneers. That night the two troubadours kept the party going until sunrise with the Pioneers' hits like "COOL WATER" and "TUMBLIN' TUMBLEWEEDS."

Early the next evening the hosts and hostesses were enjoying a well-deserved siesta when the sentry, Sue Stearns, heard a knock. She shuffled to the door in her robe and recoiled when she opened it. So did Richard Widmark when he saw her cold cream slathered face.

He stammered, "Uh, is there a party tonight?"

Sue shot back, "There is now!" before retreating inside to rally the troops. "Incoming!" How could any Texan refuse Jim Bowie a drink, or two?

Paladin, Paladin where do you roam?
Paladin, Paladin, far, far from home

Wayne as Sam Houston and Widmark as Crockett was the original billing until the studio demanded The Duke take the lead role and he cast Richard Boone as Sam Houston. The suave, debonair television star of **Paladin**, Boone was a house favorite, dropping by for parties and poker. At one meal he went on and on about the homemade mayonnaise, a recipe of McKinley Black, who had worked for my grandfather for 50 years. Like most things sinfully delicious, soon after ingesting it you could hear and feel little doors in your arteries slamming shut.

Six months later the phone rang at our home. Paladin was calling from his mother's condo in Miami Beach; she wanted the mayo recipe. The next day at school I was a star.

"Paladin called my house last night!"

"Why?"

"He's a friend of my parents." Not wanting to destroy my classmates' image of **Have Gun, Will Travel**, I left out the part about his wanting the mayonnaise recipe—that was the kind of guy I was.

When *The Alamo* opened in late 1960, I accompanied my brother Paul, Bobby Kinnan, and my cousin Jim Scott to the Paramount Theater. Arriving fashionably late, we had to sit near the top of the balcony. Youngsters who cheered the Mexican Army and booed the Alamo defenders surrounded us. As the on-screen battles escalated so did the action in the balcony. Pelted with popcorn, we returned the fire. Later salvos included milk duds and assorted candies, which we valiantly attempted to answer. My seven-year-old brain couldn't comprehend why Americans would cheer seeing Crockett, Bowie, and Travis die, but some Native Americans probably had the same reaction watching *Custer's Last Stand* or *Little Big Man*.

After John Wayne went "kablooey" and the final credits rolled, both sides were out of ammo and verbal taunts led to shoving matches. Unlike Paladin

I shot from the lip, "Oh, yeah? Well, Sam Houston asked my mother for her mayonnaise recipe!" We escaped in the ensuing confusion.

When I enjoy that pink-tinged concoction, my thoughts drift from the balcony and the make-believe movie heroes to the real defenders of the mission. And the words Marty Robbins sang in the "BALLAD OF THE ALAMO,"

And his eyes turn sort of misty and his heart begins to glow,
And he takes his hat off slowly to the men of Alamo.

My Father's Bed

My father was the only person who ever bet on a horse and won a bed. Robert and Catherine Teten were driving to New Orleans in the spring of 1946 when they stopped to browse for antiques in Opelousas, Louisiana. An early American four-poster bed captured their attention, until they saw the price tag. The two continued on to the Crescent City where they joined George and Van Meter Page and her father, Harry DeButt, the president of Southern Pacific Railroad, and traveled in his private train car to Louisville for the Kentucky Derby.

Feeling lucky

Seventeen horses were entered in the race, and the smart money was on Lord Boswell and Spy Song, not the King Ranch entry, Assault, a relative long shot. At the betting window Mr. Teten was feeling lucky, and with good reason. In 1936, he had been the lone graduate from the geology department at the University of Nebraska to find employment. Later, while working for Phillips in East Texas, he met Catherine Nash on a blind date and eventually married her. In 1944, he enlisted after giving up his draft deferment and survived the Battle of the Bulge. On a reconnoitering trip one night, his jeep was climbing a steep embankment when his sergeant whispered to Lt. Teten, "Stop!" Yards away, at the top of the berm were the gates of Munich. Quickly popping the vehicle into reverse, they returned to their bivouacked unit at dawn on April 29, 1945. A few hours later he walked through the gates of Dachau concentration camp alongside the "Band of Brothers." A week afterwards, above the STARS AND STRIPES newspaper banner headline "ETO WAR ENDS," he penned a note to his wife. "We are celebrating by drinking wine from Berchtesgaden. I got it in a wine cellar at Hitler's retreat. I am bringing home two bottles one day. I love you, Hubby."

Assault won the race by eight lengths. My grandfather, James P. Nash, and his friends Gus Wortham and George and Herman Brown had bet the favorites, and the war lieutenant drowned their sorrows with rounds of mint juleps. Betting $100 on a horse that paid $18.40 for a $2 bet can turn a pauper into a prince of a guy. Following the luxurious train ride back to New Orleans, my father treated the Pages and Mr. DeButt to a glorious meal at Antoine's before heading back to Houston.

They stopped in Opelousas and "Hubby" bought his bride that bed. A metaphor for her husband, the furniture was not ornate or showy. It was solid, dependable, and sturdy, just like the arms of her Nebraska farm boy.

Playtime and cuddling

My mother stitched an elaborate crewelwork skirt that stretched from the floor to the box springs and shielded the cavernous area beneath the bed, an inviting hiding spot for my brother Paul and me. On nightmarish nights we would silently steal into their room and climb into the bed grunting and slapping across the mattresses, announcing our arrival. We were soon comforted and allowed to remain overnight. They knew the bed would eventually help us overcome our fears, because it was really two twins that could be spread apart for changing sheets. After sleeping all night "in the crack" between them we awakened with sore spines. We had two choices: stop having nightmares or grow up to be Quasimodo look-alikes.

The posters at the foot of the bed were like firemen's poles to Paul and me. We would swing around them wildly before flinging ourselves through the air and crashing to the ground in paroxysms of pleasure. Other times we busied ourselves by loosening the finials. My father always reprimanded us softly and then set about undoing the damage created by the dynamic duo.

Saturdays were the best. No school, no plans, just a lazy early morning spent in that bed resting between two loving parents, talking about anything and everything. Or nothing at all.

The appearance of emptiness

After he died in 1991, my father's side of the bed remained empty, except for the occasional overnight stay by a grandchild. Mom could often be found reading in the bed; it was her place of refuge and solace. Sometimes Paul and I would visit her there, propping up pillows on Dad's side and resting beside her. Although the bed appeared half-empty, it was not. Bob Teten was not present, but his aura provided comfort and continuity, because the bed remained an open-air confessional after he passed away. It remained a place where grown men could still talk with their mom about anything and everything.

Final gifts

Every year my brother gives numerous gifts to our family at Christmas. Like Mom, he tries to improve our reading material and that year's author was William Faulkner. The selection he chose for me was *As I Lay Dying*, which transported me back to a day exactly 10 months before. Mom had been in the bed four days and was slipping from this life. As she lay dying, snippets from her life probably passed through her mind: thoughts of little boys swirling around bedposts; two toddlers crawling into her bed on dark, stormy nights and snuggling her on warm Saturday mornings. An intense lover of life, she also thought about the love of her life, a man who took a gamble on her affections and won her heart. Later, he took another audacious gamble that provided her with her final earthly resting place. Then she probably recalled the other note on that STARS AND STRIPES edition that read, "I wish with all my heart I was with you. Dream of me." And with her last breath no doubt she did, cradled in a four-poster bed that was solid, dependable, and sturdy, just like the arms of her Nebraska farm boy.

Death of a Bluebonnet

Part One

Telling a dying loved one goodbye is traumatic, yet brief. The hardest part is later and longer: the letting go. Some people get mired between the stages, unable or unwilling to accept reality. Others make it through on determination, faith, or both. Those things helped me bridge one such goodbye and the process of letting go. Faith was not always my strong suit, although I had an early start.

My career as an altar boy at St. Austin's Catholic Church was unremarkable; the greatest moment involved something I failed to do. At the age of 10 my body weighed about 60 pounds, including vestments. Lugging a 20-pound candelabrum up the altar steps before an Easter Vigil service nearly caused a hernia as I slung it onto the limestone table. Muttering, "Man, that thing is heavy," I retreated to the sacristy. A hidden microphone had broadcast my statement to the churchgoers. On the ride home Mom thanked me for not making "an inappropriate comment." That nearly blasphemous moment notwithstanding, the workload was a cinch. The main requirement was to look angelic while kneeling. In the old days, altar boys spent most of their time on bended knees, which prepared me for the drawback of living in a large, devout Catholic family: having to beg to sit at the grownups' table during holiday dinners.

Mom's parents had three daughters, who birthed ten grandchildren, nine of whom were born within a 10-year period, which is not unusual, because Catholics beget a lot. Every Thanksgiving, Christmas, and Easter Sunday the family gathered at the grandparents' home for lunch. The large dining room could not accommodate the whole clan, forcing some to sit in the adjoining breakfast room. In the early years, there was open seating, but that free-for-all led to the urchins' begging on bended knees to be included at the big table. Early on, I saw the handwriting on the wall and gave up, but a few cousins went down kneeling, which gave rise to place cards, ending the histrionics and banishing the youngsters to the breakfast room.

Eating in that small room wasn't bad. Flora Danica china filled the four built-in corner china cabinets and a chandelier hung above the Kittinger table.

Grandma noticed my acquiescence, and when she babysat me overnight I took my meals there. She always tried to sit with me while I ate dinner, even if she were going out that night. And she watched me gobble breakfast, regardless of her morning plans, because Grandma didn't want me to be alone. Eventually, inclusion at the big table became more egalitarian, and a respectable number of children rotated into the dining room. Yet, Grandma always told people the breakfast area was my favorite spot in the house, and she must have believed it—she bequeathed the Kittinger table and breakfast room chairs to me.

Once the dessert plates were taken into the kitchen, the five oldest boy cousins disappeared more quickly than the homemade biscuits. Hurriedly changing clothes, we reconvened in our grandparents' large yard and started the tackle football game. Thanksgiving tilts were the best, because the battle raged on for four straight days. Neighborhood kids filled out the rosters, and players came and went, but the intensity never wavered. The year I was in top form as an altar boy the Friday game shifted next door to my cousins' yard. Jim, the oldest, took the kickoff and juked past the defenders. Only my 60-pound stick figure stood between him and the goal line as his 140-pound frame lumbered toward me. Although he was only in eighth grade, Jim bulged muscles that later enabled him to bench press 400 pounds. "Oh, Lord," I thought, "Kneel down. Duck and cover." His thighs were easy targets—each was bigger around than my waist. Diving low, my arms tried to wrap them up, but one smashed my face, knocking me backward. My arms flailed trying to grab him but found only air. Everything went dark for a few seconds and, from a supine position, I heard a commotion. Both teams were yelling at Jim for steamrolling his little cousin. Stars danced in my eyes, then slowly receded, and I asked my brother, Paul, "Did he score?" Duh.

Jim helped me up, put his arm around me, apologized, and added, "I'll say this, you've got guts." So do pigs just before they are slaughtered. During the injury timeout, I promised myself the next time he charged me the outcome would be different.

In the drawing room of our grandparents' house, a large fireplace bisected the mirrored wall. Hundreds of expensive china figurines adorned the glass shelves. Jim's twin sister Anne looked like she stepped off one of those shelves and had magically come to life. Fully grown, she was barely five feet tall and weighed 90 pounds. Her skin was as pale as porcelain; her features resembled an exquisitely cast Capo di Monte figurine. Anne's saucer-like eyes would twinkle like Christmas lights when amused. Other times they were as demure as a Lladro statue.

By that Thanksgiving, the twins and their mother Mary had moved in with our grandparents, and I often stayed there when my parents were out of town. A few weeks before Jim laid me out on the football field, Anne and I walked the alley behind the house and down the steep hill to Pease Park. We went to the merry-go-round and began pushing it. I jumped on and knelt on the hard surface as my hands gripped one of the metal pipes. Anne continued to push faster, while I leaned back and looked up at the sky. As I became dizzy, the tall tree limbs looming down on us swirled together, forming darkness. The narrow circle of sunlight above me got smaller, like the f-stop on a 35-millimeter camera. "I think I'm gonna puke!" Frightened, Anne struggled to slow it down while it dragged her round and round. I jumped off, but my equilibrium knocked me backwards, and I landed in the dirt. Gasping for breath, she came and stood over me, surveying my condition. I started to chuckle and Anne feigned displeasure momentarily, then realized I had been joking and her laughter exceeded mine. Dusting myself off, I said, "Let's go to the swings."

Anne peered at me, "After that, I don't know . . ."

Pease Park's swings were 20 feet high, or so they seemed. Anne eyed me as our pendulum sways reached higher. At the height of a backswing motion, with my legs stretched out for the plummet, I yelled. "I can go higher than you!" She held back, allowing me to win, smiling all the while. On the upward swoosh, her long brown hair waved behind her like an angel in flight. After the sixth or seventh pass, my head was level with the top of the swing and she cautioned, "Don't go any higher." Not wanting to scare her, I held back and we continued floating through the air for another minute, before our feet dragged the ground and we returned to earth. "That was pretty risky," she scolded. While trekking up the tree-lined hill to the house, the topic of conversation changed as often as the shadows we walked through. Inane, idle chatter. Nothing memorable or substantive, unlike the day.

Months later, my parents went out of town, and I was farmed out to Grandma's. Anne did not have special plans, so we spent two agreeable days together. After that, she invited me for sleepovers about or four times a year. When she entered eleventh grade the visits increased.

Sometimes the cousin you bond with the most is not the obvious choice. Anne appreciated haute couture and dressing up; I wore horizontal-striped crewneck t-shirts. Anne enjoyed high brow art and reading the classics; I played sports and read Classics Comics, which were really, really abbreviated versions of her books with lots of color drawings. Anne was a 17-year-old girl interested in high school boys. I was 13 and attended an all-boys school; girls were barely a blip on my radar screen.

Late in the evenings, she would sit cross-legged on one twin bed facing me and chattering away, with her arms wrapped around a white-eyelet throw pillow. I would lie on the other bed with my arms behind my head, staring at the tall ceiling and listening. One night the topic was Dickens, Shelley, Keats, Yeats, Blake, and Tennyson. Another it was Monet, Gauguin, or some other guy painter I had barely heard of. Aware that the flood of knowledge just could not be absorbed by my non-sponge like brain, her lessons were mercifully short. After one artsy seminar, she led me into her walk-in closet. For a chap who went to an all-boys school and did not have a sister, it was an eye-opener. Dozens of shoes fastidiously lined the walls. Satin-covered hangers were draped with dresses arranged by color, as were the row of skirts and blouses. "You wear all of these?" I asked.

"Sure!"

She pointed to various garments and described the occasion where each should be worn. During the lecture, she eyeballed me to make sure my mind was not wandering. I smiled and nodded. The lecture resumed. It was like being in a movie starlet's lair. Then I was escorted to the make-up room, actually her bathroom. Hollywood lights rimmed a large mirror. Antique silver and glass sets on silver trays were interspersed with facial products, eyeliners, lipsticks, and other foreign-looking objects. Anne sat down and showed me the equally foreign concept of applying makeup and revealed how a dab here or a muted brushstroke there could attract and alter a boy's response to a girl who wished to be noticed. Those nights she unmasked the feminine mystique were instructional. More importantly, the many hours we spent together talking allowed me to observe her mind, one that was as bright as the noonday Caribbean sun.

Jim was staying with a friend one Saturday night in the spring, when Anne had a slumber party. Four of the most beautiful junior girls at Austin High greeted me when I walked into the sitting room that separated Anne's bedroom from her mother's. All of us were well-acquainted, and they quickly accepted a non-threatening boy into their midst. The record player blared tunes, and they sang along individually and as a group. Immersed in a surreal chick flick, I splashed around like a sparrow in a birdbath and let the scene wash over me.

Other diversions took place, until the arrival of the night's main event—sneaking out the car. Around 1 A.M., we tiptoed downstairs and out the kitchen door. Earlier in the evening, Anne had situated her car away from the six-vehicle carport that was just below our grandparents' bedroom. Fearful of waking them, she suggested the group push the car to the street before firing up the engine. I reminded her that when Granddad snored the decibel level was higher than the interior of a sawmill; we could take off in a helicopter and they would not hear us. My vote did not count. To our right, Enfield Road was 30 yards down the alleyway. Windsor Road was 80 yards away, in the other direction. She chose the longest distance between two points. I muttered, "Sheesh," and she climbed behind the wheel. When the three girls and I placed our hands on the trunk and pushed, the only noise on that warm night was the sound of tires crunching sand and gravel as we moved slowly down the alley.

From her position as jockey, Anne kept intoning us to push in a glorified whisper. By my estimation, 400 pounds of flesh were trying to move two tons of steel. Maybe a guy named Sven competing in the World's Strongest Man competition could do it alone, but our mostly feminine bunch was struggling. Anne barked, "Push harder!" My vital and semi-vital organs were nearing the tipping point, and I whispered loudly, "If I push any harder, my guts are gonna come out my butt!" My fellow strainers laughed, and the car rolled to a stop. Anne cracked the whip and 30 yards later we reached the street. I flicked the perspiration from my forehead with my index finger and climbed in.

The engine cranked up, Anne turned left, and we passed the house with the long stretch of lawn where Jim had flattened me. Fifty yards beyond that spot, she stopped the car. Anne looked at the girl in the passenger seat and said, "We have to go back." We had pushed the car farther than she had driven it. I yelled, "What? Are you crazy?" She was scared Aunt Mary would awaken and notice our absence. The other girls agreed. I voted for going to Nuevo Laredo or Cuidad Acuña. Once again, my vote did not count, but I did convince Anne to motor down the alley with her lights off. She cut the engine and again the only sound was crunching sand and gravel beneath the tires and the beating of our exercised hearts. Rolling her car back to its original spot ended the ordeal.

The girls went to Anne's room and I excused myself for the night. Dripping sweat, I took a languid shower in Jim's bathroom and tried to let the steamy hot water wash the disastrous experience from my memory. It proved futile. Lying in a guestroom bed, I stared at the ceiling with my hands cupped behind my head, and thought, "What a waste. What a terrible waste."

A month later I walked into our kitchen with an overnight bag, and my mother asked, "Where do you think you're going?"

"Anne invited me to spend the night."

"Come sit down, we need to talk." She stated that seventh grade boys should not have sleepovers with their 17-year-old female cousins. "It's not appropriate."

"But, Mom—"

"Mary agrees with me." The discussion was over. Again, my vote did not count.

Jim and Anne went to the University of Texas while I matriculated high school. The summer before my freshman year in college, our grandparents took the brood on a two-month vacation to Ireland. Jim remained in Austin, but the others filled the large home Granddad had rented in southeastern Ireland. Within days, Anne was smitten with our grandparents' chauffeur Barney, a short and stocky, mustachioed Irishman a few years older than she was. Why she was love struck was easy to see; he had the warmest and most engaging personality any of us had ever been around.

The estate served as home base for our many side trips. On those adventures, Barney would take the "older" cousins out for a night on the town. From Killorglen on the West Coast to Dublin on the East Coast, every bar we entered had a patron who hailed Barney. He was the most well-known non-political figure in the Republic of Ireland, although I suspected his popularity was attributable to something more than his engaging persona. The boy cousins took off for a week in London, affording Barney and Anne more time to explore the possibility of a lasting relationship. Upon our return, her smile was brighter, and she glided across the room, buoyed by "the Spirits of might and pleasure."

Days afterward, Barney took a few boys to a barren hillside dotted with a small wooden shed. Working the combination lock, he popped it off and opened the door, revealing a cache of explosives. Grabbing a handful, he walked some distance, deposited them on the ground and backtracked to us. Then he set off the blasting caps in succession. Birds scattered from faraway trees as the explosions blew clumps of grass and dirt into the sky. That was Barney's way of letting us know why he was so beloved across the country— he was a regional leader of the Irish Republican Army, the IRA. Perhaps Anne already knew of his nefarious affiliation, but we never quizzed her about it. One night at the Dunloe Castle Hotel in Killarney, a few of us sat in the establishment's large foyer with them. Barney pulled out a bottle of clear liquid and passed it around. The concoction forced a flame-like heat down my throat that coursed through my stomach and legs causing my toes to curl involuntarily. "Whoa, what is that?" I asked.

In his Irish brogue, Barney smiled, "Poteen. In America you call it moonshine."

"Am I going to go blind?"

Laughing like a large leprechaun, he stated, "No, but if you drink too much you won't see straight for quite some time." His IRA compatriots manufactured the firewater in hidden forest stills and gave away most of it to widows, who then sold the bottles to supplement their meager incomes. According to Barney, we were lucky to be able to partake, so we toasted our good fortune a while longer.

The couple corresponded for a year after we left Ireland, until a note written in someone else's hand arrived. It explained that Barney had injured his right hand in an "accident" and would not be capable of corresponding for a while. Later, we heard a rumor that he had been incarcerated. Anne never heard from him again.

Amidst the terrorist intrigue and family hubbub, Anne thrived at the estate, possibly because it evoked the same pastoral qualities as the ranch 15 miles from Austin that Granddad had bought the year I was born. Turning off that farm-to-market road, a visitor was greeted by an open, football-length field leading to a large bur oak tree that obscured the red-roofed, two-story white farmhouse built in the late 1890s. A three-board whitewashed fence surrounded the yard. Granddad had added a large family room on the back of the house that led into the old-time kitchen. Beyond that was a small pump house he converted into a dollhouse for Anne and the other grand-daughters; it was the perfect place for young girls to hone their imaginations and practice make-believe. Just over the fence from the dollhouse was a decrepit, freestanding garage held up by whitewash paint. A sand and gravel area measuring about 30 yards square separated the garage from the tractor and feed barn that was connected to a corral. South of that was a big, tin-covered hay barn the kids played in despite the parents' admonition, "There are rats and snakes in there!" Below the main house was an open field that led down to a five-acre stock tank and the grove of trees beyond it.

Dysertmore, our rented Irish estate, was also the setting for a movie, Maeve Binchy's *Circle of Friends*. The long gravel road led to an ivy-covered, two-story Georgian home. The outbuildings were hidden behind the massive structure, except for the smoke house where the young butler Jimmy cured the salmon under the watchful eye of the owner. To the right of the house a long open field led down to the Nor River where the fish were harvested. Across the water was a mountain filled with trees; an Irish National Forest enveloped Dysertmore.

Anne had skipped a rather boisterous Barney pub-crawl one evening, and when the troops dragged in around midnight they headed for the pillows. I walked into the library and found Anne curled up on an overstuffed chair, reading by soft lamplight. The paneled study was what one would expect of an Irish gentleman: cozy, full of bric-a-brac laid out in an orderly manner, a comfortable couch, and a spotless desk. Tattered spines of early edition books filled the built-in shelves that rimmed the room, which smelled of linseed oil. Peat crackled in the fireplace, warding off the chilly summer night air.

I perused the stacks of books quietly, selected one and sat down in a chair that shared the reading light. Thirty minutes later Anne stood and told me, "Goodnight." I responded, "Thank you." Perplexed, she asked, "For what?" My arm made a sweeping motion around the room. "For all of this." She smiled, understanding what I meant, and left the room. Those nights in her pink bedroom when she ushered me into the world of British and Irish authors and Impressionist painters had not been in vain. My love of reading and appreciation of art were the byproducts of her incessant teachings. Sitting in the Major's study, staring at the works of those timeless masters, showed me how far I had come. And my cousin knew it.

Resting on an ottoman was the new Rod Stewart album I had bought in London the day it was released a few weeks earlier. Removing the vinyl from its cardboard sheath, I placed it on the stereo, and Rod belted out lyrics from the title cut, "I couldn't quote you no Dickens, Shelley, or Keats," and I grinned. Along with other writers, they had formed the foundation of Anne's lectures. At that moment I was reading Percy Shelley's *Prometheus Unbound*, Act IV:

> *Let the Hours, and the Spirits of might and pleasure*
> *Like the clouds and sunbeams, unite—*

When it was published, Shelley stated, "My friends say my *Prometheus* is too wild, ideal, and perplexed with imagery." That was an apt definition of Anne. Being courted by a ranking IRA official was wild and she was idealistic to a fault. The perplexing imagery would not show itself for decades.

Before she bade me goodnight, I had re-shown Anne my prized purchase from our four-day sojourn to Paris. Rod continued singing as I unfurled it again and studied the print from the gift shop of the Musée du Jeu de Paume, Claude Monet's "Coquelicots `a Argenteuil," or "Poppy Fields at Argenteuil." A woman carrying a parasol is escorting her son in a field of red poppies. Behind her, almost undetectable is a similarly dressed woman with her child. Nestled amongst trees in the background is a multi-story white farmhouse with a red roof. Rod sang the last verses of the title song,

> *Every picture tells a story, don't it?*
> *Every picture tells a story, don't it?*

A week after we returned from Ireland, students migrated to the University of Texas for fall classes, and Deborah, my girlfriend, and I went through "rush." Fraternity rush was very straightforward; males bonded through mass quantities of beer. Sororities were more civil, ladylike, and cutthroat. Having already pledged, I was loitering around the Kappa Sigma house late one night when the summons came, and I entered the non-existent housemother's suite of rooms. Paul, Jim, and his friend Jeff were there. All three shared a bond outside the fraternity; they were members of the Silver Spurs, the organization charged with the care and maintenance of the Longhorn's bovine mascot,

Bevo. Anne was in attendance, along with her sorority sister, Sally, whose father had been a Spur.

Third period of rush for the girls had just ended, and the next morning Deborah would have to list her choice of sororities in descending order. Usually, the first Greek name on the "pref" list prevailed. Anne and Sally had befriended her over the past year when we attended fraternity parties, and they wanted to know which way she was leaning. I said, "She doesn't know if you really want her." Jim stirred the pot by suggesting his twin sister, "Call her." Anne bit her lower lip and assessed the situation. Acting on his suggestion was way beyond the Panhellenic rules and code of conduct. Doing nothing might allow Deborah to slip away. Anne looked at me. "Call her." My index finger fumbled with the small orbs of the old, black rotary phone. A familiar voice answered, and I said, "Some people want to talk to you." The Spurs nodded and smiled while the two ladies broke the cardinal rule of rush having no communication with rushees during "silence period." Jim grinned.

Eleven months afterwards, in July of 1972, most of us were together at Lake Travis. We floated on the small raft anchored in a cove and sunbathed. Anne and Sally chatted with their sorority sister Deborah. Eventually, things got quiet and I snapped candid photos of the girls. Unfamiliar with the f-stop function of the old Yashica camera, I was disappointed when the roll was developed. Most of the pictures were over or underexposed, with one exception, a snapshot of Anne. I proudly showed it to my brother, an accomplished photographer. "That was a fluke." He was right. It had an ethereal quality usually captured with the aid of a soft lens, which I did not own. Mary told me it was her favorite picture of her daughter, and she slipped it beneath the glass top of her bedroom desk where she often sat. That was my greatest moment in photography: the lighting, composition, and color. Only later did I understand how important that moment really was.

The college group gathered for a wedding in Waco, Texas, on May 5, 1985. During the backyard reception, musicians played a song by the funk group, The Gap Band, while guests danced on the large rock patio. Behind the revelers was a forest that sloped down the hillside. One morning a few years earlier, the bride's mother had gone into those woods searching for her son. She found him lying on the ground, dead from a self-inflicted gunshot. I gazed at the grove of trees where my childhood friend had died tragically and then focused on the dance floor. Anne and her friends were standing shoulder to shoulder, swaying to the music and singing along with the band. Her smile broadened and her eyes twinkled as ours met and she sang,

You dropped me to my knees,
You dropped a bomb on me.

It landed on September 10, 1990.

Part Two

An eastward moving September shower passed through Austin before the morning rush hour, dampening the Mopac Expressway. Around 8:30 A.M., my car passed beneath the 35th Street overpass and a thought invaded my mind, "Something bad has happened at the ranch." The feeling was like that Pepto-Bismol commercial where the pink liquid enters the head of an outlined figure and coats his body, but this time it was a sense of dread that coursed downward from my head and settled in my stomach.

Dad was sitting in his office when I arrived and proclaimed, "I'm going to the ranch at noon."

"Weren't you just there yesterday?"

"Yes, but I still need to go."

"Why?"

"There is something wrong at the ranch."

He pressed further, "Like what?"

I paused and said, "I don't know." Nevertheless, I stayed put.

Dad answered the phone an hour later and called out, "Tudey, Ed's on the phone. He needs to talk to you." My hand hovered above the telephone, and I stared at it for a few moments. Taking a deep breath, I grabbed the receiver and said, "Hello, Ed." His normally deep voice was laced with incredulity.

"Anne's here at the ranch." He paused briefly and my shoulders slumped, because I knew what was coming. "Tudey . . . she shot herself."

Anne's small blue car was parked against the ranch's entrance gate that opened outward. She had lost her key, which forced the 80-year-old man to climb over the aluminum gate twice. Sitting in his truck behind her vehicle, Ed looked exhausted and bewildered. I put my hand on his shoulder and asked, "Are you okay?" He gazed at the ranch house and nodded. "Ed, I'm so sorry you had to be the one to find her." He shrugged, unable to speak. "Where is she?"

Without looking at me, he responded, "Behind the garage." Removing my hand from his shoulder, I started walking away. "Tudey?" I turned around. "Yes?"

Ed's mournful expression was magnified by wrinkles that lined his face with deep rivulets. "I . . . I can't go back in. I hope you understand."

"It's alright, Ed, you've done enough."

After scaling the gate, I sprinted down the road and the day at Pease Park came back to me as the air rushed past my face, pushing back my hair. A hundred yards later I stopped, bent over, and began panting. The garage was still 30 yards away. Frightened of what was beyond the building, I refused to walk directly to it; my feet embarked on a wide path to the right of the structure. My left leg crossed over the right one following the arcing path. I repeated the motion for six slow, tentative steps, and a portion of the backside of the garage came into view. Nothing. Maybe Ed was wrong, but that was illogical: I had seen Anne's car. Denial.

Two more side steps later, a small, dark-haired head became visible. I froze and started panting again. Two more side steps brought the recognizable body into view. She looked like one of Grandma's figurines that had fallen from its shelf and crashed to the ground. A groan escaped my lips, "Oh, Anne." Tears poured down my face. I wiped them off with my right index finger and shut my eyes tightly to stanch the flow. My resolve waned, and a negative thought crept into my mind, "I can't do this." Glancing back at Ed, I thought of another old person, my grandmother, and what she would want me to do. "You never got the opportunity to sit at the grownups' table. Prove you belong there." The wind was becalmed. No birds chirping or fluttering in the sky. Bullfrogs in the stock tank were mute, as were the motionless cattle in the fields. Only my shoes crunching the sand and gravel pierced the silence, as I walked toward her.

Approaching from the side, I stopped a yard from Anne's body. She lay on her back, wearing a long-sleeved black sweater, an ankle-length black skirt with multi-colored paisley designs, black socks, and black shoes. Both arms rested at her side, palms up. With her saucer-like eyes closed and her head tilted to the left, she resembled Sleeping Beauty, except for her right hand, which still clutched the .357 magnum pistol.

Anger replaced denial and I started shaking, enraged that she had done this to herself and her family. "Dammit, Anne!" Seconds after those words were spoken, I regretted the outburst, dropped to my knees, and became an altar boy again. With my eyes closed and my hands clasped together, I began to pray. "Our Father, who art in heaven . . . ." The first prayer asked God to forgive Anne. The second "Our Father" begged forgiveness for my inappropriate comment. Opening my eyes and staring at Anne, I recited a third prayer, which was appropriate. "Hail, Mary, full of grace, the Lord is with thee. Blessed art thou amongst women, and blessed is the fruit of thy womb Jesus. Holy Mary, mother of God, pray for us sinners, now and at the hour of our death. Amen."

Ending it with the Sign of the Cross, I rose and looked around. An empty cigar box used to transport the weapon was near her feet; two yards from that the earth was in motion. Jumping the backyard fence, I ran into the kitchen, grabbed the tall aerosol canister of insecticide and went to that mound. Dozens of giant red ants were pouring out of the hole. Hurriedly shaking the can, I soaked the area around the anthill and kicked at the hole, enticing more angry ones from beneath the soil. My right index finger held the nozzle down so long it started cramping, but I kept spraying, long after the last ant that ventured out was dead until finally the canister sputtered and gave out. The ground glistened, reflecting the fluid, while the sick-sweet smell of insecticide floated in the air.

Not wanting to disturb the "crime scene" for the police, I walked back and erased the depression my knees had made by smoothing the ground with my shoe. Taking four steps to my left put me directly behind Anne's head, a yard away. Something seemed amiss in her long, wavy dark hair. A flashback floated through my mind of Anne breaking a rule that night at the fraternity house. She had not called my future wife in the spirit of sorority competition; Anne had done it because she loved Deborah. Remembering that, my eyes furtively surveyed the surroundings to make sure no one was watching. And I broke a rule, out of love for Anne. I bent down on one knee, leaned over and stretched a hand out to the top of her head. My right index finger brushed the silky, wavy locks back and forth until the part was repaired. Leaning back, I stood and ambled into the house.

On the entry hall table was the old, black rotary phone I used to call 9-1-1 before rejoining Ed. He was sitting on his front bumper when I jumped the fence. His long-sleeved light blue denim shirt was soaked with perspiration, his white work pants partially hidden by massive hands that clutched his knees.

Leaning forward, he continued to stare at the ground as I approached. A sweat-stained, straw cowboy hat shielded his eyes from the sun and the garage. Placing my hand on his shoulder, I again asked, "Are you okay?" The hat rose slowly, revealing his face. Eighty years of sunlight had deposited a leathery layer of skin pocked with sunspots, wrinkles, and tiny scars. He had the look of a beaten man. An hour or two spent thinking about Anne's death had pummeled him into submission.

Still incredulous, he gazed up and asked, "Tudey, why did she do it?" He hoped for a plausible explanation, which never came.

"I don't know, Ed. I don't know."

Her car keys were under the driver's seat. I opened the gate and moved her small sedan into the barn's carport while Ed parked his truck on the grass just inside the fence. With no more duties to perform, I went back and sat down next to Anne. In the quiet, my eyes wandered, searching for what her eyes must have focused on just before she died. It was on the other side of the fence, 20 yards away: the small wooden dollhouse with the red roof. A sanctuary of refuge she had escaped to as a child when things went wrong; a comforting room that enabled Anne to control her world. "A place where young girls honed their imaginations and practiced make believe." Grandma would have understood why I sat with my chin resting on both knees, arms wrapped tightly around my shins as I stared at Anne's lifeless face three feet away: I didn't want her to be alone.

Sirens in the distance ululated as the emergency vehicles sped over the rolling hills. The ambulance led the procession, followed by two unmarked cars and two sheriff's deputies' cars with their lights flashing. Driving past the gate, the vehicles spewed behind them as they barreled down the unpaved road toward me. An emergency medical technician jumped from the ambulance and raced over. "Sir, you can't do anything for her: she's dead. But there's an 80-year-old man with a heart condition back there by the gate. I'd appreciate it if you would check on him."

The ambulance pulled away and plainclothes men approached, and when I escorted them to her body, one peeled off and peppered me with questions. While he had to initially rule out homicide, the questions were unsettling, just the same. "Can we move back?" I asked. Noticing we were ten feet from her body, he apologized and we moved southward ten long paces. I stopped, with my back to Anne.

Satisfied that this was not a homicide, he took a different tack. "Was she depressed?" I stared over his left shoulder at the hay barn where we played hide and seek as kids. My eyes darted over his right shoulder at the stock tank and the small rowboat we paddled around the tank.

"Yes, she had attempted suicide once before, 10 years ago." Talking about it was just as difficult as dealing with it. Within minutes I was dismissed.

The house phone rang. On the tenth ring, my hand grabbed the receiver and I panted, "Hello."

"Tudey, this is Jim." My brief discussion with her twin ended with an ominous pronouncement. "I'm coming out there."

Jim's old friend Jeff already knew about Anne when he answered my call. "Jeff, Jim's on his way to the ranch. I'm gonna need some help." He arrived ten minutes before his fellow Spur. Jim swept past Jeff and lumbered toward me. "Where is she?" I stood my ground, jammed my hand against his massive chest, and said meekly, "No, Jim." Undeterred, he bulled forward and my feet skated backwards over the sand and gravel. Digging my heels into the ground, I jammed both hands against his chest and he stopped. Startled by my resolve, he stared at me and I yelled, "No, Jim!" Our eyes locked and I pleaded, "You don't want to see her . . . not like this." His mouth was closed and his nostrils flared as he searched over my shoulders for his sister, then he gazed back at me and nodded. But he said he had to see her and promised to stop when I told him, so I put my arm on his shoulder, he grabbed me tightly around the waist, and we started walking. When the backside of the garage came into view he halted. A half dozen people were milling about the area as Jim stared at his twin. Releasing my hold and slipping behind him, I stepped ten paces closer to Anne, out of his line of sight. Glancing back to ensure he was staying put, I was an unwilling voyeur: he should not have had to share this moment with the sheriff's department employees or me. I quickly averted my eyes.

Jeff and Jim departed after a few minutes. Two hours later, an unmarked van arrived and parked near the west side of the garage, blocking my view of Anne. The driver opened the back doors, took out a square object and disappeared behind the truck. Within minutes, he and a confederate reappeared carrying the black body bag. They placed Anne inside and closed the back doors, then drove away. As the van moved slowly down the road, the familiar crunch of tires reminded me of the night we sneaked out Anne's car, and all I could think about was the lost laughter of high school girls.

Shortly after I dialed my Aunt Mary's home, Mom came to the phone and told me to come by because Mary was expecting me. "I will, but I have to do something first." My mother was familiar with the terrain; a few of her long-time friends had taken their own lives.

Aware of what I was struggling with, she said, "I'm so proud of you." After muttering "Thank you," I hung up and walked to the front porch. Then I sat down and cried.

When Jim and Jeff left the ranch, Ed went home and ate lunch at the foreman's house a few hundred yards away, on the other side of the road. A Depression-era structure that could have been used in the movie *Bonnie and Clyde*, it was a worn, white-painted, one-story wooden building surrounded by a three-foot aluminum fence. A low-slung porch traversed the front of the house and framed the black screen door. Three stray dogs that had wandered into Ed's life snoozed on the porch next to him. The dogs snapped to life as my car drove up. Sitting in the rocking chair with his hands clasped together on his stomach, Ed reached for the large tumbler of iced tea on the table next to him. While I fended off the mutts, he sipped his drink, set it down, and ordered the dogs to vamoose. They scattered to the back yard as I put a foot on the porch and said, "It's over, Ed. Everyone's gone." He nodded but was not compelled to speak. Seconds ticked by, until I broke the strained silence. "I'm not going to come out for a while."

The old man responded, "I understand."

We never discussed that September day again because Ed was uncomfortable talking about it, but his last words on the subject summed up what many were thinking. He stared in the direction of the big house across the road, and said, "What a terrible waste."

Part Three

The funeral was held in the same church where she had been baptized, St. Austin's. Her five male cousins were pallbearers, along with Jeff and others. A priest eulogized her from the pulpit and told us that she was in heaven with God because God was all forgiving. Hearing those words surprised me; I had long thought suicide a mortal sin that consigned the deceased to an eternity in Hell. Traditionally, the Catholic Church did not allow church services for those who'd taken their own lives. After the Second Vatican Council in 1962-63, the Church's posture altered as its perception of the causes of suicide changed. Dogmatic theology is what we believe. Moral theology combines a truth with worldly sources and how a person evaluates those external sources, or how he or she should react to good and evil. Instead of viewing a completed suicide as murder, the Church began to see suicide as a symptom and manifestation of illness. St. Augustine said, "All things tend toward the fullness of being." Anne's illness or depression prevented her from achieving that state. As the priest spoke, the passage from Shelley came to mind,

Let the Hours, and the Spirits of might and pleasure,
Like the clouds and sunbeams, unite.

Weakened by malaise, she was unable to conjure the spirit of might, and in her opaque world of depression Anne had become incapable of seeing or feeling pleasure.

Following the service, mourners filed out of the Church and visited on the sidewalk of Guadalupe Street, "The Drag," the main thoroughfare that runs along the western edge of the University of Texas campus. Her college friends greeted each other in a scene out of **The Big Chill**, a 1983 movie about college friends reuniting after the suicide death of a former classmate. Anne's old fraternity and sorority friends hugged, cried, laughed, and reminisced about her. Two blocks east of the church was the original Kappa Sigma house.

Anne was similar to the state flower of Texas, the bluebonnet: delicate and pretty to look at, she blossomed in the spring, led a short but brilliantly colorful life, and died too quickly, and, like the wildflower, at times she could be intensely blue. She likely rationalized that her death would spare her family and friends from having to deal with her problems. Near the end of her life, she was not the person who took charge that night at the fraternity house and called Deborah. Anne had reverted back to being the 17-year-old girl who wanted to sneak out the car, yet uttered, "We have to go back," because she was unwilling to take a chance. She failed to understand that the biggest risk of all was not ending her life, but living it. So the despondent Anne killed herself and the other Anne, the one whose "eyes would twinkle like Christmas lights when amused."

She had stepped on life's carousel and stood in its center, watching the world go by. Gathering speed, it whirled around faster and faster and grew in height, stretching skyward. Like the trees that melded together before my eyes on that merry-go-round, the rising walls of the carousel trapped Anne inside an ever deepening well. Gazing up at the dwindling sliver of light that grew smaller and smaller, she could not climb out or notice the world around her. Soon, the last ray of hope was gone, and she was immersed in total darkness.

Elizabeth Kubler Ross's book *On Death and Dying* lists the five stages a person facing death and her loved ones endure: anger, denial, bargaining, depression, and acceptance. My cousin's sudden death precluded me from having to deal with the bargaining stage. The first two befell me that day at the ranch and were quickly supplanted by depression and guilt for not being able to prevent her suicide.

And no one can save me now,
If they ever really could

—Into the Great Unknown by Mary Fahl

Anne's illness was akin to a stormy night: a clear, placid sky filled with thousands of tranquil stars interrupted by a tall, billowy thunderhead that crested over the horizon, presaging trouble. Looming behind it was a darker, more ominous one. Lightning crackled and resembled raised veins on a forehead; thunder shouted in a displeased, frustrated voice. Watching it glide swiftly toward my house filled me with dread, as I somehow anticipated that which I would be powerless to prevent. An updraft of cooler, more stable air broke up the system, which dissipated the storm before it reached my doorstep. Those episodic moments with Anne occurred as frequently as springtime Pacific cold fronts swept across the plains of West Texas.

A person who attempts suicide once is at higher risk of actually achieving a completed suicide than one was has never made an attempt. I was ignorant of the danger and unaware that when someone makes the final choice to die, a burden is lifted and they become outwardly peaceful. The date, time, and location may be in doubt but, having made the decision, they are becalmed. In her last two weeks, Anne's frenetic angst dissipated like the storm clouds, and I turned away, believing a calamitous event had been averted. I didn't see the clouds re-forming, didn't see the lightning nor hear the sharp, violent thunderclap. Then again, no one else could have saved Anne; the choice was hers alone.

The night after her funeral I sat in my dining room and placed the photo of Anne, taken 28 years earlier, on the Kittinger table. For the longest time, I had fixated on the composition of the picture and missed its true significance. Her red and white checked two-piece bathing suit reminded me of the tablecloths in Italian restaurants, and I thought of Sandro Botticelli's painting, "Ideal Portrait of a Woman." The Renaissance artist's brushstrokes delineated a wavy-haired woman subject with a facial expression similar to Anne's in the photo. Botticelli spent hours studying his subject before laboriously capturing the woman's essence on canvas. When I snapped Anne's photo, her essence traveled through the lens, allowing it to be committed to film: her intelligent, methodical, and considerate personality was tinged with an aura of melancholy. The water in the background shared a quality with Anne: a shimmering surface that blinded the observer, preventing him from gauging the true depths of blue. In retrospect I had studied her, unwittingly: at the park merry-go-round and swing, on those nights in her room, sneaking out the car, at college, and in Paris and Ireland. Those forays into her mind helped me understand that the photo was an ideal portrait of this woman, the one who introduced me to Botticelli. Realizing that I had been given the opportunity to know the real Anne and commit her to film let me segue from depression and guilt to the last phase of bereavement—acceptance. And the circuitous path to that revelation had been shown to me by my cousin, who was an art history major at Texas.

Two incidents on September 10, 1990 were also appropriate. Whether Anne took her life precisely when the sense of dread washed over me as I drove to work that day will never be known, but the timeline fit. A man who leased the land for his cattle operations was there that morning checking on his herd, and he told me he left at 8:10 A.M. and saw no sign of her. That rain shower passed over the ranch a few minutes later. I remember looking for droplets of water on her face and clothing—there were none.

Some who take their own lives choreograph the death scene: the exact time and location, even the person who will find them. Anne knew I visited the ranch almost daily, and she knew if Ed stumbled upon her body his initial phone call would be to me, as the family's ranch liaison. Neither of those facts should have been comforting to me, yet they were. Anne was also aware that I had happened onto two suicides while employed at the Texas prison system and was called to the scene of a third a few years later. I was the appropriate choice.

Part Four

The process of letting go was completed months later at a 6-year-old's birthday party, an atypical event for such an epiphany, yet appropriate considering Anne's death was anything but ordinary. Releasing the heavy sorrow of her absence did not preclude thoughts of her. In some ways we continued to be tethered together, although the thick rope of our relationship that had bound us began to soften and fray with each passing year, until it was a tattered piece of twine. Thoughts of her danced across my mind in erratic intervals, usually at some function she would have attended. Most were memorable or substantive, like our day at the park. Separately or combined, those events were not capable of saving her, but in the back of my mind I always wondered, "What if?" If she had been successful in battling her illness or had managed to no longer perceive her glass as half-empty, those events could have added droplets of confidence to her life, but Anne was not there to see them.

Falling in a summer daydream
I remember what I knew
Nothing that I can't hold on to
Or return to
Even you

Where you are
Do you know I think of you
Where you are

46

Do you know
I hope you do

— From the song, "WHERE YOU ARE,"
by October Project

On the day of Anne's funeral, Deborah and I went to a house closing; the sellers were Jeff's parents, and we were buying their house. Our son William grew up in Jeff's old bedroom, went to the same high school as Jeff and Jim, and like his predecessors played football there. Graduating in 2003, he enrolled that fall at their alma mater, Texas, and was subsequently "tapped" for induction into the Silver Spurs. The summer following his freshman year, William escorted Jeff's daughter Mary Elizabeth at the Admirals Club Ball. Thirty something years in the past, Jeff had been Anne's escort. Perusing the round tables dotted with Spurs, I noticed that everyone who had been in the housemother's room back in 1971 was in attendance, except for Anne, the person most responsible for ushering Deborah into this circle of friends. Seated next to Jim was a woman who could have become much more to Anne than just her sorority sister. On April 11, 1999, Jim and Sally were married. But Anne was not there to see it.

In the fall of 1996, portions of the movie **The Only Thrill** were filmed at the ranch. The opening scene showed the actor Sam Shepard driving an old Lincoln Continental down the sand and gravel road toward the house, kicking up dust. Just past the garage, he swerved the vehicle to the left, went through a makeshift gate and hit the brakes. The camera panned, capturing on celluloid the exact spot where Anne died.

That should have unnerved me and likely would have if the process of letting go had not been completed. The epiphany occurred in April 1991, at my son's 6-year-old birthday party at the ranch. In the field between the backyard and the stock tank, little boys were dressed in cowboy hats, shirts, vests, jeans, chaps, and boots; Laura and the girls wore white shirts, denim skirts, and boots. Their imaginations were as carefree as the red bandanas each child sported around his or her neck. A football throw away, in the southwest corner of the backyard, was the red-roof dollhouse where Anne had practiced make-believe. My main function at the festivity was taking pictures and, after performing that simple duty, I took a break from the party. A girl climbed atop a square bale of hay to mount the Shetland pony for a tethered ride around the glen. Sounds of squealing children brimming with laughter chased after me as I passed the hay barn and walked to the garage with my head down, gazing at the ground and thinking. Anne was not there to hear the gleeful voices or see the smiling faces of unfettered youth. Even if she had been the denouement would likely have only been postponed, not altered. In her final troubled months, Anne felt out of place, separated from the world around her.

On the day she died I told Ed I wasn't going to come back out for a while. True to my word, I stayed away for weeks until I realized that not addressing the source of my anguish only magnified it. The first few trips, I avoided the area behind the garage for the same reason a car crash victim's family detours around the fatal intersection. Some reminders, too soon, do not have a healing effect; they only inflict more pain. Gradually, my legs led me to the area, and I began the process of letting go. That is why I stared at my feet and listened to the crunching sound of sand, rock, and gravel underfoot as I made my way to the scene of her death—to continue the process.

Familiar with the terrain, I halted a few feet away and glanced up at the spot where Anne's head had rested when I found her. In the center of that small speck of soil was a lone bluebonnet. Seemingly out of place, it was separated from the clusters of bluebonnets in the adjacent field. Attaching too much importance to serendipity would have been natural. Less than 20 percent of the non-chemically treated seeds germinate, and September is an optimal planting time, but I did not cling to those facts. Instead, I crouched down, put my arms on my knees and gazed at the flower: delicate and pretty, it was destined to lead a brilliantly colorful life before dying suddenly. Anne possessed those wildflower traits, but in the end what undid her was an incomparable flaw: she was too blue for her own good.

Reaching out, I brushed the bluebonnet with my right index finger and the plant tipped on its side and sprang back. Then I slide my finger across the backside of the flower. Seeing it was not an epiphany, merely a gentle nudge that pushed me through the final stage of healing, and I knew that the process of letting go was complete. Bishop John McCarthy described maturity as "the ability to adjust to reality." No longer did I blame myself, or her, or anyone else. Anne's illness had removed her from the grownups' table, where life's bountiful blessings are served up for those willing to consume them. I stood up, looked at the wildflower and said, "Rest in peace, Anne."

For six successive springs, I went back to that spot hoping to see another bluebonnet in the same place, but none appeared. The one I had admired, touched, and appreciated was no longer present. Like Anne, it was gone forever.

COMING OF AGE

Football's Lost Boys

Part One: Pre-Game Warm-ups

The Austin High vs. Reagan football game in 1967 created a rivalry that resembled a comet across the night sky: luminous, fiery hot, and ultimately fleeting. Three years later its lingering effect caused five basketball players from each school to break into the steamy old Austin High gym for a "statement" game viewed by no one but that ended with the arrival of the cops: it was August, and school was closed. Months later, the teams squared off in Gregory Gym. Twice. Each game drew over 6,000 spectators. At the football game that year, students from both schools' sections shared the east side stands at Nelson Field. During the second quarter, more than 500 male students became involved in a melee that swelled into a riot. It made front-page headlines in the paper and also at the University Interscholastic League, which quickly adopted a new seating arrangement at Texas high school games: students from different schools would be seated on separate sides of the field. In 1969, over 30,000 people attended the Austin High-Reagan game at Memorial Stadium, still the largest non-playoff crowd in Texas schoolboy history. What caused such interest and such mayhem? The Play . . . which was not the beginning or the end of the story, but part of the continuum.

It began in 1931, during the Great Depression, when 16-year-old Jim Tolbert walked on the University of Texas campus and became their youngest football player ever. Tolbert was massive for his age, 6'4" and 240 pounds. He dwarfed most of his teammates. Resembling John Wayne in looks and demeanor, he was soft of heart, but hard of head. Early in his playing career as an offensive lineman he had a frustrating game because one official kept blowing calls right and left. After being flagged for holding, an exasperated Tolbert walked up to the referee, reared back and punched him out, leading to his immediate suspension from the team.

Jack Gray, Sr., the student representative on the disciplinary committee, successfully lobbied for Tolbert's re-instatement at the disciplinary hearing. The jury, which included Clint Small, only needed to hear contrition from the boy before making it official. Tolbert was brought in and seated in front of the committee. He was asked, "Son, if you had to do it over again, would you do anything different?"

The young player looked down for a few seconds and then slowly lifted his head. "Yes, I woulda hit the sumbitch harder."

It would have been the wrong answer for most people, but not for Tolbert. In those few seconds while he stared at the floor, he was faced with telling a lie and extending his football season or telling the truth and being responsible for his actions. Jim Tolbert lost that season's eligibility but remained a steadfast stickler for personal accountability his entire life.

Travis Raven had played football at Austin High until his senior year when he went to the Schreiner Institute in Kerrville. His movie star looks completed the intelligent player package he brought to the University of Texas campus in 1941 as a running back. Like many others, World War II interrupted his college career while he did a stint in the Air Force. But in the years he spent at Texas, he stored voluminous amounts of football knowledge, watching teammates like Hub Bechtol—the only four-time All-American player in college history—and the legendary Bobby Layne. Some of his nights were spent in countless conversations into the wee hours with someone who knew a little about football, his roommate Tom Landry.

A few years after Raven, Glen Swenson arrived on campus. He was much shorter than the other two men and weighed only 160 pounds, not big for an offensive lineman. Swenson's battles in the trenches paled in comparison with his lifelong struggle with narcolepsy, the affliction that induced the rapid eye movement, dream-state of sleep without warning, lasting anywhere from 30 seconds to 30 minutes, regardless of how rested he felt.

In 1954, Jim Tolbert left UJH (University Junior High) to become the new football coach at Austin High. The district budget allowed two full-time assistants and he retained Raven, already an assistant there. Tolbert tapped into the University of Texas football fraternity, adding Glen Swenson. Their 0-8-2 inaugural campaign was the first winless season in the school's history. The next fall, Tolbert gathered the boys at the field house and said, "You see those pictures on the wall?" The team surveyed the photos of the all-state and all-district players who had gone before them. "None of you will *ever* have your picture up there." The motivational effect was marginal; they went 2-8. Playing in a "super district" with such powerhouses as Highland Park, Tyler, Wichita Falls, and Waco, and scheduling games against storied programs like

San Antonio Jefferson, Corpus Christi Ray, and Houston Milby made for long seasons and long road trips.

The new double-decker buses they used revealed a caste system similar to the Titanic: non-starters were crammed in steerage while the starters occupied two seats apiece in the upper deck. With that luxury came a price, starters were expected to play at all costs. Former running back Raven had the soft, deft hands of an orthopaedic surgeon. When a player staggered to the sideline with a separated shoulder, Raven popped the joint back into relative alignment and sent the boy back in the game. Once, a defensive player came off the field clutching his hand, grimacing in pain. Tolbert and Raven surveyed the damage: the mangled pinky and ring fingers were bent at ninety-degree angles at the knuckles. Only one thing to do: Raven yanked the mangled digits back in the general direction of the two normal ones, taped them all together and sent the stunned player back in. "Shake it off, shake it off, it's football," they told him. Tolbert would walk the sidelines looking for grass stains or dirt on the pants, one of his indicators of intensity. If you got in the game but only had white pants to show for it, you had better roll around on the ground when he wasn't looking or hit somebody, his other barometer of a player's desire.

During one game the defense was being pushed around mercilessly. Tolbert called time out and pulled them aside. "You aren't hitting anyone! I want you to go out there and hit someone! If you can't find anyone on their team to hit, then hit your teammate! But by God, hit somebody!" They did, partially out of fear. Tolbert, like Bear Bryant, was ahead of his time. He ceded much of the responsibility of running the program to his assistants. Raven ran the practices and Swenson instructed the linemen without interference from Tolbert, but everyone knew who was in control. At one practice a fight broke out, and Jim calmly separated the combatants. The larger player was 6'3" and weighed 195 pounds. Tolbert grabbed him by the neck and lifted him off the ground, with one hand. There were no more outbursts that season.

Despite the "old school" tactics, the players enjoyed the coaches and vice-versa. Maybe it was the post-game chicken fried steaks at the Elite Café on The Circle in Waco after the northern road games or the sincere interest the coaches took in the boys. The groundwork was forming for a successful program and help was on the way. In 1957 two more players' pictures went up on the field house walls.

The program's resurgence had a ripple effect. Near the shores of Town Lake, Little League football was thriving. The field was bordered on the east by the City Pound and on the north by a clump of trees that provided cover for the hobo camp. The 10 to 12-year-old kids didn't care; this was their Memorial Stadium. Most of them had flights of fancy that gave wings to their lofty dreams, all too soon shot down by mundane talents. Their chances of making a state championship-caliber high school football team were even lower than the Pound residents one day performing *Aida*, in Italian.

A certain group, however, caught the eyes of coaches like Harry Whitworth, Hub Bechtol, and Dick Chalmers, the Dean of West Austin Optimist Little League football. Kids from all over town participated, but one bunch seemed to possess a combination of athletic ability, football savvy, and work ethic that made a future state championship a realistic goal. That nucleus played on different teams like the Capitol City Oilers, Louis Shanks Dodgers, Capital Aggregate Aggies, and Southern Union Gas Flamers. In addition to talent, most had another thing in common: they would later attend UJH or O. Henry, both feeder schools for Austin High.

Tolbert and his assistants knew what to do with that talent. In 1957 Austin High made it to the state semi-finals before losing. Mike Cotten (UJH) and Bobby Nunis (O. Henry), both future stars at the University of Texas, led the Maroons, and their pictures went up on the field house walls. The Maroons later won district titles in 1961 and 1962, further fueling the dreams.

During those years, kids often waited outside the Texas locker room after the games, hoping to meet players like Cotton and Nunis. Their senior college season began a four-year run of Texas teams that only lost four games. A Longhorn star befriended one kid and even spent some evenings having supper with the boy's family. After one meal a chinstrap from his helmet was given to the boy, a memento of the occasion.

Austin was nutty for football and the Little League expanded to eight teams. The new television station in town KHFI (now KXAN) sent fabled sports anchor Mel Pennington and a cameraman down to the Little League field early on Saturday mornings to broadcast the "Game of the Week." The tape delay was shown at 11 A.M., followed at noon by the replay of the high school game of the week. If Texas had a home game, after watching themselves on television, kids would pile into station wagons, get dropped off at Memorial Stadium and dig into their pockets for 50 cents, the price of admission in the north end zone, affectionately called The Knothole Section (TKS). Elementary and junior and senior high students by the thousands filled the cheap seats and not only for the game. It was a social happening, because sanctioned gathering spots for kids were scarce. The boys watched the game and the girls watched the boys; it was a happy arrangement.

On November 9, 1963, TKS was packed for the game of the year. Late in the fourth quarter with Texas leading 7-0, the Baylor duo of quarterback Don Trull and split end Lawrence Elkins caught fire. They played catch all the way up the field and with 29 seconds left were on the Texas 19-yard line. The National Championship hung in the balance. High drama, and for once TKS had the best seats in the house. Trull dropped back and looked to his right. Planting his foot, he turned and fired a pass over the middle, to back of the end zone. Oh, no! TKS gasped. The Texas defender had fallen down and Elkins was wide open, but as he jumped for the ball a blur appeared from out of nowhere, having covered 15 yards since the ball left Trull's arm. Elkins stretched his hands out to receive it, but Duke Carlisle leapt at the last second and intercepted the pass, winning the game for Texas. TKS went wild. On a row below me, my brother's hand shot up in triumph, tightly clutching that memento of dinners at our home—Duke Carlisle's chinstrap.

We did not know it, but our comet of innocence would disappear 13 days later in a fleeting moment in Dallas, when John F. Kennedy was assassinated hours before his scheduled arrival in Austin. Actions by AISD would later pull down those shooting stars of Austin High, the final remnants of that comet. Reagan High School was slated to open soon in Northeast Austin, and the new boundaries would divert the player pipeline at UJH from Austin High to Reagan. Travis Raven would leave his alma mater to be the school's first head coach, taking Glen Swenson with him.

In the knothole section, beneath the light rain and gray black clouds over Memorial Stadium that day stood many of the boys who would play in the 1967 Austin/Reagan game. Also in the crowd that day was Captain Hook, who with one deft motion would chart two divergent courses for those exuberant young men still celebrating Texas' victory. One group became the foundation of a four-year run that featured a 35-game winning streak, surpassing even the great 1961-64 success of UT; the other would be consigned to Never-Never Land.

In the blink of a child's eyes it was four years later, Friday October 27, 1967, at a packed Nelson Field. Hook and his fellow Raiders marked one sideline. Across the field stood Tolbert and the Lost Boys. As the opening kickoff tumbled through the air, somewhere the Crocodile stirred, his clock and the scoreboard timepiece counting down in unison. Tick Tock. Tick Tock. Tick Tock.

Conclusion: The Arrival of Hook

October 27, 1967: a top ten tilt between #3 Austin High and #7 Reagan in front of an overflow crowd of 11,500 at Nelson Field. Austin coach Jim Tolbert often told his kids, "I'm not worth a flip during the games, I get too emotionally involved." Instead he relied on the game plan, but not this time.

Austin ran power sweeps at Reagan's three All-State defensive players, with predictable results, and trailed 12-0 at halftime. On the Maroons' first play of the third quarter they ran *away* from the trio and Robert Sidle scampered 58 yards for the score, 12-7 Reagan. The Raiders answered with their only sustained drive of the second half, a 79-yard march aided by two Maroon penalties, 18-7 Reagan. Austin then stalled at the Raider 23, a foot short of the first down. When a fourth quarter Reagan punt pinned the Maroons back on their 10-yard line, Tolbert tossed trepidation aside and allowed his signal caller to select some plays.

Just as Don Trull had against Texas years before, Austin quarterback Jim Geary caught fire. Tosses to Pat Malone and Sidle put Austin at their own 43. Reagan's Achilles heel had been found: pass, pass. Four plays later, Geary found split end Andy Laudermilk for a 3-yard touchdown, 18-14 Reagan. The majority of Reagan's defense had played both ways; they were tired and reeling from the drive. The scoreboard clock showed 1:47 remained—plenty of time. Austin just needed to recover the onside kick.

Herman Johnson's pooch kick from the 40 floated to Reagan's 35 where two Raiders collided trying to grab it. The ball hit the ground and rolled toward the Reagan sideline. Bodies flew to it like the ball was the doorway to freedom in a jailbreak. Darnell Moseley and Robby Bechtol split past a Reagan defender and Moseley, like Baylor's Lawrence Elkins years before, lunged for the pigskin. As his hands were about to grab it a blur appeared, and the ball rolled out of bounds. Bechtol had the best view, and he ran up to Captain Hook and screamed, "What the hell are you doing?" Hook ignored him, turned, and walked away. The referees signaled Reagan's ball and Bechtol went across the field, found Tolbert and said, "Coach, he kicked the ball out of bounds!"

Tolbert said, "Nah, you're crazy," and banished Bechtol to the bench. Austin's defense held, but the offense managed only two more offensive plays in the final seconds. Reagan had won 18-14.

The following morning, the team reviewed the game film and near the end, through the flickering light of the projector, the play and Hook appeared, just as Bechtol had described. Frame by painful frame showed that, as Moseley came closer to grabbing the ball, Travis Raven stepped onto the field, hooked his foot around it and kicked the ball out of bounds. The Maroons watched in stunned silence.

Tolbert's eyes found Robby's. "Bechtol, I guess I owe you an apology. That sumbitch really did kick the ball out of bounds."

The tape was rewound and they watched it again.

"Breaks—that's what football is all about," is how Travis Raven was quoted October 27, 1967, in a post-game interview. A trio of fine lawyers lodged a protest, but the UIL was not about to overturn the outcome; they had seen worse and done nothing. Years earlier, on the last play of a game, a visiting team had apparently kicked the winning extra point or field goal. Which one is not important, because as the ball approached the goalpost crossbar, "Homer," the Sheriff in those parts (as well as the end zone) fired his shotgun, and the ball exploded. Getting paid 20 bucks to officiate was one thing, dying for a replay was another. The refs signaled "no good" and the game was over.

The Maroons watched, sometimes in person, as Reagan won three playoff games by the combined scores of 67-6, then defeated Abilene Cooper 20-19 for the State title. The Raiders repeated the next year against Odessa Permian. On November 7, 1969, when Reagan and Austin met at Memorial Stadium in front of over 30,0000 spectators, the Maroons won the district title easily, 27-7. When the teams met after the game Tolbert declined to shake Raven's hand.

On the same playing field, nearly six years to the day after the Baylor/Texas game that signaled the end of our idyllic days, Austin High had won one for the Lost Boys. Tolbert probably felt the same; he soon announced his retirement from coaching. He was only 54, but he had had enough. Travis Raven led the

Raiders to the title again in 1970 and then retired from coaching at age 57. He had numerous offers, including one from the Dallas Cowboys and his former UT roommate, Tom Landry, but he accepted the job of AISD athletic director, replacing Toney Burger.

When quizzed about why he kicked the ball out of bounds, Raven responded he had a wife and three kids and thought he would've been fired if Reagan had lost. Would a school playing only its second season of UIL football and ranked #7 in Texas with a 7-0 record contemplate firing their coach? Some observers were skeptical in light of what was to come.

The biggest losers from Jim Tolbert's retirement were the players. When he arrived at Austin High in 1954, two black students were in the graduating class. In the pre-busing days of the early 60s, he quietly set about recruiting black athletes to come there. Six of them made all-district in 1966. With Tolbert's help, all of them received scholarships to play in college. Had Austin beaten Reagan in 1967 and gone deep into the playoffs, perhaps some of the players could have used that forum to garner scholarships, much like some Reagan players had. Instead, not one Maroon received a Division I offer.

When Raven quit coaching, Swenson chose not to succeed him because he didn't want a head coaching job. He joined the staff at his alma mater and coached under Darrell Royal and later Fred Akers. In 1983, Texas was making preparations to leave for the Arkansas game and Swenson was returning from his property east of Austin. During a pre-dawn hour he lost his life-long battle with narcolepsy. He fell asleep and the car drifted off the road and crashed, killing him; he was only 57. Swenson became the first of the three coaches to die, but not the first to fall.

Take the time to treat your friend and neighbors honestly.
I've just been fakin' it, fakin' it. Not really makin' it.
This feeling of fakin' it, I still haven't shaken it.

—"FAKIN' IT," Paul Simon, 1968

In February of 1974, Hook's Crocodile returned. A 16-year-old female runaway from Houston was "beat up" by a 22-year-old male in Austin, according to her parents. After she returned home, they pressed the Austin Police to investigate. Detectives visited two motels in town, which eventually led to the arrest of five individuals, including Travis Raven, who was charged with "compelling the prostitution" of a minor, a felony offense. Eighty-one days later he was convicted by a jury of the lesser offense of "compelling prostitution" and paid the misdemeanor fine of $200. Raven maintained his innocence but submitted a one-sentence resignation letter to the AISD after 28 years of service. Then he called his old roommate, Tom Landry, for help. "Travis, I'll give you money, try to help you get a job, anything. But I can't touch you with a 10-foot pole." Raven later said he thought he knew who set him up and why, but the truth was that no one forced him to go into that motel room with the underage girl. He was a pathological palliator, a person prone to making excuses to mitigate the circumstances. The Crocodile receded, again having stolen snippets of Raven's brain that controlled his judgment.

Obscured in the game story over the years was its effect on Tolbert, who also lost his chance for a state championship. He knew he could have coached a better game, but the fact was his kids played magnificently in the second half, holding Reagan to less than 100 yards and forcing three punts while his offense racked up 213 yards and never had to punt. If the two referees only yards away had spotted the transgression, Austin would have re-kicked from Reagan's 45, or been given possession at the Raiders' 20-yard line after the 15-yard unsportsmanlike conduct penalty, with 1:47 left and timeouts to spare. Tolbert felt responsible for another reason: he had retained Raven when he came to Austin High and had never spotted the man's character flaws, but Tolbert was not alone in his failure to discover them until it was too late. The Crocodile and Hook only made cameo appearances, but they spent a lifetime vying for supremacy of Raven's mind. The battle would rage for another quarter century.

The word "ironic" is inadequate in describing this story. Months before Tolbert took the helm at Austin High, in December of 1953, a musical opened on Broadway titled *Kismet*, the Turkish word for Fate. If two Reagan players had not collided going for the ball, much of this story never would have happened. If Raven had not felt the game slipping away he would not have kicked the ball. Yet both occurred. For some reason, the only Maroon player positioned to see Raven boot the ball out of bounds was Robby Bechtol whose father, Hub Bechtol, had been Raven's teammate at the University of Texas. Perhaps it was only an irony that Raven's transgression was seen by the son of one of his fellow members of the University of Texas football fraternity. Or, maybe it was kismet.

At times Raven had shown impaired judgment and an inability to reason. Although they manifested themselves earlier in his life, these traits were also symptoms of the disease that would eventually overtake him. Travis Raven has Alzheimer's. Duke Carlisle can recall his blur that changed UT football history forever. Raven cannot recall his blur at all. Like those clouds that drifted above Memorial Stadium that Saturday afternoon in 1963, his is a gray-black world. The trinity that was Raven—the Crocodile, Hook, and Travis—have been silenced forever, relegated to a Never-Never Land. Never again will Raven have to answer the question, "Why did you kick the ball out of bounds?" Never again will Raven be able to summon memories of those three state championship seasons. Also lost was his chance at redemption.

Tolbert never did receive an apology or explanation from Raven, and after a short while he stopped expecting one. Tolbert's pride would not allow him to bridge that gap and contact his old friend, fellow coach, and former Longhorn player, and Raven never was accountable to his old friend for his mistake. Even in his eighties, Tolbert never wavered from his principles; he remained a steadfast stickler for personal accountability, and he would not allow Raven to be the exception. In some ways Tolbert was still the teenage Jim who sat in a chair and faced the University disciplinary tribunal six decades earlier.

He retired to the Dallas area to be near his family. In 1996, the fortieth reunion of the class of 1956 was held. Players who formed the nucleus of those first two years under Tolbert that won only two games were in attendance on that Friday night at Jaime's Spanish Village—boys like the one that had proffered up his mangled fingers and the player Tolbert had picked up by the neck. Also there were players from the state semi-finalist team, like Mike Cotten. Many were there because they had heard who was coming. His son drove him down from north Texas and pushed the wheelchair into the room. Jim Tolbert had recently undergone double knee replacement surgery and nearly died when he contracted a Staph infection. To his players Big Jim was still a giant of a man. They showed respect, in part because they always knew where they stood with him. They had a handle on "Coach": he was still hard of head and soft of heart. It had been a painful trip for him, but he came anyway. These players had not won on the field, but they were still his boys. How soft of heart he truly was would not be revealed until after his death two years later.

Why don't we stop foolin' ourselves?
The game is over . . . over . . . over.

— "Overs," Paul Simon, 1968

The Play did not define the lives of the Lost Boys, but it helped shape them. A great majority have enjoyed successful private lives and professional careers. On October 25, 2002, two days shy of the 35th anniversary of the game, many of the players attended the letterman's breakfast at Austin High commemorating Homecoming Week. Pat Lochridge gave a rousing rendition of the contest and The Play, complete with game film. The guys laughed, as one can do only after the separation of time. The players do not solicit your pity; they merely ask that you understand.

Like all adults, these men retain a collage of childhood events, but their memory banks are unique. Some think about the game more than others do, but each fall the high school playoffs act as a pass key that unlocks the same vault for all of them. It percolates up into their consciousness, that small portion that is forever trapped in Never-Never Land. They will never know if they would have won the game, and they will never know if they could have won the State championship.

To a man they will tell you if Raven had not prevented Moseley from recovering the ball, they would have scored from the Reagan 35-yard line. After all, their shortest drive in that second half was 47 yards. Yet the difference between telling and doing can sometimes be very slight. This time it was as thin as the chalk sideline at Nelson Field. Stolen from these young men was their chance to bypass that Never-Never Land, an opportunity taken away by three adults—Raven and two officials—who failed them. Such is the fate of the Lost Boys.

In *Peter Pan* the boys only had to think "happy thoughts" and they could fly. Come fall, at the Little League field now named for Dick Chalmers, small boys wearing helmets and shoulder pads disproportionate to their little bodies will be practicing and playing football. The trees and the hobo camp have long since disappeared, but the dogs still stand watch and young boys still dream. If you happen by and are reminded of this tale, send them some "happy thoughts"; it won't enable them to fly, but it just might prevent another Hook. As the Lost Boys will tell you, one was too many.

Postlude

In April of 1968, two months before the majority of the Maroon players graduated, Simon and Garfunkel issued their BOOKENDS album. The liner notes proclaimed it "a meditation on the passage of life and the psychological impact of life's irreversible, ever-accumulating losses."

> *Time it was*
> *And what a time it was.*
> *It was . . .*
> *A time of innocence,*
> *A time of confidences.*
> *Long ago . . . it must be . . .*
> *I have a photograph.*
> *Preserve your memories;*
> *They're all that's left you.*

— "BOOKENDS" Theme,
Paul Simon, 1968

Occasionally, the entryway of a home offers insight into the inhabitants: antiques, bric-a-brac, and artwork, things that convey what the owner collects and cherishes. When Tolbert died in 1998, visitors showed up at his retirement community condominium to pay their respects to his family. Some who had not been there before were taken aback by what they saw upon entering his home; the things that the soft-of-heart Jim had prized. On the walls of that narrow hallway were pictures, pictures, and more pictures encased in simple black frames: photos of Cotten, Nunis, and others; pictures that had graced the old field house walls four decades before. For Tolbert, those pictures held a meaning that went beyond football. Like so many Peter Pans, these boys were frozen in time: a time when Jim Tolbert had not only been their coach but also their mentor and confidante. They were his memories of years spent with the boys he cherished. Amidst this gallery of individual Pans was another photograph . . . a collection of the last remnants of our comet of innocence, those shooting stars of Austin High, the Lost Boys.

You Just Never Know

My son's first Parents' Weekend at UT was on the schedule. Camp Longhorn friends were staying with our daughter. Austin High vs. Westlake High and the University of Texas vs. Nebraska were also on the agenda. Sunday was reserved for working on a newspaper article. Something happened that derailed those plans. At Scholz's Biergarten on Friday night a good friend got a frantic call from his daughter who was returning home. She described high school kids running across her street, some with bloody clothes. This was not some Halloween prank. Sirens pierced the night air, lights from police cars, ambulances, and fire trucks shot through the trees and sky like fast, multi-colored klieg lights. You just never know.

It had started innocently enough, or as innocent as any party can be when the parents are out of town. On any given weekend in Austin, dozens of similar teenage gatherings are held. Each house is like a honeycomb, attracting bees. The age of instant access ushered in by cell phones leaves invitations only a phone call away. That's when the bear shows up.

This wasn't the *Risky Business* party depicted in the Tom Cruise movie where the house was trashed and craziness permeated the residence. Except for the bear, the kids present were not the type you associate with violence; most were just relaxing and talking. One victim was stabbed walking to the car to get home before curfew. Six days before that same child had been sitting in a Sunday school class listening to Randy and Jenna McEachern talk about their miraculous story. At the party, one student stood next to a classmate when the Bowie High student walked up and began stabbing the classmate repeatedly. It was the victim's first "party." Wrong place at the wrong time.

While attending college I worked at a Huntsville prison. One day I opened the outer, solid door and peered into a dark, solitary confinement cell. An 18-year-old boy was hanging from the bars. Dashing past the "sick bay" cells that housed infirm inmates, I ran to the office, retrieved a pocketknife, returned and cut him down. The boy survived, possibly because I had been in the right place at the right time. Fred Gomez Carrasco was an inmate in one of those sick bay cells. A year later after the siege and shootout at the Walls Unit, I helped load his lifeless body into the coroner's black bag. You just never know.

On that Parents' Weekend, I sure didn't. My headline for a football story about an Austin High defeat had read "Bowie Knifes Austin."

The morning after the stabbings, dozens of students sat in the waiting room at Brackenridge Hospital, wondering how it could have happened, and the victims' parents, still numb, wrestled with their emotions. I have known some of them for 35 years and realized the only thing preventing many of us from being in their place were cell phones, fortunate decisions by some kids to stay away, or, for others who attended the party, not being nearby when the attacks occurred.

As the violence mushroomed, kids ran through the woods or tried to hide in rooms. Some attended the wounded. Meanwhile, the mind-altered bear kept searching for more honey. Eight kids were stabbed before the ninth victim, along with two others, overpowered him. Brave boys in the wrong place at the right time. The cell phones that brought some to the party may have prevented a worse tragedy. Not knowing the exact street address to guide the ambulances, some kids put their injured friends in vehicles and attempted to stanch the blood as it flowed onto the seats. At least one carload called 911 and met the ambulance at a designated location.

Following my encounter with the inmate who had attempted suicide, I went home and tossed the bloody uniform aside. It had been an unnerving experience, but he wasn't my friend. Many of the party witnesses spent hours at a police substation in far South Austin—some until 4 A.M.—seated at desks, giving their statements, still dressed in clothes soaked with the blood of their friends. If the cold steel had landed mere inches away on some victims it would have been worse. On this unluckiest of Halloween nights, at least five of them were lucky to come away with only a minor red badge of courage. Many others were fortunate to survive with only emotional wounds that hopefully will not linger like the physical ones.

As the weekend progressed, parents across west and south Austin counseled their children, trying to make sense out of a senseless act. Maybe now more of those kids will realize why you give them a reassuring hug and say, "I love you. Be careful," when they leave home to enter an unsure and sometimes crazy world. Because you just never know.

Class of 2003

The events of 9/11 did not awaken a sense of patriotism in four young people; the tragedies merely reinforced their desire to serve America. Carolyn Crenshaw said, "Ever since I was a little girl, I always wanted to join the military. When it came down to making the final decision of what I was to do with my life after high school, I chose the Navy. Watching the news coverage of the war against terrorism gave me another reason to join."

Mike Hoffman wanted to join the military after watching footage of the first Gulf War; he wanted to do "something meaningful" for his country.

John Runde knew at age five he wanted to be a soldier and, when he was 11, John announced he was going to be a Marine.

Elliott Weeks said, "Being a Marine and serving in the military has been a dream of mine for most of my life. When my recruiter asked me why I was enlisting I said, 'To serve my country.' My grandparents and great uncles served during World War II. I often think of the courage it took to serve our country during that war, and I want to honor that tradition. I am proud to be a Marine. Semper Fi."

Enlisting

After graduating from high school, all four had other options, yet each walked into a recruitment office and enlisted. Days after they turned 17, Mike and John joined the Marine Reserves, a six-year commitment that came with a "delayed entry," allowing them to enroll in college. Four days after graduating from Anderson High, Carolyn began her basic training at the Naval Training School in Great Lakes, Michigan. A month later, she was performing training exercises off the California coast on the USS John C. Stennis, a Nimitz Class Aircraft Carrier. In nearby San Diego, Mike and John were going through Marine boot camp, alternating between San Diego and Camp Pendleton. In the fall, as Carolyn sailed the high seas, Mike enrolled at UT-Austin, John went to UT-Arlington, and Elliott attended Baylor.

A decision and notification

In March of 2004, Elliott realized his dream by signing up for the Marine Corps, which is a four-year commitment. A few days later, on St. Patrick's Day, Mike and John were called up to active duty and were told they needed to take their semester finals early. They were going to Iraq. Mike left behind his 4.0 grade point average, and the two friends underwent advanced training in Louisiana and California, at the same time Elliott was going through boot camp. During that three-month ordeal, recruits have limited contact with the outside world. They receive periodic but not daily mail service; phone calls home are rare and cherished.

While the boys were roughing it, Carolyn visited Alaska, Canada, Hawaii, Taiwan, and Japan, but her job did not involve miminy-piminy, or soft and delicate tasks. She became an ABH, Aviation Boatswainsmate Plane Handler, one of the most dangerous jobs on an aircraft carrier. Much of her time was spent on the flight deck, moving and tying aircraft and operating the elevators to and from the mobile landing strip.

A letter of explanation

This group of graduates' patriotism is similar to that of Maj. Sullivan Ballou, 2nd Regiment, Rhode Island Volunteers. In a letter to his wife Sarah, written on July 14, 1861, the Major said, "I have no misgivings about, or lack of confidence in, the cause in which I am engaged, and my courage does not halt or falter. I know how strongly American Civilization now leans upon the triumph of the Government, and how great a debt we owe to those who went before us . . . And I am willing—perfectly willing—to lay down all my joys in this life, to help maintain this Government, and to repay that debt."

Fine-tuning

Carolyn was promoted to 3rd Class Petty Officer and is training to be a "yellow shirt," the crewmen responsible for guiding incoming aircraft for landing on the flight deck. She is also air warfare qualified. The USS Stennis returns to Washington State in January of 2005, and she hopes to transfer to a ship in the Middle East after that. Elliott will graduate from the Military Operations School in California on October 27, where he is an infantry rifleman in Delta Company. He will either be assigned to the 1st or 5th Marine Corps. While awaiting his designation, Elliott is actively training for a future deployment that could involve a seven-month tour of duty in Afghanistan or Iraq.

Separation

When Mike and John signed up, they were assured they would always be together in their military service, but fate interceded. With only 10 days left in their final training stint, the two went on a conditioning exercise, a 20-kilometer (12-mile) forced march. In addition to carrying his 85-pound pack, John, a mortarman, had to lug his mortar. His left foot had been hurting for days, and at the 13K mark it started swelling. He endured the rest of the trek, but the x-ray examination revealed John had previously suffered a stress fracture that was now a complete fracture of the second metatarsal. His foot was put in a cast, and he missed the pivotal specialty training required for deployment in war zones. He was very disappointed to leave his friend Mike. John returned to Austin to resume his college career but knows that someday he may be called up again.

Mike will be stationed at Al Asad Airfield, the second largest airbase in Iraq, situated 112 miles west of Baghdad, and six miles from the banks of the Euphrates River, near the Biblical site of the Garden of Eden. His 1st Marine Corps Battalion, 23rd Regiment is a heavy weapons mobile force that will patrol various checkpoints in addition to looking for improvised devices, or roadside bombs. The five Humvees in Mike's group have 40-mm automatic grenade launchers that can fire 75 rounds per minute with a "kill" radius of five meters and a "casualty" radius of 15 meters. They are also equipped with 50-caliber machine-guns that have a range of 7,400 meters, almost five miles. At Fort Polk earlier in the summer, Mike trained in both weapons and in Iraq he will ride atop a Humvee, alternately wearing his ballistic goggles and anti-shrapnel sunglasses.

A good night's sleep

Maj. Sullivan Ballou said in his letter, "I have sought . . . for a wrong motive in thus hazarding the happiness of those I loved and I could not find one. A pure love of my country and of the principles I have often advocated . . . and 'the name of honor that I love more than I fear death' have called upon me, and I have obeyed."

These recent graduates have answered the call and are doing what they love, but that doesn't keep the families from worrying about their safety. Every morning you awaken from a restful sleep, somewhere there is a grandparent, mother, father, or sibling who did not, because they endured a fitful night vexing over their loved one's safety. If part of your weekend is spent enjoying a leisurely afternoon of shopping or attending church, you do so without giving a thought to your own personal safety. That is because thousands of young graduates, including these four, are ". . . willing—perfectly willing—to lay down all my joys in this life," to protect us all.

A vested interest

All of us should take a vested interest in these soldiers. I have. Carolyn's father Charlie and her uncle Ben grew up a block away from me. Elliott lives five houses down from us. Nineteen years ago at St. Theresa's Church, my wife Deborah and I watched as the priest sprinkled holy water over the foreheads of the Hoffman twins. Deborah is Matt's Godmother; Mike is my Godson. This article was originally published on October 1, 2004, the feast day of St. Theresa. Early that morning, Mike Hoffman was scheduled to board a Boeing 777 at March AFB in California to begin his 24-hour trip to Iraq.

Godspeed

To our graduate soldiers: with boundless admiration, many of your neighbors await your safe return from far-flung deployments around the world. We anticipate the days to come, when you will be afforded what your sacrifice has given us—the opportunity to enjoy life, liberty, and the pursuit of happiness. Until then, we wish you Godspeed, for you truly are "The Class of 2003," in many ways.

Late-night Cinderella

Cinderella: "It's just no use. I can't believe. Not anymore."
Fairy Godmother: "Nonsense, child. If you'd lost all your dreams, I couldn't be here. And here I am." Whereupon, she casts her spell and sings, "Salaga-doola, menchika-boola, Bibbidi-bobbidi-boo. It will do magic, believe it or not, Bibbidi-bobbidi-boo."

Throughout the nights of October 15th and 16th in 2001, Julie and Scotty Sayers opened their home on Scenic Drive to a production company filming the movie *The Life of David Gale*, starring Kevin Spacey, Laura Linney, and Kate Winslett. Spacey portrayed a high-profile death penalty opponent who became a death row inmate himself. In my former life I had been an employee of the Texas Department of Corrections in Hunstville, where one of my unsavory chores was transporting real condemned killers from the Diagnostic Unit to death row at the Ellis Unit, 13 miles away.

Thankfully, the portions filmed at the Sayers' home were party scenes. No stranger to movie sets, my daughter Laura asked me to drop her off, which I did, while remaining an un-embarrassing parental distance behind her. That first night Kevin Spacey gave her his autograph and was cordial.

The second night after dropping off Laura and her fellow 14-year-old friends Anne Elizabeth Kay and Sterling Oles, I parked the car while the girls made their way to the Sayers' adjoining neighbors' patio to view the Hollywood spectacle.

An hour into the ordeal the youngsters found me and said Laura wanted to be an extra. The air was chilly and I was without a coat, so we piled back into the car and came home. Filled with excitement, they manufactured an outfit for my daughter and we returned to the set. They knew her chances of being picked were very slim, but the trio relished the experience.

While driving back and forth, the girls remarked the Hollywood crew members were friendlier than most of the local employees; they went out of their way to be nice to the youngsters, as Mr. Spacey had the night before. Laura was not selected as an extra. Instead, she was chosen for extra special treatment.

On a whim, one of the movie's principal makeup artists invited Laura into a trailer and sat her down in a chair. Large, bright lights rimmed the mirror as she began applying foundation on the youngster. The 30-something woman had performed her magic on big name actors: Stallone, Ahnold, Eastwood, Spacey, Linney, Winslett, and Madonna. After this movie she was the key makeup artist on *Mystic River* and *Million Dollar Baby.*

While working on Laura, the professional explained the nuances of makeup and why she had chosen certain colors and shades. Telling Laura, "You have beautiful eyes that should be accentuated," the woman used an eye-liner pencil and finished with lipstick. Then the artist moved aside, revealing her canvas. Laura stared into the mirror and smiled.

Seeing her was something of a shock. Not the makeup, which was subtle, but the expression on my daughter's face, which revealed an added dollop of self-confidence. It was also a window into the future. Laura was five days shy of her fifteenth birthday, but I realized in that momentary glance that her days as a little girl would soon be over. My baby was growing up.

My wife and I were together with William and Laura for Parents' Weekend at UT on the night she turned 19. She had grown into the young lady that was only hinted at four years before. Her stint in the makeup chair did not alter Laura's life: it was only a small step in the maturation process everyone goes through, but I have often thought of what Tonia McComas did for my daughter and the underlying reason for her largesse.

The Hollywood maven was imbued with enough self-assurance that she could treat an unknown teenage girl with respect and dignity, some of which rubbed off on Laura, along with the tincture of makeup. And maybe someone had done the same thing for Ms. McComas when she was a young girl and the artist was trying to *Pay It Forward*, the title of another Kevin Spacey movie where she had been the key makeup artist.

Halloween night many girls will dress up as Cinderella and go trick-or-treating with their parents, who will tell them how beautiful they are. As they grow older, those children will discount their parent's compliments; after all, Mom and Dad have to say nice things. Hopefully, sometime in each of those girls' lives a teacher, coach, or other adult will be able to impart to them that even though beauty is not skin deep, it's easier to display when the trait resides within.

A kind California woman helped reinforce what two parents had always told their daughter: that she was a beautiful person, inside and out. Shortly after the clock struck midnight on that October 16th, the "Bibbidi-bobbidi-boo" from the woman's magic wand was completed. Moments later, Laura exited the trailer and stood beneath the soft street light. And I silently thanked the Fairy Godmother as I gazed upon my late-night Cinderella.

Being Cool

The white dinner jackets were homages to the father of the bride Bob Kinnan, who always sported the look at similar events. To some, his six middle-aged friends looked like light-skinned versions of the wait staff at Moderno's Restaurant in Piedras Negras. In our eyes we resembled the King of Cool, Humphrey Bogart in *Casablanca*. The building had something to do with that. Situated next to the railroad track in Kingsville, Texas, the structure was built out of necessity in 1904. The King Ranch needed a way to keep their produce from spoiling on the long train trips to market, so Richard J. Kleberg and Henrietta King had the large icehouse built. Fruits and vegetables could then be packed in ice before being loaded onto boxcars. Today, a large portion of the edifice is a King Ranch museum filled with hunting cars, historical exhibits, photos, and memorabilia. The other portion of the Henrietta Memorial Center is used for weddings, receptions, and other functions. Washed woodwork frames the windows and doorways of the original red brick interior walls.

What's a nilgai?

The General Manager of the King Ranch Hospitality and Related Services, Bob Kinnan and his wife Punkie were our hosts. They put on a lavish buffet featuring one large grilled critter, the exotic nilgai. Imported for hunting purposes by Caesar Kleberg nearly 90 years ago, the antelope-like animals have thrived in the South Texas plains. Today there are more nilgai in Texas than their native India. The guests enjoyed dining on this guy; a much better choice than serving up a Texas Longhorn—half the crowd were Sooner fans.

The bride and groom, Kathryn Elizabeth Kinnan and Stephen James Idoux, attended the University of Oklahoma, and Steve is a native of Tulsa. The groom's chocolate cake was emblazoned with OU in large red letters.

After dinner, Kathryn and dozens of her Kappa Kappa Gamma sorority sisters posed for a group photo. Greeks travel in packs, and soon every woman in the building who was a Kappa swooped in for the photo. Nourished by nilgai, the ladies then encircled the bride and performed the "Kappa chant," which was not unlike a ceremonial Indian dance on an Oklahoma reservation, except for the designer dresses, jewelry, and high heels.

The ritual ended and the paid entertainment resumed. Country legend Johnny Bush and his band cranked out his big hits: "WHISKEY RIVER," "THERE STANDS THE GLASS," and "WHAT MADE OLD MILWAUKEE FAMOUS MADE A FOOL OUT OF ME." During the plaintive tunes, an irony meandered through my head. A bunch of friends were in Omaha watching Texas' baseball team compete for the National Championship, and I was in a television-less room in South Texas surrounded by Sooners. Checking my cell phone, I noticed three rapid-fire messages; each one from John S. Burns, Jr., heralding a ninth-inning strikeout by Texas pitcher J. Brent Cox. The University of Texas had beaten Florida, 4-2, in game 1 of the best-of-three series. My son William phoned. "Pops, how 'bout them Horns?" The call came from the right field bleachers at Johnny Rosenblatt Stadium. His voice sounded ebullient; he should have been exhausted.

Road warriors

Dozens of Texas Phi Gamma Delta fraternity members had made the trek to Omaha. On Friday afternoon, William and his "brothers" Justin Cole and Squire Hamilton Madden piled into a borrowed Suburban, along with recent Austin High grad Will Buchanan for the 14-hour plus drive. As the Idoux family from Tulsa enjoyed the rehearsal dinner in Kingsville, that Suburban was stopped at a Wal-Mart near the University of Oklahoma in Norman, and the boys bought white shoe polish to festoon the car windows.

Around 6 A.M. the road warriors pulled into The White House Best Western in Bellevue, a suburb of Omaha. Everything in the hotel was Presidential and "impeccably decorated" according to the hotel's website. The boys were assigned the James K. Polk Suite. Some slept as William went to the continental breakfast area and partook of the pour-your-own waffles. An early bird was already eating and motioned William to join him. The gentleman, a handicapped Longhorn fan from East Texas, had been attending the College World Series for decades and had a perk to prove it: a coveted parking pass. The middle-aged fan said he always parked in a handicapped space and offered his CWS parking pass to William, who gladly accepted it. Following a power nap, the boys' Suburban was one of the first admitted into the parking lot.

"You want the pistol, the malt liquor, or both?"

Within minutes, the father of Texas pitcher J. Brent Cox invited them to a tailgate party. Well-intentioned adults instructed the young men where to buy the cheapest liquor: Wal-Mart. The store was a short drive across the river in Council Bluffs, Iowa. Where else but Wal-Mart and America can you overhear this exchange.

"I'd like Colt .45."

"You want the pistol, the malt liquor, or both?"

The stadium gates opened and the boys scrambled to grab front row seats in right field, the best "general admission" tickets. Will Buchanan's classmate Stuart Sharpe and others joined them. Between innings, they conversed with Nick Peoples, the Horns' right fielder who scored the first run in the 4-2, Texas victory, fueled by 3-4 hitting from designated hitter Will Crouch and third baseman David Maroul. Following the game, the Suburban boys continued tailgating until the clock struck midnight, and the parking lot emptied out.

A call from Costa Rica

On Sunday, they claimed the same parking spot, but their game seats were improved. Our neighbors, Leslie and David Pohl were sitting in Rosenblatt Stadium when their son Luke called Leslie from Costa Rica, where he was watching the game on ESPN. "Mom, I just saw William Teten!" My son called. "Dad, everyone's calling and telling me that I'm on t.v." The camera showed a Texas runner on first base and William in the background, talking to me. Saturday morning, when he purchased eight general admission tickets, William had asked the ticket seller what was available for Sunday. She told him someone had just returned eight ducats behind first base, six rows up. Every wide camera shot of a left-handed batter or runner on first revealed William's group.

Moments later, David Maroul's three-run homer put the game out of reach and starting pitcher Kyle McCulloch threw the last of his seven shutout innings, before giving way to Randy Boone and closer J. Brent Cox. The dog pile ensued after the final out was registered in the 6-2 win. Beneath the broiling sun, the road warriors watched as McCulloch, Crouch, and Cox were named to the all-tournament team and Maroul received the Most Outstanding Player Award.

At midnight, the parking lot resembled the streets of Omaha—deserted. Eight people were now sharing the James Polk Suite, roughly the same number of Americans who can cite any accomplishment of the man's Presidency. Polk did keep two of his campaign promises—he only served one term and his support of Statehood for Texas occurred in 1845, during his first year in office. The next state created in his term was Iowa, famous for its presidential caucus and Wal-Marts that sell firewater and firearms.

The road goes on forever and the party never ends

On Monday evening, they entered Norman, Oklahoma, and made a beeline for OU's equivalent of "The Drag." The words written on the car windows were considered too subtle, so Justin honked the horn while William and Hamilton leaned out of the car, one waving a large Longhorn flag, the other brandishing the State Flag of Texas. Locals rolled down their car windows and spewed strident epithets that would have shaken a sailor's sensibilities. Like an ornery nilgai, Justin laid on the horn longer, drawing the ire of walkers afflicted with a genetic defect, one that prevented them from using their index fingers: instead, all of the pedestrians held up a different digit to show the Texas boys that "OU was #1."

Just before 3 A.M., the Suburban pulled onto 21st Street and stopped in front of the Littlefield Fountain, in the shadow of the UT Tower. Dozens of people milled about, admiring the Tower bathed in burnt orange with a "1" shining brightly. William spotted a friend from Spanish class with two of his buddies. All of them had been in Omaha, and the two groups converged and recounted the weekend's events. The trio had even more stories to tell than the road warriors. William's classmate was David Maroul, and his two buddies were Kyle McCulloch and Nick Peoples.

The coolest part

Growing up in Kaufman, Texas, Kathryn Kinnan probably imagined what her wedding day would be like, including having her younger sisters, Mary Margaret Kinnan and Caroline Carrier Kinnan, serve as maids of honor.

In the small Texas towns of Bay City, Benbrook, Round Rock, Westlake Hills, and others, boys a few years younger than Kathryn played baseball. They fantasized about wearing the Texas uniform and winning the National Championship in Johnny Rosenblatt Stadium.

On the last weekend in June 2005, those childhood images and fantasies played out. A girl from OU and boys from UT achieved their dreams in front of those who matter most to them—family and friends, which was the coolest part of all. Bogey would have been proud.

HISTORICAL FARRAGO

The Goliad Massacre Execution

Re-writing Texas history

People traveling to Port Aransas on the Gulf Coast often go through Goliad, past the Presidio de la Bahia and the adjoining monument to Colonel James W. Fannin and the 342 Texian freedom fighters/rebels massacred nearby. Some locals have petitioned various entities to have the wording changed from "massacre" to "execution." The local League of United Latin American Citizens (LULAC) chairman dealt the race card by saying many Anglos "still hate Mexicans, and using 'massacre' is a subtle way for them to express it" (*NEW YORK TIMES*). Or, the Anglos may have subtly consulted *Roget's Thesaurus* and learned that some synonyms for "massacre" include "annihilation, butchery, carnage, extermination, genocide and slaughter." A few synonyms for "execution" are "capital punishment, crucifixion, and shooting."

Sheer numbers can dictate the usage of the terms. The State of Texas usually carries out executions one at a time, while exterminating two people adds up to an ambush, as with Bonnie and Clyde. The Boston Massacre achieved its distinction with only five victims. On February 14, 1929, Al Capone had seven members of Bugs Moran's gang killed in the St. Valentine's Day Massacre, which also featured a unique attempt at re-writing history in midstream. One of the massacrees, Frank Gusenberg, while dying on the floor was asked by a policeman, "Who shot you?" He replied, "No one. Nobody shot me." Frank fibbed, or he had not been paying attention because "somebody" had shot him 22 times. When Hitler's Waffen-SS executed 84 American soldiers in the Ardennes on the second day of the Battle of the Bulge, it was called the Malmedy Massacre. The subsequent trial saw the employment of the Nuremberg Nazi defense, the Germans were "only following orders," which is similar to one reason given for the Goliad Execution.

Author Andres Tijerina thinks massacre is "too clumsy and insensitive a term" to describe the event at Goliad, but what happened to the Texians after they were killed on Palm Sunday in 1836 was "clumsy and insensitive." Their bodies were tossed into a mass grave, then set ablaze and abandoned, partially covered, to be picked over by coyotes, vultures, and other area wildlife. Sightseers were still discovering bones a century later.

It has been suggested the Texians might have fought to the death had they thought they were going to be massacred or executed. This almost happened in a WWII battle. General Anthony McAuliffe was the acting commander of the 101st Airborne and other troops besieged in Bastogne, Belgium, just days after the Malmedy Massacre. Word of the incident had spread among the American troops, and when the Germans encircled Bastogne and demanded surrender, McAuliffe's famous response one word reply was, "Nuts." The American forces prevailed.

A final example of a massacre took place on October 2, 1968, in Mexico City. Over 5,000 university students and union workers gathered in Tlatelolco Plaza to discuss their grievances with government officials, who never showed. They sent police and military personnel instead, who blocked the exits just before soldiers opened fire on the crowd with machine guns. Eyewitness estimates of the total deaths ranged between 400 and 500, while the government claimed the figure was 30. The officials never released the actual number, although they reportedly had the actual body count on file. Despite the dispute, October 2 has been a National Day of Mourning in Mexico for years, commemorating the Tlatelolco Massacre.

The current intent at Goliad is to rewrite the past. Next will come the revelation that some of Fannin's men were shot while trying to escape a work detail. Or they choreographed an unarmed attack by performing a Michael Jackson moonwalk toward the Mexican army, in hopes of confusing the enemy. This would explain the bullet entry wounds on some Texians' backs. Silly, but no moreso than what some revisionists are proposing. Instead of focusing on symbolism over substance, all of us— including LULAC—should heed a Cuero man's words, "My best advice to them would be to just go on to better things." One of which would be combating the lack of literacy in our State and country today.

My Arkansas Odyssey

Billy Bob Thornton was recording an album in Los Angeles and invited his long-time friend from Arkansas, Rick Calhoun, to come out and sit in on the sessions. Once there, Rick saw the engineering advances made over the past two decades and put that knowledge to good use sometime after returning home to Little Rock. He pulled a cardboard box from the closet beneath his stairway and began sifting through performance tapes of his old rock and roll band, The St. James Group. While re-mixing the music and compiling compact discs, he decided to commemorate the 25th anniversary of the group's last performance with a free reunion performance before invited guests.

Rick knew a lot about staging events. Along with his brother Mark, he had managed Calbro Productions in the 1970s. The company provided sound, lighting, and production for hundreds of concerts, including the first three Willie Nelson 4th of July picnics. And The St. James Group was no garage band: they had been successful during their 10-year run from 1968-78, sharing the stage with a wide range of artists: The Nitty Gritty Dirt Band, Jimmy Buffet, Melissa Manchester, Jerry Jeff Walker, Jim Croce, and Alabama, to name a few. Rick and I had been friends for years, and when he called to invite me to the festivities, I told him to count me in.

A secure flight

On November 9, 2003, at the Austin airport, while waiting to pass through security, I spotted Billy Gammon escorting an elderly woman through the line. She balanced herself with the cane in her right hand, while her left hand rested on his arm. They reached the area for ticketed passengers only, and Billy was forced to leave. He asked me to watch out for her. After clearing security, I searched for his friend. The woman was not hard to locate in the sea of people dressed like they were attending Disney World in July. Her perfectly groomed hair and royal blue knit suit made her easy to spot—that and the fact the local gendarmes had "orange-carded" her. Surrounded by three airport officials, the octogenarian stood with out-stretched arms as one official passed a metal detecting wand over her body and a second one inspected her cane.

Throughout the detention, she was good-natured about the inconvenience. When they released her, I informed the lady that Mr. Gammon had retained my services as her escort. We were booked on the same flight to Dallas, and for the next 30 minutes we sat together and talked in the waiting area. Pre-boarding was announced, I walked her to the gate, and she disappeared down the gangway. Everyone on the three-quarters full flight had already queued up, so I went to the end of the line. Entering the plane, I noticed the first seven rows were packed but on the eighth row on the left there was only one passenger, Billy's friend. She was standing up and leaning on the seat in front of her, waving her hand at me, and pointing to the aisle seat. When I arrived she said, "I saved you a seat, if you don't mind sitting with me." The next 45 minutes passed quickly as our conversation bounced from subject to subject. In Dallas, she was seated in a wheelchair, and I escorted her to her connecting flight. After she disappeared down the gangway for the second time, I called home and asked my wife to contact Billy and tell him, "The package has been delivered."

The concert

That evening in Little Rock, I was at Juanita's, which was voted "one of the top ten places in America to have a margarita" by MARLBORO MAGAZINE. Danny Dozier, a member of The St. James Group from 1970-1972, was there. He later played in a group whose name is unmentionable in polite society. One night, a club manager felt the same way and told the band members, "Fellas, I can't put that name on the marquee. Why don't we just call you The Howlers?" The name stuck, until the future legendary Austin band was re-named Omar and The Howlers.

Occasionally joined by former group members, Rick and his band mates, Mark Hays, Johnny Bradley, Mark Calhoun, Andy Fullerton, and Chuck Gordon, played a 20-song set and four encores. All but two songs were original compositions of the band, mixing southern rock and country. Despite only three rehearsals, the quality of music blew the audience away. People who had purchased tickets to the Alltel Arena show by Rascal Flatts, the band that had won a Country Music Award for Best Vocal Group, remained at Juanita's until Rick's band ended with their signature tune, "WILL THE CIRCLE BE UNBROKEN?"

Divertissement

The previous summer my wife Deborah and I had visited Arkansas and Rick's wife, "Miss Julie," picked us up. When we arrived at Rick's office, he was concluding a non-musical meeting with the bass player and leader of his current band, Capitol Offense. Although it was a chance meeting, Deborah jokingly told Rick's erstwhile musician friend that she was flattered he had taken the time to welcome her to the state. Governor Mike Huckabee laughed and said, "I hope Governor Perry will reciprocate the next time I visit Texas."

Governor Huckabee was in the crowd that Sunday night lending his support, and he listened as I described my escorting duties at the Austin airport earlier that day, and the plight of my elderly companion, who had informed me that she was a native of Little Rock. The Governor was surprised at the efficiency of the Homeland Security bunch at Bergstrom International Airport and asked if he could re-tell the story to his luncheon guest the following day.

The next morning my flight back to Austin was delayed, and the plane sat on the tarmac for ten minutes before the captain's voice came through the speakers and he apologized for the inconvenience. "If you want to know why we are still at the gate, look out the right side of the plane. You will see Air Force One landing." During the additional 20 minutes we remained moored to the gate, I pondered the odds: there are over 23,000 scheduled airline carrier departures daily in the U.S.; our chances of being delayed by Presidential plans were pretty remote. But not as slim as what had occurred 23 hours earlier at the Austin airport, when three airport security personnel had given the "suspected terrorist treatment" to Mrs. Jenna Welch, mother-in-law of the President of the United States.

Audacious Anniversaries

The lunar landing, Chappaquiddick and. . . Brackettville, Texas?

The airplane lifted off a New York runway and turned toward Dallas. Throughout the flight, a wealthy, well-known Texan talked incessantly to the man seated next to him in first class. The ear nodded and smiled politely and occasionally asked a question but rarely was allowed to speak. When the plane landed, the Texan thanked the ear for his time and inquired, "I didn't get your name." The ear responded, "It's Neil Armstrong."

Who could have imagined?

The word audacious has multiple meanings: intrepidly daring, adventurous, or, recklessly bold, rash. This week, July 18-20, 2004, America will mark the thirty-fifth anniversaries of two audacious events: the first lunar landing by Neil Armstrong and the tragedy at Chappaquiddick, where Mary Jo Kopechne died in a car accident. The rash driver, Ted Kennedy, made numerous mistakes in the hours after he drove off Dike Bridge and landed in the water. If someone had told me that 35 years later one man would be a virtual media recluse while the other was to be feted at a national political convention, I would have made the wrong assumption. My fellow Texan's experience explains Mr. Armstrong's reticence; the other is just plain inexplicable.

A gathering of great men

Fort Clark was an old army post in Brackettville, Texas. Its most famous resident was General George Patton, banished to the West Texas outpost to live out his military stint, until World War II rescued his waning career. After the war, the government sold the property, and it was converted into a rustic resort. My brother Paul was one of the few early risers at the summer vacation spot. He would often walk down to Alfred and Nancy Negley's house at dawn, enter the home, and pad up to their bedroom to roust the gentleman. Alfred would come downstairs, put on a pot of coffee, then read the sports section to Paul on the screened-in front porch. My brother was a big New York Yankees fan. He was five years old.

One morning in the summer of 1956, around 8:30 A.M., the human dawn patrol had not returned and my mother went searching. She didn't have to go far. Two doors down was the Patton House, then owned by George and Herman Brown, the founders of Brown and Root. Mom knocked on the door, which was soon opened by the butler. "Is Paul here?" she asked. "Oh, yes ma'am, he's having breakfast with Mr. Brown." She was mortified. "Breakfast!" The butler led her into the large dining room, where her mortification increased as she surveyed the scene. Seated at the big table were George and Herman Brown, John Connally, George Christian, Alfred Negley, Frank Erwin, Jr., Senator Lyndon B. Johnson, the U.S. Senate majority leader. . . and Paul.

Mom had seen enough. "Paul! Come here right now!" My brother dug his spoon into the cereal bowl and stuffed Raisin Bran into his mouth, wisely rendering himself speechless. George Brown diffused the dicey situation with his calm voice. "Now, Catherine, it's all right. We're having an important discussion here, and we need to consult with Paul." George smiled. "We want to ask him a few questions, if that's all right with you. We'll send him home when we're through." She was not used to losing an argument, but Mom was outnumbered. The meeting resumed following her departure.

Curve ball

The power brokers were discussing the Democratic National Convention, which was a few weeks away. The presidential nominee, Adlai Stevenson, had leaked that he was going to allow the convention delegates to elect his running mate. One of those angling for the job was a young senator from Massachusetts, John F. Kennedy. The merits of doing battle with him continued in the dining room of General Patton's house. The men consumed chorizo omelettes and pork chops as they posed a question to the cereal eater. "What do you think of Kennedy?" one chuckled. Paul's feet dangled back and forth beneath his chair, unable to reach the floor. "He's not a Yankee." They laughed. "Actually, he is a Yankee." This momentarily confused the baseball savvy boy-turned-accidental-power-broker. Paul sipped his orange juice, and asked, "What happens when you throw him a curve?" Some of the men rubbed their chins. "Hmmm."

1969

On that same weekend 13 years later, another group of America's "Best and Brightest" assembled around a dining room table in Hyannis Port, Massachusetts. Robert McNamara; Arthur Schlesinger, Jr., Ted Sorenson, John Kenneth Galbraith (by phone), and seven others discussed the previous night's tragedy, when life had thrown Ted Kennedy a curve, and he plunged his car into the water. For the first nine hours after the accident, Kennedy had done many things, but rescuing Mary Jo Kopechne was not one of them. Hence, the damage control at the Kennedy compound, which lingered through Sunday afternoon, until it was interrupted by another event.

At Mission Control in Houston, another group of America's "Best and Brightest" were trying to avert a tragedy: a manned spaceship was frantically searching for a place to land on the moon. "Apollo 11, you have one minute of fuel remaining." Neil Armstrong, who had guided his craft 240,000 miles without a mishap, surveyed the stark terrain. "You have 45 seconds of fuel remaining." In a life-or-death situation, Armstrong calmly guided the spaceship to a safe landing, with 30 seconds of fuel left. While the men in Massachusetts pondered the ramifications of the dead girl found in Poucha Pond at Chappaquiddick, Neil Armstrong marveled at the stark beauty of the moon. His Eagle had touched down in the Sea of Tranquility.

London calling

If that breakfast meeting in Brackettville had ended differently and Lyndon Johnson had chosen to run for vice-president, maybe John F. Kennedy's dream of putting a man on the moon by the end of the decade would not have occurred. And my brother, a recent graduate of Austin High, would not have been sitting on a bedroll at the youth hostel near the University of London with his buddy Bob watching Neil Armstrong take "One giant leap for mankind." In a small way, Paul could relate to the adventurous exploit by Armstrong. Paul had not taken "one small step for man," when he walked up the steps of the Patton house and knocked on the door. Yet, the two shared something in common: their audacity proved that sometimes an intrepidly daring person gets to enter a world few of us can imagine.

Four Days in Paris

In 8th grade I attended the old St. Edward's Junior High. An assistant football coach, Mr. Bruck, taught an unconventional English class, announcing on day one, "If you don't know how to diagram a sentence by now, God have mercy on your soul," and informed us the curriculum would involve a single aspect: vocabulary. His truculent manner on the football field and in the classroom prepared us well. By year's end, the mental calisthenics had forged a pedantic, didactic, and pleonastic legion. If the pen truly were mightier than the sword, the boys of Bruck could have debated the fall of Troy in 10 days, instead of ten years.

Neanderthals

A few years later, William F. Buckley, Jr., was in Austin visiting his second cousin, Beryl Milburn, and spoke at a fundraiser. Midway through the speech he unleashed a barrage of polysyllabic verbiage that left the Neanderthals in attendance slack-jawed. Asked afterwards about those words, he modestly replied that he didn't know what they meant, but his audiences anticipated and expected them.

Later, he needed to leave the Milburn's home and I offered to drive him back to his accommodations. His wife Patricia was a tall woman, yet she maneuvered into the back seat of my two-door Cutlass. She deftly dodged dozens of eight track tapes strewn across the back seat and floor before scrunching her legs for the ride to the Villa Capri Motel. During the conversation I conjured up a "Bruckism" and William F. Buckley, Junyah, said, "What an interesting turn of phrase. Do you mind if I borrow it?" What? The Human Dictionary wanted a nugget mined from my feeble brain? "No, be my guest. I have no claim on it."

Perfect gentlemen

In the summer of 1971, when my grandparents took the entire brood to Ireland, my aunt Mary Scott and cousins Anne Scott and Jerry Bell, Jr., and I flew from Cork to Paris for a long weekend. Anne had lived in

Paris while attending the Sorbonne and was worried that her rube cousins might embarrass her so she was constantly instructing us on proper etiquette and decorum. For two days I was *savoir* to Jerry's *faire* as we attended museums and dined at Anne's favorite tiny Left Bank bistro and then at La Coupole. On day three, things came apart after cocktails at the Bar Hemingway in the Ritz Hotel.

Over cocktails, Anne had instructed the two rubes on proper etiquette for dinner before we crossed the alley and entered the center of the culinary cuisine of the universe at that time, Maxim's Restaurant, and were ushered to our table. Seated nearby were David Bruce, head of the American delegation to the Paris Peace talks, and his party. Everywhere I looked there were glitterati and literati, but at our table things were simply rotty. Jerry's chair back snapped and before Anne could say, "*Garçon, s' il vous plaît,*" he raised the shattered piece above his head and announced, "My chair is broken!" Anne's hands caught her head before it hit the table, and she shook it slowly from side to side while 10 fast-acting minions of Maxim's arrived at our table. Yelling "Fire!" could not have caused a quicker response. They encircled our group, lessening Anne's embarrassment, and with instinctive aplomb changed Jerry's chair. The rest of the meal produced no more kindling, but *faux* and *pas* had lit a fire under Anne, nonetheless.

"Life is a cabaret, old chum"

Like the chair, Jerry and I splintered off from Mary and Anne after dinner, keeping our reservations at the Lido de Paris, where we saw an elaborate stage production featuring horses and waterfalls. These were sideshows to the main attractions: dozens of women whose beauty was revelatory to a former student of an all-boys school.

Following the show we walked down a corridor, turned, and saw the late-show crowd that had queued up. For a split second I felt like the guy in that Twilight Zone episode who kept getting transported from one place to another unexpectedly. In that nanosecond I thought, "Omigosh, I've gone from naked women to Vietnam!" Staring at us were 400 smiling North Vietnamese soldiers dressed in their dark gray uniforms with red trim. Enjoy the show, fellas.

"In the Heat of the Night"

Our final evening was spent in the St. Germain area, the 6th arrondissement, within blocks of the Sorbonne and Notre Dame Cathedral at La Mediterranée Restaurant across the street from the l'Odeon Theatre. The seafood was excellent; it was easy to see why the place was a favorite haunt of Chagall, Orson Welles, and Picasso. Mary spotted Rod Steiger a few tables away and they made eye contact throughout the dinner. The only thing she enjoyed more than reading was going to movies. Seeing the Academy Award winner in the flesh was the highlight of the trip, until I lit her up. She pulled out a cigarette and, being the dutiful godson, I flicked her Bic. Usually, the lighter emitted a flame akin to a votive candle. Unlike the restaurant's former neighbor, Thomas Paine, I did not use common sense and neglected to check the French-made flame first. Mary leaned over as the lighter ignited. Picture the out of control Kuwaiti oil fires after the Gulf War. No, that's too severe. Imagine someone igniting a blowtorch in your face; that's what hit Auntie M's visage. In less than a second we lost our panache and her left eyebrow. Anne was as slack-jawed as Mr. Buckley's audience and Jerry looked down at his dinner plate emblazoned with a Jean Cocteau drawing and probably said to himself, "And they thought Maxim's was bad." Mr. Steiger raised both eyebrows as the rubes gave new meaning to *In The Heat of The Night*.

Divertissement

The trip was educational and magical, largely because of Anne's determination to show us Paris through her eyes. Too bad she did not get to view it through mine the time I waited for my trio outside the Ritz Hotel. Soaking in the hubbub swirling around the Place de Vendôme early that evening, I saw a man exit the hotel and walk to the curb a few yards away from me. A female companion soon joined him; together they made an odd couple. He was balding, portly, and diminutive in his black tuxedo. Her medium-length dark hair flowed to a lithe, statuesque frame draped in an all-white summer outfit. Leaning down as he whispered something, she laughed perceptibly. Then she surveyed the landscape, our eyes met, and her face scrunched slightly, her mind trying to recall if we had met before. I smiled back, nodded perceptibly, and looked away.

The limousine arrived and the driver opened a passenger door for them. There were no eight-track tapes strewn across the backseat as Patricia Buckley stepped inside, followed by Truman Capote. The limousine disappeared so quickly I was left curbside wondering if reality or a fanciful chimera had danced in front of my eyes. And I wished that Coach Bruck could have hopped into that limo and gone along for the ride, escorting them to their destination: a party where the beautifully spoken words, rich in color, design, and texture shared space with French Impressionist paintings, and polysyllabic palaver was as commonplace as two eyebrows.

What Mick Jagger Taught Me

This is a non-musical concert review, with good reason. Attending gigs was not something I did with any regularity. Crickets inhabiting the fabled Armadillo World Headquarters music hall in Austin in the 60s and 70s saw 'way more rock concerts than I did. And the life span of a cricket is pretty darn short—about one year. The bugs do have good vision and hearing, though, which is a prerequisite for concert patrons. Supposedly, crickets are harbingers of good luck, and in my case they presaged something just short of magical. But enough prattle. On with the show.

Rolling Stones bass player, Bill Wyman, was passing time in the studio before a recording session and banged a riff on the piano. Keith Richards and Mick Jagger walked in, liked what they heard, and embellished the melody into "JUMPING JACK FLASH." The first lyrics, "I was born in a crossfire hurricane," are deemed by some music historians as an allusion to Jagger's birth at Dartford, Kent, England. Although the Blitz of London had ended a few years before, it is likely the blue-collar city suffered bombings in the summer of 1943, when he was born.

Their initial U.S. tour started in San Bernardino, California, and moved to San Antonio the next day, June 6, 1964, the twentieth anniversary of D-Day. This British invasion was much less successful than the Allied landing at Normandy but, to be fair, General Eisenhower didn't have to contend with a bunch of monkeys.

Dad's 1961 Valiant station wagon rumbled the 75 miles down IH-35 to San Antonio. By the time we pulled in front of the Joe Freeman Coliseum, my brother Paul and I were like kids waiting to bolt downstairs on Christmas morning. A blistering mid-afternoon sun sapped some of our adrenaline. Saturday, June 7, was sweltering, even by Texas standards. Jagger commented the temperature "must have been about 110 degrees," and he was referencing the inside of the arena.

Hundreds of teenagers milled about the concrete outside the Coliseum, giddy with excitement. We were among the first to see the Rolling Stones in America. What a big deal! Little did we know what awaited us inside the cavernous building.

"Teen Fest 1964" had a hodge-podge retinue that sought to imitate the popular variety shows on television that year. Organizers said the 10-day festival would feature "four changes of headline stars in order to cater to all types of teenagers." On June 7, the main headliners were the clean-cut All-American boy, Bobby Vee ("THE NIGHT HAS A THOUSAND EYES," "TAKE GOOD CARE OF MY BABY," "RUN TO HIM," and other gold records) and girl, Diane Renay ("BLUE NAVY"). Preceding them on stage was America's No. 1 country-western star, George Jones.

Articles written about the concert stated the venue accommodated 20,000. The Coliseum seating chart listed 10,000 stationary seats. Adding thousands of metal folding chairs in neat rows on the floor of the arena put the maximum possible attendance closer to the higher figure. That day there were six empty seats for each one occupied; about 3,000 people bothered to show, and a lot of them were also bothered by what they saw.

Paul was 13 and I was 11, and in our youthful naiveté we thought we were going to a Rolling Stones concert. At least seven acts were scheduled to fill the two hours. Wyman wrote that the current Rolling Stones were "the real Rock & Roll Circus." On June 7, they were just a small part of one.

The Fest began at two o'clock. My recollection of the early acts may be out of sequence; that part remains a blur. Ten minutes into the show I was sweating more than the cowboys dressed in hats, long-sleeved shirts, jeans, and boots. The Fire-Twirling Lounsbury Sisters didn't help. Those babes bounced on stage and, well, they twirled fiery batons. Already trapped in Hades, we didn't need a reminder. The minutes crept by. How many spectacular things can you do with burning batons? Next on stage was Amandis Troupe, "a teeterboard act." They came and went too slowly, as did The Pompoff Thedy Family, a Vaudeville act featuring musical clowns. A Fellini-esque movie was playing out before our eyes. This was not a Fellini crowd.

A kid yelled in frustration, "This ain't 'Teen Fest,' it's a circus! Bring on the Stones!" We got the Marquis Chimps instead—monkeys cavorting on bikes and unicycles. Then, the moment we had been waiting for: "Ladies and Gentlemen, The Rolling Stones!"

They came out like Royals exiting tumbrels on their way to the guillotine. Mick and the boys had slogged through two shows the previous day in San Antonio and were underwhelmed by the tepid response. At the end of the American tour, Richards and Wyman reportedly stuffed weapons in their underwear that went undetected by British customs agents: handguns bought during their short visit to San Antonio. Maybe they felt extra protection was needed, especially in the Alamo City.

"ROUTE 66" led their set; "NOT FADE AWAY" was another selection. During the first song a smattering of boos rippled through the audience. The crowd attracted to George Jones was not too keen on the Stones. Peering at the Brits, the cowboys saw longhaired, dope-smoking, drug-crazed kids, poster boys for this-is-what's-wrong-with-the-world-today. Jeers led to taunts and booing that did not fade away. This was the band's third San Antone rodeo/circus in 24 hours, with an evening show to go. Playing for ingrates was tough. Four years later, "STREET FIGHTING MAN" was released. The second line is, "'Cause summer's here and the time is right for fighting in the street, boy." By their third song that afternoon the band had given up without a fight. Unfamiliar with an unruly crowd, Mick and the boys went through the motions on "I WANNA BE YOUR MAN" and "I JUST WANT TO MAKE LOVE TO YOU," then exited the raised stage and rolled back to their dressing room. A tumbrel never looked so good.

Afterwards, the efforts by George Jones, Diane Renay, and Bobby Vee melted together like the remnants of ice and soft drinks on the arena floor, with one exception. Diane Renay, in her white go-go boots, sang, "*Blue Navy, blue, I'm as blue as I can be . . .*" and I gazed around. Many teenagers had a forlorn expression of profound disappointment, the type children make after tearing open the Christmas presents and not finding the gift that topped their list.

On the drive home I asked Paul what he thought. His shrug was a silent equivalent for "They stank." It didn't seem fair. The Stones had been in the wrong place at the wrong time. But is there ever a right time to follow a pack of chimpanzees? One good thing came of the gigs in San Antonio. Backstage, the band met a young West Texas musician, Bobby Keys, who appeared at the most inopportune time, yet was undaunted by the non-friendly reception heaped on the Brits. The next time all of us were in the same building the results were different.

In 1972, I was working as an assistant sergeant-at-arms in the basement of the Texas State Capitol building. The subterranean region gave visitors the sense of what it must have been like to conduct business in Hitler's bunker, without the incessant bombing noise. Sound effects were supplied by the invasion of crickets. One day I entered our one-room warren and the stench assaulted my nostrils. A nighttime janitor had swept them into a far corner, a pile two feet high and three feet wide: dead crickets, thousands of them. No one had bothered to warn me. I staggered out of the room and spied two co-workers outside our new office, but a few doors down. They were howling with delight.

A few weeks later while lunching in the Capitol's small cafeteria, a co-worker, Frank Jackson, sat down at my table. He looked bummed out. Frank had bought two tickets to the Rolling Stones concert in Fort Worth on June 24, but a conflict forced him to unload his ducats. "You want to buy them?" They were $3 each. Six bucks for tickets, 30 gallons of gas at $0.35 a gallon, lunch, dinner, maybe a tee shirt; at least 30 bucks. Minimum wage was $1.60 per hour. Did I really want to work 20 or so hours just to see another Stones concert? An internal voice whispered, "Remember the Alamo?"

"Yeah, I'll take 'em." Somewhere in the building the live Capitol crickets chirped.

The Stones Touring Party, or STP tour, was scheduled for two shows at the Tarrant County Convention Center in Fort Worth on Saturday, June 24, 1972, one at three o'clock and the other at eight. Upon learning my tickets were for the latter show I was relieved. Another Stones matinee was not what I needed. After parking a few blocks away, Deborah and I walked around the corner and spied the circus in front of the Convention Center. Participants from Friday's gay pride march in Dallas had relocated to Fort Worth. Alongside them were Students for a Democratic Society (SDS) and other anti-Vietnam War protestors. Even the Black Panthers had carved out prime real estate. A couple of other, smaller factions pissed off about something loitered in the area, but they remained a blur, like The Fire-Twirling Lounsbury Sisters.

Sauna-like heat baked the protestors, each of whom had a petition that needed signing or a leaflet that needed taking, and telling them "No" was not greeted kindly. A line from the Stones song, "You Can't Always Get What You Want" came to mind. "I went down to the demonstration, To get my fair share of abuse." And Mick thought he needed protection in San Antonio. Telling them, "Sorry, we're only here for the drugs," would have fooled no one. Deborah and I were dressed like extras from **My Three Sons**, utterly clean-cut and normal looking. Most of the audience that night was neither. My future bride and I were as inconspicuous as the Marquis Chimps.

The sold-out 14,000-seat convention center layout resembled the Freeman Coliseum setup. Rows of folding metal chairs filled the floor of the arena. The stage was at one end, and the permanent seats formed a large U around it. An usher directed us to ours in the middle of the U, high in the mezzanine, ten rows from the top. Workers scurrying about the stage looked to be the size of small primates.

A chap next to Deborah was giving a discourse to his date. One of his palms held a rainbow of pills: red, green, white, yellow, and black. He pointed from color to color and detailed the pros and cons offered by each. Deborah slowly turned her head away from the illicit pharmacy and stared at me, bug-eyed. Smiling, I motioned in the direction of the seats in front of us. Leaning forward slightly, her mouth widened, matching her eyes. The couple below us had laid out two lines of cocaine on some smooth surface, and in unison they bent down and snorted the evidence into their nostrils. The fellow next to me tapped my shoulder. "Hey, man. Want a joint?" A fat, recently rolled marijuana cigarette lay in the palm of his hand.

"No, thanks," I whispered, "I've got to drive back to Austin after the show."

He nodded and said, "I can dig it."

Surrounded by felonies waiting to be discovered, we kept to ourselves. The house lights were up. The cops were oblivious to the criminal conduct, and there were lots of cops. Between 70 and 80 coursed through the building, making the ratio one law enforcement official to every 200 druggies.

Directly below the cocaine couple, a young lad of 13 or 14 sat wearing a windbreaker. His head swiveled constantly, absorbing the shenanigans surrounding him. Wanting to show he belonged, the boy extracted a beer from a pocket of his jacket and proudly displayed the can to his neighbors. A voice shouted, "Far out, kid!" Junior figured his dad would not miss a beer. Guess who the cops hauled off?

"Hey, kid! Come here!" a policeman yelled, pointing to the boy. Our not-quite-stoned-yet neighbors became downright truculent, vocalizing their disapproval with jeers, taunts, and boos. I thought to myself, "San Antonio, all over again." Two more cops arrived and calmed the crowd with looks that implied, "Pipe down, or you're next." Things quieted down in the 'hood quickly; the drugs were kicking in.

The house lights dimmed, and the Dorothy Norwood Singers started the concert. The STP tour included the gospel group at five locales, and Fort Worth was their first. Dorothy and her gang were vital in one respect: their set and the accompanying darkness allowed the audience to fire up joints. Judging from the spontaneous combustion in the building, most of the nearly 14,000 fans were inhaling deep hits from their doobies while the ladies sang about God and Jesus. A small cloud of smoke formed on the ceiling, and as it spread the girls sang, "Oh, happy days!"

Dorothy departed to polite applause, and the house lights went up briefly as a blind man in a dashiki was escorted to center stage. Stevie Wonder hit his first note, the house lights went dark, and thousands flicked their lighters in a sign of respect. Unlike San Antonio, a love affair was beginning, one that would last for hours. Stevie's set ended with a thunderous ovation, the kind an anxious football crowd makes after the National Anthem in anticipation of the game.

"Ladies and Gentlemen, The Rolling Stones!"

No tumbrel this time. The crowd roared before the first note of "Brown Sugar" was struck. Mick belted out the saucy tune and took command of the audience. "Bitch" was the next offering, and I thought, "That's what these seats are." During the interlude I grabbed Deborah's hand and yelled over the cheering crowd, "Let's go."

Downstairs, the outer concourse was deserted, aiding our movement. Mom always told me, "Dress nicely on a trip. People will treat you better." That old adage was about to be tested. We re-entered the arena and Deborah gasped, "Oh, my gosh!" Four steps across the aisle was a metal railing, where we stopped. The left end of the stage was 10 feet away. Mick and boys were 30 feet beyond that.

The first guitar notes of "Gimme Shelter" were struck. On another June 6, in 1969 at Altamont Speedway, a Hell's Angels member stabbed a Stones fan, killing the man. Fort Worth officials and concert promoters weren't taking chances. Policemen were everywhere. Canvassing the auditorium earlier, I had selected this spot because it was the only area near the stage with a young cop. I checked my watch with the intention of timing how long it would be before we were shoed away by the 6'4", 230-pound man in blue. Jagger sang, "War, children, It's just a shot away, It's just a shot away," and I glanced at the cop repeatedly, until the crowd burst into applause and Mick started saying, "Thank you, thank you!" Our policeman never parted his lips during the song; he sucked the plentiful marijuana smoke directly into his nostrils. He wasn't going anywhere, and neither were we.

Three or four songs later, Jagger breathed in and out of a harmonica and drifted through "Sweet Virginia." The last lyrics were, "Tryin' to stop the waves behind your eyeballs, Drop your reds, drop your greens and blues," and mine searched the darkness for our seats in the mezzanine. Somewhere up there a couple dropping a rainbow of pills was spaced out. Man, were they missing a show.

My first hint something special was transpiring happened as "Gimme Shelter" ended and I re-checked my watch: the song lasted almost six minutes; the studio recording was barely four and a half. Guys with hand-held movie cameras scurried around the stage while others filmed from the floor area below. Mounds of celluloid were rolling for a film, *Ladies and Gentlemen, The Rolling Stones*. Mick and the boys had practiced two sessions in Dallas, preparing for the June 24 shows. Somewhere in the crowd, bootleggers monitored their hidden recording devices near the soundboard. The choral voices ushered in "You Can't Always Get What You Want." A figure stood in the wings on the opposite side of the stage, absorbing the spectacle. Arms folded, head cocked back slightly, he peered over his nose at the band. Eleven months before, he and I had been standing next to each other in Paris at the Place de Vendôme, on the front steps of the Ritz Hotel. A Rolling Stones concert at the Tarrant County Convention Center was the last place I expected to see Truman Capote.

The last two offerings, "Jumping Jack Flash" and the finale, "Street Fighting Man," concluded the 15-song concert with a flourish. Jagger's lyrics, "'Cause summer's here and the time is right for fighting in the street, boy," were lost in the theatrics. He tossed rose petals to the audience and disappeared without an encore. I was not disappointed.

Walking to our car, I anticipated the Sunday phone conversation with my brother. Paul: "How was it?"

Me: "They didn't stink."

Deborah slept as the car barreled down IH-35 to Austin, and I replayed the entire concert in my head. As I've gotten older, certain parts squished together and others crinkled like an eight-track tape. My memory of the night's events was shortened with each splicing, but two songs never faded. Decades later I found out why: all roads lead back to San Antonio.

I didn't get what I wanted at Teen Fest, but I got what I needed in Fort Worth. Someone else shared my sentiment. Around the time of the band's 40th anniversary, Jagger sat for an interview, which I am forced to paraphrase. A reporter asked Mick to name the worst concert the Stones had ever done. He chuckled and said, "San Antonio, 1964, 'Teen Fest.'" Paul was right! My mental calculator whirled the numbers: 40 years, 50 concerts per annum = 2,000 shows, times 25,000 fans per show: minimum = 50 million spectators. Only 3,000 had seen the Rolling Stones at their admitted worst. The interviewer asked him to name the band's best effort. Mick danced around the question, then said, "The 1972 Fort Worth concerts that made up most of the footage for *Ladies and Gentlemen, The Rolling Stones.*

I stared at the television. What were the odds of that happening, one in 50 million? Then it hit me: except for the band, I was probably the only person on Earth who could say, "I saw the best and worst performances of The Rolling Stones." A memory from Fort Worth came into focus, and I floated back 30 years to the Convention Center. Descending through the haze of illicit smoke, I reclaimed my spot along the railing next to the stoned policeman.

The audience cheered lustily after each song—guttural, throaty incantations of encouragement that Jagger acknowledged with a polite and sincere, "Thank you, thank you." He was in a rare place, where an artist uses a compliant crowd as his canvas. A unique moment when the confluence of crowd and performer meld together, creating a masterpiece.

A rhythm guitar strummed the first notes of "JUMPING JACK FLASH," followed by the 16-note riff. Jagger belted out, "I was born in a crossfire hurricane . . ." and strutted the stage like a banty rooster, cocksure of his effort. Murky images of the disaster in San Antonio were erased. Jagger was Jack Flash this night; the last stanza was directed to the little boy born in Dartford, Kent, England. "But, it's all right now, in fact it's a gas. But, it's all right, Jumping Jack Flash is a gas, gas, gas." He began jumping, and I moved down the aisle to get a better view. Dressed in a sleeveless white jumpsuit, he rose off the ground and flung his hands upward, repeatedly. From the far side of the arena, a single beam of light shone above him. While leaping, his head would eclipse the light and Jagger's dark silhouette would hang in the air for a half-second. Just before that moment, as the intense spotlight bathed him in brilliant brightness, Mick resembled a grateful angel with outstretched wings reaching for the heavens.

Some audiophiles labeled that night's rendition of "You Can't Always Get What You Want" as the Stones' definitive live version: a female chorus began, "I saw her today. . ." followed by unified male voices. Mick Taylor plucked the acoustic guitar accompanied by the horn player. Beside him, holding a saxophone was Bobby Keys, the musician from West Texas via the San Antonio Teen Fest of 1964.

A spotlight illuminated Jagger. In younger years he had sung, "I can't get no satisfaction." Approaching the age of 30 had altered his outlook. Near the song's end he stated, "You can't always get what you want, but if you try sometime, you just might find, you just might find, you get what you need. . . I'm telling the truth!" Charlie Watts banged the drums and cymbals, Nicky Hopkins tickled the ivories, then faded. Watts kept pounding rhythmically, and the choir flooded the arena with lilting voices that sounded like angels. Jagger moved about triumphantly, absorbing the essence of perfection. He wanted to give a good performance in San Antonio, but failed. He needed excellence to please the film producers and himself in Fort Worth. What he got at the Tarrant County Convention Center that night was much more: redemption for Teen Fest.

Witnessing the absolute worst in others is rare, although the odds are lower than 3,000 in 50 million. Maybe it's a co-worker, loved one, or dear friend whose betrayal is so profound and hurtful it leaves you feeling like someone made an incision in your navel, inserted a vacuum nozzle, and sucked out your stomach. Emotionally wounded, the pain sears inside your brain like hot wax and then hardens into anger, hatred, or resentment that does not easily melt away. Then you see a co-worker, loved one, or dear friend at their best. Someone who comes to your aid. Fortunately, your odds of seeing others at their absolute greatest is five times higher than viewing them at their worst, based on my concert experience. Too many people glimpse the worst in others and dwell on it and lower the expectations they have for themselves and others. They are pessimists. Another group sees the best in others and admires an effort that is as good as it can be. They are realists.

Cynics say those sexagenarians, The Rolling Stones, are still touring for the money and the rush of playing for an audience. Maybe they are right, but observing the band at their best and worst has given me a different perspective. The boy who was "born in a cross-fire hurricane" during the darkest period of the 20th century—World War II—is approaching old age. His wrinkles are deeper, his bones more creaky. Current performances are more often laced with nuance than physical bravado. Just before each concert he waits in the wings, hoping the evening produces the perfect alchemy of artist and audience, resulting in their greatest performance ever, usurping even Fort Worth. The announcer yells, "Ladies and Gentlemen, The Rolling Stones," the group bounds on stage, the frenzied crowd roars their approval, and Sir Mick Jagger grins. Because Jumping Jack Flash is an optimist; he believes the best is yet to come.

Capote and the Midnight Rambler

Filmmakers and writers descended upon Fort Worth to chronicle the event. Harold Colson wrote, "The fabled summer 1972 tour through the U.S. and Canada is revered by Stones fans worldwide as arguably the band's greatest ever, and it remains in the annals of rock lore and popular imagination as the masterpiece speedball of indoor triumph, outdoor maelstrom and backstage debauch."

Attracted by the jet-set lifestyle of rock and roll's elite and the decadence and debauchery that fueled it, Truman Capote was in town doing research for a magazine article. The nexus of the Stones and Capote on June 24 was two-fold. On a day when the world's greatest rock and roll band was at their zenith, the man Norman Mailer described as, "the most perfect writer of his generation" was at the midpoint between his professional apex and its nadir. Fort Worth was a diversionary trip for Capote's slow, inexorable death train fueled by alcoholism.

Most of the Stones' concert material came from two albums, "EXILE ON MAIN STREET" and "LET IT BLEED." During the filming on location of *In Cold Blood*, the movie's director considered Capote a distraction and banished him from Holcomb, Kansas, the scene of the murders. By then the author was very familiar with bloodletting. His opus detailed the senseless, gruesome murder of Herbert Clutter, his wife Bonnie, and their two youngest children, 16-year-old Nancy and 15-year-old Kenyon, who were home when the clock chimed midnight, ushering in November 15, 1959.

Over the next five years, Capote purloined the confidence of the murderers who bared their past and innermost thoughts, naively hoping the book's publication would somehow rescue them from the hangman's noose. Richard Hickock and Perry Smith were unlikely looking killers. Hickock elevated his medium height with an erect gait; Smith was short and shuffled lightly in a tiptoe manner, the byproduct of bad knees that never healed after a motorcycle accident.

In Fort Worth, the author probably absorbed the entire matinee, but during the evening show he appeared and disappeared with the alacrity of a ghost. Moving back and forth between stage right and the dressing rooms, he rarely lingered for an entire song. His claim of having "94% total recall" might explain his numerous departures: too many lyrics from the afternoon concert recalled something he was struggling to forget. A snippet from "GIMME SHELTER": "Rape, murder! It's just a shot away, it's just a shot away." Lyrics from "DON'T LIE TO ME": "Heard about the way you do your part, Don't lie to me don't you lie to me. Don't you make me mad, I'll get evil as a man can be." And "ROCKS OFF": "He don't come around no more, Is he checking out for sure?"

Minutes before midnight ushered in April 14, 1965, the two murderers sat on wooden chairs in a holding room at the Kansas State Penitentiary in Lansing waiting for their executions, when Capote entered the room. This was his first visit in q uite a while; he didn't come around much anymore, having already gotten from them what he wanted.

Shackled with metal chains, the condemned men sized up their confidante. Years of conversations had schooled the killers on his persona: like them, he was a taker; like them, he was an adroit liar. The executions were essential to Capote, the required denouement of his book. Until the men were put to death, the final chapter could not be written. Capote was also on hand to get something else he needed—absolution from the killers for his manipulations, false presentations, and deceit. Smith and Hickock gazed at Capote with conspiratorial, knowing smirks. What he wanted from them, although unspoken, was as transparent as the glasses he stared through. The awkward silence forced Capote to confront a grim reality: these men had no desire to accommodate him. Even worse, their smug demeanor minutes before death was, in a compartmentalized way, borne from a sense of moral superiority over Capote. The trio's relationship had begun on a level playing field of truthfulness. More often than not, it was the writer who strayed out of bounds. Because of his miscalculations, two common, run-of-the-mill thieves-turned-killers felt they were, in some respects, better than "the most perfect writer of his generation." Worst of all, Capote mutely agreed.

In the shadows offstage, Capote fidgeted as the band introduced the operatic blues tune, "MIDNIGHT RAMBLER." Jagger and Richards had penned it on vacation. Mick explained, "Why we should write such a dark song in this sunny, beautiful place, I don't know." They were in the picturesque Italian seaside village of Positano, which hugs the same coastline as Portofino, where Capote had penned parts of *In Cold Blood*. The song mirrored the movements in the Clutter home that November night: a rhythmic, methodical cadence segueing to a languid interlude, before ending with a furious, climactic flourish. Captured on vinyl, the tune was less than seven minutes long. In Fort Worth, hidden bootleggers' tape machines whirled round and round because the extended live version lasted an extra five minutes. The tapes recorded exactly 12:00. Midnight.

Film crews hustled about the stage and pit area below as Jagger sang. "Did you hear about the midnight rambler? Well, honey, it's no rock and roll show." Words to "MIDNIGHT RAMBLER" might have summoned images for the author; scenes that flickered across Capote's mind momentarily before slinking back into his subconscious, visions similar to what he may have recalled while standing in front of the killers on that April night in 1965, as he groveled, unsuccessfully. At some point, suffused with frustration and unease, Capote must have been tempted to utter in his soft-whisper voice, "You think I'm bad? Let's go back to November 15, 1959."

Did you hear about the midnight gambler?
Did you see me make my midnight call?

Shortly after midnight, a 10-year-old Chevrolet with its lights off had rolled to a stop near the Clutter house. Two men quietly exited the car and entered the unlocked home. A fellow inmate in the Kansas prison had told them Mr. Clutter kept a safe with lots of cash in his office. Unable to locate it, Smith and Hickock awakened the patriarch, who truthfully denied its existence. With their gamble now a miserable failure, the ex-cons rousted the other family members, who joined Herb in a locked bathroom. Now, what to do?

One by one they were relocated: father and son to the basement, mother and daughter back to their respective bedrooms. Orderly situated, all were bound with rope, gagged with duct tape, and left in the dark.

I'm called the hit-and-run, rape-her-in-anger.

Smith finished tying Kenyon's intricate knots in the basement and went upstairs. Hickock was in Nancy's room preparing to rape her when Smith surprised him and became enraged. Threatened with physical harm, Hickock backed off. It was the last favor granted to any of the Clutters.

I'm going easy with your cold fandango,
I'll stick my knife right down your throat baby, and it hurts. . .

The sepulchral blackness of the basement resembled a coalmine tunnel. In the furnace room, Hickock trained the flashlight's white circle on Herb's face swathed in duct tape. Unable to see much without his glasses, the father's eyes searched beyond the glare, blindly trying to find his captors. Smith plunged the Bowie knife into Mr. Clutter's throat. Blood gurgled onto the floor. Not content to just let him bleed, Smith grabbed Hickock's gun, a 12-gauge Savage 300, dropped the barrel into the spotlight inches from Clutter's nose, and pulled the trigger. Smith shuffled quickly through the darkness, into the adjoining playroom, his partner rushing to keep pace. The white circle from Hickock's light traveled over the floor until it found Kenyon, lying on the couch. Smith dropped the gun barrel into the spotlight, inches from the boy's face. The white-hot blast flashed brightly, like a thousand fireflies exploding.

The knife sharpened, tippytoe,
Or just that shoot-'em-dead, green bell jangler
You know, the one you've never seen before.

Not a single light in the house shone, which would have shuttered it in pitch-black nothingness, except for the lunar cycle. A full moon, like a giant flood beam in the sky, cast a muslin-colored hue in the rooms on the first floor. The killers ambled past them, quietly, as they walked the main hallway. Ascending the stairs, Hickock trailed behind Smith, who quickstepped in tiptoe fashion on the balls of his feet, lessening the pain of his aching knees. Moonlight splashed against the wall, outlining two dark silhouettes as they glided upward, one holding a knife and flashlight, the other carrying a shotgun.

Sixteen-year-old Nancy lay in her bed facing the wall, hands bound behind her, mouth gagged. Night cream on her cheeks and forehead, applied one hour before was now mixed with sweat. Fear. She had heard the shots. A figure entered, walked across the room, dropped the gun barrel into the spotlight inches from the rear of Nancy's head . . . and pulled the trigger.

And if you catch the midnight rambler
I'll steal your mistress from under your nose.

Clutter's wife Bonnie lay on the bed in her spartan room, hands bound in front of her as if in supplication. A muffled report from the basement had sounded in her ears, followed moments later by a second roar. Herb and Kenyon—gone. Minutes passed, and then a third blast shook the walls in her room. Nancy—gone. On her bedside table was a Bible. Resting inside it was a bookmark containing a passage from the King James Version, Mark 13: "Take ye heed, watch and pray: for ye know not when the time is." The mother knew the time was now; she heard Death approaching. Out in the hallway, floorboards moaned beneath Hickock's erect gait, masking the tippytoe shuffle of Smith's small boots. The creaking noises, rhythmic and methodical in cadence, crept closer . . . closer. Reaching her door, the footsteps paused briefly. Bonnie stared at the door, watching and praying. Then the doorknob began to turn.

Don't do that . . .
Don't you do that . . .
Oh, don't do that . . .

The door swung open and a flashlight searched the darkness, briefly, until its white circle found Bonnie's face, swathed in duct tape. Terrified, Mrs. Clutter stared into the brightness that intensified as it approached the bed. The gun barrel dropped into the spotlight and stopped, two inches from her nose. Bonnie tried to turn away.

The one who closed the bedroom door.

When the bodies were discovered on Sunday morning, Mrs. Clutter's bedroom door was closed. Beyond the wooden divide was one of the four pieces of evidence that this home was a rare place, where an enraged artist had used a compliant crowd as his canvas. Blood hung on the wall above the bed. It coalesced around her on the sheets. The shotgun blast had struck the right side of Bonnie's face at point-blank range. Her eyes were still wide open.

Did you hear about the midnight rambler?
He'll leave his footprints up and down your hall

From a dusty spot near Herb Clutter's body, law enforcement officials lifted a boot print—Hickock's. A different print, outlined in the patriarch's blood, was found nearby; it matched Smith's soles. When he was arrested, traces of Herb Clutter's blood were still wedged in the cracks of Smith's boots.

Words from "YOU CAN'T ALWAYS GET WHAT YOU WANT" took Capote back to the death house.

I saw her today at the reception;
In her glass was a bleeding man.
She was practiced at the art of deception,
Well, I could tell by her bloodstained hands.

The carnage committed in the rooms of the Clutter home was not Capote's fault, but the man practiced at the art of deception had a festering guilt of omission that needed to be expunged. Addressing Smith and Hickock, he said, "I did everything I could."

He needed to keep their blood from staining his hands. They withheld absolution, and Capote left the room.

Two songs after "MIDNIGHT RAMBLER," the Stones' offered "RIP THIS JOINT."

Ying yang, you're my thing,
Oh, now, baby, won't you hear me sing.
Flip flop, fit to drop.

Threatening weather and fear of a springtime tornado almost delayed the executions. Instead, a light rain danced on the metal roof of the prison warehouse that housed the gallows. Hickock was first. Capote witnessed the event, and during the next 20 minutes, as Hickock's body hung motionless in the air, Capote contemplated his next action. Viewing Smith's death was more than he could endure, for reasons that were two-fold. The men shared similar traits: both were small in stature and suffered residual effects from fractured and disjointed childhoods. Murmurs of a much deeper connection had coursed down the prison hallways. Capote also knew Smith was not going to "sing" the words of forgiveness the writer desperately needed to hear. The diminutive one slinked out of the building. Smith could die alone. After all, hadn't each of the Clutters?

Thirty minutes later, a vehicle transporting Smith entered the spartan building. Officials escorted him past the small crowd gathered in the bleak, dimly lit building, and stopped at the east end, where the steps led up to the dangling noose. During the killers' ascent of the Clutter stairway, Bonnie and Nancy knew the fate that awaited them. This night, as Hickock and Smith ascended the stairs, they knew the fate that awaited them. Take ye heed . . . for ye know when the time is. Smith stood over the trapdoor and an eerie quiet befell the witnesses, as if their mouths had been taped shut. A black hood was draped over Smith's head, then a knotted rope, not as intricate as the half-hitch style he had used to bind the Clutters, was placed around his neck. A lone spotlight shone down on Smith, leaving the edges of the gallows in darkness. Behind him, standing in the shadows, was the executioner, who silently moved into the white circle of light, grabbed the three-foot long lever and pulled it. As Smith dropped, a loud blast of thunder reverberated through the building, masking the noise of death. His legs twitched, in reflex: the cold fandango.

Capote later confided to his childhood friend, Harper Lee, "There was nothing I could do to save them."

She responded, "Maybe not, but the fact is you didn't want to."

He had lamented the killers' "absurd" appeals, which delayed the completion of his book, and he wanted them dead, not for the crimes they had committed, but for his own advancement.

Unlike Mick Jagger, the author was able to get what he wanted, but not what he needed. Reconciling that proved impossible as the years dragged on. Whether on the steps of the Ritz Hotel in Paris or steps away from The Rolling Stones at the Tarrant County Convention Center in Fort Worth, Texas, he couldn't shake his own failures, which followed him in the dark hallways of depression, like a flashlight. Years passed, and the self-absorbed man clung to an ever-dwindling coterie of friends. A pessimist, he glimpsed the worst in himself and others and dwelt on it, resulting in lower expectations for everyone, including himself.

After *In Cold Blood* was published, Capote reveled in fame and the attendant celebrity status that elevated him to an unequaled literary perch. It came at a terrible price. He had wanted to be in the bright, intensifying glare of the spotlight. Unlike the Clutters, there was no shotgun barrel dropped into the white circle, coming within inches of his face. Instead, it was the snout of a liquor bottle, supplemented by pills that eventually killed him 12 years after Fort Worth. His tragic denouement was as preventable as the Clutters' deaths and those of Hickock and Smith, had the killers shown restraint on that November night in 1959. Fans of Capote think concentrating on his actions during the six-year period leading up to the publication of his book obscures his body of work. A man is judged by how he ascends the success ladder and by how he reacts if a rung splinters and he begins to fall. Capote was at his very best constructing a portrait of Perry Smith at his very worst. Ironically, that occurred during a time when the writer became his own worst enemy. The two men had an unusual bond, and they also shared another trait. Like the midnight rambler who catapulted him to fame, Capote had a personality that was unique.

You know, the one you've never seen before.

SYMPHONY

Changing Lives for Generations

Marywood is an Austin institution whose stated mission is "to provide shelter and support to children, while seeking to build nurturing families for a lifetime, through maternity, adoption and foster care services." This is about the evolution of that mission and someone I know, an adoptee whose life proves the masthead on the Marywood stationery "Changing lives for generations."

In 1921, the Diocese of Austin began operating the Home of the Holy Infancy at 510 West 26th, next to the old Seton Hospital. It originally housed expectant mothers and an orphanage. In the "old days" the adoption process was not as rigorous.

One family who already had a 2-year-old son from the Home would receive a call informing them about another baby boy they might want to consider adopting. The wife would go to the Home and look at the scrawny, blond waif who was nearly three months old. She would pick him up, cradle him in her arms, and become his mother. Her husband was working out of town when his wife decided to surprise him with another boy.

The next day the housekeeper would walk in, look at the infant and think to herself, "Lord, Mrs. ___ done lost her mind!" The husband would return home and go into the nursery, expecting to see his 2-year-old boy in the crib. Instead he would gaze down on the tiny baby with a big nose and bigger ears and scream, "My God, he's shrunk!"

Over the years the adoption process evolved into a myriad of background checks, extensive interviews with highly trained social workers, and numerous home visits, some lasting up to four hours.

In 1977, the Home of the Holy Infancy changed its name to Marywood to honor the mother of Jesus and to connote a place of peace and reflection. Around that time, the institution was completing approximately 100 adoptions per year. Over the next two decades the societal attitude toward single parenting changed, and adoptions at Marywood dropped to 12 a year. Thus, in 1995, Marywood opened the Annalee House, named for Sister Annalee Faherty. It provides temporary and long-term group foster care for pregnant and parenting adolescents between 12 and 18 years of age and their children. Most of the girls come from homes with a history of some type of abuse. In addition to basic education, these young women are offered life-skills training, therapeutic services, care for their children, and a Stepping Stones program, administered in conjunction with Texas Presbyterian Children's Homes and the Annie Casey Foundation. This transitional program for women 18-21 who are parenting or pregnant helps with job training, employment group sessions, and childcare in addition to room and board.

The methods employed by Marywood changed over time, but the mission did not: the most important aspect is still to give children a loving, nurturing family regardless of size or shape, because each of us, from the Christ child on down, deserves a family. Some adopted children trudge through life with the emotional baggage of the self-imposed stigma of abandonment. Others manage to focus on the positives: a young woman in the most difficult decision of her life has committed, in her mind, a completely selfless act of love in giving up her baby for adoption. And a family relying on blind faith has been utterly willing to accept that baby into their home.

The scrawny one fell into that latter category. Whatever happened to him? He walked into Mr. Giesecke's homeroom class at O. Henry Junior High School and sat down next to the most beautiful girl he had ever seen. Seven years hence that woman consented to marry him, and she later blessed him with three wonderful children. His mother would eventually be rewarded with three additional grandchildren from her older son, the one who had not shrunk.

When families gather together over the holidays, most of them take for granted the bond forged by having such a support group. Sadly, there are over 3,500 children in Texas who reside in foster care, for various reasons. All of us should count our blessings that we were given the continuity and wealth that emanate from being members of loving families. Along with the birth mothers and adoptive mothers, Marywood should be thanked for helping place children, regardless of origin, into similar environments.

It was a very special woman who acted on blind faith and plucked a tiny baby from his wooden crib, cuddled him, and gave the boy a life more wonderful than any he ever imagined possible.

That scrawny, blond baby with a big nose and bigger ears was me. By taking a chance, the woman who took him home really did change lives for generations.

Thanks, Mom.

Life's Second Chances

In the fall of 1995, Beau Eckert was starting his freshman year at the University of Kansas. Seven hundred miles away, Bradfield Heiser was starting his sophomore year at Westlake High School in Austin, Texas. This is how a serendipitous stroll across a university campus changed their lives forever. It is about survival and an opportunity for a second chance; most importantly, it is about a gift.

Bradfield was an accomplished athlete, playing varsity baseball and running back on the Westlake football team that won the 5A State Championship in December 1996. For this 17-year-old boy life could only get worse. It did.

Three months later, Bradfield was diagnosed with acute lymphocytic leukemia (ALL), a malignant disorder that strikes only 4,000 people in the United States each year. Bradfield and his parents, Becky and Robbie, felt some hope when they took him down to M.D. Anderson Hospital in Houston, and they consulted with Dr. Charles Koller. Over the next four months, Bradfield went back and forth to Houston for the series of five chemotherapy treatments. The last one ended days before the start of his senior year in high school.

When Bradfield walked into school that first day, he felt uneasy because the therapy had caused all his hair to fall out. Waiting for him inside the school were some of his good friends from the football team. They smiled at him and removed their caps, revealing their shaved heads. With their encouragement, his family's support, and the tireless help of his trainer, Carment Kiara, Bradfield worked hard to achieve his goal of playing football again. He was rewarded two months later when Westlake played archrival Austin High. Late in the game, he walked onto the playing field for the first time that season. On his initial play, Bradfield carried the ball across the goal line. It was a more or less meaningless touchdown in the game, but the cheers and tears from the 6,000 fans validated what Bradfield already knew: he had finally achieved his real goal—to be a normal kid again. He went on to play the rest of the season, which ended on a Saturday in mid-November.

Almost on that same day, Beau Eckert walked through the student union at the University of Kansas campus. Inside, an African-American student group had set up a booth encouraging minority students to sign up for the bone marrow registry. Beau stopped and talked with the students and read the literature. He learned that the minority donor database was small, so he took the chance that he might eventually help someday. He signed up, then went upstairs and donated a sample of his blood, nearly half of which is Winnebago Indian.

Five months later and almost two years to the day that Bradfield was first diagnosed came the startling news: his leukemia was back. And this time the prognosis was much worse—Bradfield needed a bone marrow transplant. Unfortunately, no one in Bradfield's family was a match, and he could not self-transplant. His only hope was to find an unrelated donor. Becky and Robbie were told the odds of finding that donor were one in 20,000. On top of that, the survival rate after marrow transplantation for second remission patients is less than 40 percent. While M.D. Anderson Hospital performed the donor search, the Heiser family looked for the hospital to perform the marrow transplant, assuming a donor could be found. They selected the Fred Hutchinson Cancer Research Center in Seattle, Washington.

Two months later they received the good news: there were 25 possible matches. But that list was quickly narrowed to eight, then . . . two. After three separate trips to donate blood and a final round of testing, Beau Eckert matched eleven of Bradfield's twelve antigens, or markers, required for a transplant. A 90 percent match was almost unthinkable. The Heisers were told to come to Seattle.

Beau had previously made the final decision to donate his stem cells. "Well, to be honest, I was a little nervous, a little anxious; but the feeling that I could do something really good was a tremendous joy. I'm just an average guy, like anybody else, and the fact that I could do something like this was really great." Within a very short time, he began the bone marrow donation process, which lasted three days. The procedure inflicted flu-like systems upon Beau, a common side effect in many donors. It is caused by Filgrastim, a drug that increases the number of stem cells released from the bone marrow into the blood stream. On the day his procedure was completed, a special courier accompanied the stem cells from Kansas City to Seattle and a waiting Bradfield.

Then Bradfield had the transplant and, for the next five months, Becky and her son remained in Seattle before returning to Austin in late January of 2000. Bradfield, carrying a 3.5 GPA, applied to the undergraduate University of Texas School of Business and was accepted. He has since graduated. Beau Eckert graduated from the University of Kansas with a degree in history. He is now in Phoenix getting his teaching certificate because he wants to be a high school history teacher.

The two agreed to speak at the Gulf Coast Marrow Donor fundraiser in Houston in February of 2003, and they met for the first time at a press conference before the fundraiser—not to draw attention to them, but to focus attention on the need for more marrow donations. Valentine's Day is National Donor Day. But on any day, people between 18 and 60 years of age can go to their local blood bank and begin the process. The price in Austin is $55.00, which covers the cost of having the blood typed, tested, analyzed by a lab, and added to the National Marrow Donor Program. That may seem expensive to some, but then again . . . .

If Beau had not taken the opportunity to attend the University of Kansas, Becky and Robbie might not have their eldest son. If Beau had not chanced by the minority donor drive booth, Rob and Jenny might not have their big brother. If Beau had not taken that final step to become a donor, Bradfield might not have gotten what all leukemia and cancer patients dream of . . . a second chance at life. As a result of Bradfield's transplant he is now cured. All because of his tremendous determination and the gift from Beau Eckert. Who took a simple walk . . . that saved a life.

"Death, Where Is Thy Sting?"

It's around 6:15 P.M. on August 5, 2003. After dropping off a friend in Mobile, Alabama, Jenna McEachern and her daughter Bailey are driving along Interstate 85 somewhere in Escambia County, heading for Auburn University. The mother/daughter road trip was filled with chatter and excitement about Bailey's sophomore year. Six hundred miles away in Austin it is a typical evening around the Austin High track. A Run-Tex class, Gilbert's Gazelles, is finishing up a Tuesday workout on the spongy oval as the temperature dips below 100 degrees. Winding down her exercise and drenched in sweat, Jana Kay notices two friendly, familiar faces near the portable building. Randy McEachern and his best friend, Pat Kelly, working at "The Ranch," their affectionate term for the complex of playing fields at the school by Town Lake. Runners refer to them as "the coaches" because the two toil there almost daily. Randy had finished exercising on the hike and bike trail, they had plugged in a dozen sprinkler heads on the main field, and the former Texas Longhorn football players, Pat (class of 1973) and Randy (1977), were replacing a tire on the golf cart by the storage shed. A thousand yards to the west, up the hill on Veterans' Drive at EMS Station 17, technicians Matt Nealand and Jonathan Allua are milling about inside. It's been a slow, uneventful day.

The tire repair finished, Randy carries some cinder blocks back to the shed and drops them against the building, disturbing the wasp nest above the door. Pat turns and sees Randy running from the shed and goes to him. Randy says, "Some wasps bit me." They take a count: two on the back of the head, one on the back of an ear.

Pat says, "Let's go kill the nest." After they do, Randy rubs the back of his head. Pat asks, "Have you ever been bitten before?"

"Yeah."

"Are you allergic?"

"I don't think so." They discuss putting baking soda or tobacco on the wound and chuckle.

Pat says, "If you get to feeling bad, let me know," and returns to the golf cart.

Moments later, Randy becomes light-headed, staggers two steps, and utters, "Pa-." His friend turns, sees Randy wobble two steps, lose his balance, and fall. Pat catches him, spins around, and sits him on the back of the cart,

"Are you okay?" Randy's jaw drops; his head snaps back, his eyes roll white. Pat sees people by the scoreboard; he has to get their attention. Holding Randy with one arm he waves his hat with the other, "Help! Help! Emergency!" Runners see him; eight or ten sprint over. On the far end of the track, Jana Kay hears the cry for help and figures someone's overheated. She grabs the water cooler and starts running to the group. Pat tells the others, "My friend's unconscious, he's been stung by wasps." One runner has a cell phone. Pat says, "Call 911, tell them we are on the eastside of campus near the football field, near the cinder block building." Still holding Randy, Pat pours some water on his friend's head and neck. Randy's head jerks back, he's laboring to breathe.

From the EMS tape, 0:16-Runner, "Someone got bit by a wasp and they're having an allergic reaction."

Jana Kay reaches the group, surveys the chaos, and says, "I can give him CPR."

Jana looks at Randy—he's already turning blue—and says, "Does anyone have an EpiPen?" Silence. "Put him on the ground." Done. She leans over him to clear his passageway, sticks her finger in his mouth. "Ouch!" she thinks. "He bit me. Tongue's already swollen." Pat elevates Randy's legs. Jana starts CPR. Breathe, rest, breathe, rest.

EMS, 0:38- "Got'em started." Runner, ". . . giving him mouth to mouth." Randy spits up, Jana turns his head, wipes his mouth. EMS, 1:00, "Stay on the line, let me get some more help." Jana resumes CPR—breathe, rest, breathe, rest. EMS, 1:31, "I've got one on the way."

Randy spits up again; again Jana turns his head, wipes his mouth. Air isn't reaching his lungs. His throat's swollen; he's still blue. She begins breathing into his nose. His chest begins rising. She looks up, sees people crying and thinks, "I can't stop now, must keep going," She inhales a deep breath, places her mouth over his nose, and exhales. Runners return from the building with large boards and start fanning and shading Randy. Jana asks again, "Does anyone have an EpiPen?" It's hot; he's struggling-thrashing-fighting, taking guppy breaths. Jana's still breathing into his nose.

Someone yells, "Where's the ambulance?"

Matt and Jonathan rush to the ambulance and jump in. Matt prepares himself, thinking, "This is priority two: not life-threatening. A bee sting."

Pat runs to his car, grabs his cell phone, dials 911. "I am sorry, all circuits are busy, please stay-" Pat wonders, "What is this, the Cable Company?" He hears a female voice and explains the situation.

She replies, "We have the call. We'll make sure someone gets there as soon as possible." The siren blares. A thousand yards away, Pat runs to open the gate.

Bystander, "Here they come!" Siren getting closer . . . louder . . . Pat flings the gate open and waves, windmill fashion. Jana keeps breathing for Randy. The ambulance jumps the curb and speeds by Pat.

Matt can see CPR being administered and thinks, "Why are they doing mouth to mouth on a priority two call?" Matt contacts the fire department, "Priority One! Priority One!" but the fire truck from Windsor Road is already en route.

Randy is clenching his jaws. Jana, "Randy, open your mouth for me!"

EMS, 6:11. Dispatcher, "Is he breathing?"

"No!"

"No?"

"No!" The ambulance stops. Matt surveys the situation and starts EMT protocol: clears airways, puts bag valve mask on Randy. The machine starts breathing for him. Dr. Rachet, Medical Director of EMS arrives; he's been monitoring the radio. Jonathan starts an I.V.; Matt injects an epinephrine shot into Randy's arm, then lifts Randy's shirt to apply heart patches. Matt wonders, "Why are there no hives?" He checks the blood sugar—patient is not diabetic. "Is he a drug user?"

Pat, "No!"

"He's not responding." He administers the drug, Narcan, an opiate antagonist, just in case. "Was he around pesticides?"

"No!" Matt injects a Benadryl shot.

"How old is he?"

"47!" He notices Randy's pupils are still real small. The fire truck is already on the scene. Another group shows up; now there are six EMTs and Dr. Rachet. Matt, "Is he on any medications?" Pat steps 10 feet away and makes a call.

"Jenna, uh, I need you to pull off the road. We've had an emergency with Randy." Jenna, thinking he's got a broken bone, pulls off, and comes to a stop. Back in Austin, Matt injects second epinephrine shot. Pat calmly says,

"I'm here with Randy. EMS is here. I think he's going to be fine, but they need to know if he's on any medications."

Jenna says, "Not that I know of."

Pat: "He's been stung by some wasps. I need to know if he's allergic, because he's struggling." Matt gives the second Benadryl shot.

Jenna: "I don't know if he's allergic, but his father's highly allergic."

She hears someone behind Pat, "Does anybody know who this is?"

Pat turns and yells, "His name's Randy McEachern."

Jenna overhears Matt holler, "Randy, stay with us! You've got to breathe! Work with us!"

She turns to Bailey: "Your dad's in trouble, he's been stung by wasps and you need to pray for him."

Matt injects third epinephrine shot. Jonathan takes Pat's phone and says, "We have to take him to St. David's or South Austin Hospital. Which one?"

"Is my husband conscious?"

"That's a negative."

Jenna thinks, "I can't believe this!" and tells him, "St. David's." Jonathan hands the phone back. Matt injects third Benadryl shot.

Pat: "Jenna, they're taking him to St. David's." He tells Jenna he'll call back.

Bailey calls a cousin to go stay with her brother, Hays, who was at home alone. Jenna calls her mother, "Please tell my brothers and aunt to start praying for Randy."

Bailey: "Mom, call Pawpaw."

Jenna: "I will." She can't find Randy's siblings. Jenna calls Laura Kelly to go be with Hays, calls Gretchen Evans to pray for Randy. Calls others, and then pulls back on the highway, thinking of Randy and her first call, to her son.

"Hays, your Dad's been stung by wasps. I need for you, Lester, and Fred to pray for your dad."

Hays asks, "Is he going to be okay?"

Jenna pauses, searching . . . "I don't know."

Matt and Jonathan load him on the backboard . . . onto the stretcher . . . into the ambulance. Randy starts fighting, flailing. Matt thinks, "The patient's combative, can't risk further injury," so he tells Jonathan, "Restrain him!" Randy wakes up as the ambulance doors close.

Jana Kay looks at the faces of the bystanders and realizes she needs to say something; everyone's quiet, somber. Some are crying. "All we can do is pray." As she watches the ambulance jump the curb and speed away, she thinks, "I don't even know his last name."

"Stay with us, Randy! Fight it! Fight this deal!" The bag valve mask still breathing for him. Randy moans. He drifts in, hears the radio, machines, sirens. Matt checks vital signs—no radial pulse, no blood pressure—then Randy drifts out. He drifts in again and hears Matt, "Stay with us, Randy!" He feels somebody on his right, someone near his feet, two more behind him—one right, one left. Matt yells, "Fight this deal!" Randy's struggling, battling, knowing, "I can't fight much longer. . . I'm . . . shutting . . . down." With the siren blaring, they're speeding to the hospital, cutting through intersections.

Randy struggles and behind him, on his left, a calm voice says, "It's okay to relax. You can let go. It will be okay."

Randy gasps, thinking, "I can't . . . have to . . . stay here."

"Relax. It's okay to let go," the voice assures him. Randy relaxes . . . and he lets go.

Jenna has calls coming in, going out on Bailey's phone. Jenna tells everyone, "I need you to listen . . ." and explains Randy's situation. She tells them, "Pray for him."

Bailey says, "Call Paw-paw."

"I will."

"Mom, call him now. That's his daddy!"

She dials but gets an answering machine, "This is Jenna, I need you to call me immediately."

Randy: It's so peaceful now. The pain is gone. It's calm. Quiet. All the noises are gone: no siren, no machines, no voices. No colors; everything's black and white. This is a calm, soothing, gentle feeling. I'm safe, like I feel when I'm driving on the highway alone, at night. Like being wrapped in a cocoon. I'm moving down a road, someone is guiding me to a light. It's not bright, it's . . . warm. I'm floating, effortlessly, toward the warm light. A picture is moving toward me, coming into focus. It's Jenna. I'm pleased with where she is now. That's good, because if I do let go, I know she'll be fine.

Jenna passes over my shoulder. Another picture approaching. It's Bailey. She's strong. That's good. If I let go, she'll be fine. That pleases me. Bailey drifts over my shoulder. A third picture. It's Hays. He too, will be fine, because he's strong. That's good, pleasing to me. Hays glides over my shoulder. I've focused on all of them and I'm comforted; now I know they will be okay, even if I am not there. My checklist is complete. It's okay to let go.

The warm light disappears.

Jenna is busy, distracted by the calls coming in and going out. But in the quiet moments between those conversations she has time to think, "Why hasn't Pat called?"

The ambulance reaches the hospital and stops. Randy sees the back doors burst open, then his eyelids close. He can't see the hospital personnel rushing to the ambulance. He can't see them wheeling him down the hallway and into the operating room where the doctors and nurses are waiting. Randy can't see anything because he has no discernible pulse or blood pressure. He is slipping away.

Randy McEachern's eyes open, and he looks around the operating room. To his right is a doctor, to his left a nurse. He thinks, "Why are they ignoring me? Am I dead?" Then he fades out.

Jenna reaches Tuskegee and realizes she has taken a wrong turn. While backtracking to Auburn a peaceful, calm feeling overcomes her and she turns to her daughter, "I think your dad's going to be fine."

Bailey says, "I do, too."

Randy feels disoriented, like he is coming out of an anesthetic. People are in the operating room cleaning up. He wonders if he's having an out of body experience.

"Nobody is paying attention to me, I must be dead." His gurney begins to move as the nurse wheels him out of the operating room. He asks, "Am I alive?"

She looks at him and smiles, "Oh, honey, you're alive. We're taking you to ICU."

In life I know there's lots of grief, But your love is my relief.
Tears in my eyes burn, Tears in my eyes burn while I'm waiting,
While I'm waiting for my turn.

— "WAITING IN VAIN," Bob Marley

That evening Jenna talks with the emergency room doctor and gets the news Randy has pulled through. Later she learns the cat scan and other tests reveal no lasting damage to him, truly miraculous considering the circumstances.

The next morning, after dumping the carload of Bailey's stuff in the dorm room, they head for the airport. When Jimmy Evans learned the women were having trouble getting a morning flight back to Austin he dispatched his private plane. The McEachern women climb in, sit down, and buckle their seat belts. Except for a brief three-minute lapse Jenna has spent the past 14 hours composed, in control of her emotions, because she knows Randy's fate has been in God's hands. On a small runway at a rural Alabama airport, while waiting for her turn to see Randy, she finally breaks down and the tears flow. For Randy, who has survived a monumental struggle, unscathed. For Bailey and Hays, because they have not lost their father. For Pat Kelly, who didn't have to watch his best friend die. For everyone whose prayers have helped her family through this ordeal. And for herself, because she is going to see her husband again. Alive.

While the plane lifts skyward and returns to Austin, Pat walks into Randy's room and the two talk for an hour before Randy starts sleeping like a log. And the ordeal ends the way it began: Randy slipping into unconsciousness with Pat at his side, watching over his friend.

Randy McEachern was stricken with anaphylaxis, "a sudden, severe, potentially fatal systemic reaction" that can range from mild to life threatening. The best estimates reveal that as many as 41 million people in the country "suffer from severe allergies that may put them at risk for anaphylaxis." Those at greater risk are "individuals with asthma, eczema, or hay fever." The causes of reactions include food, insect stings, and, to a lesser degree, medications and latex. Reactions are fairly rare, occurring only 90,000 times per year, yet one-third of those result in trips to hospital emergency rooms. Food-induced reactions kill between 150 to 200 people a year. Deaths from insect stings are as rare as lightning deaths, about 50 per year. Yet, millions of Americans are unaware they are susceptible. Randy had been stung a few times in his life and did not know he was allergic. That is common because it is very rare the first bite will trigger a reaction. A similarly unaware man in Houston removed the cover from his boat and was attacked by wasps. He died in his driveway, next to the boat.

This does not mean everyone should live in fear of having a reaction, especially one as severe as Randy's, which was possibly enhanced because he had exercised just before being stung. Most people susceptible to anaphylaxis carry EpiPens, a prescription auto-injector that releases a set amount of epinephrine into their systems. Each injection, administered with a swing and jab motion into the thigh for 10 seconds, affords the victim between 15 and 20 minutes of relief while they seek the nearest emergency room.

A glossary of EMT terminology defines "duty to act" as "an obligation to provide care to a patient." Jana Kay is not an EMT. She works at Marbridge, in far south Austin. For nearly seven minutes on the evening of August 5, however, she performed as professionally and tirelessly to save Randy as any EMT would have. Throughout the resuscitation she saw the faces of people shocked that she put her hand into a stranger's mouth and later wiped away what he spit up before resuming CPR. Jana modestly said, "Anyone in that position would want to step up to the plate and do it, because life is so precious." To Randy McEachern, Jana Kay will never be just "anyone," she will always be The One.

Matt Nealand had worked as an EMT for over four and one-half years before taking his most memorable call. He remains appreciative of the training he received and what it allowed him to do. Helping Randy was a "good feeling; humbling, seeing the impact on the family and that he [Randy] will still be able to touch other people's lives."

When Jenna met Matt she thanked him and said, "I get my husband for the rest of my life. What price can you put on that?" Then she added, "I think I owe you a house."

A few weeks after the incident Matt's wife, Laura, was on the Internet and learned the EMS captain at Sitka, Alaska, had recently died. Having spent some time on the tiny island situated halfway between Seattle and

Anchorage, she was intrigued. As Matt said, "Every door was wide open." He applied for the job on August 29 and on September 29, Matt and his family walked through that door and left Austin for Alaska. He now lives on an island dotted with spruce forests. Only 8,800 people live there, in the midst of an Alaskan wilderness so daunting the locals don't stray far from asphalt or gravel without a global positioning device. There are only 28 miles of paved roads, but as Matt Nealand found out sometimes you don't have to travel far to save someone's life.

When Jenna thought of Pat Kelly she pondered what it had been like for him to watch his best friend slip away, wondering as the ambulance drove off if that was the last time he would ever see Randy. Yet, during the two hours Randy's life hung in the balance Pat always thought Randy was going to live.

Like Tom Sawyer, Randy was able to attend his own memorial service, or so it seemed. The outpouring of love and admiration in the form of phone calls and letters revealed to him an enormous number of lives he had touched, without ever knowing. His favorite professor at U.T. wrote; parents whose children he had coached a decade before contacted him. He was able to hear things normally reserved for family members during the grieving period. The McEacherns feel an incredible gratitude for that reason and many others.

Jenna said she was not worried during the ordeal because, "within 10 minutes of the incident I had 25 people praying for Randy." One of those, her mother, also prayed for Jenna as she pulled back onto that highway and headed for Auburn. Jenna has no memory of seeing the road in front of her during the two hours she drove those hundred or so miles. Randy and Jenna both feel they have been "slapped in the face with God's mercy and his amazing power to derail this course of action." And they have searched for the answer to the question they have posed to each other since that day in August, "Why was he thrown back?"

Providence—*capitalized*: "God conceived as the power sustaining and guiding human destiny." Many people have said, "Randy McEachern was lucky." The term implies a good result that happened by chance. If one or two fingers can count the chance occurrences, that is luck. When the number reaches eight or more, the explanation transcends luck and becomes something more. Randy and Jenna believe the hand of Providence guided Randy's helpers to that tiny plot of land near Town Lake.

If Pat Kelly had not been with him, Randy's collapse might not have been noticed until it was too late. If one runner had not had his cell phone handy, the ambulance and fire trucks would not have arrived as quickly. For years, area residents and joggers fought to have EMS Station #17 put on Veterans Drive. If it were not located only a thousand yards away from the track, critical seconds would have been lost. If Matt Nealand and Jonathan Allua had not acted so professionally and quickly, the outcome could have been different. If Dr. Rachet had not been monitoring the radio, he would not have showed up and offered his invaluable assistance.

Twice a week Jana Kay participates in a class that runs on the Austin High track. If the incident had occurred a few weeks later, she would not have been there for Randy; during high school football season they run elsewhere. Her Run-Tex class meets on Tuesdays and Thursdays at the school. If the incident had occurred the day before or after, she would not have been there. As it was, she was the only person on-site who knew CPR. If Jana did not work at Marbridge, where residents sometimes have seizures, she might not have taken a CPR class . . . just weeks before the incident.

Randy remembers the presence of four people in the ambulance: one near his feet, one on his right, and two behind him. Matt Nealand is not certain, but he only recalls seeing Jonathan Allua, and one fireman stationed behind Randy.

Randy felt the presence of everyone who attended him on his right side, while the visions of his family were on his left, along with the calm, reassuring voice he heard over his left shoulder. Matt's response was, "That's impossible." He said EMS protocol is "left ventricle recumbent," meaning the EMT is always on the patient's left side. It was amazing Randy remembered anything, considering how close he came to dying. If death is a chasm, Randy was leaning over the cliff at a 90-degree angle before he was pulled him back. Under the circumstances, Matt said, it was understandable that Randy got his left and right mixed up. Which is a plausible explanation, except for one thing: that means the presence Randy felt in the ambulance that gently guided and led him toward the light and spoke the words, "It will be okay," was on his right side.

Near the end of the interview Matt was asked to describe the inside of Austin/Travis County EMS vehicle #104. When he finished, he paused and whispered, "Oh, my God." The patient faces the back of the ambulance. To his left is the space for the emergency medical technician. The gurney is positioned hard against the right wall. There is no room for a person to be positioned to the patient's right.

"Bearing Gifts We Traverse Afar"

This was supposed to be a Thanksgiving essay, but like Columbus I got a little off course. Some humanists believe they punched a winning ticket in the lottery that placed them in the United States. Other Americans are so guilt-ridden about their good fortune in being born here that they constantly point out the negatives in our nation. This is not a jingoistic diatribe, just a simple reminder of the gifts from our ancestors who traversed afar, helping shape this great land. At the risk of offending Native Americans, Vikings, Columbus, Spaniards, humanists, etc., here is a brief list of people and things Americans can be thankful for:

The 55 members of the Constitutional Convention consisted of 50 Protestants (27 were ordained ministers), two Roman Catholics, and three others who had studied for the ministry at one time, including Benjamin Franklin. All contributed to the moral precepts that are the foundation of this country.

In Africa the ratio of primary school pupils to college students is 55 to 1. In the Unites States of America, it is 2 to 1.

After the bloodiest Civil War in history up to that time, Americans were able to come together and reconstruct a country, despite terrible suffering.

Citizens have served capably and honorably as members of the armed services throughout the centuries. Most of them risked and many ultimately forfeited their lives fighting and dying to defend our inalienable rights to life, liberty, and the pursuit of happiness.

Pioneers braved harsh elements, sometimes violent native people, and disease settling Texas and the West.

A Georgia peanut farmer, an Arkansas boy raised by a single-parent, and a man from one of the country's wealthiest families can have the same job: President of the United States.

The period from 1876-1900, which Mark Twain called "The Gilded Age" because of the rampant corruption, did not bring about the downfall of a country scarcely a century old.

The grass on your neighbor's lawn may be greener, but if your annual income is $50,000, you are in the 99th percentile of wealth on this planet. At $100,000 only 36 million out of 6 billion make more than you.

Steel, sweat shop, and underground mine workers toiled in almost unbearable conditions and propelled us through the Industrial Revolution.

We don't live in Shenzhen, China, and work at the Kin Ki Industrial factory making Etch-a-Sketch kits. Workdays last from 7:30 A.M. until 10:00 P.M., with a total of 2 1/2 hours for lunch and dinner, seven days a week—more than twice the average American workweek.

Our 13th and 19th Amendments recognized—finally—the sovereign rights and contributions of African-Americans and women in this country, respectively.

Civil rights workers struggled for and sometimes died trying to achieve equality.

You were raised a woman with college aspirations here and not in many other countries: the percentage of female students at TCU is about 56%; in Tanzania and Cambodia women comprise less than 20% and in Eritrea, which borders Ethiopia, only 13% of college students are female.

The Greatest Generation, raised during the Great Depression and World War II, spent the first third of their lives in sacrifice, making our existence easy by comparison. They later endured three other wars: Korea, the Cold War and Vietnam. Most were in their sixties or seventies when the Berlin Wall came down.

Our country is only 5% of planet's population, yet Americans consume 25% of everything produced on Earth.

Except for certain segregated inner city and suburban institutions, our public school system is still the best example of integration in this country, despite its many shortcomings.

We live in a forgiving nation, where one mistake does not define a career. In World War II, the Japanese were interred in concentration camps on the West Coast, the chief opponent of which was J. Edgar Hoover; the chief proponent was the Attorney General of California, Earl Warren, who later became Chief Justice of the U. S. Supreme Court.

We have the greatest medical facilities and physicians the world has ever seen, a major reason our life expectancy jumped from 49 to 77 in the past hundred years. In Zimbabwe or Uganda, life expectancy is 39 and 43 years, respectively.

We have the option of consuming three meals a day. "Every day, more than 800 million people worldwide—among them 300 million children—suffer the gnawing pain of hunger, and the diseases or disabilities caused by malnutrition," UN Secretary-General Kofi Annan said. About 19,000 children below the age of five die each day, roughly the population of Brownwood, Texas.

If Kwanzaa, Hanukkah, or Christmas gifts seem disappointing, think of our ancestors and the gift they bestowed on us by coming to the shores of this great continent.

And be glad you were born in a hospital instead of far away, in a manger, with no crib for a bed.

The Class of 1971

On a cold winter morning in 1971, the graduating class of Austin High assembled on a set of risers at the east side of the school for the senior photo. Interspersed among the group were a handful that became stars. The casual observer would have had difficulty selecting the future Hollywood standouts: a boy who would win the Pulitzer Prize for his play *The Kentucky Saga*, then author the screen adaptation of Graham Greene's *The Quiet American* and write the re-make of *Spartacus*: Robert Schenkkan. Or the girl who portrayed Jeff Bridges' first wife in the Academy Award-nominated movie *Seabiscuit*, Valerie Mahaffey, whose most visible recurring television role was in **Cheers**, where she played the daughter of the owner of Melville's, the restaurant above the famous bar. And another girl, one of the late bloomers, who had guest roles in various television comedies, was featured on **Lifestyles of the Rich and Famous** and graced the cover of a TEXAS MONTHLY issue on "The 50 Most Beautiful Women in Texas": Rebecca Holden, Becky Bloomer in high school.

That morning in 1971, as the sun rose slowly behind the photographer, many of us squinted as we looked at the camera with expressions that mirrored our view of what lay ahead: we gazed into the real world and the future through half-opened eyes.

After graduation, everyone searched for and found happiness, only to discover that the emotional state is not permanent: sometimes it arrives and departs at the whim of external forces beyond our control. This revelation did not cause many of us to alter our personal quests and to begin searching for contentment. Possibly because the word contentment means "satisfied, having ease of mind," and we would have perceived that as "settling." Wanting it wouldn't have made any difference, according to author Richard Easterlin who wrote in *Growth Triumphant: The 21st Century in Historical Perspective*, "In the long run, human wants and needs are never satisfied. Average satisfaction levels in the United States have not improved in half a century. People will go on wanting more and more all the time . . . never content with the fruits of their progress."

There are exceptions to Easterlin's theory—people who are satisfied with their lives and the fruits of their progress. This story is about one of the young men who stood on the risers on that cold morning. Much like the search for contentment, his story is lengthy and requires a substantial time commitment.

The Boy from Bonnie Road

Danny Robertson grew up on Bonnie Road in the shadow of Knebel Field, the old Little League ballpark. By the time he entered Austin High, he was a multi-sport star athlete. In his sophomore year, Danny was the starting quarterback for the junior varsity football team. Late in the second quarter of a game that year, he dropped back to pass, the receivers were covered, and he scrambled up field. As he tried to fake a defender, three tacklers smashed into him: from the left, the front, and the rear. Danny fell in a heap. At halftime in the locker room, his left knee had become very swollen. The trainer, a self-proclaimed jack of all trades, master of none, proclaimed it was only a slight knee sprain, and the quarterback could continue to play. Danny managed to gut it out for two series in the second half, until the pain and stiffness in his knee forced him to the sideline. The diagnosis at the hospital later confirmed the trainer's ineptitude—Danny's anterior cruciate ligament, medial cruciate ligament, and medium meniscus were shredded. He never played another down. After that, watching others play was frustrating for Danny, who knew his injury would deprive him of the opportunity to play in college. Three operations were required to repair the ligaments—before he was out of high school. Had a doctor had been present in the locker room, Danny likely could have played football his junior year and beyond. Baseball became his only option but with limited speed and mobility his second dream, playing the sport in college, was not attainable. At one point during his senior baseball season, Danny knew his playing days were almost over. Yet the injury did yield one positive result: it set him on the path to a medical career.

Training

Throughout his four years at the University of Texas, Dan, as he was now called, worked 40 hours a week while carrying a full course load and graduated cum laude with a degree in biology. Accepted into the University of Texas Medical School at Houston, he was able to work with noted physicians such as Dr. Denton Cooley, and Danny even contemplated becoming a cardiovascular surgeon. Starting a five-year residency at the UT-affiliated hospitals in Houston, Dan took an elective in orthopaedic surgery. Two young doctors a year ahead of him in the program encouraged him to take that route. Considering his medical history, it seemed a logical fit and, after his fifth year, Dan applied for a few fellowships. One offer came from the doctors for the Los Angeles Rams and Los Angeles Dodgers, the Kerlan-Jobe group, who had pioneered the "Tommy John" shoulder surgery, named after the major league pitcher whose career was resurrected by the inventive surgical technique. Danny turned them down—he would have been but one of five fellowships. Instead, he chose Dale Daniel in San Diego where, as the single fellow, he would get more hands-on training. One thing he did not need was training as the single fellow in a group, because Dan was surrounded by women: his wife Kim and daughters Melanie, Kristen, Laura, and Sara. Following that year, the family moved back to Texas, but 18 months later they returned to San Diego, where Dan entered private practice.

A wonderful opportunity

Part of his work involved additional evaluations or second opinions on many professional and collegiate athletes, and his work impressed the pros. In 1990, an NFL team, the San Diego Chargers, asked him to become their team doctor, but there was a catch: the offer was only extended to Dan individually. Accepting the job required him to leave his current group and move to the physicians' group that had a contractual agreement with the Chargers. The decision to relocate was difficult, but the opportunity was too enticing to decline.

Dan discovered life in the NFL was a pampered existence, even on the road. In those pre-9/11 days, three team buses departed the Chargers' complex, went to the airport, and were waved through security. They proceeded to the tarmac and were dropped off at the chartered plane. Once they landed in the visiting city, the entourage received similar treatment.

Life for Dan and his family was good. Eventually, they bought a home in the upscale enclave of Rancho Santa Fe, near La Jolla. If he wanted fresh avocados or citrus, Dan just walked out his back door. Somewhere on the one and one-half acre spread, his orchards were offering up ripe produce, aided by the ocean breeze and cool night temperatures. He also got to kick it around with the San Diego Soccers, a professional soccer team, as their doctor. Somehow, he found time to be a clinical professor at University of California at San Diego as well.

Hitler and the AFC Championship

During Danny's first year with the Chargers the team was really inept. Then Bobby Beatherd was hired as general manager and Bobby Ross was named head coach. The Chargers became a fixture in the playoffs. During training camp in 1994, the team flew to Germany to play the New York Giants at Berlin Stadium, the site of the 1936 Summer Olympic Games, a venue where Hitler regularly reviewed the troops. As Dan gazed around the Olympia Stadion, the ghosts of history were almost palpable. Throughout the trip, Dan said the Chargers were treated like rock stars, especially during their tour of what had previously been East Germany.

That season the team bolted through the playoffs, and in a 15-degree snowstorm in Pittsburgh they won the AFC Championship and the right to play in Super Bowl XXIX. Dan described the aftermath of that victory as the wildest locker room scene he had ever witnessed. Players and personnel puffed on Cuban cigars, drank expensive champagne, and continued the revelry on the long flight home. In San Diego, the partyers boarded buses and headed for the Chargers' complex, but the vehicles were diverted from their normal route. An announcement was made on each bus that some fans had gathered for an impromptu pep rally/celebration at Jack Murphy Stadium. None of the passengers imagined the spectacle that awaited them when the buses drove through the tunnel of "The Murph." Under the bright glare of the arena's lights, three buses drove to midfield, the victors exited the vehicles and stepped onto the turf. The roar was deafening: the 50,000 fans packed into Jack Murphy Stadium screamed their approval as the Chargers' players, and personnel were joined on the field by their families. Standing with Kim and his daughters was the culmination of a magical day for Dan.

Another momentous occasion, two years in the planning, was looming on the horizon 3,000 miles away in Miami, at Joe Robbie Stadium. It would draw Dan even closer to his girls. As an NFL team physician, Dr. Dan Robertson was in rare company: there were fewer than 30 jobs like it in the world. On a

Sunday night, in late January of 1995, only two were working at Super Bowl XXIX, when the Chargers played the San Francisco 49ers. When Dan walked the team's sideline at Joe Robbie Stadium in Miami, he had attained the public pinnacle of his profession. During timeouts in the game, he looked around and thought, "This is unbelievable." He soaked up the spectacle like a child dragging a piece of bread through the bottom of a soup bowl. Dan wanted to capture every last drop of the most grandiose sporting event in America because, in his heart, he knew it was probably his last game. After it was over, he walked off a National Football League field for the final time as a team doctor. Within months, he had resigned from the Chargers, the Soccers, and the professional hockey team he served as physician. He also gave up his lucrative private practice and left California.

Why?

It was not simply a case of been there, done that, although he did have an AFC Championship ring to go along with five soccer championship rings. Dan and Kim had spent nearly two years discussing the decision and thought the timing was right. They wanted their girls to grow up in Texas and be able to spend more time around Dan's role models—his parents, Joyce and Joe. The doctor also missed the warm Texas nights and the lakes; most of all, he missed spending time with his family. On game days, their daughters had sat in front of the television and played, "Look for Daddy." The camera showed an injured player getting medical attention, and the girls shouted, "There's his hand!" or "That's Daddy's elbow!" Dan wanted them to see the whole dad.

Earlier, he had turned down the San Diego Padres' offer to be their team doctor because of the additional travel. As it was, he was already gone too much. The Chargers' road regimen dictated an arrival in the visiting city by 5 P.M. local time on Friday, and the team often returned very late on Sunday night. Ten times each season equaled a month away from his family.

Back home

In his Houston residency days, Dan had befriended two junior residents, and the Robertsons maintained the relationship, occasionally visiting the two doctors and their families back in Texas. Dan and Kim liked the community where their friends resided, and the physicians told Dan there was plenty of work to go around.

The move surprised their friends in San Diego; his old partners said Dan was stupid to leave everything he had in California. A few years after leaving, he paid a visit to the Chargers when they played the Houston Texans at Reliant Stadium. His old team's management and owner asked Dan to reconsider coming back to the team, but Dan politely declined the flattering offer. His family was settled and very happy with their surroundings.

Had they remained in California, the girls would have attended toney Torrey Pines High, where the student parking area resembled a luxury car lot: Mercedes, BMWs and Porsches. The kids at their new Texas high school drove pick 'em up trucks.

One afternoon Dan was treating a female patient while her husband waited in the parking lot. A loud banging noise drew the attention of Dan's staff, and they ran to the window. The husband had jumped from his vehicle and quick-stepped to the back of the trailer attached the truck. It rocked and swayed as he dragged out his cantankerous cargo, and for two exciting minutes the rancher battled his donkey in the parking lot. Dan regretted not having a camera handy to capture the moment; he really wanted to send a picture to his former partners in La Jolla.

Kim had "held down the fort" in San Diego, and Dan was always happy to return the favor. When she visited Kristen at college, he was in control briefly. Hours before the winter prom at Laura's high school, the pavement in front of the Robertson home resembled a parking lot. Inside, it was backstage at the Miss America pageant; girls sat in front of every mirror in the house. Dan visited with the beauties for a few minutes, until one group commandeered the master bath area. Outnumbered, he took his golf clubs and fled to the driving range with a smile on his face.

Another wonderful opportunity

Dan's reputation preceded his arrival in town, and he quickly built a thriving practice. He began seeing so many people in the area with sports injuries that he started a free clinic for athletes on Saturdays. In 1999, he went to Winnipeg as a team physician for the American contingent at the Pan Am Games, but most of his time is near home. When the family moved in 1995, Dan accepted a part-time position that put him back in contact with athletes, yet required minimal travel. With the Chargers, he flew to vacation destinations like San Francisco, New Orleans, Miami, and New York City. For the past nine years, Dan's part-time job has required trips to smaller, less exotic locales: Bandera, Dripping Springs, Medina Valley, and Uvalde.

On Fridays in the fall when he is not traveling, Dr. Robertson is easy to find. If you drive through town, just look for the tall banks of bright lights that serve as a beacon. As you approach, the roar of the crowd will become louder. After exiting your car in the parking lot, you will be enveloped by the crisp autumn air that carries the music from trombones, trumpets, and drums. Entering the stadium, you take in the scene: the teams competing on the field, the cheerleaders moving their arms in unison, exhorting the fans in throaty chants while the bands play joyously. Somewhere along the home team bench you will notice the tall, angular man with an athlete's stride, a full head of hair, and a ubiquitous, ingratiating smile that dazzles as he encourages the players. When one is hurt, the parents' fears are calmed as Dan examines the injury. The crowd sees a former NFL team doctor, but you see something different—a man who has come full circle.

The boy from Bonnie Road, the one who rested on a table in the dingy locker room with a mangled knee and questioning eyes, has become the person he did not have that day but desperately needed: a doctor who is always there for the kids. A man who has found contentment living in the Texas Hill Country: Dr. Dan Robertson, the official team physician of the Battlin' Billies of Fredericksburg High.

Mothers' Gifts

David Edwards, a junior defensive back for San Antonio Madison High, had covered Westlake receiver Coy Aune during the game. When one made a good play the other would offer a compliment; they were two great kids enjoying friendly competition, until the scoreboard clock registered 2:22 left in the game. Beneath an overcast sky, Coy reached for a pass and saw David coming toward him to make the tackle. After an awkward collision both fell to the turf. Coy got up but David lay motionless on the ground. Within seconds, silence steamrolled down the stands as 10,000 stunned spectators stared at the stricken player. For many agonizing minutes the only sound at Chaparral Stadium was the wailing of his grief-stricken family, later joined by the mechanized noise from the approaching ambulance. David's mother, Faye Stanton, cried in anguish for her son, but her sobs were also a plea for help.

Guest in our house

Coy's mother, Marci Aune, watched as David was sped away to Brackenridge Hospital. The Chaps' first ever home playoff game had resulted in serious injury to a guest, and she knew "the Westlake community needed to take ownership of David." Along with her husband Jon, she went to the hospital and met with the family, including Faye's husband, Walter Cedric Stanton, and the Madison coaches while David underwent a five-hour operation. The next day David inquired about Coy and the two talked, not in front of thousands but in the solitude of a hospital room. That evening Coy and his mother were discussing ways of showing support when Marci thought of putting an orange #5, David's number, on the Westlake helmets and dedicating the game to him, which led to David Edwards Day at the school the following week.

During her frequent visits to the hospital, Marci learned she and Faye had many things in common. Both held deep religious beliefs, were blessed with extremely supportive husbands, and each had two boys and two girls children who were close in age. At some point it hit Marci; what was that large family going to do for Thanksgiving? She fired off e-mails and in a short time had three free hotel rooms, turkeys with all the trimmings, and more than enough food for David's family. Some friends called first while others just appeared at the Aunes' door, gifts in hand. At Christmas time the exercise was repeated, with Internet networking filling the wish list for David and his sisters, Diera and Deandra, and his brother, Divon. One specific e-mail request was answered when an envelope was left on the Aune doorstep: inside were tickets to Fiesta Texas. Money jars appeared in many Westlake stores the day after David's injury. Within a week $120 in small change had been donated. By late February the community had stepped up and raised over $100,000, much of it through the booster and Chaps' clubs, headed by Gina Reese, Jill Durkee, and Anne Moning. The donors did not seek or expect attention for those deeds; tapping into their own goodness was reward enough. Many who donated their time and money were at the stadium that day. They were affected by the strength and courage of the young man and his family. To many, David Edwards was a present to the Westlake community, a gift they felt compelled to reciprocate.

Strength

Throughout the ordeal, Faye's church and the Madison High family have been very supportive. Head coach Jim Streety said, "I coached one day too long," because a coach never wants to see that injury befall his player. Streety travels to Houston on a regular basis to visit David at The Institute of Rehabilitation and Research where the boy's room is festooned with jerseys from Earl Campbell and Lance Armstrong. An apartment association in Houston helped the family relocate there. A golf tournament and auction were held near Boerne, and KB Homes in San Antonio is donating a new one-story house that will accommodate David's needs. Helping a family as close-knit and wonderful as the Stanton/Edwards clan is easy. Cedric works in the Bexar County sheriff's department, and Faye had a daycare center where all the children, including David, pitched in when they could. A family devoted to protecting others is being rewarded.

David's strength and outlook guide him through the days. "There's no point in getting frustrated. You have to think positive. If you don't, you're never going to get better." He was told he would always need to be on a ventilator; by March he was breathing on his own.

Moviemaker

Film director Peter Berg was a frequent guest of the Aunes' while shooting *Friday Night Lights* in Austin. He was at the game and has brought gifts to David during his trips to the hospital. Wanting to do more for the boy, he instigated the Gridiron Heroes concert and cajoled Tim McGraw, Billy Bob Thornton, and others to spend Easter weekend in Austin for the benefit. The singers also visited David in Houston. The public relations and proceeds from the concert helped the fledgling foundation that aids football players who incur spinal cord injuries during games. Founded in 2001, the organization hopes soon to expand nationwide. In one of many strange coincidences, Peter Berg had acted in the movie about a New York Jets player who became paralyzed during a game, *Rise and Walk: The Dennis Byrd Story*.

Coincidences

Coy Aune's jersey number was 1, David Edwards' was 5. Coy's birth date is the 5th, David's is the 1st. The accident took place on 11-15. David is scheduled to go home on May 14. The next morning he will wake up in his own bed for the first time since the injury occurred, exactly six months ago. The date will be 5-15. After the game, while the Aunes remained with Faye and her family at the hospital, the person in Austin most qualified to be with their son took Coy to dinner. Seated across the table from the distraught young man at Kenichi Restaurant was the actor who had portrayed Dennis Byrd, Peter Berg.

Gracious ladies

Faye and Marci found themselves by happenstance, but it was no accident they became friends; these gracious ladies are reflective of everything that is good in their respective communities. Marci's father passed away on February 3; the day of the funeral she received a special phone call from Faye. They talk two or three times a week, exchanging news, sharing birthdays and anniversaries. Sometimes Faye, knowing the grief her friend is struggling with, calls simply to check up on Marci, just as Marci has done for Fay since that day in November of 2003.

The bond of motherhood naturally extends to the children. At the Gridiron Heroes concert, Diera slid her arm through Marci's as the two walked the grounds of Auditorium Shores. After one visit to the Aune home, Marci took the Edwards children to lunch and during the meal Diera told Marci, "I think you're going to be in my wedding someday!" The mother was flattered but later confided to Faye, "Does she know how old I am?"

David's injury was tragic, but it was a miracle that two strong, resolute women found each other, resulting in a ripple effect of goodness that goes far beyond mere dollars. And with constant medical advancements being made in spinal injuries, Marci's prayers will be answered and her dream will come true: the day David Edwards walks through her front door. Until that event, Faye Stanton and Marci Aune must be content to share their support, friendship, and love. Gifts, from one mother to another.

Days of Future Passed

When Texas played Auburn in 1983, I was sitting in Memorial Stadium with my brother Paul. After an Auburn punt the Horns' offense trotted on the field. Before they broke the huddle, I turned to Paul and described the play Texas would run. That precise play unfolded, and I predicted the seven successive plays, exactly, until Texas crossed the goal line. Paul looked at me and asked, "How did you do that?"

Uncertain and confused, I inadvertently punned, "Texas' offense is predictable." Neither one of us pointed out the obvious—it was the first game of the year.

Jose, can you see?

Calling something "intuition" is acceptable; labeling it "psychic" will often elicit condescending grins or nervous laughter, which is understandable. I was skeptical myself before that night. Reading Yale Professor Jose Delgado's explanation didn't help; it could make dizzy even a seasoned whirling dervish. "Psychic energy may be considered a main determinant of the quantity of intellectual and behavioral manifestations." He also tossed out that "each person is a transitory composite of materials borrowed from the environment, and his mind is the intracerebral elaboration of extracerebral information." Okey-dokey, but, Jose, can you "see"? I bounced this subject matter off some well-known and very well-educated Austinites. None of them scoffed; at some point in their life each had been around someone who possessed "intuition."

Fat Chance

The New England Patriots were ahead 17-10 in the fourth quarter when they punted inside the opponent's 10-yard line. A thought came over me, "Game over," followed by, "linebacker Teddy Bruschi intercepts a screen pass in the right flat and runs seven yards for the score." On second down the quarterback looked right and . . . welcome to the world of psychic phenomena if you "knew" Teddy would snag the pass and score.

By now grinners are thinking, "This guy's nuts." Savvy readers are thinking, "T-man, let's go to Vegas!" Fat chance. In my pre- "pre-cog" days, Texas played Virginia in a 1977 football game. On a bet, I took Virginia and 60 points. Sixty points! Call me Count de Money, right? The final score: Texas 68, Virginia 0, and the Count minus $5.00. Virginia's administration was so disgusted they closed down the football program for five years. My disgust continues to this day.

"Keep your mouth shut"

In 1992, Texas was playing Virginia Commonwealth in the Central II Regional baseball final for a berth in the College World Series. Trailing by a run in the bottom of the eighth inning, Texas loaded the bases with one out. Left-handed hitter Brooks Kieschnick stepped into the batter's box. Seated two rows below me was 78-year-old Jack Balagia, Sr. (who recently celebrated his 92nd birthday with a little help from me).

The pitch count was 1-0 when Kieschnick whiffed badly on a curve ball. "Strike one!" Jack jumped up, turned to me and yelled, "Tudey!" Mr. B. looked like he was having a gallbladder attack. I shrugged, and Jack sat down. Kieschnick waved his bat at the next swing. "Strike two!" Again, Jack jumped up, turned and yelled, "Tudey boy!" Now Mr. B. appeared to be trying to pass a kidney stone. Wanting to leave the rest of his stones unturned, I yelled over the growing vocal angst of the crowd, "Double play ball to the shortstop . . . but don't worry Jack, he'll boot it." Kieschnick smashed a grounder to the shortstop and the Rams' best defensive fielder positioned himself to receive the ball, but it glanced off his glove, rolled up his arm and over his shoulder into center field. After two runners scored I glanced down to check on Jack's health and noticed we were the only people in our section looking at the field. Everyone else was staring at me like I was a freak in a circus sideshow.

Why now?

So, why am I going public now? I do it for the people who have the trait but endure it silently, fearful of the ridicule of the grinners and laughers. Some have a benign strain: they think of someone, the phone rings, and it's that person. Most of them have premonitions or feelings that are injected into their lives, some of them unpleasant. My trait is not limited to the relatively frivolous world of sports, but to quote Forrest Gump, "That's all I have to say about that."

Occasionally, I watch sports with a fellow who predicts fumbles and interceptions with regularity. We exchange high fives after these occurrences, partly to celebrate his exactitude. Mostly, he does it because he can share the knowledge with someone who, unlike that UT baseball crowd, will not stare at him as if he's a freak.

Gentle Ben

On Friday, September 17, 1999, I walked into the original Maudie's Restaurant and spotted Scotty and Julie Sayers and Ben and Julie Crenshaw seated at the middle table against the mirrored wall. Soon, they would be leaving for Brookline, Massachusetts, and the Ryder Cup matches. Ben, the American Captain, knew I was rarely at a loss for words, so when I walked over to wish him good luck, he smiled and asked, "Tudey, what should I tell the boys?" referencing the team's 12 golfers. A pregnant pause lingered for six seconds until I gave birth to, "Tell them to relax and have fun." I quickly excused myself and rejoined my party, certain the foursome was thinking, "We waited six seconds for that?"

I didn't watch the first two days as the Americans dug a deep hole for themselves. By Saturday evening it looked bleak: Captain Crenshaw's boys needed to win eight of the 12 individual matches and tie another on Sunday to regain the Ryder Cup. At the afternoon press conference, the passionate Captain was pelted with questions about his boys' abysmal showing. Ben ended the negative discussion when he pointed a finger at the reporters and said, "I'm a big believer in fate . . . and I have a good feeling about this. That's all I'm going to tell you." He stood, grabbed his bottled water, and walked off the dais.

The comeback

On Sunday I watched the first two holes of Tom Lehman's match before exiting the house. The rest of my day was spent running errands and piddling in the yard, but each time I re-entered the house my eyes found the television. As Justin Leonard sank his famous putt, I plopped down on the couch and remained there after the final grouping hit their tee shots on the 18th. As they walked up that final fairway, the gallery pressed in behind Colin Montgomerie and his American opponent, Payne Stewart, who was clad in his signature "plus fours," plaid knickers with knee-length socks.

I went outside but returned later and heard an analyst repeatedly saying the feat was "the greatest comeback in Ryder Cup history." Standing on a rooftop balcony of a clubhouse, Ben and his boys were spraying champagne on each other and the exuberant crowd below. Somewhere in that golf gallery were many Austinites, including Mark Eidman, Bob Kay, and Pat Oles. My happiness for them was not tinged with jealousy as those days of history had passed before their eyes, because I had been there briefly, 10 nights before.

Fate?

Ben believes in fate, I am an observer of ironies. Ten months after that weekend, Ben and Scotty invited my alter ego, Uncle Sam, to ride with them in the Tarrytown 4th of July Parade. Our transportation: one of four official Ryder Cup golf carts from the 1999 matches. Seeing the cart always reminds me of that Friday night at Maudie's, when Ben posed his question and "things" immediately entered my mind. I had seen the fairway gallery following behind two golfers, one wearing plus fours. And I had heard the phrase, "the greatest comeback in Ryder Cup history."

The Most Amazing Thing

Many sons "go away to college"; mine merely "crossed Lamar," the Boulevard. The proximity works out great, except on those occasions when he brings a truckload of dirty clothes home, and his mother might as well have "laundress" tattooed on her forehead. Recently, he breezed in without a cleaning request, so it was obvious that something was up. William needed guns and ammo for a college freshman right of passage—the senseless shooting spree. In the old days, the description was, "If it's flying, it's dying," which narrowed the scope to the avian world. Nowadays, the expedition is all-inclusive, like the Spring Break hotel packages in Mexico. Quizzed about the quarry, my son said, "I think it's, 'If it moves, shoot it.'" Relax, PETA, the hunt was cover for an overnight trip of male bonding, where mouths shot off more frequently than guns. Bambi, Thumper, Rocky Raccoon, Sammy Squirrel, and the other creatures of the forests and glens of Burnet County were safer than their city-dwelling counterparts, judging from the boys' meager haul and a cursory trip over West Austin's asphalt.

A few nights later, we called William home and informed him that one of his best friends since middle school, Charles Beaman, had been diagnosed with Ewing's sarcoma, an extremely rare type of cancer. It primarily afflicts children between 10 and 20 years of age, and the most commonly affected areas are the pelvis, thigh, and trunk of the body. Treatment involves chemotherapy followed by surgery and/or radiation therapy. Although it is treatable, the news shook up our son, who forgot to retrieve the little used hunting equipment from his truck and returned to his apartment.

The next morning he discovered everything had been stolen: his shotgun, my father's .243 rifle that I used to bag my first buck at the age of 12, the camo ammo bag, and an extensive CD collection. After the police left and following a morning class, William did what many males do when stressed out—he played golf; that is he walked down 24th Street to the Frisbee course at Pease Park. While playing, he probably thought about special times with Charles. The week spent in San Miguel de Allende three summers earlier and the long drive down, when we stopped in Real de Catorce for a horseback ride through the old village, movie location for *The Mexican*. The times Charles would return from Phillips Andover prep school, borrow a car from his parents, Joe and Lisa, and show up at our house, where the boys would sit in the small television room playing guitars or quietly enjoy each other's company. Or Charles' first OU-Texas game when the boys were in seventh grade. A wonderful young lady had given us a sideline pass that the boys swapped throughout the game. When the game ended, we couldn't locate Charles. After a few anxious moments William tugged my shirt, pointed, and said, "There he is!" All of the UT players were jumping up and down and hugging each other as they rushed to midfield to greet the vanquished Sooners . . . except for one player. He was bringing up the rear, oblivious to the pandemonium on the field and the stands singing "Texas Fight." His left arm was draped over the left shoulder of the five-foot tall Charles, who held the player's helmet in his left hand. The two were talking as they ambled across the storied Cotton Bowl turf alone, together: Ricky Williams and a young boy.

While walking the eighth hole at Pease Park, my son spotted something out of place. He approached a man-made clump of brush, bent over, and parted the tree limbs, revealing the thief's treasure: William's shotgun, the .243 rifle, the camo ammo case, and the CD collection. The camouflage case of the shotgun had caught his eye, and he was ecstatic. Unlike Ali Baba, he did not say, "Open, sesame." Instead, when the phone rang, my son exclaimed in an excited voice, "Dad, the most amazing thing just happened!" The only sight more amazing would be the thief's expression, if he learned his stolen stash had been retrieved by the person he burglarized!

Three nights later, a group of boys watched the OU-Texas basketball game. They probably thought about William's good fortune and Charles' misfortune, but no one connected the two or couched the event as a going-away dinner for Charles before he began his treatments, because he did not want special attention. Indeed, he would consider this essay excessive attention; he never wanted anyone to make a big deal about his predicament. Which was hard, because to many people Charles Beaman is a big deal.

A few days later, his friends departed for Spring Break and Charles walked into a Houston hospital, fortified with a positive attitude and an understated inner strength. Unlike his lucky friend, Charles' journey will not be a short walk; it will require months of chemotherapy followed by surgery. His many supporters are filled with hope the doctors at M. D. Anderson Hospital, like modern day Ali Babas, will restore to the soft-spoken young man what has been stolen from him—his good health. And when that day arrives, the phone will ring and my son will exclaim, in an excited voice, "Dad, the most amazing thing just happened . . . ."

Constructing a Miracle

The previous essay begins the story of 19-year-old Charles Beaman and his struggle with cancer, with a cameo appearance by Ali Baba. Six months later representatives from the U. S. Navy attended a solid freeform fabrication presentation at the Navy Shipyard in Newport, Rhode Island, hosted by a different Ali Baba. Why the two are remotely related dates back more than 20 years.

Charles was born in August of 1984. Around that time, a UT mechanical engineering professor and a graduate student both wondered if there were a technique by which manufacturing molds could be built more quickly. Their first construction was a crude cube within a cube. The computer-aided design (CAD) essentially tells the machine how to build products from the ground up in a layered structure, like a pyramid. A thin layer of powder drops down, and a laser zaps the computer-designated locations into a solid. The process is repeated, layer upon layer, until the completed product is formed, which usually takes two hours.

A NEW YORK TIMES article on March 2, 1987, chronicled the progress of the idea. Seed money and materials supplied by B. F. Goodrich led to DTM, a University of Texas spin-off company. Eventually, more than 150 people in the Austin area were employed by Harvest Technology, located in Temple, and DTM, which subsequently merged with 3D Systems, a California company. The first showing of the UT-designed machine was in 1991, and in 1995 the machines were being sold to auto makers and aerospace companies. By 1997, the University of Michigan had adapted the process into the medical field, doing early work on facial reconstruction. That same year, Charles was the star point guard of his sixth grade basketball team.

Charles went to Phillips Andover near Boston for high school. During that period solid freeform fabrication was expanding. Stereolithography, a liquid process utilizing photo polymers, had been supplemented by direct metal laser sintering and other applications. Siemens, the German company, could take a surface catscan of a person's ear canal and make custom-shaped hearing aid shells using the technology. Boeing created a subsidiary company, On Demand, that supplied parts to the plane manufacturer. An airplane part that used to require 16 separate pieces could now be quickly made as a single, solid part used on a jet fighter. Another company, Invisalign, created a clear mold that could make a set of teeth conform into perfect alignment gradually, by periodically replacing the solid sets that acted like temporary braces. Many industries realized the cost effectiveness on small lot production that this process allows. The U. S. Navy became interested because this process might allow "smart weapons" to become a reality. If a gun fell into enemy hands, that weapon could be manufactured to recognize the person to whom it was assigned and refuse to fire if it did not recognize the person handling it.

Meanwhile, the medical field continued rejoicing. By 2002, orthotics and customized prosthetics had become a $900 million per year industry. Utilizing the process, UT mechanical engineering professor Dr. Rick Neptune won the DaVinci Award for his work on orthotics for the lower leg. Solid freeform fabrication grew from a $100 million industry in 1993 to an expected $700 million in 2005. Instead of designing for manufacturing, engineers can now manufacture for design.

Which brings us back to Charles Beaman, who was a freshman at UT in the fall of 2003, when he began experiencing pain in his hip. The diagnosis was Ewing's sarcoma, an extremely rare type of cancer. Charles endured months of successful treatments and, as the date for operation neared, the doctors were offered the services of the fabrication process. A CAT scan of Charles' afflicted hip was sent from M.D. Anderson Hospital to the UT Health Science Center in San Antonio and then to the UT mechanical engineering department in Austin. In the cave-like basement of the campus building on East Dean Keeton Street, various Ali Babas constructed a solid freeform fabrication of Charles's hipbone on one of their machines. Surgeons at M.D. Anderson were studying the tumor-laden bone three days after taking the CAT scan and its replicated replacement. Surgeons walked into the operating room, and constantly referenced the model during the delicate and successful four-hour procedure.

Days later, a man returned to his office, but his emotional co-workers did not see an Ali Baba. They were happy to hug the man they knew as the chairman of the UT mechanical engineering department and the co-inventor of solid freeform fabrication, Dr. Joe Beaman, Charles' father.

When something bad happens to a child, every father hopes to be able to remedy the situation. In 1984, while his wife was giving birth to Charles, Joe Beaman had an idea that played a material part in the recovery of his son.

The people involved in the treatment were all members of the University of Texas family: M.D. Anderson Hospital, the UT Health Science Center in San Antonio, and the mechanical engineering department at UT-Austin. Charles attends UT-Austin. No one appreciates that fact more than Dr. Joe Beaman, a devout family man whose vision 20 years ago helped keep intact the most precious things in his life: his wife Lisa and his children Justin, Clark, Lilly, and Charles. All children are miracles, yet some are exposed to more miraculous events than others, something Joe and Charles are happy to have in the Beaman family.

Return to Marywood

Two years ago I wrote "Changing Lives for Generations." In it I thanked my mother, Catherine Teten, for plucking me from the orphanage at Marywood. Along with my father, Robert P. Teten, she "gave the boy a life more wonderful than any he ever imagined possible." In the 1980s, to repay a debt to my parents and the institution, I became the first adoptee board member of Marywood. My tenure was unremarkable.

My main contributions were the discussions with the pregnant girls who resided there. We met in the girls' dayroom and sat on couches and chairs in a small circle. During each session certain questions always came up.

"Do you ever think about your birth mother?"

"Yes."

"Do you resent her for not keeping you?"

"No." My answers were followed by lengthy explanations, but after three years of meetings it was hard to tell if they were having a positive impact on the girls.

On a sunny spring afternoon in 1985, while sitting in the building's new chapel, I came across a story that helped me understand that Marywood was more than a haven for the girls. The institution also gave counsel and help to those in need.

A 26-year-old female nursing instructor at a hospital became engaged to be married, but the Irish woman's family did not approve of her fiancé. Over the next few months, she realized their assessment was correct, and she called off the wedding. Her difficult decision was compounded by the knowledge that she had become pregnant.

Abortion was not an option: the man and woman came from large Catholic families. Her ex-fiancé had eleven older siblings: one was a priest, two others were nuns. The pregnant woman packed her suitcase and walked across the threshold of Marywood to await the birth of her child.

The staff at Marywood considered her a very sweet and patient young woman, whose personality allowed her to befriend others easily. She worked in the nursery, assisting the infants and orphans. One toddler had trouble adapting to his environment, and she spent a great deal of time working with him.

Eventually, she gained his trust and exposed him to the world outside the nursery. His first unsure steps became purposeful, and soon the two walked slowly down the marble halls together, the Irish woman holding his left hand while the fingertips of his right danced across the wall searching for the stability he could not see. He was blind.

On the threshold of a dream

Today, Marywood still handles adoptions, and through their Stepping Stones program they also furnish housing for homeless mothers between the ages of 18 and 21. Like that blind child, most are feeling their way through the hallways of life, searching for a stable future, scared of falling again. Like the Irish woman, Marywood takes the girls under its wing and nurtures them lovingly.

Recently, a young woman walked across the threshold of Marywood with her baby and a dream: to become a chef and support her child. A year later she graduated from a culinary institute. Now she is living in an apartment with her child and working in the kitchen of a prominent hotel in another city. She has found stability.

As the months passed, the Irish woman kept working in the nursery, but she always found time for the blind boy. Despite her doting, he still resided in a world without a mother or a home. If he suffered a nightmare or cried out in despair, she was soon at his side, regardless of the time of day or night. She would lift him from the crib, and the two would sit together in a rocking chair. He would lie at her side with his hands resting on her womb and his head nestled near her shoulder. Her free hand would gently stroke his hair as she kissed his forehead and softly whispered, "God loves you, and I love you. Everything's going to be all right." They remained in the rocking chair until the tears and despair evaporated or he fell asleep. And then her feet would lightly tap the floor, and they would rock a while longer.

Are you sitting comfortably?

A few years ago another Stepping Stones candidate came to Marywood with her child and a feeling of despair, unable to retain a job for more than a few months. Nestled in the comforting arms of the staff, the young girl persevered

154

and graduated from a technical school. For the past two years she has worked in a doctor's office and is no longer homeless. She lives with her child in an apartment where the two sit comfortably each evening, in part because of Marywood's assistance.

The Irish woman left Seton Hospital with her newborn and stayed at Marywood a few more days. When she heard her baby cry out, she was soon at his side. A nun checking on the infant would peek in at night and see a familiar scene in the darkened nursery: the moonglow coming through the slats in the long windows, casting soft rectangular rays of light over the hardwood floors and white cribs . . . a woman seated in a rocker, a child nestled in her arms. The nun retreated, allowing the two some final moments of privacy.

The Irish woman gently stroked her newborn's hair and softly whispered, "God loves you, and I love you. Everything's going to be all right." Then she kissed his forehead and added, "You will have a fine life." They remained in the rocking chair until he fell into a dream state. Then her feet lightly tapped the floor and the two rocked a little longer, until it was time for her to leave. She laid the sleeping baby in his crib and left Marywood forever.

Upon leaving Marywood, each birth mother retraces the steps that brought her to the brick building. She exits the home with suitcase in hand, descends the stairs, and walks along the thin sidewalk to a waiting car. As the automobile departs, she carries inside of her the hopes and aspirations for the child left behind.

Her thoughts of that child dissipate and become faint over the years, obscured by jobs, marriage, and subsequent children, with one exception, the birthday of her Marywood baby. On those special days, the birth mothers have secret, stolen moments; times when they wonder what became of their little ones, each one hoping that her baby was taken in by a loving and caring family like I was.

I spend part of every December 17 with my mother and I always thank her for giving me a wonderful life, although the visits now take place at her gravesite. The north end of Mount Calvary Cemetery touches East 26th Street. Upon leaving, my car retraces the steps to Marywood, located at 510 West 26th.

My eyes always find the bank of second-story windows near the southeast corner. Today it houses the chapel where I first read about the Irish woman. Prior to renovation, that room had served as the nursery for the blind boy and other children in need. In a secret, stolen moment, I send a thought to a blue-eyed brunette with fair complexion who gave me life: that 26-year-old Irish woman. "God loves you, and I love you. And my life turned out fine, just like you said it would."

The Last Dance: A Lenten Suggestion

This is a loose interpretation of some quotes from the Reverend Nicholas Cirillo of Connecticut because many people forego something during Lent.

Even if you consider your own free time terribly important, my suggestion is not about sacrifice; it is about gift: capturing your grandparents or elderly parents on film. That doesn't mean you are supposed to go barging into Granny's home and set up extra lighting, then plunk the camera on a tripod in front of her, stuff a microphone in her face, and shout, "Action!" because her first thought will be, "I guess the test results weren't good." Being tactful helps.

If you give something up, as most people do, your sacrifice should help you recognize the blessings that we take for granted most of the time.

After my grandfather died in 1979, the family realized we did not have any audio or video to commemorate his years on earth. Following that discovery, numerous cousins made entreaties to our grandmother, Anne Thornton Nash, to no avail. Unfazed, I walked into her sitting room one day with notebook and video camera in hand. For the next minute, her 92-year-old heart raced as she told me, in a most demonstrative manner, what she thought about being captured on film. Defeated, I said, "Well, Grandma, I guess that's enough aerobic workout for one day." The chess game continued for months, as my crazy Bobby Fischer matched wits with her cool Boris Spassky. Fate intervened when my brother became engaged, because Grandma was a sucker for weddings. One month after his nuptials, she awakened at three in the morning on July 29, 1981, to watch Prince Charles and Lady Diana Spencer get hitched, and she remained glued to the tube until after noon. That evening she gave me a complete rundown.

Our chess game had concluded the month before. The winning move was an appeal to her sentimental side. Ten summers before, Anne and James P. "Big Jim" Nash had taken 14 family members to Ireland. Those two months were memorable for us all, largely because we were constantly in their company. On the wall next to the recliner where she often sat was a weathered linen towel fitted with dowels on the top and bottom that displayed the inscription of an

Old Irish blessing. One day in June, I showed up with a cassette tape player and explained what I wanted. Grandma glanced at the cloth hanging on the wall, then looked back at me, and smiled. Checkmate.

The toasts at the rehearsal dinner in Chicago had ended when I stood up, and said, "One person could not be here tonight, but she wanted to say something to the bride and groom." I held the cassette player up to the microphone, and her sweet voice permeated the room. "May the road rise to meet you. May the wind be always at your back. May the sun shine warm upon your face, the rains fall soft upon your fields and, until we meet again . . . may God hold you in the palm of His Hand . . . Love, Grandma."

The day after Thanksgiving in 1987, she passed away, one week shy of her 99th birthday. Grandma was ready to go, a fact the family accepted, grudgingly. After the graveside service concluded, I stood and faced the family. "Grandma never got to say goodbye. If she had, this is probably what she would have told us." I unfurled the weathered cloth and read the Old Irish Blessing. Some relatives became choked up, recalling those magical days in Ireland; others were misty-eyed remembering her voice at the rehearsal dinner. Still others were sad because they knew she would never utter those words again.

Christ was always aware of his Father's sustaining presence.

Big Jim died three weeks shy of his 87th birthday, on April 3, 1979. The night before the funeral, a rosary was held at the mortuary, followed by fellowship at his home. Late in the evening, the only ones left in the card room were the five adult grandson pallbearers, who ranged in age from 24 to 30, and four other similarly aged men. Although the others were not related to Big Jim, he had been like a grandfather to them. All of us were dreading the funeral; we were ill prepared to cope with his death. Granddad came from a generation that relished big cigars, but not big tears. Everyone in the room was unsure how he would hold up at the service. None of us wanted to let Granddad down.

Around 11:30 P.M., I asked, "Why don't we go to the funeral home?"

My odd suggestion was met with another question. "Why?"

Two words: "Irish wake." To the Irish, grieving and drinking go together like fish and chips. One fella fished out a prized, 50-year-old bottle of single malt scotch from the liquor cabinet. A box of Cuban cigars was discovered, a recent Christmas gift to Granddad from one of the non-grandson pallbearers. Beer in a spare refrigerator was transferred into two coolers, and the group slipped quietly out the kitchen door.

The night watchman at the funeral home heard a pounding noise on the side door and went to investigate the disturbance. He opened it, stepped back, and fled. Apparently, he was unaccustomed to midnight intrusions by nine fairly sizable guys chomping on unlit Cubans and carrying ice chests, while holding cups of beer and whiskey.

The funeral home's chapel was deserted and dark, except for two low-light sconces near the open casket, and a spotlight that shone down on Big Jim. Some in the group sat on the first pew, as others pulled up chairs, forming a large circle near the coffin. Stories about Granddad flowed, and we pictured him in our minds' eyes. When a speaker quoted him, we imagined it was Big Jim's voice.

Nine years earlier, a family member in attendance had hosted a nocturnal varmint hunt at Big Jim's ranch. During the carnage, one of Granddad's cows had accidentally been shot "stone cold dead." The shooter's true identity had been cloaked in secrecy, but the host family member was forced to spend the summer as an indentured servant at the Kash-Karry grocery store. The premier sack boy's salary had been garnished to offset the loss of Big Jim's moocow. Around 1 A.M., at the funeral home, the real shooter finally fessed up to nailing the "white-faced deer."

"The what?"

"Hey, it had two horns." The revelation stunned the group. "So, you thought you were shooting a spike buck with a white face that just happened to weigh 800 pounds?" The group found that more amusing than Granddad had at the time. That admission opened a new area of discussion. Everyone told stories of how Granddad had kept them out of or had rescued them from trouble. When each storyteller finished, he silently excused himself from the group, walked to the casket, and stared down at Big Jim. The time each person took to say goodbye varied—some staying at his side briefly, others lingering. A few of us walked outside and sat down on the steps. Each of us lit a Cuban cigar and, as it burned, thought of Big Jim. And in the wee hours of the morning, we reflected on the dying embers of our relationship with him. On returning to the group, each of us was red-eyed and silent.

Around 4:30 A.M., someone said, "We've got to be at the house in less than five hours," and the group hurriedly reclaimed the evidence of our visit. The ceiling light illuminated Granddad's face, and we knew that it was the last time we would see him, and the final time he would be in the spotlight. The nine men gathered in a semi-circle around the open casket, together we lifted our glasses, and said, "To Big Jim."

At the funeral, we heard the soft crying of family members behind us. Leaning forward, I looked down the pew at the other pallbearers. They wore dark suits, white starched shirts, muted ties, and the same facial expression: a serene, almost conspiratorial calm. The last lesson he taught us was that collective grief can be the best elixir. Big Jim would have been proud of his boys.

Lent is designed for one purpose alone: to lead us to recognize the presence of God in that which is right before our eyes.

Everyone delights in watching their parents or grandparents dance through life. Some of them tango, others foxtrot, or waltz. We turn away briefly and, when we look back, the dance floor is deserted. The last dance is over. All that remains are memories and what we captured on film, either in photos or videos. Our family recognized the presence of God in our grandparents but never committed their goodness to film. The weathered cloth that contains the Old Irish Blessing remains in my possession, but it can't speak to me. I keep the small cassette tape, because it can.

The Patient Man in Seat 10E

I used to be as patient as a starving monkey in a zoo, but a transformation occurred on the last leg of a family vacation to Italy. The trip ended the same way it began—with a traveler's nightmare. We stood in the airline check-in line for 90 minutes and spent 15 more going through airport security. The family was worried; curlicues of steam were rising from my tousled hair. Our flight to Cincinnati on December 23 arrived early, but we waited on the tarmac for 50 minutes until a gate became available. The town had received 18 inches of snow in the preceding 12 hours, its entire average annual snowfall; airport personnel were overwhelmed.

We sprinted to make our connecting flight and boarded at 6:20 P.M. just before they closed the doors for the first time. Captain Brian announced we would take off after the wings were de-iced. An hour later, he said we were waiting for some passengers from a connecting flight. When they boarded, he stated we were now waiting for a few more passengers from another flight and, "By the way, one-half of your lavatories could go out at any time."

No prob, Brian, we only have an eight- or nine-hour flight ahead of us; we can hold it. A stewardess took the microphone and spoke in Italian. She was probably telling us we might want to hold onto our cups, but at least she did it in a lilting, poetic, vowel-laced voice. Captain Brian, the pathological liar, then explained that airline potties performed differently in the air than on the ground. That unpleasant visual gave new meaning to the term "fly over country." It was now 8:30.

Twenty minutes later someone actually began de-icing the plane. Not the entire structure, just the wheels. Seems the aircraft had been sitting there overnight and no one had snapped to the fact that 18 inches of snow pack might take some time to melt. Passengers were treated to free water and pretzels. Whee!

Once in a while the plane would lurch a few inches before jolting to a stop. The iceberg around the wheels was not going down without a fight. A strong kerosene-type odor wafted through our enclosed airspace and took its toll. The woman behind me placed a moist paper towel over her nose to filter out the foul smell. Most passengers were so used to it they didn't notice, or they hoped the fumes would put them out of their misery. A three-year-old walked down the aisle with his dad; it was the boy's thirtieth trip to the bathroom in four hours. Now I know why some species eat their young.

At 10:45 P.M. we taxied to the runway. Three planes were in front of us, waiting to be de-iced. Thirty minutes later a truck with a crane similar to the ones used by the telephone company appeared outside our window. At the end of the one-man compartment housing were four bright lights that illuminated the wings. The machine's operator aimed the stream of de-icing fluid at the plane. A howling wind dispersed half the fluid, and the 15-degree weather caused steam to rise as chunks of ice slid off the wings and, finally, at midnight the plane lifted off runway K2-27 and reached skyward. Beneath an almost full moon, the lights of Cincinnati twinkled amidst a blanket of snow. We had been in the plane for more than five and a half hours. It was Christmas Eve.

On our visit to the Vatican, we stared at Michaelangelo's ceiling fresco in the Sistine Chapel. To complete it, he had to rig a contraption on wheels that rode back and forth on the narrow molding near the ceiling. The artist spent five years on that makeshift scaffolding, painting his masterpiece. His other contribution to the room was "The Last Judgment." That project, which covered an entire wall, spanned six years; all that patience was lost on me.

Our return flight left Rome 45 minutes late. We missed our connecting flight and spent three extra hours at Hartsfield Airport in Atlanta on New Year's Eve night, before boarding the plane. My tired troops sat across the aisle while I occupied seat 10D. Once the flight took off, the lights dimmed and my family went to sleep. By my calculations, they had been awake for 21 hours. I turned my attention to the man in 10E, who was about my age. Our row was just past the first class section and he reached into the pleated receptacle attached to the partition and handed a box drink to the passenger in 10F. After placing it back in the holder, he doled some of the contents of a snack bag into the hands of his seatmate. Glancing at the floor I noticed the unseen passenger in the window seat was barefoot. The toes were splayed; they did not touch each other. I leaned forward and saw they were attached to a young man who was about 18 with blonde hair and blue eyes. The boy had Down's syndrome.

They had been visiting relatives up north for the holidays and were coming home. It was difficult to imagine how much energy this man had expended taking care of his son, who was virtually incapable of speaking. My thoughts reverted to Michaelangelo, working on his masterpieces in the Sistine

Chapel. The painter knew he would finish those projects in a finite amount of time. The occupant of seat 10E knew his commitment to his son was open-ended and would cease only upon his own death or that of his son. Michaelangelo managed his ceiling work with a contraption built on wheels. The man in seat 10E needed a wheelchair to escort his son on and off the airplane.

I felt sorry for the dad because he would never get to watch his son perform on an elementary school stage or play baseball or walk across the Erwin Center stage to receive his high school diploma—things most fathers take for granted. Their relationship seemed frozen in time, like the snow that had surrounded our plane's wheels in Cincinnati.

I was wrong. The boy placed his left arm around his father's neck and pulled his dad toward him. Then he kissed his father and their embrace lasted three or four seconds before the son released his arm and Dad returned to an upright position. No words were exchanged in the interlude; they were not needed. A son conveyed his love and a father showed his appreciation with a simple pat of the boy's leg.

During our conversation I told him about my children's exploits, yet the father never appeared envious of my situation. In spite of some of the shenanigans his son perpetrated while we talked, he never got angry with the boy or boasted about what a loving parent he was. Each morning he awakened, the father probably hoped his child would have a good day and that their relationship would deepen. The son, despite his mischief, understood that he could always trust his dad, who was there to protect him and ignore his shortcomings.

Watching them interact brought to mind a familiar passage spoken at many weddings. While the words are appropriate for couples, they exemplify the essence of the father in seat 10E. "Love is patient, love is kind. It does not envy, it does not boast, it is not proud. It is not rude, it is not self-seeking, it is not easily angered, it keeps no records of wrongs . . . It always protects, always trusts, always hopes, always preserves."

Flight #71 from Atlanta lasted 150 minutes. In that time, the boy repeatedly slipped his arm around his father, pulled him close and kissed him in a lingering embrace . . . more than 100 times. And I no longer felt sorry for 10E. Sure, he could not experience the joy of coaching his son in baseball or watch him excel in another endeavor, yet this dad was granted what many fathers dream of having—a child's unconditional affection. The man in seat 10E was rewarded because he understood that "Love is patient, love is kind . . . ."

163

COMEDY

A Great Hunting Trip

Many successful bird hunts are shown on the weekend outdoors shows. This trip did not fall into that category.

It began when an anonymous group of fathers and sons decided to embark on a season-ending goose hunt. They started at McBride's gun store by amassing more ammunition than the Columbia drug cartel. Then they drove to Eagle Lake and checked into a motel that catered to the NRA Camo Soldier of Fortune crowd, during the "high season." During the "low season," the motel's owners slashed their rates and became a romantic getaway destination for the trailer park social elite seen on the television show "COPS." The marketing ploy was successful, judging from the paneling, which in most rooms was dotted with plaster repair jobs ranging in size from fist to bowling ball to roughly the circumference of the blast of a 12-gauge shotgun fired from across the room. After a lively debate over which room offered the most ambience, the hunters set about the chore of securing indoor plumbing for one room by mastering the art of transferring water from the shower stall to the toilet basin, via ice chest.

After getting the requisite four hours of sleep, they headed out to the field. There they trudged about in the pitch black staking hundreds of "rag" decoys into the ground before sitting down in the "spread" and loading their guns. As dawn approached, a misty fog appeared and the group anxiously awaited the hunt and bragged about all the birds they would nail.

The first shot hit the bird dog. The perpetrator swore that Beau ran in front of the low-flying goose, but the canine world hasn't bred a dog that will "take one" for a bird. It was such a bad shot that Beau only absorbed one BB pellet and recovered rather quickly, but he spent the rest of the morning with a keen awareness of the perpetrator's whereabouts.

The boys quickly re-learned a valuable hunting lesson: aim higher than dirt-level. Their hunting style closely resembled "shoot early and often." Countless salvos were launched, mainly at birds flying in air space usually reserved for commercial aircraft. Into the valley of the shadow of death flew the 600 hundred geese, and out of the valley flew about 591. The nine that did not make it were four kamikazes and five who suffered massive heart attacks from the concussion of gunfire. Had this cadre of hunters been on the ramparts at the Alamo, Colonel Travis would have personally tossed them en masse over his line in the sand.

But this hunt was not about the bird count: it was a quest for something much more important: memories. It was an opportunity for some boys to spend part of a weekend of their ever-dwindling youth with their friends and dads. For too soon these young men, like the geese, will spread their wings and fly away. And if many years from now, long after the resilient Beau has been laid to rest, the boys can look back and smile about the good times they spent on a glorious Saturday morning in a rice field in Eagle Lake, Texas, then it truly was a great hunting trip, especially for us anonymous Dads.

Ode to Elvis

On the 25th Anniversary of his Death

If you got excited about the anniversary and were searching for a place to celebrate, I would have recommended, without a moment's hesitation, going to the original Maudie's. There you can get a hunka hunka burning salsa and really good Tex-Mex food while viewing an extensive gallery of Elvisiana, including two obligatory Elvis paintings on black velvet. For those not so inclined, here is some "lighter" fare.

Elvis left the building for the absolutely last time on August 16, 1977. Leading up to that date each year in Memphis is Elvis Week, billed as a huge family reunion, although some of the attending families won't have many tines on their genealogical forks, but they can probably strum "DUELING BANJOS."

The genesis for this article was the mandatory college tour which required a trip to Memphis, which further mandated the obligatory trip to Graceland. Shortly after exiting Highway 240 onto Highway 51 South (partially renamed Elvis Presley Boulevard) in southwest Memphis, my son and I entered a two-block area that should be called the Emirate of Elvis, an exaltation of excess. On the right was Elvis Presley's Heartbreak Hotel (a "fashionable boutique hotel") perched in a nest of campers and recreational vehicles. Just past the hotel were Graceland Plaza and Graceland Crossing, two small strip centers with shops named Gallery Elvis and Elvis Threads. We chose the latter but were unable to fill little sister's request for an Elvis jumpsuit. My son passed on the 5x7 jungle room diorama complete with water weeping through the bricks ($49.95), and chose instead the most understated tee shirt in two stores for his sister. After 20 minutes of intense searching/shopping and multiple sensory overloads we were, well, all shook up, uh-huh. So much so that we passed on the Graceland Outlet Store. Now, some might accuse Lisa Marie and Priscilla Presley of being sElvish, but we did not see anyone pointing a loaded, fried peanut-butter-and-banana sandwich to any visitor's head and forcing the patron to purchase Presley paraphernalia.

Pressed for time, we opted out of the Platinum Tour Package ("Best Value" at $25.00), two-and-a-half to three hours long and the Graceland Mansion Tour ($16.00), 60-90 minutes, both of which ended with "a quiet visit to the

Meditation Garden" where Elvis is buried. We selected the economical, expedited tour—i.e., a "drive by," which was fairly popular judging from the traffic at the turnout in front of Graceland. As we drove away my relieved son said, "Thank you. Thank you very much."

Upon leaving I pondered, is there a prototypical Presley fan? It would probably not be the guys with three first names who spot Elvis at 4 A.M. on a Red Man chewing tobacco restocking run after having spent six hours slamming down mass quantities of Schaefer beer with their buddies from the planet Xorlok, the same misguided aliens that always seem to search for intelligent life on Earth on a Thursday night in *really* rural Alabama.

To be certain, the crowd gathered for the anniversary likely did not resemble the one gathering on April 4, 2003, a few miles away from Graceland at the Lorraine Motel to mark the 35th anniversary of the assassination of Dr. Martin Luther King, Jr. But a diverse group did make up the estimated 150,000 fans from homes in places like the Tonya Harding Doublewide Estates and migrate to Memphis the next week. And who could blame them? Planned festivities included the Rock-A-Billy Pool Party, the Elvis Week Art Contest/Exhibit (no velvet here), Elvis Barbeque Cruises, and The Tao of Elvis. The highlights were VigilCast 2002, a live webcast from the Candlelight Vigil, followed the next night by a live concert at The Pyramid featuring "thirty live musicians" and Elvis. . . on Memorex, which makes him the only dead performer to sell out a live concert. Twice.

Like me, lots of folks make fun of Elvis and his fans. But many people who joke about his followers are guilty of some bizarre devotion, either as Grateful Dead "deadheads" or as pilgrims to Strawberry Fields in Central Park or to the Dakota to pay respects to John Lennon.

There is no typical Elvis fan. Some admired him because he served two years in the military at the height of his career, without asking for special treatment. Others liked him because he was so generous, once raising $100,000 for the *USS Arizona* memorial at Pearl Harbor. Most of his fans liked him because he was able to simultaneously uplift, inspire, and entertain, which explains why one of his Hawaiian concerts drew a larger American audience than the first lunar landing.

You are free to disagree with my assessment. In fact, you can do anything . . . but don't you step on my blue suede shoes.

The Wedding Gift that was a "Hit"

Those who combine the career paths of prison and the securities business usually go from the latter to the former. I was that rare exception. In early 1973, I made two important decisions: to get married and to lend my 20-year-old brain to solving the prison ills in Texas, which showed I would be the average husband—correct half the time. While going to school, I worked full-time at the Diagnostic Unit of the Texas Department of Corrections. This granted me contact with some of the most degenerate flotsam and jetsam that flowed through Texas prisons during the mid-70s: Fred Gomez Carrasco, the mastermind behind the prison siege in 1974 and professed murderer of over 50 people (sad, basset hound eyes); Elmer Wayne Henley, Jr., who aided and abetted Dean Corll in the murders of over two dozen teenage children (the most liquid, striking blue eyes I ever saw); and Ronald Clark O'Brian, "The Candy Man," who laced pixy sticks with cyanide, killing his two children for insurance money (lifeless, inkwell dark eyes).

This essay may appear jaded to some and, after spending over 8,000 hours surrounded by inmates, I plead guilty as charged. My mentor and the retired head of the Prison System, Dr. George Beto, said inmates were cunning but not smart, otherwise they wouldn't be in prison. One of my convict workers, Paul, was a prime example, as featured on **America's Most Wanted**. A second-generation cop, he landed in the slammer on a robbery conviction. Old habits die hard and, 10 years after his discharge from the TDC, Paul staked out a bank depository and got the drop on the armored car personnel after they finished toting in the moneybags. Paul was lugging the thirteenth sack of unmarked bills to the trunk of his car when the good guys arrived. Questioned later why he had taken so many bags, he explained, "I figured out that 13 bags equaled one million dollars." Poor Paul, he had figured wrong: *each* bag was worth a million dollars.

The exceptions to Dr. Beto's rule were two former lawyers who made ambulance chasers seem scrupulous. Leon looked like Hank Hill from **King of The Hill**, but his innocuous looks belied a sensationally creepy personality. Even the other inmates gave wide berth to his wide girth. Most miscreants start at the bottom and ascend the crime pyramid one step at a time. Leon had taken the elevator straight to the top. He was decades ahead of his competition and, if he had any scruples, he chose to ignore them. A hip prison psychologist pronounced Leon "a sick puppy," Sam, on the other hand, was the Top Dog, in prison parlance. He bore an eerie resemblance to Mr. Burns on **The Simpsons**, except his choppers did not stick out: they were removable. Sam was the first of four consecutive mayors of Pasadena, Texas, indicted on felony or misdemeanor charges. A successful criminal defense attorney, Sam's avocation as a crime lord got him into trouble. Apparently, he had really ticked off somebody, because there was a contract on his life for $100,000. In 1974, the average Major League Baseball salary was just over $24,000 per year, meaning someone thought a supine Sam in a casket was worth more than the entire infield of the Minnesota Twins.

Into this murderous maelstrom walked innocent Tudey, fresh from West Austin. My only brush with death had been a pet parakeet. One day, I plopped a *TEXAS MONTHLY* issue about "Five Unsolved Murders in Texas" on Sam's desk. Hours later, Leon stuck his head in my office and said with his sheepish grin, "We solved three of them: Sam did two, and I did one." Leon "Owl Eyes" wasn't joking, but my superiors told me this "confession" would not hold up in court.

At the age of 20, my namesake Tudey Thornton worked and had friends in high places. At the age of 20, I was surrounded by thousands of convicted criminals and worked with the Gruesome Twosome, who had committed mortal sins more frequently than cloistered nuns prayed. At least they weren't my friends. That changed one evening, while I sat on a bucket outside Sam's cell, and he said, "Tudey, you've been a good friend to me. I know you are getting married, and circumstances limit what I can give you for a wedding present, but if you ever want somebody taken care of just let me know."

Whoa, Sam! You shouldn't have. I envisioned the party where friends would view the gifts: between the tables of china and crystal would be a 12-gauge shotgun, with a photo of a casket and a note, "This could be you, if you make the happy couple mad. Love, Sam"

I told the former mayor that my bride would not be writing him, because Emily Post's Etiquette Book did not have a proper thank-you note for the gift of murder. Her letter probably would have read, "Dear Sam, Imagine my surprise when I learned of your thoughtful gift. Tudey and I will cherish it, 'til death us do part, which hopefully won't be soon, or by your henchman's hand. Sincerely, The Woman who promises to love, honor, and obey Tudey and really, really makes him happy."

Sam went on to lead a long, unproductive life in prison and died about 16 years ago. Leon got out soon after I left in 1977 and continued to set the curve in crime class, committing what a federal judge called, "one of the most bizarre, heinous criminal plots": Leon had mailed officials of multinational corporations letter bombs, diseased insects, poisoned food, and assassination threats. He signed the letters B.A. Fox.

When a bride opens her gifts and gets one she deems to be a white elephant, she will think, "This is the worst wedding present ever," but she will be wrong. Trust me. I know.

April Foolers

Friends of John S. Burns, Sr., and Robert Ammann, Sr., breathed a sigh of relief every April Fool's Day, because the two men ceded that date to amateurs. Everyone, except their victims, acknowledged the two were professional pranksters of the highest order.

One repeated target of John S. was his dear friend Tom "Top Cat" Wommack. Returning from a trip to Europe, Tom discovered his bedroom furniture in the back yard of his home on Winsted Lane. It was almost midnight, Tom was tired and needed sleep so he and his wife Virginia changed and padded out to their bed. Sleeping beneath the stars was fine until around 3 A.M. when the MoPac train blew by, causing Tom to jump about three feet. Another time, Chris Brandt was driving down the highway while Tom, seated next to him, enjoyed an adult libation. From the back seat John S. got Chris's attention by waving a firecracker, which he lit and tossed at Tom's feet. The sudden explosion caused Top Cat's drink to shower the inside of the vehicle. Then there was the time John S. had promised to bring Tom some venison, so he showed up at Mr. Wommack's office in the old Scarbrough Building with a Rylander's grocery store bag. He unloaded the contents onto Tom's desk and a six-foot rattlesnake bounced off the furniture into Tom's lap. After a few skipped heartbeats, Tom realized the slithering snake was dead and he took off after John S., running down the hallway yelling, "You crazy $#@!" One evening, Tom left a party and discovered his car had been stolen. The police came, filled out a report, and drove him home. When they saw a car matching that description in his driveway they began to question his sobriety. He probably responded by saying, "Who would do something like this to me? The same person who threw a lit firecracker at my feet in a moving vehicle, tossed a rattlesnake on my desk, and moved all my bedroom furniture into my back yard. But that's just a guess."

Bob Ammann often performed pranks on his good friends. While Judge John Wood and his wife were on a post-Christmas cruise, Bob took out an ad in a San Antonio paper asking people to bring their Christmas trees to the address in the ad. This was years before the recycling craze, but that did not stop over a hundred people from dumping their old Tannenbaums on the Woods' expansive front lawn. What stopped the recycling effort was the intervention of the Health Department.

The weather was cold and damp and everyone was bundled up when the Ammanns and my parents visited the Great Wall of China. My father put a hand inside his coat pocket to keep warm and felt something hard. He didn't need his geology degree from the U. of Nebraska to know what it was—a chunk of the Great Wall. At some point during the tour Bob Ammann had backed up to the edifice, pulled out a small hammer, whacked off a piece of one of the Seven Wonders of the World, and slipped it into my father's coat pocket. If caught, my father would have been eating rice with chopsticks the rest of his life, but Bob thought it was pretty funny.

A group of couples went to Laredo for the weekend, and on Sunday they loaded up for the trip home. Bob's car got stuck in reverse. It was suggested he call a mechanic to fix the problem, but he responded, "There's no issue here; we'll see you in Austin." The others sped away in disbelief. Bob and John S. proceeded to drive from Laredo to Austin in reverse. Bob observed the speed limit, which wasn't hard to do; it would have been pretty tiring driving hundreds of miles backwards while doing 70. Imagine what people thought as they saw a car coming toward them that was actually moving away.

That was not the only spectacle the two caused on the northbound lanes of IH 35. They were in John S.'s Chrysler sedan, coming home from a successful hunting trip when they pulled onto the shoulder near San Marcos and stopped the car. Soon motorists began slowing way down as they neared the car with its hazard lights on and spotted a deer hunter's worst nightmare. A massive, ten-point South Texas buck was in the driver's seat with his front legs on the steering wheel while Bob and John S. lay draped over the hood, their hands bound.

Breakfast at Barton Springs

Bob and John S. planned a pre-dawn breakfast at Barton Springs every summer. The guests had little warning, often receiving a call at 5:30 A.M. to be at the site in one hour. Failure to appear put the absentees on the "pranks list." After a decade-long sabbatical, they held the event to indoctrinate their friends' grandchildren. The last event was special, watching Bob prepare the meal under the attentive eye of his confederate, and it brought closure to a fanciful tradition that allowed two people to coax their friends out of bed with the promise of nothing more than a hearty breakfast, a beautiful sunrise, and the opportunity to celebrate and grab hold of life. John S. used to say, "Eat dessert first," which was hard to do when the first course was a practical joke.

Tarrytown Fireworks

*"I am the god of hell fire and I bring you: Fire, I'll take you to burn.
Fire, I'll take you to learn. I'll see you burn!"*

— "Fire," Arthur Brown, "The Crazy World of Arthur Brown"

In the 60s, it was legal to sell fireworks inside the city limits and Tarrytown was seasonally dotted with stands run by entrepreneurial youngsters. Occasionally, a mishap occurred. One location nestled on the grass at Casis Village was destroyed, after suffering a direct hit from a roman candle during operating hours. Hearing the explosion, people left Rylander's grocery store and watched the small structure go up in flames.

It was not the only time there was such a display in West Austin. Steve and Mark Chalmers, with careful guidance from their father Dick, opened shop on a vacant lot near the southeast corner of the Windsor Road and Exposition Boulevard. It appeared to be a safe location, nestled between the Church of the Good Shepherd to the west and the Fire Station to the east. Nothing bad could happen; even if God allowed some twist of fate to intercede, surely the firemen would come to the rescue. The twist of fate arrived one evening in the form of a misguided, mischievous miscreant who lobbed an M-80 into the stand. The Child Protection Act outlawed M-80s and "cherry bombs" in 1966, too late to save this fireworks enterprise. Congress banned M-80s because these gunfire simulators were extremely powerful, although they only contained flash powder. Today, aerial reports like rockets and shells can each hold 129.6 milligrams of "pyrotechnic composition," and we can legally buy a 50-milligram firecracker. The M-80 last seen re-visiting the fireworks stand at Windsor and Exposition contained 2,916 milligrams, approximately the size difference between a young spider monkey and a western lowland gorilla. Young Mark Chalmers was manning the stand and knew how to spot a lowland gorilla when he saw one, pyrotechnically-speaking. He fled the small wooden building, exhibiting the deft moves and speed that later led to a professional football career. Why the rush? Tossing a tiny spider monkey into a small enclosure filled with other small spider monkeys would cause a minor ruckus; tossing a lit gorilla into that same enclosure filled with lots of gorillas would create a sizeable reaction. This stand contained lots of M-80s.

The explosion was not on par with the one near the end of *The Alamo* when John Wayne/Davy Crockett tossed a burning stick into the munitions depot, but it was close. The incredibly loud boom was caused by the explosive disturbance of air. Parts of this same surge of air traveled across Windsor Road, over the parking lot, and into the Tarrytown Shopping Center, exploding the plate glass windows of the storefronts. The firemen arrived quickly but discovered they weren't dealing with an ordinary fire: aerial reports of rockets and shells were reporting; sparklers were sparkling; firecrackers were cracking; bottle rockets were rocketing in every direction; and roman candles were roamin.' The story would have ended then, but this happened in December, and the Optimist Club had set up their Christmas tree lot next door. By the time the firemen arrived, the roamin' candles had found the old Tannenbaums adjacent to the fireworks stand. To paraphrase another near disaster, *Apollo 13*, "Optimists, we have a problem. Pessimists, we have Armageddon." Curiosity seekers showed up as the firemen battled through the rainbow of smoke caused by a variety of smoke bombs.

This story has been stretched farther than a fireman's hose, so to recap: there were shattered storefronts with glass everywhere; a fireworks stand on fire with some residual noises and explosions; and 99 more burning bushes than Moses had to contend with. Which would have been the end of the story, except for the indigenous, or rooted trees on the southside of the lot. For those of you scoring at home, add a forest fire to the mix. The firemen got everything under control within a reasonable amount of time, but the next morning passersby were stunned to see the half-acre of hell. What looked like a Norman Rockwell painting the day before now resembled *The War of The Worlds*.

Fortunately, this wonderful tale is the F.M. (fuzzy memory) version and, like most memorable events, it has been embellished over the years. The real story goes like this: two boys were tossing smoke bombs at each other when one struck the fireworks stand and splattered against the wooden structure. Within moments the building was on fire and young Mark fled as fireworks flew and the building blew. Christmas was saved for all because no trees were burned, but some of the pyrotechnic projectiles shot across the street and blew out windows in the shopping center. The firemen never arrived, they remained spectators on the lawn of the firehouse. Mr. Chalmers asked them why they did not respond. Their answer was, "Nobody called us," which was probably enough to transform Mr. Chalmers into a human smoke bomb when he imagined what could have happened.

The morals of this story are three-fold: don't play around with fireworks *at* the stand; don't believe everything you read; and, if you operate a display make sure you have a working cell phone handy, because you never know when a gorilla will appear, pyrotechnically-speaking.

"COPS" Comes to West Austin

The short, crescent-shaped street is connected on both ends to a minor arterial in West Austin. In between, it leads to a "no outlet" street and two cul-de-sacs that are smaller than river eddies. Not much runs through it.

Around 11:15 P.M., we returned home from a party and I was changing clothes in our bedroom while my wife Deborah was in our youngest daughter's room, singing to an amused Laura and her friend, Mary Catherine Jarvis. A low-flying helicopter passed overhead on its way back to Camp Mabry, or so I thought. The chopper circled back and hovered above our house, casting its giant spotlight across the backyard. Either the Publishers' Prize Patrol was about to drop $10 mil on me, or there was a bad guy nearby. My wife was still belting out a show tune when the bullhorn ordered, "Come out with your hands up!" Either Simon from **American Idol** was issuing a cease-and-desist order to my bride's vocal talents, or there was a bad guy nearby.

Sobering sight

Standing on the curb, we noticed a police car chase had ended near the intersection of our street and the minor arterial. Four marked police cars formed a roadblock that halted the suspects' vehicle; behind it was an un-marked police car, all within 100 feet of our front door. The perpetrators, who appeared to be in their late-teens, were already in custody. One was spread-eagled on the ground in the middle of the street; the other two were on opposite curbs handcuffed and kneeling.

Frightened neighbor

Eventually, the chopper attracted a larger crowd than the Christmas Star; the initial neighborhood responders were a half-dozen teens armed with cell phones. My son William drove up from the unblocked west-end of the street. There was too much activity at his apartment and he needed a good night's sleep before one of his finals at the University of Texas.

William walked through the open front door, which I had left ajar after gating our dogs in the kitchen thinking it would let the canines feel involved in the action. The pooches had stopped barking and everything was going according to Hoyle, until the wildcard was played. Son ran outside and yelled, "There's a bird in the house!"

A distracted cell phone reporter asked, "What's in the house?"

Another replied, "A bird. Pay attention."

Frightened by the chopper blades, noise, and lights, a female cardinal had sought refuge in our home. She flew into the kitchen and darted above a whirring ceiling fan. The dogs sprang into action. "So *this* is what all the fuss is about?" The 17-year-old Corgie mix, a mostly deaf, half-blind, hip-transplant recipient, spun around in a tight circle, yelping courageously at the intruder. The Labrador tried retrieving the bird, but her only success was leaving the kitchen looking like a barroom brawl aftermath. Thinking she could jump like a springer spaniel, the lab knocked over chairs and stools and slammed into the refrigerator repeatedly. The bird entered the pantry, found nothing to her liking and swooped past the frustrated and berserk dogs, heading for Laura's room, which also had a ceiling fan. My son called for backup.

Outside, to the tune of "The 12 days of Christmas," we now had, "four marked police cars, three perpetrators, two lonely adults, and a helicopter hov'ring overhead."

The crowd "swells"

The helicopter departed and, from the west-end of the street, a dozen new pedestrian teens moved aside as a large car drove up. Our three suspects were seated beside their car as the new arrival quizzed me. A few minutes later, the large car backed down the street and departed. The bright lights of the chopper had briefly attracted an FBI agent.

William came on the porch and shouted, "Laura, you have a new pet!"

The cell phone reporter asked, "What did he say?"

Another replied, "There's an alien in Laura's room."

Laura went inside with my son's backup, James Edsel. His mother Nancy walked up with Hilary Ramirez, noted television and radio spokesperson for ABC Pest Control. I asked if she would help with the pest removal, but Hilary stated emphatically, "I only *talk* about pest control." The women noticed my wife's smashing ensemble—aqua suit with white shell and floral shoes—and immediately voted Deborah "best-dressed at the crime scene."

181

Six carloads of teenagers materialized. We now had the makings of a high school dance, with over 50 students milling about, burning up free weekend cell minutes.

Catch and release

During the fashion show, Laura had plucked the bird into a pot and William slapped a plate over it. The cardinal was released on the porch and the crowd sang "Born Free." The bird probably wondered, "What's the deal with all the blades in this neighborhood?"

The non-free perpetrators were getting more attention: two additional marked cars showed up. A policeman approached the teens. Anyone driving the minor arterial would have seen: six marked cars with lights swirling, three handcuffed perps on the ground, a policeman talking to a ton of teens and my wife, and that driver would have thought, "Must have been a pretty wild party at the Teten house."

Among the assembled kids, I noticed some that were probably experiencing horrible flashbacks as the police lights and handcuffs reminded them of Halloween night the previous year: They were at a house off Stratford Drive when a boy stabbed nine of their classmates. (See "You Just Never Know.")

Things change

Around midnight, cops dispersed the crowd. At 12:35 A.M. an officer peered past the open driver's door into the perps' vehicle. Spotting something beneath the car seat, he leaned inside. Retrieving an object, he backed out and held it against a patrol car's headlights. It was a handgun. He checked its magazine, then slammed the cold steel weapon against the car's sheet metal hood. Off came the handcuffs, spread-eagled went the boys, again. I followed Laura and Mary Catherine inside, grabbed some water, and returned. Thirty minutes later another unmarked car drove up. Two marked cars sped away, quickly replaced by another. Out popped four dark blue t-shirts emblazoned with APD on the front in white letters. The water break caused me to miss the narcotics discovery; the drug detail doesn't descend upon the scene unless invited.

At 1:45 A.M. a police car marked "supervisor" came from the west and killed its lights and watched as the engine idled. Fifteen minutes later the car backed down the street, turned around, and departed.

At 2:40 A.M. the suspects were put in squad cars and the caravan departed. Moments later, our nighttime neighbors arrived: an armadillo waddled across the empty street headed south while a possum and raccoon skittered northward. Order had replaced mayhem.

The beginning

The suspects' car had been involved in a robbery of a business earlier in the day. The boys, students in a school district north of Austin, had panicked when a policeman attempted to stop them. A chase ensued and careened for miles through sinuous west side streets like a lethal snake. An event hours and miles away had started a chain reaction that slithered right to my front door.

You just never know

Had the young driver panicked for a second time and reached for his gun, our street might have been filled with bodies. An eight-point buck walked over the spot where the human conflagration had nearly played out. He halted, sniffed the air, and scampered away as I walked inside our house. We were probably thinking the same thing: you think you live in a safe, quiet neighborhood where bad things never materialize, but in reality you just never know.

Dead Men Driving

The Last Ride of The Magnificent Seven

The term "dead man walking" refers to a condemned criminal walking outside his death-row cell. This story's title is over the top, but so were the actions of the Seven. Most men are incapable of accepting total blame for anything; it's genetic. I will honor that chromosome with a lengthy explanation of the one percent the Seven were not responsible for. Like most excuses, it will take a while.

Camo

In the bird world, males are festooned with bright, colorful plumage. Females are muted in earth tones, camouflaged from predators. For centuries, men matched women powdered wig for powdered wig, and red high heels for red high heels until the original Dandy, Mr. Beau Brummell, invented black tails. He died penniless in an insane asylum in France in 1840, after realizing what he had done.

In the 1890s, some guy in New York invented tuxedos, thereby restricting men's nighttime wardrobes. Women liked the idea, because it detoured additional clothing dollars in their direction. Somewhere along the line, husbands were hoodwinked into thinking older tuxedos were more prestigious. Guys believed it, and soon were proudly announcing, "Yep, this thing is 30 years old." Man is gullible and pliable. How else can you explain wearing the same article of clothing to dressy functions six times a year for 30 years? What woman would wear the same dress to 180 events and brag about it? Woman is not gullible or pliable.

In the 1950s, tuxedoed man began to fidget, until woman said he reminded her of Fred Astaire or Gene Kelly. In the 1960s the compliment was updated to, "You look as dashing as James Bond." Never mind that man looked in the mirror and saw the physique of Goldfinger or Odd Job. Man is gullible, pliable, and stupid. If the 700 hundred women at a large fundraising gala went to powder their noses at the same time, the ballroom would look like a maitre d' convention. When the plumage returns, the men are transformed back into camouflage. Seven hundred guys dressing alike is mandatory, but nuclear fallout blankets the party when two women are spied wearing the same dress. "Poor __ and __, can you believe it?"

Even when man breaks the mold he reverts to form. The Admirals Club, the old adjunct to the Austin Aqua Festival, created another spiffy, dressy uniform: a powder blue jacket with gold epaulets, braids, and a naval hat, which I was wearing one day in front of the Four Seasons during Aqua Fest. An elderly woman saw me and asked, "Excuse me, could you hail a cab?" After saluting her and obeying her command, I opened the cab door, and she handed me a dollar. Whether tuxedo or faux military, when man is duded up he's just working for tips.

Recipe

The party preparation process for a large gala reads like a recipe. Men: shower, shave, and put on tuxedo. Prep time: 20 minutes, add five for non-clip-on bow tie. Can do ahead: yes. The female recipe assumes that manicures and pedicures have been outsourced. Prep time: 2 hours, minimum. Can do ahead: absolutely not. Women: select two dresses from closet, call friend to check what she is wearing. Put dresses back, select two more, and then take luxurious, extended bath. Pat dry, call another friend to double-check clothing selections. Send husband out to buy new pair of hose. "Honey?" No answer. She remembered hearing him say something like, "Dear, I'm going to have a drink with the guys," while she was talking to her friend on the phone, but it didn't register until she needed him. Women don't spend arduous hours of primping in an attempt to impress men. Remember fellas, your tuxedo camouflages you. Or so the Magnificent Seven thought.

Hair

This category is critical, and the most mutable accessory in the repertoire of the budget-conscious gala-goer. After spending 30 minutes with the curling iron, woman asks, "How does my hair look?"

Man always responds, "Fine."

"Oh, what do you know."

"Plenty. I can talk for 30 minutes about why UT can't beat OU, but I know diddly squat about hair, because I'm bald!" But man doesn't actually say that, because he is evolving.

Charlotte Robinson, the grand dame of Austin society, knew hair. On a cruise with seven friends, she spent the week instructing them on the nuances of hair and makeup. The last evening, the group of 70-somethings waltzed into the dining room looking like Loretta Young: perfect hair, bejeweled to the max, their chiffon dresses whisping as they passed through the packed dining room. Once seated, their coiffure conversation continued, until a man at the adjoining table had heard enough. Turning to his friends, he blurted out, "See, I told you they were hairdressers!"

Mrs. Robinson's friends raised their glasses, "To Charlotte, the head hairdresser."

Oh what a tangled web we weave/When first we practice to deceive.

—Sir Walter Scott (*Marmion,* 1808)

The Magnificent Seven sat around the table, toasting their subterfuge as they took in the surroundings: the barroom of a two-story building at 5906 Old San Antonio Highway, now named South Congress Avenue. In the 1950s, the establishment was out of the city limits; the Seven were out of their league. One guy checked his watch, "Hey, we're running late. Somebody needs to call their wife." ET, phone home—okay. Men behaving badly, phone home—bad idea.

A volunteer approached the bar, dialed home and nodded confidently to his friends. "Hi, honey. We're finishing up here and we'll be home in a few minutes."

The friends sent telepathic messages, "Hang up, now!"

He didn't. She inquired, "Exactly, where are you?"

Shocked by the question, and imbued with the truth serum of liquor, the dolt stammered, "We're at Hattie's." The phone went "click," only because AT&T could not adequately register the sound of a receiver being slammed down. "Hattie's Place," was a bordello. Sheriff T. O. Lang, who raided the joint a hundred times in seven years, called it a "bawdy house." Call it what you want, just don't call from it.

The room went silent as Hattie sidled to a safe location behind the bar; she had seen this before. One tuxedo screamed, "You idiot!"

Another slapped his head and said, "Someone call the funeral home, because I'm a dead man."

A third, still in disbelief, yelled, "You told her the truth?" Unlike Mr. Brummell, the talky tuxedo pleaded temporary insanity.

Hattie chimed in, "Shouldn't you boys be leaving?" Chairs toppled and they bolted for the door like penguins leaving an ice floe.

A fourth tuxedo passed Hattie and said, "Leaving? I never was here. You got that?" She nodded, and knowingly thought, "You are a dead man."

The chase

The back door flew open. Seven Gene Kellys and Fred Astaires danced through the parking lot, searching for their cars. Two guys had hitched rides, so the five engines revved and popped into gear. Tires spewed gravel and dust in all directions. Some cars backed out as others went into overdrive. The parking lot became a demolition derby for the well heeled. As they drove down the street, over the bridge and up the hill, the lead changed hands repeatedly. Autos swerved past one another like a stock car race, in an effort to get home and plead for a stay of execution. Everyone knew the governor would not be calling with a reprieve.

A mile away, at the top of the hill, two homeless chaps were enjoying wine curbside, staring across the street at Hill's Café, "October was a great vintage for Ripple." The second was drinking Mogan David 20/20. "Perhaps, but I appreciate the consistency of the Chateau de Double Twenty." The first car crested the hill and went airborne, then slammed against the asphalt. The muffler sprayed sparks everywhere as the vehicle hurtled past these chaps. Their eyes followed the car until the second one appeared. It floated farther than the first, before landing and grinding against the pavement like a 4th of July sparkler. The wine spectators' eyes were transfixed. After the third hurtled past, Ripple said, "Man, my neck is getting sore from all this back and forth."

M. D. added, "This is why I gave up my box at the U. S. Open."

The last two cars blasted over the hill side by side, and the curbside sommeliers lifted their feet just before the cars smashed against the street. Ripple: "Boy, that was close. What the heck was it all about?"

M. D.: "Those boys were leavin' Hattie's Place. My guess is, one of 'em called home and let slip where they were. Which means the wives know. Which means they ain't gotta prayer. Those boys are what you call 'dead men driving.'"

Ripple watched the last taillight disappear up Congress Avenue. "That is why I will never get married."

M. D.: "I'll drink to that."

How do I love thee? Let me count the ways.

—Elizabeth Barrett Browning

A car pulled into the driveway and the first tuxedo opened his front door, slightly. "Hi, honey, I'm home!"

"You don't have to yell. I'm right here."

Entering the foyer, he saw an iceberg disguised in a ball gown, and said, "You look ravishing."

The wife squinted her eyes. "As ravishing as those trollops at Hattie's?" Trick question. Answering, "Yes," would open a can of worms. Saying, "No," would open a 55-gallon drum of the night crawlers.

When faced with danger, all creatures choose the safest route, which is avoidance. "Shouldn't we be going to the party, dear?"

Once there, the invisible rope of guilt tethered him to her. Eventually, she began to thaw. "Oh, that is a beautiful new necklace __ is wearing." The sound of a cash register jangled in his ears. She added, "I wonder if __ bought that dress at Nieman Marcus?" Cha-ching.

"What kind of lowlife. . ."

Days later, the Seven gathered in a downtown coffee house for a debriefing, and they agreed it was the most costly night ever at Hattie's. They were wrong. A few years after their ill-conceived cocktail congregation, two gun-toting robbers cleaned the place out of $25,000 in cash and a watch valued at $15,000. Hattie was the star witness at the trial of the mastermind. What kind of lowlife would stage a robbery of a bordello? My friend, Sam Hoover. The former mayor of Pasadena was incarcerated in the Diagnostic Unit of TDC when I worked there in the early 1970s. (See "The Wedding Gift That Was a Hit.") Convict Sam took a shine to me, although I tried to buff him out. He learned I was getting married and said, ". . . circumstances limit what I can give you for a wedding present, but if you ever want somebody 'taken care of' just let me know." The mayor had offered to "whack" somebody for me. How nice. My wife was the only bride ever registered with the Texas Department of Corrections.

Finding religion

Hattie's Place burned to the ground in March of 1960, but Ms. Valdes soon fired up the biz again. The doors were shuttered for the last time shortly before her death in February of 1976. The Magnificent Seven never rode there again. Their wives had taught them a valuable lesson: there is no such thing as an innocent cocktail in a cathouse. Hattie's daughter, Betty Jean, didn't darken the door either; she became a professional recluse. The men found religion and stayed on the straight and narrow, perhaps with some help from Betty Jean. Like her mother, she worked in a building staffed with other women, but with a different purpose. She joined the Sisters of the Holy Cross, in South Bend, Indiana, and became a cloistered nun.

Fishing, Hunting, and Hunting Fish

This offering is like a summer salad filled with a green, a tomato and an onion. Unless you desire a disastrous outdoors experience, don't emulate what follows.

Bob Ammann was always a man of decisive action dating back to his Austin High days before WWII. One day the teacher left the room, and Bob enlisted the aid of his confederates in the chemistry lab. They closed the windows and vented a gas jet that quickly filled the room with the dangerous, noxious odor. When the teacher returned, the students were splayed on the floor, lab tables, and chairs, overcome by the gas. She went screaming down the hall for help as the students jumped up, closed the valve, opened the windows and fanned the odor away. Bob enjoyed practical jokes, except when he was the victim.

Fishing

Later in life he decided to show a group of youngsters the best way catch fish. The group piled into a boat and set out for the cove on Lake Travis he knew was teeming with bass. No need for messy worms, minnows, or cumbersome cane poles with bobbers, those were too slow for Bob. His decisive action a few days before was certain to bring quick results. In the boat were the only tools he needed: a generator and some wire. He planned to attach the wires to the generator, drop them in the water, crank up the generator and voila! With stunned fish floating everywhere, he would let the kids scoop up the keepers with nets. He was the acting professor of Fishing 101. Right before he turned the fish into real live wires Bob spotted a boat with two passengers speeding toward his classroom. "Uh oh, game warden!" All hands went to their battle stations. Aided by his students he heaved the heavy generator overboard, creating an enormous splash. A minute later the brand new generator was 40 feet below the surface when the game warden's boat veered off and Bob waved weakly at a man and woman out for their Saturday morning pleasure cruise.

Moral: if you want to generate an illegal catch, bring along a good pair of binoculars. That way you might actually know who's watching.

Hunting

After closing the gate of the hunting lease in South Texas, Wally Scott and Don Weeden loaded their shotguns for the mile ride to the main house, just in case they saw any birds. Don drove while Wally sat on the long hood of his friend's Delta 88. They barreled down the gravel road until the Oldsmobile flushed a large covey of quail and Don slammed on the brakes. If you remember going to the circus and seeing a guy shot out of a cannon, that was what Wally looked like. Except for two important differences: the circus guy had a net and wasn't holding a loaded shotgun. Wally had the gun part covered, but not the net. He crashed into the ground and rolled over a few times, coming to rest in the general direction of the car. Opening his eyes Wally peered through the gravely dust and saw the Delta 88 coming at him. "This is how I'm going to die?" The car was almost on him when it stopped. Wally could have used Bob's generator to jumpstart his heart again. While Don exited the car with his gun Wally checked his body to see if any bones or vital organs were protruding through his skin. Don leaned over his fallen friend and yelled, "Wally, did you see which way they went?"

Moral: hunting from the hood is unsafe, at any speed.

Hunting Fish

Decades ago on a Saturday night, dozens of men, women, and children were fishing on the Port Aransas pier when someone yelled, "He's caught a shark!" People ran to the railing and watched the angler reel him in. As the shark neared the decking the fisherman leaned into the railing then thrust his rod tip toward the middle of the pier. The onlookers saw the shark clear the railing and float skyward in their direction. Like a school of baitfish, they scattered just before it landed on the wood planking. The audience yelled and cheered as they formed a 20-foot circle around the flailing shark.

Shouts of "Kill it!" and "No, it'll die eventually," rang out until a gentleman sporting a ribbed tee shirt of the wife-beater design pushed his way through the crowd. Like Bob Ammann, he was a man of quick and decisive action. Holding a beer in his left hand he walked up to the shark, took a sip, and then reached into his shorts pocket with his right hand. He pulled out a pistol and fired six rounds into the shark. "Boom, boom, boom, boom, boom, boom!"

After the shooting stopped, you could have heard a fish hook drop. No one complained because they couldn't remember if he had used all of his bullets. Testing a guy with a beer in one hand and a gun in the other late on a Saturday night is not a good idea. Men quickly grabbed their wives, kids, and gear and sidled off, wondering how to explain a gunfight between an unarmed shark and a doofus with a fully loaded Saturday night special. Owning a combination hunting/fishing license does not mean simultaneous usage is permitted.

Moral: if you see that subduing the catch du jour will require firearms, just cut the line.

The Wonderful World of Wrestling

City Coliseum was a giant dilapidated Quonset hut near the banks of Town Lake that housed charity garage sales, rock and country music concerts, the opera **Carmen**, and many other festivities. The venue's highest and best was the wonderful theater and rustic ballet performed by the gladiators of wrestling. Fans preferred the sweaty, gritty one-act plays to real theater because you can't drink beer or yell and scream at the actors during **The Iceman Cometh**. You could, but that would be unseemly, a word not contained in the lexicon of wrestling.

"How to win friends and influence people"

My friends at the Phi Delta Theta fraternity house had purchased two dozen tickets and asked me to tag along, saying the dress code was Obnoxious Preppy. Donning an Irish tweed jacket, shirt and tie, khaki pants and topsiders, I fit in with the nattily attired entourage that marched into the dingy arena. It had the desired effect: we got noticed. The same way a group would if they waltzed into the predominantly black Sweet Home Missionary Baptist Church in Clarksville dressed in Klan outfits. Dale Carnegie was not a Phi Delt.

A bleached blonde, tanned, cocky grappler named Johnny Valentine was the most hated man in wrestling. We cheered him, which made us guilty by association. When he pulled some unseen object from his black, oversized Speedo the crowd tried to warn the referee, who never saw the object, coming or going. The ref was like a French soldier—appropriately clothed, but incapable of stopping anything. Johnny could have packed a chainsaw in his briefs, and the ref would have missed it.

There are lots of ways to view wrestling; the crowd that night had chosen "while drunk." Adoring fans yelled, "You suck!" and other pithy, unprintable epithets. We couldn't tell if those words were for Johnny or us, until the first food salvos landed in our ringside section. Our support for Johnny, the evil one, did not sit well with the crowd, so they stood up, because it's hard to throw things with any accuracy while sitting down.

Snow cones, half-empty beer cups, and half-eaten hot dogs with mustard and relish splattered the preppies. Some of the Phis returned fire, and I thought, "Yeah, *that'll* diffuse the situation." Like pre-game calisthenics, both sides were just warming up.

From my fourth row seat on the aisle, I noticed an octagenarian woman glaring at me from an adjoining section. She sat on the front row framed by her misanthropic son on the right, her walker and umbrella on the left. Granny was displeased with our choice in wrestlers. Incoming! Soft drinks, nachos, fudgesicles, and M&Ms rained down on us. I sure could have used that umbrella. Between fights we sipped our coats and dined on our shirts, while the crowd rushed to the concession stand to reload.

La grande procession

Will "Wilbur" Price, the ringleader of our group, had pre-arranged our movement at the matches, and this was the scheduled time for us to temporarily vacate our seats. He led us to the west end of the building where we stood outside the dressing rooms and prepared for the main event. Minutes later, the most beloved "rassler" of all time, Ivan Putski, walked to the ring. Standing 5'9" inches, and weighing 280 pounds, his bio said Ivan was chopping wood in the Polish countryside one day when he was "discovered" by scouts for the Southwest Texas State football team. The critical-thinking college boys knew better.

The locker room door opened again, and the crowd gasped. Picture a 450-pound, white Shaquille O'Neal with an Afro. Yes, it was the actor who later carried the movie *The Princess Bride*: Andre the Giant. We escorted him past thousands of Putski fans for 30 yards until he reached the ring. The friendly Phis waved tiny French flags and held up signs that read, "Andre, s'il vous plaît!" "Le Giant est très bien!" and "First Napoleon, then DeGaulle, now Andre the Giant." Mark Chalmers, Maurice de Chalmare, carried a boom box that blasted the French national anthem, "THE MARSEILLAISE."

We spouted the only French words we knew, "Pommes frittes!" The crowd obliged and began tossing French fries at us. This was David vs. Goliath. And you can't spell Philistines without the Phis.

"You not Putski!"

The wrestling match went back and forth, with Ivan occasionally getting the best of our hero. The crowd cheered the Polish warrior while he stomped around the ring and beat his chest, proclaiming, "Me, Putski!" About the fourth time he did this the crowd had become complacent and sat quietly on their hands, but not my cousin Philip Bell.

He stood up and shouted, "You not Putski, you Joe Bednarski from Travis High School!" Philip repeated the statement as he pointed to the South Austin high school's yearbook with Joe's picture that he held up for all to see. My first thought was, "Cuz, you might not oughta done that." In the annals of history this gross miscalculation ranked right behind the Charge of the Light Brigade. We went from being a nuisance to a cadre of communists in an auditorium filled with McCarthyites.

Our section was inundated with eggs, lettuce, and biscuits. A tomato exploded against my face. "They sell tomatoes at the concession stand?" With their retail arsenal depleted, our enemy had called upon the reserves—the contents of their home refrigerators. The four food groups were launched at us and a pyramid of garbage piled up quickly in section one. It was an ugly scene.

It got uglier. Temporarily blinded, I sat down and felt a presence in the aisle. I could make out a silhouette standing beside me, its raised right hand holding some object. Whack! The umbrella bounced off my noggin.

"Granny?"

Bam! During the buffet blitzkrieg she had come over, with the aid of her walker. Bam! Bam! I was Janet Leigh in the shower scene from *Psycho* and Granny/Norman Bates was strumming my head.

"Kill him!"

"Get the jerk, Granny!"

One Phi yelled, "Take her down!"

Again, I thought, "Yeah, *that'll* diffuse the situation." Whack!

Eventually, her troglodyte son dragged Granny away, after her aerobic workout on my cranium. The crowd weighed in on me, "You, Putz-ski!"

I envisioned the conversation at the Phi Delt house the next day.

"How was the match?"

"Great. Teten got beat up by an old lady on a walker."

195

Somewhere, there's a 110-year old lady in a nursing home still talking about the time she "kicked that frat boy's ass!"

Denouement

I think Andre won the match on some trumped up disqualification, but my brains were scrambled like the eggs on the concrete floor. We were allowed to exit alive, probably because my body had been offered up as the sacrificial lamb of appeasement.

The rebellious pranksters learned a good lesson about toying with the emotions of a wrestling crowd. As Jim Croce sang, "You don't tug on Superman's cap, you don't spit into the wind, you don't pull the mask off the ol' Lone Ranger, and you don't mess around with" . . . them.

IMHO*

---

*In my humble opinion.

Westlake and Waverly

Sour grapes, regardless of the fermentation process, yield only a bad whine. This is not either; it is the extension of a heartfelt suggestion, by way of a story, to my friends in Westlake. Another essay in this volume chronicles the courageous battle of one Westlake's former players (see "Life's Second Chances."). This is about two schools, Westlake High School in Austin, Texas, and Waverly High School in Waverly, Ohio, and how others perceive them and why. So let's begin, and may Spalding, the god of football, have mercy on my soul.

In many ways Westlake football is a model program. Other schools, given their limited resources, would be well served to cherry-pick the positive attributes at Westlake they could implement. Yet one aspect of Westlake football does not rise to the level of the rest of their program, and that is sportsmanship. After witnessing nine of the annual bloodlettings called Austin High vs. Westlake High, a familiar pattern emerged, the most egregious example of which occurred in 1995. In that game Westlake threw a 45-yard touchdown pass that made the score 49-0 . . . in the second quarter. Leading 56-0, Westlake was playing non-starters on defense when Austin High moved down inside the Chaps' ten-yard line and had first and goal. That's when Westlake sent their first-string defense back in. One Westlake sideline veteran explained that an impulsive, instinctive voice shouted out, "goal-line defense," which was comprised mainly of starters. So they marched back out onto the field. Maybe you could see that happening with one eye shut and the other in full squint. Perhaps a forgivable mistake on first down, but not for the second, third, and fourth downs. My immediate thought was of the Westlake non-starters. Were they angry and embarrassed at being jerked out of the game against a rival? Were their parents thinking, "Is my son not good enough to play even when we are ahead 56-0 with two minutes left?" What message was sent to those hardworking kids?

While that may be ancient history, the pattern has continued. In 2002, Westlake's starting quarterback attempted a 40-yard pass into the end zone with Westlake leading 42-7. . . in the fourth quarter. The following year an Austin defensive secondary player turned his ankle but was not replaced. By coincidence, on the next play Westlake's starting quarterback threw a 49-yard touchdown pass over the injured Maroon defender . . . in the fourth quarter, making the score 50-23, Westlake. Perhaps the Chaparrals were scared of a miraculous Maroon comeback, but they had outscored Austin 44-14 in only 28 minutes after falling behind 9-0 early. The offensive non-starters for Westlake finally got on the field two possessions later, with less than three minutes left.

When questioned about this behavior, some Westlake fans shrug their shoulders and offer, "It's the coaches' fault." Although it is easy to blame the schools and coaches, they are a merely a reflection of the parents whose silence is their tacit approval.

Here's hoping that next year Westlake "gets it." Their incredibly successful football program should be highly thought of by all, but class and respect are not birthrights. Like Boy Scout badges, they must be earned by effort. If you think The Heretic (moi) is being too hard, I am just making a simple request that is printed in Texas' University Interscholastic League (UIL) Manual: "Behavior expectations of the student athlete: 'Treat opponents the way you would like to be treated, as a guest or friend.' Behavior expectations of the coach: 'Display modesty in victory . . .'" and "Instruct participants and spectators in proper sportsmanship responsibilities and demand that they make sportsmanship the No. 1 priority."

For better or worse, high school football coaches in Texas are the highest paid teachers on campus. At many sites they are judged primarily on their wins and losses, but they are teachers of young men, first and foremost. During the season boys spend more time in the company of their coaches than with any other male role model, with the possible exception of their fathers. From the UIL Code of Conduct for League Coaches: "always pursue victory with honor; teach, advocate, and model the importance of honor and good character by doing the right thing even when it is unpopular or personally costly."

Two small schools in Southern Ohio are fortunate to have wonderful role models. Northwest High coach Dave Frantz called Waverly High coach Derek DeWitt during the week of their game with a proposal. He had a player who suffered from "Chromosomal Fragile-X," the most common cause of inherited mental retardation. The boy was a senior who had showed up for practice every day and dressed out all four years but had never played a down during a game. You see, Jake Porter was unable to take a hit; it was just too dangerous. Northwest was playing their last home game of the season, and Coach Frantz asked Dewitt, "If the game's not at stake on the last play, I

[want] him to come in and take a knee." Northwest practiced the play all week after Coach DeWitt agreed to the scenario. During pre-game warm-ups DeWitt ambled through the field, stopping to talk with Jake and some of his teammates. The conversations made DeWitt change his mind. With five seconds left in the game Waverly led 42-0 and Northwest had the ball at Waverly's 49-yard line. Coach Frantz called timeout and met Coach DeWitt and the referees in the middle of the field. Frantz was explaining the agreed-upon scenario to the referees when DeWitt interrupted, "Coach Frantz, we'll let him score."

Dave Frantz was stunned; he had only asked for a simple handoff to Jake, who would then take a knee. He returned to the bench and told Jake, "You're takin' it to the house!" Young Jake's eyes widened, and he ran onto the field. The quarterback took the snap and handed it to Porter. Excited and confused, Jake reached the line of scrimmage, turned around, and started running the wrong way. A referee and some teammates jumped in front of him and pointed Jake in the right direction. The other 21 players stood motionless and cleared a path for Jake and he tentatively walked through the line. After crossing midfield he broke into a run. With every step he took, more cheers erupted from both sides of the field. After crossing the goal line, he ran to the back of the end zone and turned around. Still holding the football he raised both hands above his head. His teammates mobbed him. His mother said that one act of kindness changed his life forever.

After the game, DeWitt said, "At Waverly, we didn't do anything special. We were just happy to be a part of that. Our guys didn't care about the shutout, those stats went out the window. When you're involved in a moment like that, you want to make sure you end the game with class, decency, and respect." A former coach once said, "If you tell people you are making a sacrifice, then it ceases to be one." Coach Dewitt downplayed losing the shutout for that reason and out of respect for Northwest.

For schools like Westlake, shutouts are more readily achieved; for programs like Waverly they are not commonplace. What Coach DeWitt did not mention was the Waverly defense had given up an average of more than four touchdowns per game before facing Northwest.

To assume the above examples are apples and oranges would be wrong. Sure, Jake Porter is "special" and not every team or child should be given a "free" touchdown. That is not what is being suggested of Westlake. Only this: recognize that there is a little bit of Jake Porter in every opponent, a child who plays for the love of the game. A child who deserves to be treated "with class, decency, and respect."

Coaches Frantz and DeWitt have been feted nationwide, one for what he did, the other for what he did not do—preserve his team's shutout. In life, a man is not only judged by what he does, sometimes he is measured by what he refrains from doing. And sometimes Spalding or perhaps a much Higher Being intercedes. The week after playing Northwest, the Waverly Tigers won their final home game of the year, defeating Cincinnati Mariemont. The score: 7-0.

What's the Matter with Kids Today?

In the movie *Bye Bye Birdie*, Paul Lynde asked the musical question, "What's the matter with kids today?" Four decades later the same question is being posed regarding sportsmanship in athletics.

A racially diverse high school football team loses a playoff game and boards the bus. As they attempt to exit the parking lot, racial epithets are shouted at them and then salvos of rocks are hurled, breaking out windows.

A ninth grade football player lies injured on the field late in the game. After patiently allowing three minutes for a diagnosis, a mother from the other team (seated directly in front of me) stands and yells, "He doesn't have any broken bones. Let's get him off the field and finish the game!" Unfortunately, she was wrong: my son had two broken bones.

A coach, fed up with the refereeing late in the fourth quarter, removes his team from the court and leaves the gymnasium. It was a seventh grade boys' basketball game.

A lacrosse player pushes his opponent to the ground and falls on top of him. Then he raises an elbow and drives it into the groin of the defenseless and unsuspecting boy. As the injured player attempts to crawl off the field, some opposing players come over and offer their unique brand of apology, "Get up, you wussy!" Or something that sounded like that. Then the parent of the "elbow" yelled out to the referees, "All he did was fall on him." Which brought chuckles from other parents of "elbow's" team . . . all of this while the injured boy was attempting to crawl off the field.

A player parades up and down the sidelines during a game tossing out more expletives than the Easter bunny has eggs . . . in front of his coach, teammates, and parents.

All the above are random and isolated incidents that have occurred in Austin or to Austin schools. The students perpetrating these acts are children of privilege; they were not forced to grow up on violent streets; they were raised in affluent, safe neighborhoods. Logging 3,000 car miles and viewing over 60 high school sporting events including baseball, football, volleyball, lacrosse, and basketball in one year revealed to me, at least to a degree, an inverse correlation between sportsmanship and the wealth of a school, whether public or private. This arrogance and egotistical sense of being immune to the rules of the game is what led to Enron and, to a lesser degree, the dotcom debacle.

So who is to blame—the referees? Barely. Like teachers, referees must receive support for their actions from coaches and parents, not verbal abuse, which only compounds the problem. Often, teams mirror the personalities of their coaches. If a coach does not punish "elbow," his teammates feel emboldened to push the boundaries even farther. Many of these kids are in that gray area between being under their parents' thumbs and total independence, constantly seeing what they can get away with. Sadly, they can get away with much more in sports than in a classroom. And that goes for coaches, too. Coaches are teachers, but could you imagine a Latin club "coach" stalking out of a Certamon with his students in tow? Or an AP English teacher allowing "cussin' boy" to perform in class as he did on the field?

We grew up playing pick-up games, policing our own. Nowadays, a lack of field space and a fast-paced lifestyle result in highly structured events, under the watchful eyes of parents, some of whom apparently need to live vicariously through their kids, others with competitive urges that must be going unsatisfied in their own personal and professional lives. When elbow was a toddler he probably explored an electrical socket with his fingers and his father swiped his hand away and admonished him with a stern, "No." Sixteen years later this father is joking about his son's sucker-punching another person in the groin. What happened during those years to change them? Maybe the father is like some of the aforementioned parental examples.

Another parent on the team said that elbow's father had been a problem for four years. There is a direct correlation between the other parents' tolerance and the fact elbow had been the star goalie during those years. If this boy had been a bench-warmer, his father would have been chastised in the first year. A different adult also said the boy reacted "in the heat of battle." The Alamo was a battle. Antietam was a battle. This was a Saturday morning lacrosse game. Parents who offer excuses or apologies instead of trying to correct the problem are becoming a problem themselves. By lowering the bar of acceptable behavior, we are all getting closer to the gutter.

So what can be done? Students caught engaging in destructive or pugilistic endeavors should be forced to perform agrarian maintenance at the offended school's campus, preferably on a Saturday morning. Kids who throw elbows or temper tantrums should be treated like kindergartners—put in "time out" for a game or two. Of course this will prompt some parents to call their lawyer immediately!

Which brings us back to Mr. Lynde. What's the matter with kids today? It is easy to blame the schools and coaches, but they are a merely a reflection of the parents whose silence is their tacit approval. Parents and their children are not being responsible and not being held accountable for their actions; they are to blame for this boorish behavior. If Junior is old enough to drive, he is plenty old enough to know the difference between right and wrong, and he is plenty old enough to suffer whatever punishment is appropriate. As a society, we need to invoke that infrequently used word: NO. Otherwise, we will be enabling and nurturing a generation that could inflict more damage than a sore groin. Just ask the employees of Enron.

The Filtration Device on the Media Spigot

One fear about the looming consolidations by large media conglomerates is that our flow of information will be adversely affected. In Austin, Texas, we already feel the effects as Cox Newspapers has swallowed up the daily as well as the weekly media outlets in and around Austin: the Bastrop Advertiser, the Lake Travis View, the North Lake Travis Log, the Pflugerville Pflag, the Smithville Times and the Westlake Picayune. A few examples of filtration follow.

A new trend is quietly creeping into college campus commencements nationwide, but, before we get there, you can't have a commencement without a speaker.

The mainstream media reported that when Chris Hedges, the New York Times Pulitzer prize-winning reporter-turned-commencement-editorialist, spoke at small Rockford College northwest of Chicago, a problem arose. School President Paul Pribbenow said, "He delivered what I guess I would refer to as a fairly strident perspective on the war in Iraq and American policy" without mentioning the graduation. Eschewing the free speech doctrine, some in attendance stormed the stage and twice pulled the power to the microphone. This intolerance deserved coverage.

Yet little was made of the time when it was not a beautiful day in the neighborhood of Hanover, New Hampshire. That year Dartmouth College alum Fred Rogers was asked to give the commencement address. Seems Mr. Rogers had spent too much time tying his tennis shoes, donning his sweaters, singing "You Are Special" and playing with hand puppets to suit the "progressive" students who found him objectionable because he was not "a human rights activist." Hmmm. "Okay, boys and girls. Our word for today is intolerance. Can you say intolerance?" Pause. "I knew you could." Just up the road in bucolic Georgetown, Texas, last year the commencement speaker at Southwestern University was Dr. bell hooks [sic]. She told those assembled, "The radical, dissident voices among you have learned here at Southwestern how to form communities of resistance that have helped you find your way in the midst of life-threatening conservatism, loneliness, and the powerful forces of everyday fascism which use the politics of exclusion and ostracism to maintain the status quo. Every terrorist regime in the world uses isolation to break people's spirits." Applying those bombastic remarks to bastions of higher education reveals that everyday fascists and terrorist regimes run many of those institutions, because they willingly practice exclusivity while ostracizing and isolating students . . . at commencements. Voluntarily, of course.

There are "Lavender Graduations" for gay, lesbian, bisexual, and transgendered students at UCLA, Iowa State, and UC Santa Cruz, and many others. Michigan State University, Eastern Michigan, Wayne State, and Oakland College hold "Black Celebratory" commencements. Schools along the East Coast hold similar events for African-American, Jewish, and Native American students, and many universities hold "Raza Graduations" for Hispanic-Americans. In Austin in 2003, the University of Texas held separate graduations for Native American, Hispanic, and African-Americans but not for Asian-Americans. These ceremonies are optional and supplement the larger, university-wide graduations, but it is not known how many students attend multiple events. At Oakland University, the director of OU's Office of Equity said, "Our whole goal is inclusion, not exclusion. We are celebrating the inclusion of these students into the workforce." A commencement is a rite of passage that should reflect the shared campus experience. Imagine the uproar if hundreds of white students requested a segregated ceremony.

Also in 2003, students at Taylor County High School in Butler, Georgia, held a single, integrated prom for the first time in three decades. The next year some white-sheeters reverted to a whites-only prom, in addition to the integrated dance. Not a shock, considering the Crackerland Country Fair is held in nearby Howard each year, "cracker" being a mildly pejorative term for people whiter than Michael Jackson. The crush of media covering both years was warranted. Yet most of the exclusionary university commencements did not draw attention. The majority of these were implemented at the request of students, which seemed to contradict the spirit of Dr. King's civil rights movement that railed against segregation and divisiveness.

In 1998, two straight men savagely beat and murdered a gay Wyoming college student, Matthew Shepard. The case garnered worldwide media exposure and the WASHINGTON POST ran some 80 stories about it over the next 14 months. Almost a year later, a murder in Rogers, Arkansas, was virtually ignored by the national media: Jesse Dirkhising, a 13-year-old seventh grade boy was the victim of repeated sexual abuse by two gay lovers before they asphyxiated him. The *Washington Post* ran one article, in a local edition. The paper's ombudsman said the editors only print murder stories they feel impart a lesson or are newsworthy if they occur beyond the borders of the District of Columbia. *Time Magazine* senior editor Jonathan Gregg echoed this sentiment by saying, "The reason the Dirkhising story received so little play is because it offered no lessons. Shepard's murder touches on a host of complex and timely issues: intolerance, society's attitudes toward gays and the pressure to conform, the use of violence as a means of confronting one's demons. Jesse Dirkhising's death gives us nothing except the depravity of two sick men. There is no lesson here, no moral of tolerance, no hope to be gleaned in the punishment of the perpetrators. To be somehow equated with these monsters would be a bitter legacy indeed for Matthew Shepard." The elevation of one murder, by its implication, devalues others. Imagine Dirkhising's family and friends' sad exasperation upon learning there was "no lesson here, no moral of tolerance, no hope to be gleaned in the punishment of the perpetrators." And that his murder did not touch on "a host of complex and timely issues" like "the use of violence as a means of confronting one's demons," merely "the depravity of two sick men." Reporting this story would not have "somehow equated . . . these monsters" with the legacy of Matthew Shepard; that "bitter legacy" is Jesse Dirkhising's alone.

The arrogance and subjectivity displayed in the lack of reporting this case shows an evanescent employment of balanced reporting; it comes and goes. During a citywide election in Austin, a reporter "got the goods" on one candidate and wrote a scathing expose. He was told the article would not be printed unless he "got the goods" on the opponent, who had no "goods" to be got. The story was killed, and the reporter resigned. Fortunately, in this case the omission of the story did not affect the outcome of the election.

These examples beg the question: How do you know you're missing something if you don't see it? Without access to a variety of sources, it is difficult to spot filtration devices on media spigots. This paranoia and cynicism go away, though, don't they, when you look at the masthead quote of the *New York Times*, "All The News That's Fit To Print."

We wish.

Unbridled Political Correctness and The Victimization in America

In the movie *The Matrix: Reloaded,* two of the bad guys are twin albinos. A pigment-challenged spokesman has registered a complaint, claiming the film portrays albinos in a bad light. Following this claim the National Organization for Albinism and Hypopigmentation (NOAH) wasn't exactly flooded with support. The exact number of twin albinos in America is unknown, but they could probably hold their national convention in a phone booth.

With this sense of political correctness, many feature films will have to be rewritten or have almost any physical characterizations deleted. The one-armed man from *The Fugitive* would be gone. The diminutive denizens of *The Wizard of Oz,* the Lollipop Guild, would be given short shrift because they depict vertically challenged tough guys. The cannibal-barbecue scene in *Fried Green Tomatoes* remains because the "blue plate special" was a physically abusive white guy, but the non-fiction *Alive,* which featured real intra-species dining would have to go because it served up some South Americans in an unsavory manner.

Robin Lakoff, who teaches linguistics at U.C. Berkeley said, "I think people use these terms like 'PC' or 'politically correct' as a way of cutting off what should be a legitimate discussion. People on the political right who are saying 'PC' are really saying, 'Shut up, we don't want to hear about this anymore.'" Which means no one should invoke the term 'PC' after the family in Michigan filed a complaint against a high school teacher because he uttered a racial slur while reading aloud from Mark Twain's *The Adventures of Huckleberry Finn.* He used the "N" word. The student alleged a teacher at Cousino High School in Warren spoke the word while reading from the novel and later during class discussions about the book. The student was offended, and his family intends to file a lawsuit against the district whose initial response alluded to the fact the slur is in the book. In California, an Irish-American has recently found the term "paddy wagon" offensive, because it conjured up the stereotype of the drunken Irishman. It's as if David Naughton has subliminally reprised his old Dr. Pepper commercial "I'm a Pepper, he's a Pepper . . ." but the words now are, "I'm a victim, he's a victim, she's a victim, wouldn't you like to be a victim, too? Be a victim, in the USA!"

A classic case of victimization occurred 10 years ago at the University of Pennsylvania when Eden Jacobowitz, after asking some students to quiet down so he could study finally yelled out 20 minutes later, "Shut up, you water buffalo!" The students were black. Although many epithets were shouted that night from other dorm windows, Jacobowitz was the only one who "fessed up" to what he said. By confessing, he messed up. Soon he was penned to the proverbial wall and faced severe sanctions including expulsion. Five years earlier, Louis Farrakhan had spoken at the University of Pennsylvania, and he had been so inflammatory that school President Sheldon Hackney's subsequent statement admitted Farrakhan's comments were "racist and anti-Semitic and amount[ed] to scapegoating" but, "in an academic community, open expression is the most important value. We can't have free speech only some of the time, for only some people. Either we have it, or we don't. At Penn, we have it." Obviously a widely promoted speech given in a public forum had "it," but words spoken at 12:30 A.M. to specific individuals did not. Jacobowitz's problems lasted over four months before charges were finally dropped, despite the school's being educated early on that "water buffalo" was a Hebrew slang term for a "rowdy or thoughtless person," and water buffalo are indigenous to Asia; none are found in Africa.

Had the racial identities been reversed in the recent Fort Worth trial of the black woman who struck a white man with her car and left him to die in the windshield, some opportunists would have labeled it a hate crime.

The victimization industry in America is doing everyone a disservice by trotting out marginal examples on an almost daily basis. When so many groups are shouting at once, the public, like a person with hearing aids, hears only noise. People get few chances to garner attention, after which they become like the boy who cried wolf: no one will listen to their pleas. This constant barrage also diverts attention from real victims, like the ones in Central Africa today. Indeed, there exist more than 4,000 websites worldwide devoted to anti-Semitism, which is at its highest level in Germany since World War II.

Through a quirk of fate my father's WWII experiences placed him alongside the real Band of Brothers for the period that was depicted in the last two episodes of the HBO miniseries. On what would have been his eighty-ninth birthday my family sat and watched episode nine, the liberation of Dachau. In the 40 years I knew my father he spoke of that day only once, on a warm August night on our patio. When he began speaking, the fireflies disappeared and night gave way to the post-dawn hours in Germany on April 29, 1945. He and his fellow soldiers had no idea what awaited them until they spotted the boxcars filled with bodies on the tracks just outside the camp. On entering the concentration camp gates they saw what Col. William W. Quinn, 7th U.S. Army later described as, "one of history's most gruesome symbols of unhumanity [sic]. There our troops found sights, sounds, and stenches horrible beyond belief, cruelties so enormous as to be incomprehensible to the normal mind. Dachau and death were synonymous." The shock was so enormous that one American soldier snapped and machine-gunned some SS soldiers before his superiors could stop him. My father never mentioned the day's events again. Maybe it was too painful or perhaps he knew the details would be seared in my mind's eye forever. He was right. The almost-anything-goes HBO network did not attempt to replicate the horrors. They couldn't.

Now, when some trivial, perceived slight is announced, I keep hoping the 21st century "victims" will begin to pick their chances to be heard, using their freedom of speech wisely. And I think about that cold spring morning in Bavaria when a Nebraska farm boy walked through the Gates of Hell and saw the carnage of real victims whose cries of injustice only the executioners heard.

The Weak(ly) Reader

As another school year begins, it is easy to blame teachers for the lack of literacy in our country, but the bulk of the blame belongs to the parents and children. Years ago, the national question was, "Why can't Johnny read?" Today the query should be, "Why does Johnny stop reading after 4th grade?" A 1992 study by International Educational Achievement showed that U.S. fourth graders ranked second, behind only Finland, but a recent RAND Report revealed, "U.S. 11th graders have placed very close to the bottom, behind students from the Philippines, Indonesia, Brazil, and other developing nations." Many American kids don't read for pleasure; nearly 30% of high school seniors said they "never or hardly ever read for pleasure." In 1998, the Nation's Report Card said 6% of high school seniors read at the "advanced" level; only 40% were considered "proficient," the level the National Assessment Governing Board said all students should attain. When Johnny gets to college, he is not alone in having poor reading habits. A writing instructor at Northwestern University, Barbara Shwom, said, "When I meet freshmen, one third read quite well, one third do not. If we were to read something and discuss it, they would get it wrong. A third don't read. To get them to read at all, you have to say the magic words: 'It will be on the test.' They're all bright . . . but there's no patience for [reading]. So they become much less skilled from lack of use, and it spirals."

Concern for the poor performance by American children is mistakenly assuaged by statistics, like these: per capita income in countries with literacy rates less that 55% averages about $600 per year, while the amount balloons to $12,600 for countries with literacy rates over 96% (UNESCO, 2001). Sounds good, until you discover there are five levels of literacy, and Level 1 means a person can: "sign one's name and total a bank deposit slip, but not locate an intersection on a road map or two pieces of information in a sports article" (Radford University). When 50 million Americans have difficulty entering information on a social security application, that's a problem. Numbers also show this is not an imported malady; only 15% of Americans with limited literacy skills were born beyond our shores, and only 5% have learning disabilities. Our reading is bad enough, but we fare worse in science: only 18% of high school seniors are "proficient," leaving 82% mired in the "basic" level, or lower.

While there are highly literate people in lower paying jobs and wealthy persons in Levels 1 and 2, these are anomalies. For the vast majority of Americans, literacy is like currency—people in the lower rungs often earn one-third the amount of those in the top level. In a certain nationwide assessment test, company presidents scored the highest average on vocabulary, a full 15 percentage points above the next profession. The testing company says, ". . . words are the instruments by means of which men and women group the thoughts of others and with which they do much of their own thinking. They are 'the tools of thought.'" It used to be that Johnny said, "you know" a lot, as he stumbled to foment a cogent thought. That term was supplanted by "I mean," then "well" and now "like" or "it's, like." Today, a typical declarative sentence by Johnny goes something like this. "Well . . . I mean, it's like . . . you know, cool." The boy could learn a thing or two by listening to the Vicars of Verbosity, Don King and Jesse Jackson, because Johnny commands only four polysyllabic words: his name, "awesome," and his two favorite food groups: pizza and cheeseburger. Sadly, over 60% in literacy Level 1 and over 90% in Level 2 think they read "well" or "very well," and maybe they do read well enough to adequately perform their jobs. There will always be demand for menial or low-paying employment, but people are not forced to remain in those jobs, because vocabulary is not a trait, it is acquired. As a result, two problems surface. First, America is moving toward a service-based and hi-tech economy, with fewer manufacturing jobs. The former require more critical and independent thought. Without improving their skills, the people mired in menial jobs will put even more distance between themselves and better paying, more rewarding jobs. Second, those left behind are perpetuating an underclass in America. This has fostered an adversarial haves vs. have not's mentality that is exploited by some for personal or political reasons. But no amount of wishful thinking, class envy, or affirmative action can bridge the chasm between the groups. In spite of our instant gratification society, there are no shortcuts to improved literacy or vocabulary.

On average, inmates in the Texas prison system have a tenth grade education, but most of them inhabit the two lowest levels of literacy. As previously pointed out, the literacy bar for those levels is set lower than the stick at a limbo contest for ferrets. It also costs over $18,000 a year to keep them locked up (the inmates, that is). The average tuition/room and board at a public university in Texas is just over $12,500, with the University of Texas at Austin the highest, at $16,100. Not all inmates need to attend college, but a little preventive medicine is in order, including additional help and encouragement at home. The current battle over who should administer the Head Start program ignores the statistics in articles like this one, which is dangerous. Whether states or the federal government manage that program is less important than finding out why Johnny gets a head start on reading but jumps ship by age 10, because without parental involvement, the ship starts taking on water. Instead of arguing, the feds and the states need to start tossing out life preservers, because Johnny and his friends are sinking.

I am preaching to the choir, but we all need to start singing loudly before the congregation disappears. There are almost 21 million Texas residents. Nearly 700,000 are in the criminal justice system, either in prisons, local jails, or on probation, with the state prisons housing 126,000 of that total. If you took everyone in Abilene, threw them in the crossbar hotel, and tossed in all of Lockhart and Luling you would equal our prison population. Speaking of Abilene, they are going to be sending one to the big house soon. A man who was shy, in a hurry, or possessed a limited vocabulary walked into a local bank and handed the teller a one-word note, "robbery." He was captured 30 minutes later, along with the $2,000 in cash. The criminal had just been released from a Florida prison for another bank robbery committed in 1999. Lest you think criminals outgrow their tendencies, the man, H.L. Hunter Rountree, is 91 years old. We need to spend our money helping our children get a good education and improve their life skills, because most of them will eventually be spending their own hard-earned money locking up the students who fell through the cracks.

While literacy does not prevent larceny, ask yourself this: if a guy steals your car, or breaks into your home, is he risking a jail sentence so he can make off with your copy of the latest *Harry Potter*?

The Bad Apples of Abu Ghraib:
A Little Perspective

Perspective: *"the capacity to view things in their true relations or relative importance."*

My flibbertigibbety persona has ceded this week's column to a Tudey Tirade. Before arriving there, a little detour to the Abu Ghraib prison in Iraq where some of the non-distinguished, soldier prison guards have said they did not receive sufficient training. Apparently, 300 hours wasn't enough. How many does it take to discern right from wrong? Another excuse employed by the guards was the old canard, "We were only following orders." That didn't fly for the German soldiers at the Nuremberg trials following WWII, and it won't take flight now. On March 16, 1968, a helicopter pilot swooped down on a Vietnamese village, placing himself between armed American soldiers and nine women and children. In countermanding an order, he risked his life but saved that small group and helped end the My Lai massacre, where more than 500 women, children, and elderly were slaughtered. Somebody at Abu Ghraib should have been as brave.

Bad vs. terrible

What befell those detainees was bad; what happened to Nicholas Berg was terrible. Eschewing perspective, the mass media marketing machine has run cover stories in national magazines and countless television news reports that have dragged on for weeks. Coverage of Nicholas Berg's beheading barely made it through one weekend before it was allowed to fade away, presumably because it was an isolated incident, an aberration. The mistreatment at Abu Ghraib was not? Most of the soldiers involved worked the night shift in one area of the prison, Tiers 1A and 1B.

Over-exposure of Abu Ghraib is not about prison abuse. It is a way for those against the war, but who profess, "We support our troops," to pile on at the first opportunity. If it were about prison abuse, where were those champions of human rights in the '90s, when the federal government took control of prisons in two states because of chronic, rampant abuses? Looking for the bad in America has become endemic to the major media. An innocent citizen is roughed up or worse, murdered, and hundreds flock to protest the unjust treatment under the watchful and lingering eyes of cameras. Yet, at the annual march and ceremony to honor law enforcement officers slain in the line of duty, where are the crowds?

Stripping the detainees was bad. Blowing up 22 innocent workers at the United Nations offices in Baghdad was terrible. Dogs frightening detainees was bad. Murdering four innocent American civilians, then dragging their burned, mutilated corpses through the streets of Fallujah while crowds cheered was terrible. Forcing detainees to sleep naked on concrete floors was bad. Watching hooded assailants attack a bound Nicholas Berg from behind, then saw his head off was terrible. If a few American soldiers were bad, what does that make the murderers of those 27 innocent victims?

Our damaged reputation

Americans are told Abu Ghraib has severely damaged our credibility in the Arab world. What about the credibility of the Arab world that produced 19 Saudi citizens who crashed planes into buildings in our country on 9/11, killing over 3,000 innocents? If people in the Middle East were upset over discomforting photos at Abu Ghraib, how would they react if 19 Americans commandeered planes and crashed them into high-rises in Mecca or Riyadh, killing over 3,000 Saudi innocents?

Photos of prison abuse flood our media outlets, yet the documentary of Saddam's tortures in the same prison a few years ago receives mention on page A21 of the *Washington Post*, without photos. Media counterparts in the Middle East also splash abuse photos on television screens, but few have mentioned the murder of Nicholas Berg. No wonder our reputation continues to plummet in that region.

Puzzled people with perspective, like myself, do not wish to deflect attention away from our shortcomings; we merely want them placed in their proper context.

A measured response vs. the immeasurable

Our bad apples make Americans sick to their stomachs; the enemy's bad apples kill Americans. Fellow countrymen turned in our bad apples, and most of those apples will serve time in prison. The enemy's bad apples have yet to be turned in by their countrymen; they remain free to join the throngs protesting the harsh treatment of Iraqi detainees. Our bad apples were stopped over four months ago, and safeguards were put in place to prevent further harm to Iraqi citizens. The enemy's bad apples continue to murder Americans. Our bad apples used leashed dogs to intimidate; the enemy's bad apples are unleashed around the world: to the Khobar Towers in Saudi Arabia, to American embassies in Kenya and Tanzania, to discotheques in Bali—resulting in more than 2,400 injured and 479 dead.

Forgive and forget

Since 9/11, no single event has received as much attention as Abu Ghraib. On September 12, 2001, if we were told we would not see another terrorist act on our shores in the ensuing three years or more, we would have been comforted. Since then, we have become so comfortable in our country that we waste this peaceful interlude decrying an event that would barely rate a footnote in the written history of a conventional war. Which this is not; just ask Spain. When the Moors were tossed from Granada in 1492, it marked the end of a reign that began in 711. On March 11, 2004, a series of bombs exploded on trains in Madrid, killing 191 and injuring 1,100 more. Immediately, Al Qaeda took responsibility and proclaimed, "This is part of settling old accounts with Spain, the Crusades, and America's ally in its war against Islam." Within days that "death squad" caused "one of the pillars of the crusade alliance, Spain" to announce their troop withdrawal from Iraq. While we distract ourselves with prison abuse, "narco-terrorists" finance their explosives and missions with drug money: 66 pounds of hashish bought the 220 pounds of stolen dynamite used by the Moroccan murderers in Madrid. According to the *L. A. TIMES*, "a Spanish police commander said, 'Until now, Islamic terrorism and drugs were two separate areas. Now you are not sure where to look.'"

Instead of looking at prison photos for a month, Americans should be looking south, to Mexico. The blueprint for bombings in Madrid makes us susceptible to similar carnage, because there is a well-established drug cartel in Mexico, supported by the larger network in South America. Hundreds of thousands of illegal immigrants stream into our country from Mexico, and not all of them are our southern neighbors. Some are from Eastern and Western Europe and the Middle East. Maybe a few are just coming for illicit vacations, but others have a sinister purpose. Those bad apples want to plant the seeds of their jihad in an orchard near you. "The train bombers caught international counter-terrorism agencies off-guard" and that is possible in America, where valuable resources and eyes are focused on a cellblock in Iraq.

The Garden of Eden was in Iraq. The United States is perceived as the modern day Eden because of its liberty, wealth, security, and vast natural resources. When Ferdinand and Isabella drove the last remnants of the Moors out in 1492, Columbus discovered America on an expedition funded largely by the riches regained while defeating the Moors. Over 500 years later, some of the vanquished are committed to claiming what they feel would have been theirs, had they won that war. Terrorists coming into America through its southernmost gateway, near Brownsville, would be ironic. Named for a Catholic priest, who was also a freedom fighter, Matamoros translated means "kill the Moors."

As events over the past months have revealed, our bad apples perform their work at night and put hoods over the eyes of those they mistreat. Our enemy's bad apples operate in broad daylight when our eyes are wide open . . . then they kill us.

Separation of Church and State

The one constant in this debate is inconsistency. Strict separationists note the phrase "under God" was inserted into the Pledge of Allegiance in 1954, followed by "In God we trust" being added to all paper currency in 1955 and then chosen as our national motto in 1956. They say these Acts of Congress are relatively new, but our current Age of Enlightenment only began in 1947, when the Supreme Court ruled in *Everson vs. Board of Education*, "The First Amendment has erected a wall of separation between church and state."

The Supreme Court in the 1844 case *Vidal vs. Girard* must have had it wrong when they opined, "Why may not the Bible, and especially the New Testament be read and taught as a divine revelation in the schools, with its general precepts expounded and its glorious principles of morality? Where can the purest principles of morality be learned so clearly or perfectly as from the New Testament?" In 1892, the Supremes cited 87 precedents in their ruling on *Church of Holy Trinity vs. United States,* "Our laws and our institutions must necessarily be based upon and must embody the teachings of the Redeemer of Mankind . . . our civilization and our institutions are emphatically Christian."

The 1947 Everson case referenced the First Amendment, which states, "Congress shall make no law respecting an establishment of religion, or prohibiting the free exercise thereof." The phrase, "building a wall of separation between church and state" is not found in the Constitution, Bill of Rights, or Declaration of Independence; the words are contained in a letter written by Thomas Jefferson. Up until 1833, many states had officially-designated denominations, and Jefferson was responding to the Danbury, Connecticut Baptists, who were upset with that state's official church: Congregationalism. Jefferson thought the subject was a states' rights issue and didn't think the Supreme Court should intervene. "But the opinion which gives to the judges the right to decide what laws are constitutional, and what not, not only for themselves in their own sphere of action, but for the Legislature and Executive also, in their spheres, would make the judiciary a despotic branch." (September 1804 letter to Mrs. John Adams.) Jefferson was not anti-religion, "We have solved, by fair experiment, the great and interesting question whether freedom of religion is compatible with order in government and obedience to the laws." (Reply to Virginia Baptists, 1808)

A Sampling of Contradictions

All of this apparent confusion has led to some interesting dichotomies. "The Ten Commandments are depicted in three locations on the United States Supreme Court building. There is a big oak door separating the courtroom from the central hallway where the Ten Commandments are depicted alone"; actually, just the roman numerals. Yet the two tablets above the Chief Justice's chair in the courtroom are rounded at the top and flat on the bottom, like the ones Chuck Heston carried in The Ten Commandments. Separationists say those tablets are the Bill of Rights, which is a necessary explanation. Otherwise, how could one reconcile Chuck's tablets in the U. S. Supreme Court building, but not allow them on a courthouse lawn in Montana or the State Supreme Court Building in Alabama?

The State that gave us Goofy is at it again. Three Commissioners of Los Angeles County voted to remove the cross from the County Seal, even though the entity's website states, "The cross represents the influence of the church and the missions of California." The officials thought it offended some people living in the county of "The Angels." Forget the fact the town was founded as a Christian mission. The officials did not have a problem with other emblems in the flag: the Roman goddess Pomona (agriculture); the tuna (fishing industry); or Pearlette, the championship cow (dairy industry).

"The current U. S. Senate chaplain's duties include spiritual care and counseling for senators, their families, and their staffs—a combined constituency of over 6,000 people—and special Bible study groups, discussion sessions, and prayer meetings, including a weekly Senators' Prayer Breakfast." The Senate chaplain makes $136,000 per year, the House chaplain $155,500. (CRS Report to Congress, updated 4/7/04). The Supreme Court ruled in the 1983 *Marsh v. Chambers* case that a chaplain "is deeply imbedded in the history and tradition of this country." But you should not attempt to pray in public schools.

A principal removed a Christmas tree from her school because she said it was too big, when compared with the menorah and crescent and star. She sent a memo to her teachers asking them to, "Bring in Muslim, Kwanzaa, and

Jewish secular symbols. I would like to display these religious symbols equally," sans the Xmas tree, of course. The principles of Kwanzaa escaped the principal; the holiday is secular. Nguzo Saba (Seven Principles) of Kwanzaa do not reference religion, even when describing Imani (Faith). The name of this school? Thomas Jefferson Magnet School of Humanities in Flushing, N.Y.

The original "Dubya"

The following descriptions and words are excerpted from Washington's Inaugural Address of April 30, 1789. (National Archives and Records Administration: Washington, DC, 1986, and taken from *www.ourdocuments.gov*). "After repeating this oath [of office], Washington kissed the Bible, and read his inauguration speech. 'No People can be bound to acknowledge and adore the invisible hand which conducts the affairs of men, more than the People of the United States. Every step by which they have advanced to the character of an independent nation seems to have been distinguished by some token of providential agency.

"Since we ought to be no less persuaded, that the propitious smiles of Heaven can never be expected on a nation that disregards the eternal rules of order and right, which Heaven itself has ordained . . . ." When the speech concluded, he and the members of Congress proceeded to St. Paul's Church for divine service.

And in Austin . . .

The Tarrytown 4th of July parade participants mass together on and adjacent to the grounds of the Episcopal Church of the Good Shepherd before starting their secular, celebratory march. Mr. Jefferson would have approved of that union of church and state, or so his words seem to imply. "One of the amendments to the Constitution . . . expressly declares that 'Congress shall make no law respecting an establishment of religion, or prohibiting the free exercise thereof, or abridging the freedom of speech, or of the press,' thereby guarding in the same sentence and under the same words, the freedom of religion, of speech, and of the press; insomuch that whatever violates either throws down the sanctuary which covers the others." (Draft Kentucky Resolutions, 1798)

Foot-in-Mouth in D.C.

The Fruitcake, the Whore, and the Man who Disgraced his Race

*People demand freedom of speech as a compensation
for the freedom of thought which they never use.*
—Soren Kierkegaard

*"It has always seemed strange to me . . . . The things we admire in men,
kindness and generosity, openness, honesty, understanding and feeling,
are the concomitants of failure in our system. And those traits we detest,
sharpness, greed, acquisitiveness, meanness, egotism and self-interest, are
the traits of success. And while men admire the quality of the first they
love the produce of the second."*
—John Steinbeck, ***Cannery Row***

In 2002, Toronto Mayor Mel Lastman flew to Mombasa, Kenya, to help lobby for the 2008 Olympic Games in his city. En route, Lastman told a reporter, "[Why] the hell do I want to go [to] a place like Mombasa? Snakes scare the hell out of me. I'm sort of scared about going out there, but the wife is really nervous. I just see myself in a pot of boiling water with all these natives dancing around me." True to his name, Mel was the last man to mention "a pot of boiling water" and "natives dancing around me" in the same sentence, without getting scorched by the media. Although his smooth lobbying efforts did not win many friends or votes in sub-Saharan Africa, back home he has won the Humanitarian of the Year Award and is the only politico to garner Marketer of the Year for Canada, presumably not for his airplane chatter.

In the summer of 2004 an event occurred that may be used by name-callers on elementary school playgrounds this fall to elevate their game. In a recent U.S. House Ways and Means committee meeting, after Chairman Bill Thomas, R-Cal., tried to choo-choo through some legislation, tempers reached the boiling point. Rep. Scott McInnis, R-Colo., said, "Shut up," to Rep. Pete Stark, D-Cal., who snapped back, "You think you are big enough to make me, you little wimp? Come on. Come over here and make me. I dare you, you little fruitcake, you little fruitcake. I said you are a fruitcake!" Mr. Stark repeatedly invoked a term considered by many to be a gay slur, but McInnis is married, apparently heterosexual, and not hearing-impaired. Winnie Stachelberg of the Human Rights Campaign gave Mr. Stark a hall pass, without detention. "I think Congressman Stark's use of the word, he probably regrets having used it. I think he meant nothing by it, but . . . it's probably a poor choice of words. But it's also important to note that Congressman Stark is one of the gay community's staunchest allies." Translation: He's a hot-tempered jerk, but he's our jerk.

Stark later explained, "'Fruitcake' means inept, crazy, a nut cake to me. Sometimes I feel so passionate about an issue that I am not as diplomatic as I should be . . . I did exchange words that were not becoming of my office. I regret that."

Earlier in the meeting, Rep. Stark-Raving-Mad purportedly called Chairman Thomas a three-syllable slur that ends in "sucker," and another word that defies detailing, even in impolite society.

Rep. Mark Foley, R-Fla. said, "This isn't the first time. That's the problem here. The Democrats fail to recognize this is an ongoing problem." Which is like saying the *Titanic* had "an ongoing problem" with water. Pistol Pete has shot off his mouth at targets before, once referring to ex-Health and Human Services Secretary Louis Sullivan "as close to being a disgrace to his race as anyone I've ever seen." Dr. Sullivan is an American of African descent who served in the first President Bush's cabinet from 1990-93. Old Pete offended blacks and gays but needed to add women to win the trifecta. Despite long odds, he crossed the finish line ahead of Earl Butz, when he let slip that Representative Nancy Johnson, (R-Conn.) was "a whore," who learned everything she knows about health care via pillow talk with her doctor husband. The most outrageous parts of Pete's performances were what followed them: no condemnations by the NAACP or the National Organization for Women. Rep. Stark attempted to become an equal opportunity basher when, in 1991, he called Rep. Stephen Solarz, D-N.Y., "Field Marshal Solarz in the pro-Israel forces."

Dr. Louis Sullivan, M.D., has been "a disgrace to his race" by graduating magna cum laude from Morehouse College and later graduating cum laude with a medical degree from Boston University. He taught medicine at both the Harvard and Boston University medical schools and was the founding president of the Association of Minority Health Professions Schools. Dr. Sullivan helped found and then served as the first dean of Morehouse School of Medicine in Atlanta, where he is the current president. The doctor is certified in hematology and internal medicine. He has received 50-plus honorary degrees and professional honors and has served on the boards of the Boy Scouts, United Way, General Motors, Bristol-Myers Squibb, 3M, Georgia Pacific, and CIGNA.

As for the "whore," Mrs. Johnson's proselytizing includes being, "a tireless advocate for quality health care all across America. There's no more strong advocate for making sure Medicare meets its promises than Nancy Johnson," the current President Bush stated in 2004. She was the first Republican woman to be put on the Ways and Means Committee and is a Radcliffe College graduate. She is married and has three daughters and three grandchildren.

Stark's gaffes rival another politician who suffered from foot-in-mouth disease, the late Earl Butz, who was the Secretary of Agriculture in President Ford's administration. Asked about the Pope's stance on abortion, Earl said, "He no play-da-game. He no make-a-da rules!" Secretary Butz was forced to resign over a comment he made about African-Americans, uttered while traveling on a plane (cf. Mel Lastman).

Meanwhile, Pete prowls the halls of Congress offending many Republicans and too few Democrats. This double standard reveals that politicians can trump their stupid remarks as long as they adhere to the correct ideology. The problem with double standards is that they usually devolve to the lowest common denominator, with the ultimate losers being Integrity and Civility, which cheapens all of us.

John Kerry vs. the Swift Boat Vets: A View from the Back of the Bus

This article is being written for the younger readers. Although bright, articulate, and well informed, they have trouble relating to the Vietnam War. Hopefully, telling this story through younger eyes will overcome that minor handicap.

The easiest way to explain the emotional debate is to climb aboard the bus. Austin High was playing a football game in Corpus Christi in September 1970. As seniors, Peter Barbour and I got the bright idea to rent a bus and charge our fellow students to ride to the game. There were many takers, because our dim idea was to travel sans chaperones. The principal required parental releases. Some of the students probably filled out the forms personally, without consulting others (i.e., parents). Like some of John Kerry's self-penned "action reports," the veracity of our documents went unquestioned as they passed up the chain of command to the principal. Kerry made it a few decades before he was questioned; our grace period ended the following Monday morning.

Rumors of atrocities

During homeroom period a voice came over the school-wide speaker system, "Peter Barbour and William Teten, report to the principal's office immediately." We knew a medal ceremony was not forthcoming. The principal rattled off a list of larcenies that roughly tracked the route and timeline of our bus trip, and then he quizzed us about each incident. After we successfully repudiated the half-dozen felonies that spanned from San Marcos to Karnes City and various stops in between, I smirked at #7.

The principal was not amused, so I responded to the charge. "Sir, we don't own any pistols. Even if we did, do we look like we would rob a convenience store at gunpoint and use a school bus as a getaway car?" After dropping felony charge #7, he said he had "heard" a girl had been raped on the bus. That news stunned us, but it came as a bigger shock to the purported victim. The attractive young lady was incredulous, as were the six girls she sat with throughout the bus ride.

Hearsay evidence

Rumors of our supposed atrocities whispered down the school's corridors. The young girl laughed them off, but the other charges lingered; finger pointing, sniggers, and crude jokes.

In his appearance before Congress in April 1971, John Kerry enumerated a list of felonies—including rape—perpetrated by his fellow soldiers in Vietnam. The sweeping generalities implicated an entire army. Kerry did not speak from first-hand knowledge; he merely repeated what he had heard, as did our principal and fellow students. Hearsay evidence is permissible in school hallways and congressional hearings.

In our case, the effect lasted only a few days, but some Vietnam vets have felt the burning pain of enduring the whispers of atrocities for decades. Their anguish never faded. It continued to smolder, until recently, when Senator Kerry's Vietnam exploits resurfaced and fanned the fires.

"I-Feel-Like-I'm-Fixin'-To-Die Rag"

On Friday, the bus hurtled down the highway toward Corpus Christi on its crime-free spree while we listened to the **Woodstock** soundtrack on a boom box. The "I-FEEL-LIKE-I'M-FIXIN'-TO-DIE RAG," a song by Country Joe and The Fish, was playing. Crammed together on the back half of the bus, 30 junior and senior students sang loudly: "Well, come on, mothers throughout the land, Pack your boys off to Vietnam. Come on fathers, don't hesitate, Send 'em off before it's too late. Be the first one on your block, To have your boy come home in a box."

An anti-war activist requested a reprise of the song. Someone whispered in my ear, and I told our disc jockey to pick another selection. He asked, "Why?"

I replied, "Arthur Scruggs." A grade ahead of us at Austin High, Arthur had entered the military and had been shipped off to Southeast Asia. On June 18, 1970, Arthur was killed in action in Vietnam.

The disc jockey asked, "So?"

I pointed to the bus driver. "That's Arthur's father."

I made my way up the aisle and sat behind Mr. Scruggs. The bus had grown silent as he continued driving down the highway, occasionally glancing at me through the rear-view mirror. His expression, a mixture of forlorn sadness and heartache, did not change during my apology, except for the tears that welled in his eyes. When my feeble apology ended, he nodded his acceptance and I returned to my seat.

All of us wished he had lashed out in anger, but his disciplined, silent rebuke had compounded our shame and humiliation. He never displayed anger, although he could have. Mr. Scruggs probably wondered why Arthur's schoolmates could be so insensitive toward someone with whom they had shared classes and hallways.

Missing the Boat

Pundits who call the swift boat ads a purely political ploy are missing the boat. Those of us who did not serve have trouble relating to Vietnam veterans. We did not slog through rice paddies or navigate swift boats through narrow rivers dotted with mines. We were never the point man of a nighttime patrol in booby-trap infested jungles.

Kerry and most of his crew view his four-month stint in Vietnam through the eyes of the official "action reports," many of them written by the Senator himself. More than 200 soldiers that served in boats mere yards away have a different perspective. Like Mr. Scruggs did that day, they are looking back on history through a rear-view mirror, where written words appear backwards.

Unlike Mr. Scruggs, the "swiftees" do not offer a silent rebuke to Kerry's anti-war stance. His congressional appearance angered them. They wonder how someone they shared the Vietnam experience with could be so insensitive to his fellow soldiers. Michael Moore and these vets are entitled to their version of the truth.

The "swiftees" speak not only for themselves but also for others. Less than one percent of Americans served in Vietnam; those who committed atrocities were probably a similar percentage. In their minds, the swift boat veterans are speaking for the mothers and fathers that didn't "hesitate" to "pack [their] boys off to Vietnam," parents like Mr. Scruggs, who was "the first one on [his] block . . . " And for the more than 58,000 American soldiers like Arthur Scruggs, who came home in a box.

The Missing Acronyms:
WMDs and the UN

I found the weapons of mass destruction but, before revealing their location, please permit a slight detour. A quick synopsis of United Nations history is boring, yet the signposts lead to the missing weaponry. Tuesday marked 19 months since the UN Security Council passed the resolution on Iraq by a vote of 15-0. The document referenced 10 prior resolutions that Saddam Hussein had ignored, dating back to 1990. The verbiage included the standard language of condemnation; the word "deploring" appeared four times. "Determined to ensure full and immediate compliance by Iraq without conditions or restrictions with its obligations . . ." the Security Council was ". . . expressing the gravest concern at the continued failure by the Government of Iraq to provide confirmation of the arrangements as laid out in that letter . . ." dated October 8, 2002. And, "by this resolution, a final opportunity to comply with its disarmament obligations . . ." was given to Saddam. The UN saw "the need for full compliance" within 30 days, "in order to secure international peace and security." Their summation "recalls, in that context, that the Council has repeatedly warned Iraq that it will face serious consequences as a result of its continued violations of its obligations."

Miscalculations

Saddam misjudged the first President Bush and he, along with the UN, repeated the mistake with the current President. UN Secretary General Kofi Annan, appearing on **Frontline**, was asked if the world's response to the next Rwanda-type massacre would be different. "I am not convinced that we will see the kind of political will and the action required to stop it." America's will and action in Iraq surprised not only the Security Council but also the entire UN. The President's decision was based on history, because the UN is like the well-intentioned boy on the playground who tries to stop the bully from pounding a fellow student. "You better stop!" The bully pauses and asks, "Or what?" The do-gooder responds, "Or else I'll get all your classmates to sign a declaration deploring your behavior and mandating you cease and desist, within thirty days." The bully resumes pummeling the helpless victim, just like he did in East Timor, Sierra Leone, the Balkans, Sudan, Rwanda, and Somalia.

Bones in the Balkans

The UN wants the cachet of being the world's policeman, with the U.S. as their enforcer, the operative word being "their." When America acts on a UN mandate, we are damned. When we fail to create a mandate, we are damned. Secretary General Kofi Annan said the massacres in Bosnia were "one of the most difficult and painful" lessons for the UN. "No one laments more than we the failure of the international community to take decisive action to halt the suffering and end a war that produced so many victims." In 1995, Serbian forces committed gendercide, killing between 8,000 and 10,000 Muslim men in Srebrenica, Bosnia, even though the town had been declared a UN "safe haven" two years earlier. Annan further washed his hands of blame by saying the UN was "not given the mandate or resources by member nations to fully take care of Bosnians or do anything to stop the war," that caused over 200,000 deaths, many directed by Slobodan Milosevic. What member nations mandated the bombings and supplied the resources that ended that war? NATO, led by the United States. Damned if you do.

Ghosts of Rwanda

In 1994, over 8,000 Rwandans were killed every day for 100 days; a Srebrenica-type massacre on a daily basis for over three months. Those 800,000 deaths wiped out 10% of Rwanda's population, the equivalent of everyone in California being slaughtered in the United States. Boutros Boutros-Ghali, who was the UN Secretary-General at the time, talked about his meeting with President Clinton. "Based on this discussion I had with him, Rwanda was a marginal problem. He said [he was] not so sure if [the United States] was ready to help to send soldiers, but he was not interested in this problem." Damned if you don't. No mention of France and Germany, both of whom had historical ties to sub-Sahara Africa, or China and Great Britain. Major Brent Beardsley, executive assistant to UN forces commander, had a different take. "We could have packed up dead bodies . . . flown to New York, walked in the Security Council and dumped them on the floor in front of [them]. And all that would have happened was we would have been charged for illegally using a UN aircraft. They just didn't want to do anything."

The killing fields

Pol Pot and his Khmer Rouge army killed over 2,000,000 in Cambodia between 1975 and 1979, before a Vietnamese invasion forced him to retreat to the hills. The UN "peacekeepers" arrived on the scene with $3 billion to help rebuild the country . . . in 1992. Pol Pot was never tried for war crimes.

Weapons of mass destruction

When President Clinton ordered the bombing of Baghdad in 1998, it was in retaliation for Saddam's tossing the weapons inspectors out of Iraq. Like President Bush, he relied heavily on intelligence supplied by the CIA and its head, George Tenet, a Clinton appointee. The UN inspectors said they were searching for WMDs, but they were merely seeking the implements or tools of the real WMDs. So where are the real ones? They reside in minds. Like Pol Pot, Saddam Hussein, Slobodan Milosevic, the Rwandan rebels, Adolf Hitler, Joseph Stalin, and others. With the exception of Hitler and Hussein, none of the others used chemical or biological weapons. The implements of death may have become more sophisticated, but the end result never changes: orchestrated deaths, usually in the form of genocide. Hitler had over 1.2 million gassed at Auschwitz during WWII. The Rwandans killed two-thirds that number in one-tenth of the time, all without "weapons of mass destruction." For 100 straight days, real WMDs woke up every morning and killed the numerical equivalent of every student at Austin, Anderson, McCallum, and Westlake High Schools, combined.

Those who cannot learn from history are doomed to repeat it,

—George Santayana

The dust from the Twin Towers that fell on September 11 cascaded northward for six miles, depositing residue on the doorstep of the UN General Assembly building. "Lots of those eyes still haunt me, angry eyes, or innocent

230

eyes. But the worst eyes that haunt me are the eyes of those people who were totally bewildered. They're looking at me . . . and saying, 'What in the hell happened?'" Those were not the words of a New York policeman. General Romeo Dallaire, commander of the UN forces in Rwanda, spoke them when questioned about the holocaust in Rwanda. Maybe the Security Council acted on Iraq because of their proximity to the Twin Towers. Perhaps they have read Santayana and want to change, although the failure to act on the massacres in the Sudan raises doubts about that theory. Regardless, the Iraq resolution shows the UN is getting closer to realizing there must be a bite associated with their incessant barking. The denouncement of the coalition forces' invasion of Iraq via that mandate reveals many in the UN think they are getting too close for comfort.

CSI: Washington
An Apolitical Postmortem

I have surreptitiously obtained the script of an upcoming television special, **CSI: Washington**. The grisly references in the script have been deleted and the "bodies" are neither wraiths nor real; they're mannequin cadavers. Remember that this show airs on CBS, which is famous for allowing their shows that last 60 minutes to take literary and dramatic license.

The scene: a morgue in Washington, D.C. Bodies of Democratic presidential hopefuls lie on autopsy tables throughout the large room. The show's star, William Petersen, enters and approaches lead assistant Marg Helgenberger.

Petersen: "What have you got?"

Marg: "Lots of Democrats in suits, but there are a few Republicans in the next room. Every one of them expired in November, but in different years."

Petersen: "How do you know that?"

Marg: "All of them are wearing 'I voted' buttons."

Petersen, looking dubious, asks: "Anything else?"

Marg: "Yes. None of the ones in this room have even a trace of Southern blood, except for those two in the corner." She points to a body sporting a Planters Peanuts gimme cap and another one wearing a University of Tennessee cap.

Marg: "Jimmy Carter and Al Gore."

Petersen: "What's Gore clutching in his hands?"

Marg: "That would be his lock box."

The Switzerland of the Civil War

Petersen: "Carter and Gore were from Georgia and Tennessee, so why are they here?"

Marg: "Well, Gore lost to a fellow Southerner, Bush #43, and Carter had his own unique set of problems: 20% inflation and that whole Shah of Iran/Ayatollah/hostage crisis."

Petersen: "When did this trend begin?"

Marg: "Apparently in 1948, when a New York Republican named Tom Dewey lost to Harry S. Truman. I know! Truman was from Missouri, which was the Switzerland of the Civil War; apparently neutral beats Yankee almost every time. After that, the smartest man ever, Adlai Stevenson, lost twice to General Eisenhower, who some people considered just an unengaged golfer, in spite of the fact that he did plan the largest amphibious assault in history, D-Day, and at one time he was president of Columbia University. Oh, and Eisenhower was born in Denison, Texas."

Petersen: "But how do you explain John F. Kennedy getting elected President?"

Marg: "Simple: he had a Texan, Lyndon Baines Johnson, as his running mate. Despite that, Kennedy only won Texas by 46,000 votes and he eked out Illinois by some 9,000 voters. He was the last Yankee elected and that was, gosh, 44 years ago."

Petersen: "Don't forget that Kennedy was shot in Dallas, Texas. And since then, both of the Massachusetts Democrats who've run for president, Dukakis and Kerry, have been beaten by Bushes, both Texans. Interesting."

Marg: "Nixon came back and beat Humphrey, who was from Minnesota and McGovern, who was from South Dakota. Tricky Dick was from California, which didn't reach statehood until after the Civil War."

Petersen: "And following Nixon, Carter beat Gerald Ford, who was from Meechigan."

Marg: "Nice accent. Speaking of Texas and California, do you realize that Johnson and Bush #41 and #43 are all Texans?"

Peterson: "What's that got to do with anything?"

Marg: "Adding the two Nixon wins and the two Reagan victories to Johnson's and the Bushs' means that eight of the last 11 presidential elections have been won by residents of those two states. Look at Gore: he lost to a fellow Southerner, just like Bush #41 did. And the only three elections that a Texan and Californian didn't win were won by guys from Georgia and Arkansas—Carter and Clinton."

Petersen: "So what's the formula for success?"

Marg: "Being a war hero sure doesn't help. Three of the last four losers were: Bush #41 in '92, Dole in '96 and Kerry this week."

Bill Clinton, choirboy

Petersen: "Aside from his charm, how did Clinton win?"

One of the young male hunks on the show, George Eads appears. "I've got the answer to that." George looks at his notes and continues, "When Clinton lost his re-election bid for Governor of Arkansas he got religion, literally. His wife belonged to the biggest Methodist church in Little Rock. Bill studied the Sunday church shows for the best camera angle. Pretty soon after that, he joined the largest Baptist church in town. Every Sunday for one hour, a fixed camera showed the preacher and seated just over his shoulder in the most visible chair—Bill Clinton, wearing his choir robe. Say what you want, that man knew the value of a photo op."

Peterson: "That's great, George. Go get some coffee."

Eads leaves and Peterson whispers to Marg: "That guy held out in a contract dispute this summer. I'll be darned if I'm going to give him more camera time."

Marg: "So, Chief, where are we?"

Peterson rubs his chin: "I don't know. You think the Democrats will run Hillary Clinton in 2008, knowing that a Yankee has won the White House only once in the last 60 years?"

Marg: "She's from Chicago, by way of Arkansas and Washington, D.C., before she went to New York. Maybe a hybrid will work. The Democrats have only won three of the last 10 presidential elections, and two of those victories were by her husband. Do you remember the cartoon of the kid trying to enter the School for the Extremely Gifted? He was pushing on the door, but the sign clearly said 'pull.' Most Democratic Presidential candidates come off looking like brusque New Yorkers, always trying to push Americans in one direction or the other. Maybe because he was a good old Southern boy, Clinton knew the best way to get people to follow was to lead, not push."

Petersen: "That jibes with something I read by the novelist Tom Wolfe in THE GUARDIAN on Monday. I cut it out, because it seemed so dead on, so to speak." Petersen pulls the paper from his shirt pocket. "He was saying Americans don't want to be governed by, ': . . East-coast pretensions. It is about not wanting to be led by people who are forever trying to force their twisted sense of morality onto us, which is a non-morality.' Maybe that's a simplistic answer, but voting isn't complicated; it's visceral, not mental."

George Eads returns with a tray loaded with three cups of coffee. Petersen takes one, and grabs a crumpled piece of paper from the platter. Petersen: "Thanks for the caffeine. What's this?"

George: "I found it in Al Gore's lock box!"

Petersen: "You pried it open, you nitwit?"

George nods and says, "Very informative piece of evidence, Chief."

Petersen stares at the sheet. "It's a map of the United States broken down between the red and the blue states, presumably from the 2000 election."

Marg: "How can you tell?"

Petersen: "Scribbled across the top of the page are the words, 'I was robbed!' And a signature, 'Al Gore, December 2000.'"

George laughs: "That's funny!" The other two stare at him, not getting the joke. He continues, "Almost every elected President was able to deliver his own state. Gore couldn't even win his beloved Tennessee. He didn't even win one of the eight states that border Tennessee. If he had been victorious in one of them, just one, Florida would have been a moot point. Heck, when Fritz Mondale got drubbed in '84, the poor guy only got 13 electoral votes, but at least he won his own state of Minnesota, along with the District of Columbia."

Marg: "How do you know all of this? Are you from Tennessee or something?"

George: "No. Fort Worth."

"Ohio"

The director yells, "Cut." Petersen starts walking between the manne-quin cadavers and stops at John Forbes Kerry, whose Silver Star, Bronze Star, and three Purple Hearts are pinned on his "Vietnam Veterans Against the War" jacket. Peterson thinks about Bush #43, who served in the National Guard, and of the Crosby, Stills, Nash & Young song about four students who were shot and killed in 1970 at Kent State University, during a Vietnam War protest. The song was named for the state where the shooting took place— "Ohio." The protestors were shot by members of the National Guard. Ohio proved to be a most pivotal state in the 2004 election.

Petersen's eyes drift across the rest of the blue-state tinged presidential hopefuls. He thinks aloud, "This year the Democrats spent as much as the Republicans, they registered a ton of young people, the overall turnout was the largest since 1968, and they still lost for the seventh time in the last 10 elections. A baseball player can make millions batting only .300, but my show would be cancelled if I only solved 30% of the cases. Making a 70 on a test in school is barely passing. Why good Democrats across this country are willing to accept a 70% failure rate in presidential elections is a mystery. Now, there's a case I want to solve."

A voice in the background screams, "Aaarrgghhh!"

Petersen: "What was that?"

Marg: "George spilled some of his hot coffee on Al Gore."

Petersen: "Which means he's still alive."

Marg: "Apparently so." She turns and sees Eads peering over Al Gore. "George, get away from that lock box."

Hurricane Katrina: a Cycle of Nature

Four cycles played out last week in New Orleans. The first, fallout from Hurricane Katrina, was more predictable than the storm itself. Media members, politicians, and some victims began assigning blame for the slow response. Most faulted the federal government—President Bush in particular. He deserves a degree of guilt, as do others.

One popular potshot: "If the National Guard troops were here instead of Iraq, the problem could have been solved much sooner." Last year Florida suffered four hurricanes, yet that state got by, even though a number of their Guard troops were in Iraq. The Department of Homeland Security was lambasted for being flatfooted in the face of imminent danger and its horrific aftermath. Days before Katrina made landfall the head of FEMA (Federal Emergency Management Agency) went on television imploring New Orleans residents to evacuate.

The second cycle was also predictable. Ray Nagin loved New Orleans so much he took an 80 percent pay cut to become Mayor. The magnitude of that responsibility overwhelmed him. With a category five storm bearing down on his city, the Mayor told people to evacuate. His order was not mandatory, nor was it enforceable, and his citizens knew it. That's the way it's been in the Crescent City for a long time.

According to one source, the police force has only 60% of the officers required to effectively control the city. Statistics confirm the shortfall. Beginning in 1993, Louisiana had the most violent crime rate in America. New Orleans is the murder capital of the United States. You're 7.5 times more likely to be shot in The Big Easy than in The Big Apple. The New Orleans Police Foundation says over 40% of serious crime cases have been dropped by prosecutors in the last three years. Less than a quarter of the murders end in a conviction. As Katrina approached, more than 10% of the Big Easy's officers disappeared, making it impossible to enforce a mandatory exodus.

Despite a check for $750 million from the federal government, the State of Louisiana and the City of New Orleans did not have a coherent disaster plan in place. When Nagin urged everyone to leave, he didn't have to tell the white people; they had left a long time ago. The city was founded in 1718. Slaves arrived in 1719, and by 1724 freed slaves had their movements restricted.

President Andrew Johnson sent General Philip Sheridan and his troops into Louisiana to contain civil unrest in 1867. The soldiers didn't depart until 1877. Whites drifted to the suburbs, and today only three in 10 residents are non-black. Thirty percent of New Orleanians live below the poverty line. An estimated 100,000 failed to evacuate. How were the poor, the elderly, and the infirm supposed to flee the city? Two hundred school buses and 300 hundred mass transit buses were available. If each bus carried 50 people and had made four trips, the Crescent City could have been emptied. But where were they to go?

Contrast that lack of initiative with Houston, which ended up housing thousands in the Astrodome and other venues on 14 hours' notice. And Alabama, whose governor called up 500 National Guard soldiers before the first zephyr filtered through the trees along that state's shoreline. Like a deer in headlights, the Big Easy's bureaucracy shoveled 20,000 stragglers into the Superdome.

The Army Corps of Engineers has come under fire for building a levee system that can only withstand a level 3 hurricane. More than one President, one Congress, one Louisiana governor and legislature and New Orleans mayor failed to upgrade that system.

The third predictable cycle does not involve human nature, but nature itself: Katrina was long overdue. "From 1900 to 1996, twenty-five hurricanes, including twelve with winds faster than 111 mph [level three], have hit Louisiana, says the National Hurricane Center." (*USA TODAY*, 5/17/2005). "On average, since 1871, a tropical storm or hurricane should be expected somewhere within [Louisiana] every 1.2 years. A hurricane should make land-fall every 2.8 years. (*www.nws.noaa.gov*) Before Katrina, four of the 10 most powerful hurricanes in American history hit Louisiana. Betsy in September 1965 and the September Hurricane of 1915 both flooded New Orleans. The city was first inundated with water by a hurricane in September 1722, four years after it was founded.

A number of victims of Katrina will not return to New Orleans. Hopefully, those decisions will enrich their adopted hometowns, which is part of the fourth cycle. Before Katrina, Hurricane Hugo and the Isle of Derniere (Last Island) Hurricane of 1856 were tied for the tenth most powerful storm. Hundreds died in the mid-19th century storm south of New Orleans that, along with subsequent erosion, reduced Derniere to the Isles of Derniere; a small collection of glorified sandbars. New Orleans businessman James

Martin lost his wife in the massive storm surge of that killer storm. Crestfallen and left with only a four-year-old daughter, Martin remained in New Orleans until the girl graduated from Ursuline Academy. The two moved to Austin in 1871, where he opened the first shoe store in town, on Congress Avenue. He helped raise funds for the new St. Mary's Cathedral and his daughter married. For 85 years her husband and son were reporters, covering the Capitol for the GALVESTON/DALLAS MORNING NEWS.

Another part of the fourth cycle is the most predictable one of all: the largesse displayed by people in the states that border Louisiana and beyond. The massive destruction caused by Katrina is unmatched in our nation's history, and so is the flood of aid, compassion, and love exhibited by Americans for the inhabitants in Louisiana, Mississippi, and Alabama. Every thoughtful gesture will benefit future generations and will be appreciated by those who came before us. My sister-in-law Virginia is a native of New Orleans. Last Friday my brother Paul was on the road, picking up his mother-in-law, Nancy and her aunt Arlene who were hunkered down in the Garden District.

Although more than 300 million people live in our vast country, somehow we are all connected, often in surprising ways. On that same Friday night, my wife and I dined with group that included Susan Parker and her cousin Susan Johnson, who was displaced from her suburban New Orleans home by Katrina. Longer ago than she cares to remember, Susan Johnson was a math and science teacher at a private school in New Orleans. One of her students was Virginia, Paul's future wife.

The four cycles will repeat themselves: the media and politicians will play the blame game, elected officials will disappoint, and hurricanes will lash our coastlines. Citizens of this disparate melting pot will band together in a crisis, as we have done for centuries. Preventing the first three is problematic; continuing the fourth is what sustains us. With apologies to the songwriter, A.P. Carter, "WILL THE CYCLE BE UNBROKEN?" By and by, Lord, by and by.

HOMAGE

John S. Burns

The elderly man had finished his swim in Barton Springs and was smoking a cigarette, perched on his favorite rock overlooking the pool. He came here often after retiring from the downtown bank he founded, City National, which later became part of Frost Bank. A young man approached him and said, "Sir, you can't smoke here." John S. Burns eyed the do-gooder and said evenly, "Son, I've been smoking on this spot for over 50 years and I'm not about to stop now." Chastened, the young man retreated. John S. looked down at the cigarette that rolled back and forth between his thumb and index finger. Then he glanced at the clear, cold waters of the pool and remembered the day that a cigarette saved his life.

It was 11:55 A.M. on January 6, 1945, in the Lingayen Gulf off the coast of Luzon, Philippines. In the distance he saw them charging toward him, the Four Horsemen of the Apocalypse. Familiar with the Book of Revelation from the Bible, he knew the fourth horseman, ". . . his name that sat on him was Death, and Hell followed with him." Burns figured he would be dead within minutes and reached for his last cigarette.

John Simeon Burns was born on December 18, 1917, in Coleman, Texas, into a devout Baptist family. He dreamed of attending Baylor University and then Baylor Law School. His father was the district attorney until the day he suffered a fatal heart attack in the courtroom. The Depression offered few employment opportunities in Coleman for the Widow Burns so she moved the family to Austin.

John S. graduated from Austin High and then attended the University of Texas, where he worked odd jobs to support his education. He used a push mower to groom the complex of intramural fields off 19th Street (now the site of Jester Hall). Another chore involved looking after the fruit flies in the biology department, which his friends found appropriate: with his incessant practical jokes John S. himself was sometimes a pest.

As a Sigma Chi fraternity pledge he had to roll a full keg of beer from East Austin to the fraternity house west of The Drag. He didn't mind hard work, especially if it resulted in a good time for all.

John S. worked at the Capital National Bank after getting his BBA in Finance from UT and joined the Naval Reserves. When the Japanese bombed Pearl Harbor he was called up to active duty.

He served on two destroyers before joining the *USS Walke* (DD-723) in September of 1944. In a letter to Commander R.L. Nolan with the Fleet Administrative Office in Boston he wrote, "As you can see I am at last where I have wanted to be all along and I am happy. Haven't shot any Japanese yet but they say there's plenty of time. But of course I have not been here long enough to grow tired of it as they tell me I will. Sincerely, Johnnie"

The *Walke* had returned to the East Coast for repairs, having been shelled off the shores of Cherbourg after supporting the D-Day invasion. The 5' 6" inch Burns boarded the ship as it traveled through the Panama Canal. Dr. Robert "Linky" Link, the ship's physician, quickly became his best friend.

The doctor was the only person allowed to requisition liquor, and at every depot and port Linky and John S. went ashore and got Four Roses blended whiskey which they locked inside the hold of the ship, with Linky retaining the key. Their growing stockpile caught the eye of the Admiralty, who wanted to know why so much booze was being requested. Burns sent a short reply, "It's for medicinal purposes."

The ship had been commissioned on January 21, 1944. Except for a few officers, the crew had remained intact since that time. It was an egalitarian vessel; the enlisted men were treated with the respect usually reserved for officers. Each sailor could name the other 379 men on board. The *Walke's* crew was decades ahead of the civil rights movement. The six black sailors were treated the same as the rest of the crew.

All of the men eagerly accepted their new second in command, the affable Lt. Burns, who was a nice complement to LTJG (Lieutenant Junior Grade) Edward G. Burnham, the oldest man on the ship. "Pops" had risen through the ranks of enlisted men to become a gunnery mate. Burnham was in his late thirties, possessed a booming laugh and loved to tell jokes. Burns was 26 and his jokes were of the practical kind. From short-sheeting bunks to sneaking up on a sleeping Dr. Link and drenching him in cold water, Burns relieved the wartime tension.

A black cook, Lewis Grey, was a strikingly handsome and soft-spoken 20-year-old from Ohio. At 28, Linky was like an older brother to the men, including Grey. Most of the crew were between 19 and 22 years of age and treated their fellow shipmates like brothers. They had to because they were steaming toward war. Somewhere in the Pacific Ocean waters the Four Horsemen of the Apocalypse were waiting.

Commander George Fleming Davis was a deeply religious man who was already a highly decorated sailor before taking command of the *Walke* on November 26, 1944. A graduate of the Naval Academy at Annapolis, he had survived the attack at Pearl Harbor while on the *USS Oklahoma*. Almost 400 of his fellow crewmen did not. Davis had recently received the Legion of Merit, with combat "V" for heroism in numerous battles including Leyte, which occurred one month before he assumed command of the *Walke*. At 34, he was the second oldest man on the ship.

Davis was familiar with the "Kamikaze" (Divine Wind), Japanese suicide planes that attacked Allied ships. They were named for the typhoon that saved Japan by destroying the 13th century Mongol invasion fleet. Before embarking for the invasion of Ormoc Bay, Davis gathered the crew and "instilled in their minds that suicide plane crashes could not sink a ship if the crew was determined to save their ship." Burns also wrote that the Commander's "uncanny foresight and preparation was largely responsible for the crew's performance" when the attack occurred.

At the invasion of Ormoc Bay on December 7, 1944, they saw their first kamikaze. Another destroyer, the *USS Mahan* was in the wrong place at the wrong time. A majority of kamikaze attacks occurred near sunset. Their success ratio was 50 percent when targeting a screen, or formation of ships. The percentage increased to 75 percent when battling a single ship.

The *Mahan* was on radio picket, separated from the other destroyers; the ship was a sitting duck. At 5:23 P.M. six kamikazes descended upon her. The gunners managed to shoot down three, but the others crashed aboard and 10 minutes later the order came to abandon ship. The *Walke* spent nearly three hours pulling sailors out of the water. Butch, a cocker spaniel wearing a life jacket, was pulled on deck and the *Mahan's* mascot was introduced to the *Walke's* mascot, a lady named Rosy.

Around 8:30 P.M. Davis ordered the 40-mm and 20-mm guns to fire on the crippled ship, sending the *Mahan* to the bottom of the waters off Ormoc

Bay. While en route to San Pedro Bay the next day, the *Walke* shot down its first kamikaze.

Suicide planes weren't their only worries. After supporting the assault on Mindoro, more than 85 ships had retreated 300 miles off the coast of Luzon on December 17, when the seas began building. The next morning the typhoon hit the flotilla of carriers, cruisers, battleships, and 50 destroyers. Fires broke out on three aircraft carriers when planes crashed in their hangars. In all, 146 planes were lost. A cruiser, three destroyers, and five carriers were damaged by the waves that caused some ships to list between 60 and 75 degrees.

Visibility ranged from 1,000 yards to zero. Wind and waves sheared off masts, stacks, and lifeboats. By early afternoon the wind was "in excess of 100 knots; the sea became mountainous; the air was filled with foam and spray; and the surface of the sea was white with driving, boiling foam."

In the worst weather-related American naval disaster since 1889, almost 800 men perished and 80 were injured. Three destroyers capsized, including the *USS Hull*. Almost 100 men were trapped inside the ship when it sank. More than 120 that jumped into the water died when the massive waves crushed them against the foundering ship.

Two jumpers and Fireman Second Class Roy Morgan managed to evade the wreckage, but within minutes a wave stripped him of his lifejacket. His friends held onto Morgan through gale force winds as the giant waves pounded them. In the darkness they watched helplessly as the lights from other ships disappeared in the distance. Eventually, they were rescued and the three collapsed on the deck of the ship. They had been in the water for 31 hours.

Burns and his crewmates were fortunate; they were on the outer edge of the small typhoon. They deserved some luck. Between December 2 and January 6, six of the nine ships in destroyer squadron 60 were hit by kamikaze planes and two were struck twice. Casualties in the squadron reached 22 percent. One ship was sunk.

On December 29, the *Walke* was anchored in San Pedro Bay beneath a penumbral lunar eclipse, a phenomenon where all of the full moon is visible, but there is a slight, dark shading that is imperceptible to the naked eye. Eight nights later when the moon phase shifts from waning to last quarter, 16 members of the *Walke* would be dead, dying, or missing in action. Nearly 30 others would be injured. The attack would change the survivors, forever. After January 6, 1945, their hearts and personalities would be slightly shaded with a darkness imperceptible to the naked eye. Like the penumbral lunar eclipse that bathed the waters of San Pedro Bay.

On January 4, the *Walke* was off the coast of Luzon, Philippines. At 5:24 P.M. a kamikaze crashed into the bridge of the *USS Ommaney Bay*. Ten minutes later her sailors abandoned ship.

The activity increased on January 5. At 5:13 P.M. a kamikaze hit the *USS Louisville* on the bridge. At 5:48 the *USS Stafford* was hit amidships. Five minutes later the *USS Halligan* was hit. Two minutes after that a suicide plane crashed into the *USS Manila Bay*.

On January 6, the *Walke* provided cover for the minesweepers that usually entered the harbor area three days before a planned invasion. Somewhere behind them General MacArthur and 68,000 troops were counting the days. At 11:52 A.M., the minesweepers had been operating in Lingayen Gulf for 90 minutes. The *Walke* was at general quarters, or battle stations. The ship was a sitting duck, and every man knew it.

In the ship's hold were a series of valves and pumps. Attached to them were the fire hoses that coursed upward through the ship and lay on the deck. In minutes the valves would open and the pumps would force salt water through the hoses to the firemen fighting the blaze.

During World War II, over 16.1 million served in the armed forces, millions of them in the Navy. Fewer than 2,700 seamen received the Navy's second highest medal, the Navy Cross. The highest award, the Medal of Honor, was granted to only 57.

At 11:54 A.M. Dr. Link was walking to the aft, or rear of the ship. He had the run of the destroyer, along with the two pharmacists' mates. The crew was protective of their medical staff, knowing their lives could be in the hands of the three men at any moment. That moment was eight minutes away.

LTJG Burnham stood at the 40-mm gun near the bridge. Next to him was Lewis Grey, whose secondary job was ferrying replacement ammunition to the guns. Commander Davis stood on the open deck of the bridge. One level below him, Lt. Burns peered out of the rectangular opening of the cramped combat information center.

One of these men would later get the Bronze Star; another would receive the Navy Cross. A third would be awarded the Medal of Honor, posthumously.

All five would be gathered on the deck that evening for the burial at sea. Three of them would be in body bags.

At 11:55 A.M. the lookout saw something off the starboard bow, flying low on the water. Six miles away and closing fast; four kamikaze planes. John S. figured he had minutes to live. Instead, his next move granted him an additional 53 years. His right hand reached into his pants for a lighter as his left hand dug into the shirt pocket for a cigarette. The one that would save his life.

On January 6 just after 11:55 A.M., the kamikazes were five miles away from the *USS Walke*. Like Gary Cooper in **High Noon**, it was four against one, and help was not on the way.

Two of the planes broke formation and began to climb. In the combat information center (CIC), Lt. John S. Burns lit his cigarette and told the other three men in the cramped observation room, "When they're 1,000 yards away, get down!"

On the open bridge one deck above them, Commander George Fleming Davis ordered the 5" guns and all starboard 40mm to fire on the lead plane at 11:56. Black smoke clouds from the guns' exploding shells dotted the sky as machine-gun fire peppered the water beneath the low-flying plane. At 11:57 the kamikaze was hit and burst into flames before disintegrating. Davis shifted attention to the second plane that was now only 1,000 yards away. Burns cupped his hands over his headphones, trying to hear the orders. The cigarette dangled from his lips and he yelled over the gunfire, "Hit the deck!" The other three scrambled to find floor space in the small enclosure.

The second kamikaze came in low and was peppered repeatedly. At 500 yards it was aimed at midship on the starboard side, but the pilot lost control and the plane started to climb. It passed just above the ship's mark-12 antenna and exploded. Pieces of the aircraft flew through the air and splashed into the water just yards from the port side.

The third plane had climbed to an altitude of 3,000 feet. At 11:58, it turned and attacked from the port bow. All of the port machine guns started shooting; the kamikaze returned the fire, strafing the ship. Davis refused to leave the open bridge and continued issuing orders. Beside the starboard 40-mm gun, LTJG Edward Burnham and Lewis Grey quickly checked the ammunition.

The gunners hit the plane, but it kept coming and increased its speed. The pilot made a slight turn to defeat the effectiveness of the 5" and machine guns. Five hundred yards away, the kamikaze went into a glide. Men in the targeted area ran for cover. Commander Davis stood on the open deck, encouraging his gunners, resolutely.

Burns glanced down at his men, and the cigarette slipped from his lips. Thinking it might burn one of them he bent over and searched for it in the darkness. One second later, the plane slammed into the bridge and pilothouse on the port side, but its dud bomb did not. The 250-pound cylinder filled with gasoline shot downward and blasted into the CIC. It whistled two feet above the stooped over Burns before blowing a hole in the wall next to the men and crashing into the water. If he had remained standing, John S. would have been cut in half.

The kamikaze's explosion sprayed the deck with gasoline as a giant fireball expanded upward for hundreds of feet, and cascaded below the CIC. Burns checked on his men, stood up, and looked through the opening of twisted metal and shielded his eyes from the heat of the flames. He ran back through the hallway and bounded up the stairs, two at a time.

Outside, the fire fighters pulled hoses up the steps leading to the bridge. When they climbed over the open deck they recoiled in horror. Standing before them, engulfed in orange-red flames was Commander Davis; he was a human torch. The inferno raged on his legs, torso, arms, and face. Flames reached several feet above his head. Through the burning heat, he saw the shadowy figures. His right arm waved them on as he shouted, "Save the ship men, save the ship!" They aimed the first hose at him and the strong stream of water staggered Davis backwards a few steps, then he stiffened as the fire was doused.

Burns arrived and ran toward him as the Commander pried open his blackened eyelids, shook the salt water from his eyebrows, and searched the sky for the fourth plane.

The kamikaze began his dive on the starboard quarter at 12:01 P.M. The few starboard machine guns that were undamaged, the number three 5" mount and the 40-mm and 20-mm guns sprayed a fusillade at the plane. Dr. Robert "Linky" Link was standing near the rear of the ship, watching the kamikaze bearing down on him a hundred yards away. For the first time in his naval career he thought to himself, "I could die out here." The plane exploded and Linky ducked as it flew over him, missing his head by 10 feet. The debris crashed close aboard on the port side. He started running toward the fire on the bridge, but he never made it. Along the way he encountered too many injured and dying.

The firemen fought "with unusual efficiency and ability," in the words of Commander Davis, who months before had "instilled in their minds that suicide plane crashes could not sink a ship if the crew was determined to save their ship." By 12:15 the fires were out, and the firemen surveyed the human damage.

Edward Burnham lay dead near a 40-mm gun; other bodies were scattered nearby and on the bridge. The pharmacist's mate and his assistants were helping Dr. Link tend to Lewis Grey and dozens of others. Commander Davis knew the *Walke* would survive and felt the adrenaline seeping from his body. He turned the vessel over to Burns, and then his legs buckled and his body slammed against the deck.

By 1:40 P.M. the *Walke* had returned to the protective cover of the ships in Task Group 77.2.1. Lt. Commander Burns checked the damage report. The superstructure had lost all communications, radars, gyro repeaters, and electrical circuits and suffered extensive damage to the bridge itself, as well as to her gun and torpedo directors. The kitchen was inoperable, and all of their food supply had been destroyed.

Nearly 50 men were unable to man their battle stations because of injuries and deaths. One kamikaze had removed almost 20 percent of the *Walke's* fighting force, in addition to destroying many of the forward guns. At 2:45 the undermanned force opened fire on a kamikaze that was headed for the *USS Minneapolis* and helped down the plane before the pilot could hit the hospital ship.

Dr. Link and the mates worked furiously, dressing the shrapnel wounds, supplying burn victims with I.V.s, and dispensing pain medications. Three seriously wounded men filled the available bunks in the officers' staterooms on the main deck and three more, including Davis, filled the small sick bay. Others were "bunked in the passageways where light and ventilation [was] very poor and special treatment [was] rendered difficult."

By the time Link made his way to Grey, the beds for the critically injured were filled. Lewis was taken to his own bunk, and the doctor leaned over the badly burned cook and said, "Grey, I've got to go check on the captain, but I'll be back." Grey nodded through the pain. Dr. Link gave him a shot of morphine and rushed to sick bay. Thirty minutes later Linky re-entered the room and walked to the bunk. His shoulders sank at the sight. For a few moments the doctor gazed down, sadly, at the lifeless body of Lewis Grey. He thought to himself, if the cook had been the only one injured, perhaps I could have saved him. But Grey wasn't the only one: there were dozens of injured, many of them critically. Dr. Link took a deep breath and tried to exhale the sorrow. Then he charged out of the room. The one thing he didn't have right now was time to spare.

Burns visited the men in the officers' staterooms. Third-degree burns had fried their nerve endings and they were in relatively good spirits. He told Link, "They seem okay." The doctor pulled him aside and whispered, "They'll all be dead in the morning." Burns ordered the whiskey to be dispensed. In the end, his words to the Admiralty were prophetic; the liquor was consumed "for medicinal purposes."

The pharmacist's mates hauled the cases up from the hold, left them on deck and walked back to the staterooms to ask Dr. Link where he wanted the cache. "Bring it here," he replied. They went topside, but the booze had mysteriously disappeared. Apparently the injured and dying weren't the only ones who needed liquid comfort. A mate located a bottle and sheepishly gave it to Linky.

Following the unsuccessful sunset attack on the *HMAS Australia* by four kamikazes, the *Walke* transferred eight critical casualties to the *USS Minneapolis*, but not Commander Davis. He never regained consciousness and died at 4:30.

At 10:30, all off-duty seamen had opted to remain in their rooms. Some slept. Most just lay in their bunks, thinking of home. Others huddled in small groups and sipped whiskey. They did anything to distract themselves from the event playing out on deck. It was just too painful.

The moon's glow glistened off the waves. Stars filled the sky. Lights from the surrounding ships stretched as far as the eye could see. Standing on the side of the ship were Linky, John S., the pharmacist's mate, his two assistants and the chaplain. They didn't notice the beautiful night. They were staring down at the twelve body bags laid out before them. Inside the white canvas coffins were three officers and nine enlisted men. The six observers watched as two other men finished their jobs. They had put a heavy 5" shell in each canvas bag before sliding the body of their shipmate inside. Then they sewed them shut with a heavy needle and thread. The chaplain performed the service and then walked up to each white body bag and spoke about the fallen comrade that lay inside. After he finished, the stitchers placed a wooden board at the ship's edge.

Commander Davis was first. The two stitchers lifted his body and placed him on the board, then raised the head end upward until his body slid off. Burns, Linky, and the rest heard the splash, seconds later. Burnham was next, followed by Ensign Pinegar, Lewis Grey, and the rest, until all of them were gone. Linky and the others trudged off, in search of sleep. As Burns walked the ship, he noticed a crewman on the bridge staring straight ahead. The man had been unable to look. John S. understood why. It was just too painful.

At latitude 16-40-00, longitude 120-05-00 E, the dark waters enveloped the 12 white canvas body bags that floated downward in formation, led by George F. Davis. Even in death the men of the *Walke* followed their Commander.

The next two days were slow. Burns traversed the ship, boosting morale. The men were still shell-shocked and grieving. They were like an offensive football team that had lost it quarterback and all of its receivers and backfield (five officers), except for Burns, the fullback. Without replacements, the new, untested signal caller had to pencil in a makeshift lineup because injuries had depleted his options. Many men were forced into unfamiliar positions. John S. was walking an eight-man front to the line of scrimmage with only himself in the backfield. In front of them was the full complement of the Japanese defense.

On the ninth of January, a Japanese plane dropped a bomb 50 yards off the starboard beam, but the shrapnel did little damage. They transferred another nine wounded to the *USS Rixey* hours after the first assault wave hit the beach. Before dawn on the tenth, enemy torpedo boats hit three ships in the Task Group. Midget subs were reported in the area. By 7:14 A.M., they helped down another plane, and at 7:04 P.M., the *Walke* splashed their last kamikaze, less than a thousand yards off the port bow.

The *Walke* passed under the Golden Gate Bridge on February 7 and entered the Mare Island Navy Yard in Vallejo. No welcoming committee or brass band was waiting for them. John S. and Dr. Link gazed down at the solitary figure standing on the deserted dock—the mother of Lewis Grey, clutching her purse with both hands. Exactly one month before, a man had come to her door and told her that her son had been killed. Since then, she had been waiting to hear one thing.

The two men exited the ship and walked up to the mother. She searched their faces and her eyes filled with tears as she clinched her purse and asked, "Can you tell me how my boy died?"

That afternoon, Burns was summoned by Admiral Tisdale, who told the Acting Commander to convey his gratitude and appreciation for a job well done to the men of the *Walke*. John S. was occupied with official duties until the following afternoon, when he took a car and drove the 22 miles to Berkeley. Pulling onto Carleton Street, he craned his neck looking for #1221 until he found it. He stopped the car and admired the view. Six blocks away was San Francisco Bay and the Golden Gate Bridge, and beyond that, the waters of the Pacific. Eleven families of the *Walke* could not see their loved ones' gravesites. Every time Mrs. George Davis stepped to her sidewalk, she gazed upon the water that led to her husband's.

John S. left the car and straightened his uniform. His well-polished shoes climbed the steps and he rang the doorbell. Mrs. Davis ushered him into the living room, where a two-year-old boy played with blocks. In the corner was a playpen where his seven-month-old brother slept.

The late afternoon sun infused the room with soft golden light as Lt. Burns and the widow sat on the couch. He recounted the last six weeks of the Commander's life, at length. Then he took her hands in his and told Mrs. Davis how her brave husband died.

Fitted with a new commander, new steel plates around the bridge, and fully repaired, the *Walke* shipped out in early April, with John S. as second-in-command. On July 31, 1945, Burns got his orders. It was six days before the atomic bomb was dropped on Hiroshima. He spent his last few hours on the ship with Dr. Link, and then quietly departed the *Walke*. In September when his orders came, Dr. Link slipped silently off the ship. Neither man could bear to say goodbye to their shipmates. The crew understood: it was just too painful.

Dr. Link was awarded the Bronze Star; Lt. John S. Burns received the Navy Cross. Commander George Fleming Davis was given the Medal of Honor, posthumously, and the *USS Davis* was named for him, along with a room at Bancroft Hall, a large residential hall for midshipmen at his alma mater, the US Naval Academy at Annapolis. Destroyer Squadron 60's tragedies led to fire retardant clothing being recommended for all men stationed on the bridge of destroyers. Steel plates were also added for additional protection.

Dr. Link started his private practice in 1950, far from Texas, with a loan from his favorite banker, John S. Burns. They remained good friends, forever. Linky came for OU-Texas games. Afterwards, the two would head for Laredo.

Sometimes they hooked up with their shipmates at reunions. One was held at a crewman's ranch in rural North Carolina. The men of the *Walke* enjoyed the barbecue as they imbibed "for medicinal purposes." Most of the crew over-medicated themselves that night. Lt. Commander Burns organized a convoy for what he knew would be a dicey drive back into Mayberry. He made the mistake of actually stopping at the only red light in town, which caused a four-car pileup involving no one but the members of the *Walke*. The local Barney Fife was determined to throw the shipload of elderly sailors into the hoosegow. Burns called the rancher, who contacted the local Andy Griffith. "If they're out of my county by 8 A.M., I'll forget about this." Burns was an early riser.

Dr. Link thinks about the men of the *Walke* "every day." John S. was no different. His mind was similar to a ship's bow: waves of memories would crash into his consciousness, spraying his mind with thoughts of his crewmen that would hang there like sea foam, before dissipating. At Barton Springs, he noticed a dark-haired man playing with his two young boys and thought of Davis, who never had that chance. And of the Commander's two sons, now middle-aged, whose lifetime physical connection with their father was limited to sliding their fingers across his Medal of Honor.

Burns saw young men flirting with girls on the hillside and thought of Grey and the others, who never had that opportunity. Unlike John S., they never got to marry a special woman like Hallie Bremond Houston, nor have three children like "Peaches," John Jr., or Billy. John S. made his mark in banking and civic endeavors. Grey's and others' lasting marks were on their hometown squares, where their names were etched in WWII monuments.

A cigarette prevented John S.'s name from appearing in Coleman, Texas, and he never forgot that, or his crewmen. For more than half a century, he conducted himself in a "nobly chivalrous and often self-sacrificing" manner—he did "go gallantly." His parents raised him that way, but he did it for another reason: to honor the memory of those who fought beside him and died, the men of the *USS Walke*.

A Gathering of Men

In the span of a decade, Mrs. Damon Philip Smith, Jr., buried her mother, husband, daughter, and a grandson. "Chu Chu" Smith was so devastated that her oldest son, Damon III, promised her, "You won't have to bury me." He was good with math and figured the odds on not keeping that pledge were one-in-a-million. On November 27, 2004, he died from Creutzfeld Jakobs disease, which strikes about 325 Americans each year. The one-in-a-million affliction would not be on anyone's short list of ways to go.

On December 3, I attended the graveside service in Damon's hometown of Llano with no intention of writing about it. Before the service my car passed Laird's BBQ, where a large group of men were spilling out of the restaurant. Twenty minutes later a nice convenience store clerk pointed me in the right direction to the cemetery where three dozen men were sporting the same fashion accessory. When the service concluded, I approached Chu Chu, but she was surrounded by a large contingent of friends, so I hugged her only remaining child, Hatch, then talked briefly with other relatives and walked to my car. Across the gravel road from the cemetery stood the old abandoned high school and its football field. I drove around the bend in the road and parked the car. Walking to the 50-yard line of the football field, I tried to absorb the simple setting. The words of an old rock song popped into my head, because the scene was a corollary to Damon. The song was released in 1971, the year Damon received his MBA from the University of Texas. As my car exited the Hill Country, the tune blared on my speakers. Certain lyrics seemed apropos to Damon's life, death, and funeral.

Late that night and the next, I wrote a 1,250-word letter to Chu Chu. Part of it was about my first gun-toting deer hunt at the age of 12, which took place on the Smiths' ranch. It was never my intention to the share the correspondence publicly, but the following weekend Ed Sharpe gave me some background on the gathering of men at Laird's BBQ, and he later e-mailed me the photo they had taken. Subsequent follow-up conversations with Ed and Sandy Watkins fleshed out the group, which was no stranger to tragedy. One member was unable to attend because he was convalescing from two weeks spent in a coma—fighting Bubonic plague. He survived but lost both his legs. One week before this article was published, a man in the photo was coming back to Austin from

Llano when he was involved in a one-car accident. He spent months in the Intensive Care Unit of Brackenridge Hospital, fighting for his life. He did not survive. The group has also encountered many other personal tragedies.

I asked Chu Chu if my letter to her could be re-worked into article form, and she consented. The personal contents have been excised and the role of the gathering of men has been expanded.

My great-uncle and namesake, Tudey Thornton, spent his career covering another gathering of men: for the first half of the 20th century, he was the Capitol reporter for the DALLAS MORNING NEWS. The original Tudey possessed five essential traits of a good writer/reporter. In no particular order, they are fair-mindedness, a sensitive and caring heart, a practiced ear, alert eyes, and an expansive vocabulary to formulate thoughts. In my brief career as a writer/reporter, a certain quadrant of our readership has accused me of possessing none of the above. Thankfully, the story requires only three. Damon's funeral was laced with an incongruity, just like life. It was sad, yet uplifting—a result of the tribute to him and his family made by a gathering of men. At least that's what I saw and heard and felt in my heart while standing in the Llano cemetery on that cold gray December day.

Damon Philip Smith III
"Pure and Easy"

Creutzfeldt-Jakob disease (CJD) is one of the prions, "a group of rare, invariably fatal brain disorders which occur both in humans and certain animals . . . which reportedly affects around one person per million per year," with 85 percent "occurring for no, as yet, known reason," (CJD Foundation website). The disease is a spongiform encephalopathy, the human equivalent of Mad Cow disease.

Damon Smith was dying from CJD and slipping away quickly, as Dr. Bill Birdwell flew to New Canaan, Connecticut, to say goodbye to his best friend. Their relationship had begun nearly four decades earlier, when they were college roommates for three years at the University of Texas. Bill sat with family members as Damon struggled to "be there" for the people he loved most. The doctor's daughter, Bonnie, called to express her love for Damon, who listened, and remembered that she had given birth to a daughter the month before. Damon mouthed into the phone "Love that baby."

The following morning, Damon had difficulty speaking. Bill prayed with him, held his hand, and said, "God loves you, and so do I." The dying man summoned the strength to squeeze his old roommate's hand tighter, and said, "God loves you." Bill soon left for the airport, comforted by those final words from his best friend. Six days later, Damon died.

At the cemetery in Llano, hundreds of people dressed in black endured the damp, 50-degree weather and a light wind. The sky looked like someone had pulled a dull, flat gray sheet across it. Part of the eulogy given by Damon's fraternity brother and business partner, Tex Gross, caused me to think back to the early 60s and a deer hunt on the Smiths' ranch. Dad had placed me in a concealed spot next to a dry creek bed, walked 50 yards away, and hidden himself. I was 12 years old; it was my first gun hunt and shivering in the freezing dawn air disguised my nerves. The sun rose through the trees and I squinted, seeing what looked like a tree limb move, then suddenly stop. Morning dew glistened off the dozens of limbs; the sun's glare shielded the shadowy figure. Dad saw it, and whispered, "Shoot it." My eyes searched for the buck, but the rising sun was blinding. Dad jumped up, his long white coat flapping around him as he stalked up the creek bed toward me. Pointing at the deer, he yelled, "Shoot it! Shoot it!" Frightened, the deer moved away from my father, and the safety of the sun's glare. The deer was running toward me swiftly through the thick brush. At close range, the gun's scope was useless. My finger squeezed off a shot that had no chance of finding its mark.

Minutes later, my father and I were standing over the dying buck. A one-in-a-million shot had pierced the deer's spine, and he jerked involuntarily for a few more seconds, took three shallow breaths, and expired. As we observed the magnificent animal, I explained my earlier predicament to Dad and he apologized, unaware of my struggle with the sun's glare. I had refused to tell him while it was happening. Back at camp, Philip and his sons, Damon and Hatch, were ecstatic for me; the eight-point buck was the third largest one bagged in Llano County on that opening day.

During the eulogy, Tex spoke of Damon's struggle with something infinitely worse than a blinding sun and of the man's refusal to tell others what he was enduring. Damon never revealed to most people that he had CJD; he just told them the name of his illness contained a bunch of long words. He was aware that if his friends learned the disease's name they would search the

Internet . . . and learn the prognosis. Men as majestic as Damon are rarer than the buck I saw. Maybe that was the reason some came to Llano on December 3: they respected the magnificent man who was felled by a fluke—a one-in-a-million disease—yet suffered his agony in quiet dignity.

Sprinkled throughout the throng of mourners on that hillock were dozens of men wearing burnt orange bow ties. The expression of solidarity was moving and no doubt comforting to the deceased man's family and friends. Damon's trademark had been bow ties, usually orange or burnt orange. During his visits to Austin for meetings at the University of Texas, Damon always wore a blue pinstripe suit and a burnt orange bow tie. The idea had come to Bill during that final visit with his best friend. After returning to Texas, Bill had scoured the Internet and found "Beau Ties," a small mail-order business, located in Middlebury, Vermont. They had to be burnt orange, but nothing on the website seemed quite right. A woman at the company named Jody assured Bill that tie #6306 was the one, so he ordered two dozen, then sent e-mails to a group of Damon's friends, informing them of the planned tribute. The quick response forced him to up the order to three dozen. Damon's sudden passing made it a rush job, and Jody enlisted extra help to make the silk shantung ties by hand. They arrived at Bill's home two days before the funeral.

On the day of the funeral, the group congregated at Laird's BBQ in Llano before the service, had lunch, and then donned the "pre-tied" neckwear. Damon was a purist—he only wore the "freestyle" models—but he would have agreed with this small concession, because he knew this group very well: tying bow ties was not their thing. All of the men in the photo were members of the Delta Tau Delta fraternity at UT with Damon between 1965-1969, and their sons. The one exception was the business partner of Tex and Damon. Tex thought it would be funny to have the Texas A&M grad sporting something burnt orange.

When these Delts entered UT, girls wore dresses to class, even in winter, and boys wore slacks and sport shirts. Two years later, pressed jeans were considered dressy. The group was buffeted by the Vietnam War protests, Charles Whitman's shooting spree from the UT Tower, contentious racial protests, the sexual revolution, and the advent of the drug culture. Those upheavals tested the resolve of the college boys but not their friendship. They became good friends, in part, because they shared a similar upbringing. Few hailed from the wealthy neighborhoods of Dallas, Houston, or other big cities in Texas. Most had been reared in the small towns of West and East Texas or the Hill Country. Their core values and beliefs ran as deep as the roots of the pine and post oak trees that had offered them shade during the hot summer months of their youth. It was an unpretentious bunch that joined the Delta Tau Delta fraternity and formed life-long bonds.

As they spilled out of Laird's BBQ, some of the middle-aged men lamented not donning the bow ties for Damon the previous April at the UT Delts' centennial gathering, months before the disease invaded his body. They lined up for the photo, then went to the graveside service, where their silent tribute was more than a celebration of his life: it revealed what his friendship meant to each one of his Delt brothers. At beautiesltd.com, all of the solid-color ties have names that are inventive reflections of the colors they represent, with one exception: #6306. The tie's name reflected the feelings of the Delts as they stared into the camera, a moment that truly was "Bittersweet."

Across the gravel road from the cemetery is the original high school football field, where Damon played for the Llano Yellowjackets. A few rows of sandstone rock bleachers were carved out of the hillside, like a Greek amphitheater. Above the stands, resting on stilts, is a dilapidated wooden press box the size of two deer blinds. This relic of football and Damon had been constructed the same way: pure and easy, which is also the title of a 1971 song by the rock band The Who.

The note is eternal
I hear it, it sees me
Forever we blended
Forever we die

Damon infused many people with his personality, and over the years it blended into his friends and especially his family. To some, he was the most generous person they had ever known; others considered him their best friend. Damon was someone who just gave and gave. After his death, his friends and family realized that they still carry a little bit of Damon inside them.

The noise that I was hearing was a million people cheering
And a child flew past me riding in a star

He probably touched the lives of hundreds of thousands of people through his extensive municipal bond business, and his church, community, and UT endeavors. As he went about improving the plight of others, his son Philip ascended into heaven. Two other Delts in the group had had sons die in car accidents. Bill Birdwell said, "When my son was buried, Damon was there." He always was. Damon knew the fragility of life's existence: he had experienced it, firsthand.

We all know success
When we all find our own dreams
And our love is enough
To knock down any walls
And the future's been seen
As men try to realize
The simple secret of the note in us all

His successes dwarfed the accomplishments of most people. And he also found his own dreams, because he reached out to others with love, understanding, and humility, which helped knock down the stereotypical walls of his post-collegiate environment, one that was vastly different from Llano, Texas. At Damon's memorial service, more than 1,200 mourners packed St. Mark's Episcopal Church in New Canaan, Connecticut. They wept at the passing of their fun-loving and humble Texan who had settled in New England.

He had found what many seek but fail to realize: inner peace. Damon never tried to be anything but what he was—a simple boy from the Texas Hill Country. His career had taken him far away from his childhood home, but it did not change the man, because Damon carried his roots with him everywhere he went.

There once was a note
Pure and easy
Playing so free, like a breath rippling by
There once was a note
Listen

The graveside mourners came from various backgrounds, cities, and professions, yet they shared a common experience that led them to that hilltop in Llano on a cold wintry day. At different times in their lives, all of them had listened to a note playing free as it floated through their lives, like a breath rippling by. It was pure and easy. The note was Damon Philip Smith III.

(Dr. Bill Birdwell contributed immensely to this story.)

The Strong Family

A Sooner Came Later

On a Wednesday night in 1996, my phone rang at 10 o'clock; it was not a social call. The voice on the other end belonged to Nannie Mae Strong, someone I had known a long time. My mother hired her when I was 12. By her own admission, when she stepped into our kitchen that first day, she could barely boil water. Mom's cooking prowess was legendary. Through hard work and determination Nannie Mae's culinary skills soon surpassed her employer's.

Her home in Clarksville was across the street from the legendary Italian restaurant Casiraghi's, until both were razed to make way for the Mopac Expressway. She moved to a house on Eason, behind Nau's Drug Store and Anthony's Cleaners, with her husband Freddie and their two children, Sandra and Wayne, both of whom went on to graduate from Austin High. Sandra enrolled at the UT School of Nursing and graduated cum laude. Later, she married Dr. Farris Blount and had two children, Farris, Jr., and Joshua. The Blounts now reside in Sugar Land, south of Houston, where Farris has a family practice.

Wayne played basketball and ran track in school. On Sundays he sang in the church choir, just as his father had. He explored various occupations after receiving his diploma from Austin High, until he started working at the Sigma Alpha Epsilon fraternity house on Pearl Street.

Long before then, Nannie Mae had transcended being an employee. In addition to raising her own brood, she was instrumental in rearing my brother Paul and me, a full-time job by itself. Later, our wives and children knew her simply as "Nannie," a nickname bestowed upon her by close friends and family. Despite that informality, she always addressed and referred to my parents as Mr. and Mrs. Teten. This seemingly stilted appellation was not out of deference but respect, which was reciprocated. Over the years, her workload at Mom's decreased, and Nannie Mae replaced that free time with younger and more lucrative employers, but she never traded in Mrs. Teten. Loyalty was one reason, but there were others.

Sweet Home Baptist Church in Clarksville was founded in 1871, and the current structure was erected in 1936, long before air-conditioning. On a sweltering Saturday in August, Sandra was married there. Mom was listed as the "Wedding Consultant."

Early on the day of the wedding, Freddie brought the gladiolas and greenery to Mom's house, to keep them from wilting in the stifling heat at the church. Mom's kitchen and breakfast area were jammed with water buckets filled with the floral displays for the ceremony, which were removed at the last possible moment. The decorations held up throughout the service.

In the wedding photos, Nannie Mae looked radiant in her mother-of-the-bride dress. The wedding consultant had picked out the fabric on their shopping trip and lent Nannie Mae some of her jewelry to complete the ensemble. Their relationship may have surprised some, but it shouldn't have. On days at the house on Possum Trot, and later at Mom's condo in Woodstone Square, many workdays were full and busy, with minimal chat. Before a party, there was always a bustle of activity. At erratic intervals between those events, the mothers would talk while working in the kitchen or seated at the breakfast table—conversations that often remained confidential, a hallmark of their mutual respect and friendship.

Mom tried to keep a few things from her friend, with mixed success. Late in 2002, she hid the onset of physical pain from others. Nannie Mae was the first to perceive a slight change in her health and alerted our family. Subsequent tests revealed the diagnosis—terminal cancer. After a short hospital stay, she came home for the final time and two days later confided to Nannie Mae, "I want Paul and Tudey and my rosary. . . I'm ready to go." Twenty-five hours later, to the minute, she passed away with her family and Nannie Mae there.

Days later, Paul and I joined Nannie Mae in the kitchen, handed her a small cream-colored bag with a drawstring and told her, "Mom wanted you to have this." She opened it and gazed at the large garnet ring. Then we told her the story. On December 27, 1997, our family was on vacation when Mom led the troops into Romancing the Stone, a jewelry store off the main square in Santa Fe. Scouring every display case, she waved off various offerings from the overly attentive and somewhat exasperated clerk, who finally asked, "What exactly are you looking for?" The pointed response: "I'll know when I see it." Mercifully, something came into view, and she tried it on. The daughters-in-law agreed it was the perfect selection. Holding out her hand and admiring the sparkle, she added, "Good, because someday it's going to be Nannie Mae's."

The home remained fully furnished for a long time, and Nannie Mae dropped by every day to water the plants or putter around the condo. Other times she just sat in a small chair on the back patio, gazing at the small garden. Letting go was harder than saying goodbye. Providing a respite from her grief was small consolation. I remembered the time my words were inadequate, that Thursday night when she called at 10 o'clock with the news about her 34-year-old son.

"Tudey, Wayne just died." Fifteen minutes later, Deborah and I were in a hallway at Brackenridge Hospital. My wife remained with Nannie Mae, and I went into the hospital room, which was dark except for the flickering images emanating from the television. Wayne was lying on the bed. The peaceful repose belied the battle he had waged with a rare blood disorder. His hands were folded together on his chest, above the sheet and blanket that covered him from the shoulders down. Freddie was leaning against the wall next to the bed, still standing watch over his son. A half-hour later he visited Wayne's young son, Fred, and the boy's mother, Loretta, and informed them of Wayne's passing. Days later, Freddie sang at Wayne's funeral.

Years later, Fred played football and basketball and ran track at O. Henry. At the end of his eighth grade year, he told Jenna McEachern he was not going to play football in high school. Jenna's home was filled with her two children, Bailey and Hays and Lester Simmons, but she always thought of Fred as her "fourth child." She jokingly told him, "You can't quit, you make my son look good!" Then she asked him who held the Austin middle school record for the longest pass reception. Fred didn't know. "You do, 99 yards from Hays McEachern." The pass covered five yards, Fred did the rest.

Wayne never got to see his son play sports, but Fred kept his memory alive. He brought some maroon-and-white block "A" athletic letters, the kind put on letter jackets, to O. Henry for a class project. They were his father's, from Austin High. Early in his freshman year at Austin High, Nannie Mae, Freddie, and Loretta asked Debbie Hanna to be Fred's academic mentor. She helped map out his course curriculum and was his advocate at the large school. The two were in constant communication, which continues to this day.

The Hannas' affinity for Fred grew from their relationship with his father. Debbie's husband, Mark, was president of the SAE House Corporation during the seven years Wayne worked there, and Wayne was often a guest in their home. He enjoyed being around people. As Nannie Mae said, "Wayne never met a stranger." That truth was evident on a day in 1992, when Mark drove Wayne to the fraternity house for a surprise induction ceremony. The active members presented Wayne with a proclamation making him an honorary member of the Sigma Alpha Epsilon fraternity.

The SAEs also raised funds for Fred's college education. With capable stewardship from Don Sanders, the amount escalated in value. Before he died, Wayne had confided to Debbie, "I dream of Fredrick going to college." Fred, the third generation choir singer, was well on his way. As it turned out, he didn't need the money for his education.

Every year in high school, Fred would confide to the McEacherns that he wanted to drop football. Every year Randy counseled him to continue, reminding Fred he possessed a gift few athletes are granted: unsurpassed talent.

Hays' and Fred's senior year they played a rival school whose students sported t-shirts that read "Fred is ugly" beneath a photo of the wide receiver. Trailing 38-0 in the third quarter, quarterback Hays suggested a play to the coach, who didn't think much of the play but agreed to let Hays run it. Taking the snap, Hays scrambled around and lofted a 30-yard pass to Fred, who had slipped past two defenders in the end zone. Fans on the other side even asked, "Where's that play been all night?" Fred languished as a decoy much of the season, but his talent did not go unnoticed. A shoebox at Nannie Mae's soon filled with letters from universities and colleges that wanted Fred to play for them. When one recruiter promised Fred's grandmother he would bring his boss to her residence for Fred's home visit she was a little skeptical. Until it happened.

Fred was selected for the all-district team and the academic all-district team in football his senior year. Debbie joined him on recruiting trips to college campuses. Tours of the facilities were followed by interviews with head coaches, offensive coordinators, and specialty coaches. The recruit watched game film with the coaches. They fired intricate football questions at Fred, who handled them with aplomb. Debbie enjoyed helping the young man; he was always quick with a hug, a smile, and a "Thank you."

Still undecided after his visits, Fred called Jenna. "G-Momma, can we talk? Right now?" G-Momma went to his house and picked up Fred. Jenna and Randy were guardians of Hays' and Fred's teammate and friend, Lester Simmons, who gave her the nickname Guardian Momma, which the boys abbreviated. Fred and G-Momma drove around Austin for an hour as Fred weighed his options and their respective pros and cons. Jenna finally asked him, "Who wants you the most?"

On January 14, 2004, Austin High was playing basketball against the school with the t-shirt collection. Late in the game, Fred was fouled and went to the charity stripe. Three hundred students from that school erupted in singsong, "Fred is ugly, Fred is ugly." The object of their ire smiled while shooting the free throws. He made both of them. Austin High won by two points. Fred was bemused by the boorish attention, but he also grinned because he knew what awaited him at his grandparents' house: the two men who would make Wayne's dream come true.

The Clarksville neighborhood contains some unique history, as Judge Joe Greenhill and his wife Martha found out driving home one night after a party. Wanting to show my mother where the couple lived when they first moved to Austin, he drove to the area. The Greenhills had resided in a new rent house for nine months, until WWII broke out and Joe enlisted. Pulling onto Eason Street he pointed to it and Mom broke out in laughter, "That's Nannie Mae's house!" As Fred drove home after the basketball game, the one-time residence of a former Chief Justice of the Texas Supreme Court was preparing to welcome the head football coach of Oklahoma University.

Assistant Head Coach Bobby Jack Wright had told Nannie Mae months before, "Bob Stoops is going to be in your living room." True to his word, the two waited in the car for 30 minutes until Fred arrived and then followed him inside. For one hour, Bob Stoops sat in her living room selling the virtues of Oklahoma to Fred's mother and grandparents. A prior commitment prevented me from attending, but there was a suitable replacement—Nannie Mae's brother, Donald Holmes. Fortunately for the coaches, Donald's vote didn't count.

Bob Stoops was not accustomed to The Donald, who sat in a corner dressed in his burnt orange TEXAS shirt, eyeing the men. "Coach Stoops, what happened to you guys against LSU?" The Tigers had recently defeated the Sooners in the National Championship game. Bobby Jack and Bob took it in stride and stressed not only the athletics but also the academic support offered by the institution. Fred was already sold; Donald went down fighting. The visit concluded with a photo session. Flanked by both smiling coaches,

Donald grinned, raised his hands and gave the Hook'em Horns sign as the flash went off.

Fred's uncle wasn't the only one having trouble with the choice. In church a few months before the photo shoot, Fred whispered his intention to the head usher, who relayed the news to the pastor, who informed the congregation. Immediately, Nannie Mae was bombarded with questions, "OU? OU?" "You're letting him go to OU?" In hindsight, Fred was smart; at least his grandmother was in church where no cursing was tolerated.

On National Signing Day, Fred inked his commitment in the Austin High cafeteria. Randy McEachern, a former UT quarterback, was the master of ceremonies, and ended the festivities by saying, "Boomer Sooner." The comment wasn't only for Fred; Hays McEachern was going to walk on at OU. He is now the third-string quarterback, the same spot his father was in, until the second quarter of the 1977 Texas-OU game, when Randy came off the bench and led Texas to an undefeated season before losing the title game to Notre Dame.

Fred red-shirted his freshman year but still suited up for games and received the gold watch awarded to the Big XII Champions. Before leaving for the National Championship Game in Miami, the family opened Christmas presents. Nannie Mae's gift from Fred was a frame with two team photos. One was taken at the Cotton Bowl after the 2004 game, celebrating five years of beating Texas; the other was snapped following the Conference Championship game. Fred knows how much she likes the Longhorns, but she proudly displays the gift in her hallway. He gave his grandfather the gold watch.

Sprinkled in the burnt orange contingent at this year's game, a group of SAEs will be rooting for Texas. They will also offer encouragement to Fred, returning a gesture extended to them by his father, the man who "never met a stranger." The walls of the chapter room at their house on Pearl Street contain two pictures of the previous SAE residences at UT. Over the years many notable and famous alumni were initiated; none of their portraits appear on the walls. The lone photo in the room is of Wayne Strong, next to the proclamation naming him an honorary SAE.

Wayne knew human existence resembled football; both are filled with spectacular victories and devastating losses. He understood that the most important aspect was how a person conducted himself throughout the game of life. On the night Wayne died, the television in his hospital room was tuned to a football game, his second passion. His first was spending time with Fred, who often thinks about his gentle, loving father, especially on OU-Texas weekend. Wayne Strong passed away on Wednesday night, October 9, 1996, and he was buried on Saturday; the day of the OU-Texas game. Boomer Sooner, Fred, Boomer Sooner.

Alec Beck

A Tribute

An hour before Alec Beck's memorial service on April 17, 2006, Tarrytown United Methodist Church was packed with mourners. Friends continued to stream in and were diverted to the Fellowship Hall, Choir Room, and other parts of the Church. This is not an obituary; it's merely an observation on why people endured the hottest April day in Austin's history to pay their respects.

(All lyrics are from "ANGEL," by Sarah McLachlan)

Spend all your time waiting for that second chance.

When we lived in Northwest Hills, my family invited friends to the N. W. Hills 4th of July parade. After we moved to Tarrytown in October 1990, those former guests asked, "Now, what do we do on the 4th of July?" I suggested starting an annual Tarrytown Parade. The idea lay dormant, until Alec got wind of it. Within weeks, he had assembled a committee of two dozen volunteers. Some people fear failure; they spend time waiting for someone else to act first. Alec Beck was not one of those people.

I need some distraction, oh beautiful release
Memories seep from my veins

Everyone he met can recall his smile. When Alec approached you, his face beamed. His smile was genuine and sincere and went much deeper than the dimples that formed on his cheeks: it sprang from his heart.

He was also a "hugger." That physical activity was a metaphor for his human existence: Alec Beck embraced life. Few people possessed more "joie de vivre." And whenever something positive occurred, which it often did around him, Alec would demonstrably utter his favorite phrase, "That's what I'm talking about!"

Alec's most striking attribute was his positive attitude. It not only defined him, the can-do spirit he exuded is what caused many to follow him into various community endeavors without reservation.

Every one of his projects presented challenges. If a seemingly insurmountable obstacle was placed in front of him, Alec found a way to hurdle it. If a roadblock appeared, he created a detour around it; his vision was not limited to the straight line.

Most artists do not see the world in black and white, or follow a predetermined route. They delight in exploring opaque areas, and their vision allows them to see and paint vibrant colors that others miss. Alec was an unconventional artist; he used his community as his canvas. That first parade notwithstanding, he understood that thinking outside the box was often required to make a successful project, and in doing so he helped create vibrant, colorful showpieces, including the YMBL Sunshine Camp, St. Andrew's Upper School, and the Austin Golf Club, to name a few.

Where some people saw a simple parade, Alec envisioned a grander tableau: the opportunity for parents to help children design and decorate parade bikes . . . the opportunity for neighbors along the route to host large, family-based picnics as they cheered on the parade participants . . . the opportunity for neighbors, families, and friends to congregate at the end of the parade route, and revel in the gifts we Americans have been so blessed to receive.

A man had built a first-class playhouse for his five-year-old daughter. Even without the roof attached it weighed a ton. He needed help transporting the building from his father's garage to his own backyard a few blocks away, so he called Alec, who showed up around 4 P.M. with two of his workmen from Stripling-Blake Lumber Company, a heavy forklift and a long flatbed truck used to transport lumber and trusses. Alec admired the craftsmanship of the playhouse: custom front door, insulation in the roof and walls, double pane windows, electricity, and wood floors.

When the roof was attached to the backyard playhouse two hours later, Alec refused the man's offer of payment, and Alec and his men climbed into the truck and drove away in the darkness. It was 6 P.M., on Christmas Eve.

Alec liked the little house so much he got permission to duplicate the structure, and the first two built by the lumber company were donated to the Junior League of Austin, who sold them at their annual Christmas Affair gala. Bidders paid over $5,000 for each at the silent auction.

In this sweet madness, oh this glorious sadness, that brings me to my knees

Alec thrived on competition; people said he abhorred coming in second. But even when he finished first he was not always pleased, because Alec was never competing against anyone else, only himself. And his standards were very high.

That is why others joined him in community endeavors; they knew Alec would give his best effort, and make the project noteworthy.

In the arms of an Angel, fly away from here

Alec perished in a helicopter accident, but I choose to believe he did not experience much pain. Words from one book concur and provide comfort to his cohorts and family; the same individuals who smile when they think of Alec's first words in heaven.

In her book ***Embraced by the Light,*** Betty Eadie described her near-death experience and concomitant journey to heaven. "When we 'die,' my guides said, we experience nothing more than a transition to another state. Our spirits slip from the body and move to a spiritual realm. If our deaths are traumatic, the spirit quickly leaves the body, sometimes even before death occurs. . . [the] spirit may be taken from [the] body before [we] experience much pain. The body may actually appear still alive . . . but the spirit will have already left and be in a state of peace."

Upon arriving at that state of peace, Alec likely surveyed the immense beauty of his celestial surroundings, smiled, and said, "That's what I'm talking about!"

You're in the arms of the angel; may you find some comfort there

Alec Beck fully embraced life, up until the moment he was embraced by the Light. He has found comfort there.

Throughout his life, he mentored many individuals, especially his family and close friends. Although he is no longer here to lead them through life's parade, they will continue on, in part because of his teachings. But they are not alone in the journey. Thousands of people share the same immutable thought that consumes his family and friends. We miss you, Alec.

Brian Newberry: "A Wonderful Life"

In the movie *It's a Wonderful Life*, Clarence the Angel says to Jimmy Stewart's character, "You see, George, you've really had a wonderful life." George Bailey and Brian Newberry have things in common: both raised four children and became pillars of their respective communities. Their disparities were glaring. Bailey spent much of his life in quiet desperation, longing to leave his hometown of Bedford Falls. Brian longed to remain in Austin for a lifetime. Most importantly, George was a figment of a writer's imagination, viewable only on a silver screen. Brian Newberry is real.

Helen Newberry gave birth to Brian on March 30, 1945, in Colorado Springs, Colorado, where her husband Jack, a/k/a "J.D." worked in the intelligence service for the government. J.D. and his brother Gatewood had graduated from Baylor University with business degrees, and when J.D. returned to Austin the two men looked for a business to purchase together. A pharmacy that opened in Tarrytown on December 8, 1941, was for sale and they bought it. Gatewood later sold his interest to J.D.

Brian and his younger siblings Neal, Keith, and Sharon lived in a house on Cherry Lane. Their backyard neighbor was Veldon Lemens, who later worked with Neal for two decades at the Tarrytown Texaco/Shell service station. When the Newberrys moved to Mt. Laurel Lane, there were only eight houses on the street; the terrain behind the home was a giant sprawling forest. The kids spent countless days and hours exploring the virgin land, hunting with BB guns, building hideaways and secret forts. Living in West Austin back then meant never having to leave; nearly everything was available in the Tarrytown Shopping Center. Jack Ritter's men's shop, Bettis Electronics, a hardware store, gas stations, restaurants, a 5 and 10 store (now the Post Office), and a barber shop were located in the center. The freestanding building on the East Side of Exposition Blvd housed Dr. Archer's family practice and Dr. Fuller's dentist office. Every store was family-owned.

For a brief period, you could even find religion there. Before The Church of the Good Shepherd was built, members held their first service at the Center. Tarrytown Pharmacy was in the space now occupied by Seattle's Best Coffee. Just inside the door, to the right were pinball machines; ahead was the cash register and the comic book stand. Just beyond that, the soda fountain stretched almost to the back, where a wooden phone booth stood. Kids would come in and order a burger and shake, put it on their parents' charge account, and read the comic books for free while they ate at the counter. After eating they would stuff the comics filled with their greasy fingerprints back into the bins. J. D. never raised a fuss.

The first job for many young Austin men was being a soda jerk at the fountain. Future UT Chancellor Dan Burck was one, although his altercation with one particular chocolate milkshake almost abruptly ended his career. Laverne Lundquist was another, although he dropped the "La" from his name before he became the voice of the Dallas Cowboys, and later an announcer for CBS.

J.D. expected his sons to get their health cards at the age of 14 and pitch in. Brian started as a soda jerk at 13, working for $0.24 a night. The fountain shut down at 9 P.M., an hour before the pharmacy closed, and the cleanup usually took 30 minutes. Upon finishing, Brian would go next door to the gas station. There were usually a few drops of gasoline trapped in the pumps, and he meticulously emptied the fuel into his Cushman scooter. If he was lucky, the night's haul would yield 1/10th of a gallon; enough to allow him to fire up the scooter and go shooting down the streets of Tarrytown, exploring the quiet neighborhoods as the wind brushed through his hair.

The streets weren't always bucolic. On Halloween night in 1958, a few hundred teenagers suddenly appeared at the intersection of Windsor Road and Exposition Boulevard. Within minutes they cordoned off the area with chains they connected around the four corner telephone poles. The dance party ended with the arrival of the police, but the event made headlines in papers across the state. The bar had been set for future teens. Halloween night four years later a group of boys stood atop the doctors' building and shot bottle rockets at fellow miscreants perched atop a building 30 yards away at Broaddus' gasoline station. A cop was called to the scene and stopped the fireworks war before anything, or anyone, went kablooey. The local gendarme went after one fireworks fanatic on foot, and the chase coursed through the adjoining streets and lasted way too long. The policeman returned to the center empty-handed and found out the juvenile wasn't the only thing that got away. His patrol car was on cinder blocks. The tires were gone, and so were the boys. The following Halloween, J.D. and John Schooley, a pharmacy employee, stood guard on the roof of the establishment. They weren't taking any chances.

Brian ascended the workforce chain from soda jerk to manning the front cash register and eventually became the deliveryman. He drove the pharmacy's old Chevy pickup. The first car he bought was a 1958 red Oldsmobile 88 convertible with power windows and a tilt steering wheel. J.D. was still puttering around in a 1953 VW Beetle and chuckled, calling his son "Diamond Jim." In spite of his needling, Brian's father was proud of his son, because the boy had worked hard to earn the money for the automobile.

At Austin High, Brian played cornet in the band. He enrolled at Texas in the fall of 1963, the year of the school's first National Championship in football. Later he became the rush captain of the Pi Kappa Alpha fraternity and orchestrated a rush party at the River Oaks Country Club, where his fellow Maroon alumnus Al Staehely performed with his band. Two of the rushees at the party were Neal and Veldon.

After graduating from Pharmacy School at UT, Brian's career decision was easy. His parents had always been his role models, pillars of the community. He was attracted to the community-oriented world, and in those days most pharmacists were independents or worked for one who was. His parents poured their jobs into Tarrytown, and their lives. Their son did the same.

Brian bought out his father in 1973. The soda fountain commanded 20 percent of the store's space, the grease wafted over all the store's merchandise and it competed with the Holiday House. His first official act was traumatic: he shut down the restaurant portion of the store. Two days after Brian tore out the fountain Mike Levy came in. To Mike, Tarrytown Pharmacy served up the quintessential All-American burger and milkshake. He told the new proprietor he would always be a loyal customer, but he would be an even more loyal customer if the fountain remained. Brian said, "If you want to sublease the space I'll let you run it." Mike kept his word, and like many others he has remained a loyal supporter to this day.

The Vietnam War was winding down, but Brian joined the Army Reserves at Camp Mabry as an enlisted man, along with 28 other recruits. Twenty-eight were placed in a medical company; Brian was put in a supply unit. He later changed to the Air Force Reserves and immediately went from enlisted man to Second Lieutenant.

Brian knew the value of working in an environment where people got along with each other. Mrs. Tiemann and Dorothy Polvado both worked at the Pharmacy for over 40 years. Numerous employees stayed with him for two decades; the stock manager has been there for 15 years, and many of the pharmacists have dispensed prescriptions and offered advice for more than a decade. It is a good place to work, patronized by a good clientele.

Mike Levy said that walking into Brian's establishment is like a time warp: you re-enter an era where people who wait on customers care about them, and it's comforting, knowing you're dealing with friends you can be trust. Perhaps some prescriptions can be bought for less somewhere else, but you know at Tarrytown it will be done right . . . and by friends.

Running a neighborhood family business for more than three decades allowed Brian to hire hundreds of youngsters and pass along his work ethic to them. For the majority of them it is their first work experience, stocking the shelves and running the cash register, the same as it was for Brian and his brothers. His wife Gail has also been a mainstay, having salved the pain from the demise of the soda fountain by adding a first-rate gift and retail section to the pharmacy, which moved to its current spot in 1985.

Brian's egalitarian approach extends to his patrons. Many governors, from Coke Stevenson to Rick Perry have trusted Brian and his staff. Congressman Jake Pickle and President Johnson were clients. Brian treated all of his constituents the same way. Duke Covert would call Brian to get an explanation of the medicines. After Brian was diagnosed with pancreatic cancer a few years ago, Duke often stopped by the store to discuss the situation with his friend. If Duke had to catch an early flight and was out of medicine, Brian would meet him at the pharmacy and open up just to fill a prescription. He opened the doors late at night to help people, too. That's what Brian Newberry is all about: helping others. Not in a flashy, showy manner. He does it the manner his father taught him—with selfless concern for others.

A childhood friend, Dr. Malone Hill, said, "He is a mentor of mine. I've learned from and admired Brian throughout my life."

Duke said, "He is the epitome of a good father, person, businessman and friend. His integrity is impeccable."

Integrity was the most referenced word on Merriam Webster's online dictionary last year. The definition is "firm adherence to a code of especially moral or artistic values." Brian's life has been defined by integrity.

His four children: Paige, Blair, Mark, and Joe mirror the values and commitment to community their father learned from his parents. Mark recently took over the pharmacy, and the others still live here. Brian remains close with his three siblings, and their five children. All nine of the cousins are good friends. At the rehearsal dinners last year for Mark and Joe, their siblings and cousins performed skits. The Newberrys support and thrive on each other.

Brian notices the same characteristics in his neighborhood. "Despite the societal changes, it is amazing that the Tarrytown community has held together and still has a small town feel to it. Many people can afford to buy a larger home in Westlake but they purchase a smaller home in West Austin, because they are willing to make a sacrifice to be near their parents and the community that raised them." Those who enter the pharmacy are a testament to that observation: a lot of them are third generation customers.

At the 2002 Fourth of July Parade Brian and Neal were co-Grand Marshals. When Brian spoke he asked the crowd to "Stop and think about how lucky we are to live in the best country, the best state, the best city and the best neighborhood on Earth. We are so blessed." For decades he expended innumerable hours making this neighborhood special, through his involvement in so many endeavors they are too numerous to mention.

What type of man is Brian Newberry? As his life draws to an end, he muses that he could have done more for others. The number of citizens who have done more for this city than Brian can be counted on the fingers of one hand. Yet he has few regrets, because he truly had a wonderful life. It involved a copious amount of hard work and resolve, but the rewards are incalculable.

One of the last lines in *It's a Wonderful Life* is a toast by Harry Bailey to his brother George, "To the richest man in town!" Brian is that man, in every way that matters. And we are the beneficiaries of his largesse because each of us, whether we realize or not, have benefited from Brian Newberry. The children he raised, those he nurtured with employment, the many he helped heal, and the countless number aided by his generosity continue to ripple through our community, enriching us all.

Standing on the porch of his home a month ago we hugged and I repeated what I first told him a year ago. "Each of us has a small list of role models; people we try to emulate. We have even fewer heroes. You are both to me."

A fanatical supporter of UT, Brian attended every home game in 2005 and the Ohio State game in Columbus. Mark had tickets to this year's Rose Bowl, but his plans changed. He spent the evening with the crown jewel of the Newberry clan, his father, "Diamond Jim." On January 4, when Texas played USC, Brian and Gail watched with their children and spouses, and Neal. Boisterous cheers preceded high fives throughout the whole game at the home on Windsor Road. Afterwards Brian said, "I've seen all four National Championships." It was a great night for UT, but an even more memorable one for the Newberrys.

This past Monday night some old neighbors from Cherry Lane got together: Brian, his younger brother Neal, and the kid from across the back yard, Veldon Lemens. For over five decades they lived and worked in close proximity to each other. For three hours that night the trio traveled back in time to a period when Tarrytown was the epicenter of their universe. It still is for Brian, and with good reason. For more than three decades Brian has been the center of the Tarrytown Shopping Center.

Jimmy Stewart was asked to explain the success of *It's a Wonderful Life*. His response could have described Brian's life, which began 54 weeks before Stewart's favorite movie began production. "It's simply about an ordinary man who discovers that living each ordinary day honorably, with faith in God and a selfless concern for others, can make for a truly wonderful life."

The Black Swan

Part One: Early Years

In the winter of 2001, a few players decided to surprise our old basketball coach Jim Haller. The 1971 graduating class of Austin High was holding its 30-year reunion four months later, and the organizers wanted this meeting included in a commemorative video. Jim had come from McCallum High to Austin High our senior year, and after a few seasons he moved on to coach at McLennan County Junior College and then Baylor University, before becoming a banking bigwig in Waco. His love of basketball endured and on that Tuesday night in 2001 he was the color analyst for the University of Texas game televised on the Fox Sports Southwest network. A confederate from our grade worked at the network and was in on the prank, and he placed Jim in front of a camera on the floor of the Frank C. Erwin Center. As our former coach provided a taped pre-game commentary, he did not see Mark Jones, Ben Wear, and me creeping up from behind. Seeing three of his least important players in the flesh again really was a surprise.

Being the team motor mouth, I grabbed the microphone and asked him to describe our squad. Without skipping a beat, Coach Haller looked into the camera, grinned, and said, "You couldn't shoot, you couldn't dribble, and you couldn't pass, but you were the smartest team I ever coached." His last observation was the most accurate. Peter Barbour published his first novel in 2006. Mark Looney, writing under the name Mark Doyle, has authored numerous books, and Ben Wear is a columnist for the AUSTIN AMERICAN STATESMAN. We writers were among the most eloquent members of the team, and the dumbest.

Ben asked him, "Do you remember our record?"

Jim spouted, "24-9."

Stunned by his memory, Ben posed a follow up question, "How did you remember that?"

"Because you were the only championship team I ever coached."

According to the University Interscholastic League archives, Austin High's 19 trips to the boy's State basketball tournament are the most by any school, even though the Maroons' last appearance was in 1961. From that date until the late 1990s, the school managed just two or three district championships. Someone suggested listing those championship seasons on banners and hanging them from the rafters in the Roosevelt C. Nivens gymnasium. Historians did a pretty good job of researching the records to ensure all the winners were included; only one squad was omitted—the 1971 team. We were an easy bunch to overlook, except for one person. What follows is about that exceptional exception as viewed through my eyes. To better understand what follows requires a short backdrop.

The original Austin High School opened its doors in 1881. Three years later, the first high school for blacks in Austin, Robertson Hill School, opened on the corner of East 11th and San Marcos Streets. Two of the three subsequent moves occurred while Laurine Cecil Anderson was principal. The son of slave parents, Anderson was born in Tennessee in 1853. After attending Fisk University in Nashville, he came to Texas. Governor Oran M. Roberts made Anderson the head of Prairie View Normal and Industrial College (later renamed Prairie View A&M). He was the first elected president of the Colored Teachers State Association and later accepted the position of principal at Robertson Hill School in 1896 and remained there for 32 years, until he retired. The school was renamed for Anderson's brother in 1909, but two days after Laurine Cecil Anderson passed away in 1938, the Austin School Board unanimously renamed the institution L.C. Anderson High School.

All blacks, regardless of where they lived, had to attend Anderson, including those in Clarksville. Settled in 1871, that area northeast of West Tenth and the current Mopac Railroad tracks became home to a large portion of Austin's black community led by its founder, Charles Clark, who bought the initial two acres from a Confederate general. Many of the freed slaves worked in the homes or businesses of the affluent white neighborhoods that surrounded Clarksville. Yet 80 years after it was settled, fourth-generation Clarksville students were still forced to ride the bus to Anderson High.

Most of them walked past the all-white Mathews Elementary on their way to the bus stop. They paid a nickel and boarded the bus that carried them eastward, down the steep bank of West 12th Street and up another hill, past the Austin High campus at the corner of Rio Grande and West 12th Streets, a distance of 7/10ths of a mile. The bus continued on for five or six blocks, then skirted around the State Capitol Building and motored onto 11th Street for another six blocks until it crossed over East Avenue, which later became Interstate Highway 35, the physical divide between black and white Austin. Traveling down 11th Street, the bus passed the original Anderson location and the black-owned establishments that lined the road. In the old days, the public transport would veer right at the fork in the road where 11th Street joined with Rosewood Avenue, and drift past the elementary school the students had attended, Blackshear. Starting in 1953, when the new Anderson was built, the bus driver veered left at the fork and rambled past Kealing, the first black junior high school, and deposited the Clarksville students at the Anderson campus, 3.2 miles from home. It was reverse busing: sending black students that lived in the white part of town to the black part of town to be educated.

Albert Sidney Johnston High School, named for a general in the Confederate Army, opened on the east side of town in 1960 with a racial mix of 10% white, 30% hispanic, and 60% black. From its inception, Johnston was allowed to compete against the other schools in the Austin Independent School District. L.C. Anderson High School was not added to the mix until the 1968-69 school year. The majority of other high schools in Austin were either all-white or predominantly white except for Travis, which was mostly hispanic.

To achieve some semblance of balance, in the late 1950s the school board gave students living in the Anderson and Johnston areas the option of attending Austin High. The number of minorities went from a handful to more than 50% within a decade. In terms of integration, Austin High was years ahead. From January 1970 through May 1971, *Time* ran 40 articles on desegregation, and one of those talked about Austin High, because the institution was among the most racially diverse high schools in America: 40% white, 30% black, and 30% Hispanic. Most of my classmates thought the integration problems had been solved, but in some ways they were only beginning, which is where we now take up the story.

Sportswriters referred to the contest held on January 20, 1968, as the "game of the century." The UCLA Bruins, led by Lew Alcindor (who later changed his name to Kareem Abdul-Jabbar) were riding a 47-game winning streak and playing the University of Houston Cougars, led by Elvin "the big E" Hayes. It was the first regular season game shown on national television and the inaugural basketball contest in the cavernous Astrodome. Alcindor suffered from double vision, the result of a scratched eye a few days earlier,

281

and Houston eked out a 71-69 victory paced by Elvin Hayes' 33 points. Each time Hayes scored, the giant Astrodome scoreboard flashed a blinking, giant "E," and the 52,693 in attendance would chant "E" in syncopation. But the Bruins seemed unfazed by the enormous, partisan crowd; Alcindor did not allow himself to be intimidated.

Weeks afterwards in Austin, the O. Henry Junior High Mustangs played the Martin Junior High Eagles. Neither school's gym could accommodate a large crowd, so the powers that be shifted the game to a neutral site: Austin High. That was the official reason given for the unprecedented change; the real one was less palatable.

During the summers of 1965-1967, race riots broke out in some of the larger metropolitan cities in America, the Ku Klux Klan was terrorizing desegregation protestors throughout the South, and the angst and frustration seeped into the Austin community, which numbered less than 200,000. No problems surfaced on the courts during district games, but the possibility frightened the school district enough to move the junior high tilt to a neutral site.

The Eagles relished taking on a bunch of rich kids from the west side, although none of the Mustangs' players resided in the big houses in Old Enfield and Pemberton Heights; we lived in average middle class homes. Their perception was as ill-founded as the comment we had heard: if you drove down East 11th or East 12th Streets at night, the sidewalks would be teeming with pimps, prostitutes, and drug dealers.

When we strode into the antiquated gym that February afternoon, the stands weren't filled with rich kids and drug dealers; the north side bleachers were filled with 500 Mustangs' supporters, almost all of them white. Across the court, 500 fans of the Eagles, most of them black, sat in anticipation. At 6'2", Jack Nash was our biggest player, and he crouched down at center court as the referee prepared to toss the jump ball into the air to start the game. Jack's opponent in the circle was a skinny 6'6" player from Martin, Tyrone Johnson, who soared above Jack and flipped the ball to a teammate.

We kept the game close for about 30 seconds. Regardless of where Tyrone received the ball, he elevated, raised his long arms high above his head and, at their apex, released a shot that usually went in. He was unstoppable, which made the final score of 65-53 almost a victory for O. Henry, because Martin had annihilated their first eight opponents by at least 30 points.

The Eagles' trash talking was new to us. The ever-present jawboning was often spoken in jest. At other times it was a verbal beat down that coincided with their dominance on the court. Throughout the contest, Tyrone never said a word; he just played the game. In the first quarter, a group of Martin students who were wedged in the corner beneath the scoreboard started playing drums, and their classmates started singing African songs in a foreign dialect. Until that point, the idea of actually winning was still in our heads. We got psyched out and never recovered. Late in the game, I was standing next to my teammate Peter Barbour at midcourt while someone attempted foul shots and said, "Never again." He appeared non-plussed by my comment, so I explained, "We will never be this intimidated again." Peter nodded, but his expression said, "Yeah, okay, whatever you say."

The squads queued up for the customary post-game handshake and, wanting to be last, I went to the end of our team's line. When Tyrone extended his hand I said, sotto voce, "We sure could use you at Austin High." He threw his head back and laughed, then patted my shoulder and moved on. I watched him walk back to the Martin bench. There was no swagger from beating the "rich kids," only the self-assured gait of a boy who knew he had performed well. He seemed oblivious to the racial overtones that pervaded the gym—he was there simply to play basketball. With his graceful moves and gracious demeanor, Tyrone reminded me of a black swan, and I wanted him to choose Austin High over Johnston for a reason other than sports: he was a class act, a person I wanted to befriend.

Weeks later, I took the bus over to Gregory Gym on the University of Texas campus. Built in 1930, the un-air-conditioned structure was the site of the University Interscholastic League boys' high school State championships. The Houston Wheatley Wildcats, the scourge of the all-black Prairie View Interscholastic League for more than a quarter century, had made the finals in their inaugural UIL season. Opposing them was a perennial visitor to Austin in March: the Thomas Jefferson Rebels from Dallas. The Rebels had won the title in 1962, and finished third the next year. Jefferson drew its students from an affluent part of Big D; the team was all white.

After paying for my ticket, I entered the old gym and climbed the stairwell to the mezzanine; the game was underway and I knew the floor level was full. I entered the arena and looked around. A stage marked the east end of the lower level, which was filled out by ten rows of wooden bleachers that formed an intimate U around the basketball court. The steep concrete rows of the mezzanine were fitted with wooden planks for seating. Whites occupied one-half of the gym, blacks packed the other. I had wandered into the "other" section and had two choices: walk across the long aisle and join the white people or plop down somewhere close and soon—my lily-white skin was attracting attention.

An elderly black man on the first row nodded at me and I took that as a positive sign. "May I sit here?" He nodded again and squinched against the person next to him, creating an aisle seat. I smiled, sat down, and said, "Thank you, sir."

Puzzled, he asked, "Son, you lost?"

I shook my head, "I, I don't think so."

"You pulling for the Wildcats?"

"You mean the 'Mighty, Mighty Wildcats'?" He laughed and returned his attention to the game.

The term "hully-gully" has been used in Texas basketball circles for decades, probably dating back to 1968 when major newspaper reporters started covering Wheatley on a regular basis. The word they used to describe the mayhem that was Wildcats' basketball means "haphazard, disorganized, inconsistent, *loosey-goosey*," and a joy to watch. Throughout the game, my seatmate explained the intricacies and nuances of the frenzied action, and the hully-gully pace began to make sense. When a long shot was attempted, the elderly man yelled, "Face!" I had no idea what that meant, but he was not the only one around us who shouted it. At the end of the 32-minute contest, Wheatley had prevailed by the score of 85-80, an almost unheard of point total for a State championship game. A doorway into a new world opened for me that day. Four years later, I was back at that gym for another championship weekend, and the lessons I had learned from my elderly companion and Tyrone enabled me to make sense of it all.

When I wasn't being schooled in basketball, my time was spent in a loftier endeavor: the annual ritual of 9th grade boys at O. Henry—building a houseboat. Lake Austin was lowered in late January every year in hopes that a late winter freeze would kill the bane of boat propellers—duckweed. Normally 200 yards wide, the water level was squeezed down to the size of a creek, unveiling the treasure desired by 15-year-old boys: 55 gallon drums. Walking through muck up to our rear ends, we emptied the water out of the metal cylinders and rolled them back to shore, where the mechanically inclined guys soldered the holes. Soon, the 40-foot by 20-foot structure began to take shape at one classmate's waterside home, an inlet across from the Laguna Gloria Art Museum.

Two dozen boys had ponied up $25 each to purchase the necessary wood. It was not enough, which led to another time-honored tradition employed by our boat-making predecessors: pilfering. A man whose home was being built at 2607 Maria Anna noticed some lumber was missing from the project. He heard about a little construction effort going on near the lake and paid a visit to our site. Standing in our classmate's backyard, the man gazed down the cliff at the houseboat. Most of it had been painted white, but we had not gotten around to whitewashing the roof, and one of the 4x8 plywood planks contained writing in red spray that stared back at the man: 2607 Maria Anna. We bought him replacement pieces.

A favorite destination was the small waterfront park adjacent to Tom Miller Dam, where we picked up classmates and friends who rewarded us with beer. The next winter when the lake was lowered, one of the more intelligent basketball players sped to a carpet and tile store owned by the parents of a boat member. He came back with large carpet remnants that we draped around the boat. The parents bought the idea that we didn't want to walk through the mud to reach the houseboat. Our quick-thinking partner had an ulterior motive: he didn't want the receding water to expose the thousand empty beer cans that surrounded the moored vessel.

Weeks before school started, the houseboat chugged up the narrow lake on a sultry August night. Eight or ten "jocks" were on the long, white flat roof. Some sat cross-legged; others lay on their backs staring at the crescent moon and stars. The topic of our first year in high school was tossed about, with everyone having predictions on how the next three years would go. No one mentioned the possibility of racial problems; we couldn't see it in the distance. Being athletes, the topic centered on sports. Baseball was easy; we had the most talent by far. Reagan had won State in football the prior year and was loaded with talent; no chance of winning district there. Basketball was not even brought up; we had finished the 9th grade season tied for third with few prospects of improvement. I listened quietly and stared at the stars, which transformed into thousands of screaming fans cheering us on as we captured the district title in basketball. A lofty and unrealistic dream until a few weeks before when I had heard the good news: the Black Swan was coming to Austin High.

Part Two: Junior Year

Tyrone was going to be the first 6'6" defensive back in the history of football until he suffered a career-ending injury while attempting to make a tackle in the first week of practice our sophomore year. His fashion statement during the fall semester was a neck brace, and he sat out the entire basketball season.

America's involvement in the Vietnam War peaked in the spring of 1969, with over 500,000 troops involved in the conflict. Race riots in major cities like Philadelphia stretched through the summer, which culminated with Woodstock in mid-August. Days later, with virtually the same musical line-up, the Lewisville Pop Festival was held in the Dallas suburb. As the Summer of Love came to an end, students returned to Austin High for the 1969-70 school year with expectations of a great year. Disappointment set in early.

The racial unrest did not explode in one day, it crept up insidiously: an incident here and there, two or three times a week. The tension in the hallways was palpable: like a rubber band pulled tight, with all of us waiting for the final snap that would unleash a full-scale riot.

One morning in September, I was walking down the west corridor of the second floor when a teammate exited the bathroom with a pale expression on his face, and I asked, "What's wrong?" He said, "I was at the urinal and two black guys pulled a knife on me . . . for a quarter." A week later, a black student was late for class and four white students cornered him before he could escape. Both incidents served the same purpose; groups were staking out their turf, reminding those of a different color that they weren't going away, and they weren't going to be intimidated. The effect was counterproductive: it left everyone wondering if the next time might be the one that triggered a cataclysmic event.

Leaving school did not always offer a refuge. Jack Nash often took black players home after football practice. One evening he was driving his new

Monte Carlo down East 11th with Ken Campbell and John Holmes who were slumped down in the car, their heads barely visible. Jack stopped at a light and in the darkness curious black men encircled his vehicle. One of them noticed John, who informed them that Jack was "good people," and not to bother him if they saw him riding through East Austin.

Playing sports gave all of us a chance to develop relationships with people of different races. To be successful we had to rely on our teammates, and such bonds turned out to be far more substantial than those enjoyed by the rest of the student body, friendships that have endured. Jack still takes a deer harvested from one of his hunts to Hudson's Meat Market and pays for it to be processed and, just as he has for the past 35 years, Ken Campbell picks up the venison and shares it with his church members.

Basketball gave us a refuge from the strife. We started the season 5-0 and headed for the San Angelo tournament with confidence. Two teams, Thomas Jefferson of Dallas and Wichita Falls Rider, were ranked in the state's top ten. With only six combined losses, the eight entrants were very good, and the others shared another distinction: they were all white. Our Friday opponent was Thomas Jefferson of Dallas. We trailed 30-26 at halftime, but wilted under their full court pressure in the second half and got obliterated, 75-46. Tyrone played the worst game of his life and scored one point.

In the locker room, he sat sullenly on the bench, uncommunicative. Coach Gay Walker pulled some of us aside and explained, "This is the first game he has ever lost." Tyrone had played three years in junior high without tasting defeat. But our big man lingered in the shower for a long time trying to wash away the bitter taste of something else. Things the referees missed: rabbit punches to his kidneys, ribs to the elbows, tugs on his jersey while he jumped for rebounds, and the ubiquitous and incessant racial slurs whispered in his ears as he ran up and down the court. Tyrone was mad at himself for his dismal showing, but he kept the other part of his disappointment to himself: when he needed us the most, his fellow Maroons had not been there for him. We didn't have his back.

Saturday morning, Rider beat us by one in overtime, and we lost the third game later in the afternoon. Between games, we crowded into a motel room and watched the Texas Longhorns' football team beat Arkansas. The victory enabled the Longhorns to win the National Championship. They were the last all white squad to do so.

Two weekends later, we traveled to Corpus Christi to play two more homogenous teams. The vans pulled into a dilapidated motor court in the seedy part of town, and Coach checked-in and handed us our room keys. On a double bed in one room, the threadbare, white chenille coverlet had a red bloodstain the size of a basketball. A teammate said to the guys assigned to the room, "Look, you get to sleep underneath the Japanese flag." Horror stories about the accommodations were compared at a gathering in the parking lot. A redneck and his female companion appeared in the doorway of their room and he yelled, "Hey kid, come here, I've got something to show you." When I got close he flashed the centerfold of a PLAYBOY magazine in my face and laughed, along with my teammates.

Coach said the school district's budget was to blame for our lousy digs. I stood in the parking lot and looked at Tyrone, Phil Miller, and Don Hill, and thought it might have something to do with the color of their skin—the decent motels didn't want us. The rest of us were getting an inkling of the discrimination they had faced their entire lives.

In the two months following San Angelo, the team went 10-1, until we lost to Johnston by five points at their gym, which was nothing to be ashamed of because they made it to the State semi-finals that year.

On January 20, 1970, the principal spoke to the school while we were in homeroom. "We discourage you from going to the game at Anderson tonight, but if you do attend, don't wear anything that identifies you as an Austin High student. This includes band members and cheerleaders." I fell out of my chair, laughing. Our female septuagenarian teacher towered over me and asked, "What's so funny?"

I informed her, "Like their not going to know who our cheerleaders are rooting for—they're white!"

Up to that time, each team member had been responsible for finding his own transportation to away games in town. That afternoon a bus was parked outside our gym flanked by two Austin police cars. The caravan took a circuitous route to Anderson and dropped us off behind the school, far removed from the gym and the main parking lot.

In the visitors' locker room, a bank of thin windows divided the west wall from the ceiling; most of them had small round holes. One player asked, "Hey, are those bullet holes?" Nervous laughter ensued, but as we changed into our uniforms all of us glanced up at the broken panes and wondered.

Tyrone sat mutely, mentally preparing himself. Although he would have attended Johnston instead of Anderson, the Yellow Jackets resented him for not staying on the east side. In their eyes he was the anointed one: the best roundballer in the history of East Austin, and he spurned them and his heritage by coming over to Austin High.

We entered the gym from the south end. To our left were the bleachers. Anderson fans occupied 90% of the seats; the four dozen Austin supporters sat in a clump near the door to our locker room. To reach their seats, they had to walk past 500 screaming Yellow Jackets' fans. Directly across from our faithful few was the Anderson bench, which was separated from ours by the scorers' table. Behind us was a large stage hidden behind massive black curtains that did not deaden the noise. Like most schools, the Anderson students had an R-rated cheer. During warm-ups they let loose with a doozy. "Chewin' tobacco, chewin' tobacco, makes you wanna spit. If you ain't a Yellow Jacket, you ain't _ _ _ _!"

The defending champions had a district record of 1-5 coming into the game; they had saved their best minutes for us. Exhorted by the raucous fans, Anderson led 32-30 at halftime. When the Yellow Jackets were on defense, their students often chanted, "Spit on the floor, spit on the wall, come on niggah, get that ball."

Metal chairs rimmed the north end of the court. The first occasion I had to inbound the ball, I felt a sting on the back of my thigh. Someone had reached over and plucked a few hairs from my leg. The second visit was less painful: the man just spit on my leg.

Tyrone fouled out late in the game after scoring 13 points, yet his biggest contribution was holding the man-child from Anderson to only 15 points. My cousin, Jerry Bell, Jr., sank one free throw with 30 seconds remaining in the game, and another one at the 15-second mark that tied the score at 63. Anderson missed a shot and somehow I ended up with the ball in the front court where a Yellow Jacket fouled me with only six seconds remaining. Their coach called time out to "ice the shooter," hoping the additional time to think about it would cause me to miss the front end of a one-and-one free throw attempt.

Seated in the metal chairs, Coach Walker bent down and addressed us, "Now, after Tudey makes the free throws . . ." which was Coaching Psychology 101: instill confidence in wobbly-kneed player. When the timeout ended, the other four players took the court and Tyrone put his hand on my right shoulder and stood perpendicular to me. His eyes concentrated on a spot at the end of the gym and he said, emphatically, "We aren't playing overtime." A grin creased his face. I walked onto the court and saw what had captured his attention. None of the Anderson players had left their bench; half of them stared me down and I wanted to shout to Tyrone, "There's no U in we!" But I did not want to spoil his moment: the other Yellow Jacket players were glaring at Tyrone, and I didn't need eyes in the back of my head to know that he was still returning their attention with a smile.

With my pre-shot ritual completed, I bent my knees and started the shooting motion. That's when somebody starting firing a machine-gun into the crowd. In reality, it was a roll of Black Cat firecrackers an Anderson student dropped beneath our fans' seats, but as I turned my head I expected to see a crazed gunman mowing down the small contingent of Maroon fans. Instead, I saw the first "half wave" in history as my parents and others jumped out of their seats. Students on the first few rows sprinted onto the court to avoid the fireworks.

Tossing the ball to the ref, I pivoted and walked off to collect myself. I bent over and wiped two very sweaty palms on my maroon and white striped leggings. Cocking my head toward our bench, I saw a concerned look on the faces my coaches and teammates, with one exception: Tyrone. A towel was draped around his neck and he held the two ends in hands that rested on his chest. Our eyes locked and he flashed a huge grin.

I don't recall shooting the free throws, only the relief I felt after they went through the net. In the ebullient post-game locker room, the topic of conversation centered on the fireworks display.

Tyrone, Phil, and Don went home with their families, because they lived in the neighborhood. Our revelry ended after we showered and changed into street clothes. Two policemen led us down a long hallway that was pitch black, except for the red "Exit" sign on the distant door. None of us spoke a word as we carried our game bags; the only noise in the hallway came from the heels of our shoes as they made contact with the tile floor.

Sandwiched between the police cars the bus traversed East 11th Street, past vibrant storefronts, the historic Victory Grill, and the original site of

L.C. Anderson High School's predecessor, the Robertson Hill School, which was now a parking lot for the Ebenezer Baptist Church. This was our three teammates' environment; for a few hours on Tuesday night the rest of us had been mere interlopers. The Yellow Jackets had put an unseen bull's eye on Tyrone's jersey; he was the one they most wanted to beat. Now Tyrone would not have to endure their verbal jabs and taunts. He led our team in scoring with a 22-point per game average, and on those nights he was not prolific, our other big man, Mark Chalmers usually rescued us. Against Anderson, Mark, Phil, and Jerry had scored 44 of our points. My contribution was one point more than a dead man, until those last two free throws. Anyone else on the team would have made them, I was just fortunate to have the opportunity, which ushered me into the company of our best players in one respect: on the night he needed us the most, we could truthfully say, "We had Tyrone's back."

Ten days later, the season began to unravel. The school was abuzz about the away game at Reagan that night, until the rubber band was pulled tight and the chatter reverted to race. Between morning classes, a black student found a note taped to his locker. "Go back to Africa, nigger." The alleged author was a noted hippie-hater and, by syllogism, a racist. Classrooms on the west side heard a voice screaming, "Help! Help! Somebody help me!" Students looked out the windows and saw the suspected scribe sprinting down West Avenue with six black guys in hot pursuit. He found refuge in the corner gas station before they could nab him.

Our junior varsity team's departure was delayed; a few black players wanted to discuss the incident, and a spirited dialogue flowed so long that the team arrived with little time to warm up. It was the only game they lost all year.

We had beaten the Raiders by eight in December, but with five seconds left in the game we trailed 49-48. A teammate's errant shot caromed off the rim seven feet from the basket where it fell into my hands. Another teammate under basket shielded his man from me, providing a clear path to basket. I dribbled twice, banked in a four-footer and was carried off court by my fellow Maroon players. Well, that is what *should* have happened, but it didn't. I dribbled twice and froze. With a second left I tossed the ball to my shocked teammate beneath the basket, and he attempted a wild shot as the buzzer sounded.

One stunned Maroon player ran up to me and shouted, "What the hell were you thinking?" A second yelled, "Why didn't you shoot the ball?" A Raider slapped me on the back, "We oughta give you the game ball," and cackled.

While my teammates showered, I sat on a locker room bench with a white towel draped over my head; the initial embarrassment of my indecision was supplanted by a severe case of self-loathing and disgust. Someone came up behind me, and my body tensed, waiting for another barrage of anger. Tyrone put his large right hand on my back, leaned over and whispered through the towel, "Shoulda shot the ball." He patted my back softly, twice, and re-treated. No recrimination, no rancor, just a statement of fact. Tyrone knew I felt worse than anyone, and he understood that no amount of screaming or yelling would deepen the pain festering inside me. In his understated way, he was really saying, "You screwed up, but next time you'll know what to do."

One day, seasoned student protestors from the University of Texas and local malcontents coalesced on a sidewalk across the street from the north end of our school. During breaks between classes, Austin High students took in the newfound ambiance: a multi-cultural protest, complete with professional and hand-drawn signs, emphatic chants and strains of "We Shall Overcome." A Maroon student ambled across West Avenue to address the leader of the event, and he purportedly told the man Austin High did not need this attention; we could handle the minor problems internally. The gentleman responded, "That's cool," and the student turned to leave. The protestor called out, "Hey, man!" and our classmate looked back just as the heavy rock smashed against his face, splattering blood on his shirt and the protestor's clothes.

Within minutes, Principal Robbins came over the P.A. system and asked the football team to report to shop class, a room that was on the southwest corner of the ground floor of the main building. Coach Tolbert instructed the players, who glanced repeatedly out the window at the re-energized and vocal demonstrators. The football team lined up, not in clumps of black, brown, and white; they amassed in the form they were accustomed to—as one unit. They filed out and walked silently to the curb on the east side of the street. Protestors continued chanting, yelling, and waving signs as athletes quietly formed a single line on the sidewalk. Some folded their arms across their chests, others rested them at their side, and a few stuffed their hands in their pockets. They stared at the protestors but never spoke, and they remained in position until the police arrived to disperse the demonstrators.

We lost the next two games and any hope of winning district. Even so, that 1970 team was probably the best squad in school history that never won district, because they had to compete against Johnston, one of the greatest groups ever assembled in Austin, and they had to contend with the external forces of overt racism and the internal strife at school, which manifested itself daily. Following that anomalous game against Thomas Jefferson of Dallas, our senior leaders had molded us into a cohesive unit that supported and genuinely cared about each individual, and if that is the true yardstick by which a group is measured, the 1970 basketball team may be the finest Austin High ever produced.

Our next-to-last game was a good example. Unbeknownst to the team, Coach Walker was successfully interviewing for a new position with the school district that would start in the fall: director of busing. Aware that his coaching career was winding down, he prepared a game plan that was different from anything we had employed: full-court press, three guards, Jerry at high post, and Tyrone down low; as close to hully-gully as we would ever get.

The evening of February 13, 1970, I tried to chat up Tyrone in the locker room before the game. "Got my first date with Deborah tonight!" During free throws at practice I had told him of my years-long infatuation with her, and he was genuinely happy when I informed him that she had agreed to go out with me. But on this night his mind was focused on the large post player for Anderson who was an inch shorter and forty pounds heavier than Tyrone, who had fouled out trying to guard the bruiser in the first meeting and did not want another early exit.

The newspaper said "Big Tyrone Johnson" controlled the boards in the second quarter, before leaving midway through the stanza with his third personal foul and most of the 9 points and 13 rebounds he contributed for the game. With our seniors, Mark, Phil, and Jerry all scoring in double figures we were ahead 61-42 early in the fourth quarter, and I had a glimpse of how good we could have been. Johnston and another state tournament squad from San Antonio had not dominated Anderson this badly. Subconsciously, we throttled back, and won the game 77-65, but the closeness did not diminish the Anderson players' anger. Embarrassed by the drubbing, one Yellow Jacket had words for me in the final minute as he dribbled up the left side of the court. "You think you're great because my aunt works for your mother." Tyrone had told us to "Shut up, and play ball," when confronted with trash talk. Instead, I parroted his words to my opponent. During a timeout, I started thinking about my date with Deborah and forgot about the conversation, but others had not.

The final buzzer sounded while I was guarding a Yellow Jacket by the free throw line near our bench. With my back to the action, I shook my opponent's hand and never saw it coming. Mark Chalmers did and he ran onto the court but got there too late. The biggest and baddest Yellow Jacket had snatched the game ball, sprinted toward me, and stopped six feet away. He reared back with it in his right hand and, as I turned around, fired it as hard as he could into the right side of my face.

Stars flashed inside my head, I blacked out, and crumpled to the floor. Seconds later I came to and propped myself up into a sitting position. Jerry and Mark struggled to restrain the huge Anderson player who wanted to finish with his fists what he had started with the basketball. Tyrone had locked arms with the Anderson coaches, his long wingspan preventing the Yellow Jackets' bench players from joining the fray. Six policemen helped usher out the Anderson fans, followed by the Austin supporters, and then they monitored the parking lot.

I showered quicker than an automobile passing through a car wash, hoping to avoid Tyrone. My altercation was initiated by an exasperated Yellow Jacket, yet it could have been prevented if I had kept my mouth shut. Pulling a sweater over my head, I saw Tyrone standing next to the open door of my locker. His right hand clutched the long towel that encircled his waist. Steam from the showers rolled into the dank room and he used the small towel in his left hand to wipe moisture from his face. Leaning against the lockers with his left elbow, Tyrone blocked anyone from overseeing our conversation.

He knew the Anderson player must have been provoked and I was the likely suspect.

"So, motor mouth, what did you say?"

I told him and Tyrone studied the welt on my face for a few moments. "Was it worth it?"

Closing the locker, I turned and faced him. "What do you think?"

We looked at each other silently and listened to teammates' laughter coming from the showers. Tyrone noticed a seam from the basketball on my cheek and joked, "Lucky Deborah. She's got a date with Mr. Basketball head."

Part Three: Senior Year

Tyrone wanted to gauge our progress over the summer, and he scheduled a scrimmage against Reagan's starting five. After breaking into the Austin High gym, we opened all the windows and doors, which stirred the August heat like a convection oven. Four of the Raiders were returning two-year starters; only one was white. Tyrone was our lone returning starter and, with the graduation of Phil and Don, the lone black player for the Maroons.

We won the first half-court game; what had started as a friendly scrimmage evolved into something else. In the second, Reagan players starting complaining, "Aw, c'mon. You're calling that a foul?" and the testosterone level escalated. Short of having his forearms detached by a meat cleaver, Tyrone was not going to cry "foul." Predictably, the Raiders won the second game. During the rubber match, I threw my 143-pound frame into my stockier counterpart, Reagan's point guard, and he hit the deck. Bouncing up, he got in my face and said, "That's the way you want to play? Fine, I like it rough." With Mark Looney and Peter Barbour bombing from outside and Jack helping Tyrone inside, we were coasting to victory when the school district's cops arrived.

Words like "trespassing" and "breaking and entering" got our attention. Peter begged for our one phone call, which he made from the foyer office. The man on the other end was a friend of his stepfather and a high-ranking official in the AISD. After exacting a promise from Peter to refrain from further felonies, he told the cops to let us go.

Joking about the incident on the way to our cars, I looked over and saw the Raiders' players. They were standing beside their vehicles with basketballs under their arms, staring at us, and I knew what they were thinking: "If those guys hadn't been here, the cops wouldn't have let us off." Tyrone had scheduled the game to make a statement. Unfortunately, the one they remembered added fuel to the fire that burned inside them.

Peter and I rented a bus to go to the Austin vs. Ray football game in Corpus Christi. To cover expenses, we had to expand the invitation list to include students whose parents had open minds, because our transportation was not chaperoned. Their free-spirited children sat at the front, expanding their minds with marijuana, while the rest of us hovered over an adult beverage cache more voluminous than a small town liquor store. By the time we arrived at the stadium on the Naval Base, the 30 or so passengers were in various states of coherency.

About 400 Ray students packed their portion of the small stands. Next to them, Tyrone and two dozen Maroons sat by themselves; our band, cheerleaders, and Red Jacket drill team had gone to the wrong stadium and did not show up until the second quarter. Tyrone had chartered a bus that was chaperoned. Some white students labeled it "The Congo Bus," even though our teammates Coalter Baker and Woody Robinson were aboard.

Tyrone said, "We brought two cases of beer." A person from my group responded, "Heck, Tyrone, I brought two cases just for me." To prove his point, the fellow blasted a five-second belch that was so violent it made his neck quiver. Pleased with his effort, he smiled, said, "Have a nice day," and went in search of others to impress.

A hurricane had passed through days before, necessitating movement of the game, but this field and its sidelines were also a quagmire. Without cheerleaders, I jumped into the mud with Danny Robertson and we cajoled two black girls to join us. Short on memory, we kept the cheers simple, "Uw, ungawa, we got that magic powa'" and other all-time cheerleader favorites. Austin High scored and we broke into the ersatz fight song whose melody was the same as Notre Dame's famous tune. "Beer, beer, for old Austin High, bring on the whiskey, bring on the rye. Send those freshman out for gin, and don't let a sober person in. Oh, Lordy, we never stagger, we never fall, we sober up on wood alcohol, all you saints from Austin High, and we're out on the drunk again." Across the way, parental binoculars noted the embarrassing transgressions.

The official representatives of the school—the band, drill team, and cheerleaders—were aghast when they saw us. Dark overcast skies had dumped an inch of rain, soaking our clothes to our skin, and no one seemed to care. There was no line of demarcation to our seating: the 50 or so students—black, white and hispanic—mingled like adults at a cocktail party. We couldn't understand the stares from our recently arrived classmates. We thought this was what high school was supposed to be about: having fun and interacting with people who often did not look or think the same way you did.

During the game, one of our linemen, Rickey Guerrero, suffered a severe ankle sprain. Days later, a blood clot went from the injured area to his heart, and he died. The school forgot about race relations, at least for a few weeks.

Student council members were elected by their homerooms, and that body reflected the white majority of those classes. Minorities demanded redress, and student representatives spent three days in the cafeteria hammering out an at-large voting compromise. Not everyone was satisfied with the maneuver. A popular white student was pulled aside as he entered the room. A bespectacled, wizened female teacher warned him, "Don't let those niggers get control of the council."

On the first day of basketball practice, we learned that our new coach, Jim Haller who had come over from McCallum High, was a noted high school roundballer. His team had won the 4-A State Championship in 1962 and placed 3rd in 1963. Jim's alma mater was Thomas Jefferson in Dallas.

Unwittingly, Tyrone tested our new coach at an early practice. Jim saw our big man repeatedly retrieving something from his gym shorts and placing it in his mouth. Coach had the rest of us do a drill, and he took Tyrone into the foyer and asked, "What are you eating?" Tyrone pulled a bag of Fritos from inside his shorts. Trying not to laugh, Jim told him that he, too, would like to eat during practice but that was something no one was allowed to do. Tyrone nodded and kept his hunger pangs to himself the rest of the season. Coach Haller said of Tyrone, "He was the nicest, most cooperative, and mild-mannered player I ever coached," which balanced out the rest of team. In early December, we had a pedestrian 5-5 record. In hindsight our schedule was brutal: seven of our nine losses for the year came at the expense of district champions. Low on confidence, we were slaughtered by San Antonio Jefferson in the second round of the AISD tournament. Tyrone gave away two inches and 50 pounds to their big man, Rick Bullock, but he scored 16 points and matched Bullock's defensive effort. Tyrone's teammates offered no support: we mustered only 17 points and fell, 47-33.

297

Our reward for the lackluster showing was a 10:00 consolation game at Reagan against Alamo Heights from San Antonio. Trailing by eight points after three quarters, Coach decided to wake up the troops by employing a full-court press. Short on guards, he was forced to play me, even though I had done nothing the night before. My punishment was giving my best effort of the season in front of ten fans—the smallest crowd in AISD history.

With 15 seconds left the score was tied and Coach called time and diagrammed our options: a) "Mark Looney shoots from the baseline"—not open; b) "Dump a pass into Tyrone down low"—not open. Frantic, Mark looked at me and created option c, as in "Crap don't throw it back to me." He did. My defender did not bite on my pump fake. Tyrone was in front of the basket and had come open, so I chunked a 17-foot fade away pass that looked suspiciously like a shot. He was helpless as it sailed over his head and into the basket with four seconds remaining.

Alamo Heights called a timeout and three of my oncourt teammates mobbed me while Tyrone stood beneath the basket shaking his head in amazement. I felt bad about not connecting with him, but after the timeout he let me know it was okay. Placing his hand on my back, he steered me out of earshot of the others and whispered in my left ear, "Shoulda shot the ball." I cocked my head toward him and Tyrone starting laughing so strenuously he had to grab his stomach, and he didn't stop until he reached the other end of the court.

The next practice was brutal. Coach pushed the rebounding drills mercilessly, and all of us were exhausted as we took to the baseline for the suicides: non-stop sprints from baseline to free throw, and back, midcourt and back, far free throw line and back, opposite end line and back. Coach figured we were done when Tyrone burst through the heavy metal doors that led to the foyer, because he was almost indefatigable. That day everyone's gray practice shirt was charcoal black with sweat. After the second one, Coach Haller smiled, "That was so much fun, let's do another."

Dragging like we were running through molasses with ankle weights, our lungs felt as if someone had poured hot coals into them. Tyrone crashed through the doors while the rest of us wobbled to the end line and collapsed. Leaning over, I watched droplets of sweat form a small pool on the floor beneath me. Guys were prostrate on the floor and one gasped, "Will somebody just . . . shoot me . . . and put me out of my misery . . . please?"

298

Twenty seconds went by and Tyrone had not returned. After a half-minute, Tyrone flung open the door and walked to the end line. He stared at the other end of the court and said, "One more."

Coach Haller smiled as we lined up and blew his whistle. The first up and back, little voices inside us whispered, "You can't do this; you won't make it." Halfway through, a resolve began to push them away from our ears. Someone shouted encouragement as we slapped the floor and started for the far free throw line. Others joined in, and by the time we made the turned for the final dash, all of us were running as if it were the first suicide, not the fourth.

Tyrone burst through the door and we followed him; in part to drink from the water, but mostly to keep him from returning to the gym for another drill. I heard their hoots and hollers fade as they descended the stairs into the locker room. Walking back into the gym, I eased onto the first row of wooden bleachers, rested my elbows on the row behind me, and my eyes retraced our steps.

Tyrone knew that it took more than talent to win. You had to have the right mindset; you had to believe you could accomplish it. He was the only one who had ever won a basketball championship, and he wanted to take us where we had never been, which required him to push us beyond our perceived limits. In that simple drill he succeeded; he had instilled a shared confidence that catapulted us to our goal.

Including the Alamo Heights game, that started a span of 20 games where we went 19-1, including a 16-game win streak that shot us into a top 5 ranking in the state, which was unwarranted because our competition was not that stiff, with two exceptions. Missing two starters at Anderson, Tyrone was forced to exceed his 26-point season average, often with two or three defenders draped on him, and we eked out the victory.

Reagan fell 57-53 in our first meeting at Gregory Gym, in front of 6,000 fans. Trailing by nine at halftime, we did not seal the victory until Jack Nash scored a basket with seven seconds left.

Tyrone fouled out of the playoff game just before regulation ended. An opponent's desperation half-court shot at the buzzer in overtime sailed through the net and we lost, 57-56, ending our season. The signature moment of the season had come the previous Saturday, in the rematch with Reagan in Gregory Gym.

In the first minute of that game, a Reagan player stole a pass. Peter raced back and put his stick figure in front of the basket, hoping to draw a charging foul. The Raider, an All-State football player, busted through Peter on his way to making a lay-up. My teammate crashed into the basket stanchion and slumped to the floor. Removing his glasses from his mouth, Peter put them on just as the referee pointed at him and said, "Foul on number 30, white!" It was going to be one of those days.

Coach Haller told a reporter, "Our inside men were not ready to play this game. We had a complete discipline breakdown offensively and defensively." Reagan had lost another district game, and win or lose, we had already clinched the title. After two years of hard work, setbacks, and struggles, the team was physically and emotionally spent. Even Tyrone had a bewildered look during the contest; after three quarters he had scored only eight points, and we were getting blown out, 65-43. Mark Looney was our single bright spot, scoring 28 points.

I was told to check in, because Coach Haller wanted to press Reagan. Having lost my starting job when I missed the Anderson game because of illness, I knew my chances of seeing the court in the playoff game were slim, and I was right: I didn't play a second of it. Tyrone had been the co-captain by example and I was supposed to be the court leader, but my infatuation with an up-tempo, hully-gully style consigned me to the bench.

As Coach barked instructions, I thought about Lew Alcindor in the Astrodome, and the promise I had made to Peter at the end of our game against Tyrone and Martin Junior High. We took the court and I called out, "Hey, T!" Tyrone glowered at me; he was in no mood for a motor mouth monologue. My eyes narrowed as I looked up at him and asked, "Intimidated?"

The Reagan coach said, "I wasn't too worried about losing, but when you have to play with three starters gone, it gets ticklish. Our reserves weren't used to coming in under that kind of pressure." The first one fouled out at the 5:33 mark, the second exited with 4:49 left, and the third sat down with 3:41 to go. All of them fouled out trying to guard Tyrone.

He swiped a rebound, fired an outlet pass, and sprinted down the floor with the speed he exhibited as a defensive back in football. Once there, we passed him the ball. A photo in the yearbook captured one of the next moments: Tyrone skying for a jump shot surrounded by three flat-footed Raiders staring at him in awe and wonderment. He scored ten points in the first four minutes of the quarter.

None of us was doing it for the school or our fans; we were following Tyrone's lead. We were just boys at play.

With each stoppage, the Raiders glanced at the clock, willing it to move faster. If I had not missed the front end of a one-and-one at the three-minute mark, we might have won the game. Reagan scored a bucket with 1:38 left, and later added a free throw. Those were their only points in the last eight minutes. Prior to my missed attempt, we had run off 15 unanswered points, and for the quarter, we outscored them 20-3. The final score was Reagan: 68, Austin: 63.

The Raiders spent three quarters building a beat down that Tyrone nearly demolished by himself, with his teammates providing the crowbars. Frustrated by our comeback, the Reagan point guard retaliated. Mark "Pee Wee" Andrews dribbled the ball across midcourt in the last minute and the stocky opponent slammed into Pee Wee so hard that he went flying into the second row of the stands and landed in my mother's lap.

While the referee fished our diminutive guard from the stands and tried to placate a bunch of angry Austin High moms, I got in the face of the Reagan player, put my nose six inches from his and said, "If you want to fight, pick on someone your own size." His eyes filled with anger and his neck started shaking, and my body tensed as I waited for him to punch me out; something I knew he had wanted to do since that hot August afternoon in the Austin High gym.

His eyes darted over my left shoulder for a split-second, then fixed again on me. Moments later, they softened, and he shrugged and retreated. I turned around and saw what had momentarily diverted his attention. Standing 20 feet away, with arms akimbo like the Green Giant: Tyrone, our protector.

Their eyes stayed locked until the Raider turned his head and conceded the staring contest. Tyrone shifted his attention to me, "What did you say?" I told him and he nodded. Then he departed without saying a word.

My on-court career with him ended the way it started: with my watching him walk away. Memories of games flashed through my mind, especially the bad ones: Thomas Jefferson of Dallas and San Antonio Jefferson. In spite of his teammates' shortcomings and failures, our big man's loyalty never wavered. He always had our backs.

Part Four: Later Years

Tyrone enrolled at Tyler Junior College, and four of the other seniors attended the University of Texas and joined fraternities. Following a holiday party one Saturday evening in December, I went to the Kappa Sigma house with three senior members. The pantry/liquor cabinet was locked. They asked me, "Where can we find Meeks?" Kenny, the elderly house porter, had accidentally taken the keys home, and they knew I had befriended him over the past few months. "I have an idea where he might be."

The late model Pontiac sports car went under Interstate 35 and traveled down East 12th Street. My brothers' nervousness increased the further we went. It was midnight and cold, but the sidewalks were filled with black people milling about. Pointing to the north side of the street, I said, "There it is." Our driver did a U-turn and parked; if trouble broke out, he wanted to be headed in the direction of home. Exiting the car, I noticed we were still dressed in suits we had worn to the cocktail party. "I think we blend in pretty well, don't you?"

Inside the bar, I planted myself next to the front door while my compadres went in search of Mr. Meeks. A man at the nearest table stared up at me and sipped his longneck beer. I shifted my eyes toward him and he said, "You look familiar."

"I was on Tyrone Johnson's basketball team."

He smiled. "How's he doing?"

"Great. He's playing for Tyler Junior College."

Our conversation ended, and as I searched for my friends I heard a chuckle. The man had seemed familiar to me, too. Their laughter was likely the result of his telling his friends "Remember me telling you about that kid from Austin High, the one I plucked leg hairs from? That's him."

The neighborhood storefront bustled with patrons who obviously recognized many familiar faces in the crowd. With my fraternity brothers in the back pool room, I was the lone Caucasian in the main bar of The White Swan. And I had an appreciation for what Tyrone had endured: countless hours practicing, traveling, and playing basketball with a bunch of neighborhood kids who did not share his skin color. My epiphany continued three months later.

Jerry Bell, Jr., and I had planned to meet at Gregory Gym on March 10, 1972, for the 4-A basketball tournament. The talent assembled that weekend was the gaudiest in Texas schoolboy lore. In the evening semi-final, San Antonio Jefferson defeated Plainview and then lost in the championship the next day even though Rick Bullock (Texas Tech, New York Knickerbockers) tallied 44 points in a losing effort. The other semi-final match up pitted two all-black schools, Dallas Roosevelt and Ira Terrell (SMU, Phoenix Suns) against Houston Wheatley and Eddie Owens (UNLV, Kansas City Kings). From 1948-1961, Wheatley had won nine Prairie View Interscholastic Leagues titles and placed second twice. After joining the UIL, the Wildcats won three straight titles in 1968-1970, and finished second in 1971. In a sportswriters' poll conducted by the *Austin American Statesman* in 2006, Wheatley vs. Roosevelt was voted the second best game ever played in Gregory Gym, including college contests. It was the greatest high school game in Texas history. My first hint should have come when I saw the street sign near the gym, which read "Speedway."

Jerry and I snagged floor seats behind the basket on the west end of the court. The gym filled quickly and with the exception of the sportswriters gathered near the scorer's table and some of our old teammates—Coalter Baker and Ben Wear—we were about the only white folks in the overflow crowd of more than 7,800. The Roosevelt Mustangs' fans did a cheer that was answered by Wheatley's students and supporters. Clapping their hands together, they swayed back and forth like participants at a revival and sang, "Everywhere we goooo, people want to knoooow, who we are, so we tell them, 'We are the Wildcats, the Mighty, Mighty Wildcats!'"

The teams congregated at midcourt for the opening tip-off, and when the referee tossed the leather sphere into the air, the floor resembled a pool table after a cue ball strikes the rack: players scrambled in every direction. On average, a shot was attempted every 10 seconds, and a basket was scored every 17 seconds . . . for 32 minutes. The crowd welcomed foul shots and timeouts—chances to collect their breath. Roosevelt outscored Wheatley 17-6 in the last 2:52 of the game. The three-point shot was not implemented until 1985 or 1986, which makes the final score even more outrageous: the Mustangs won, 111-109.

Both squads played a high-stakes game of h-o-r-s-e, laced with machismo. Each outlandish pass or shot was answered by an equally eye-popping one, but this was much more than a basketball game. Months before, a federal judge had decreed that all Texas schools with more than 90% minorities should be closed and the students bused to predominantly-white institutions. The blacks in the gym that day did not know if or when the two schools would be shuttered; they were in Gregory Gym to enjoy their teams' success. More importantly, they came to celebrate the pride and tradition of the storied institutions the players represented.

Descending the steps after the game, I understood what Tyrone had given up, and why some in East Austin thought he had forsaken them by coming over to Austin High. Additionally, had he gone to Johnston, Tyrone would have played in this game his junior year. With him, they might have made it to the championship game and won it all. The exposure would have meant a four-year scholarship for Tyrone right out of high school. I wanted to ask him a question but didn't, because I was unsure what his answer would be to "Was it worth it?"

The University of Texas offered Tyrone a basketball scholarship, and he moved back to Austin. One August afternoon Woody Robinson and Mark Elbrecht, two former Maroons who played for Concordia University, and Tyrone broke into the Austin High gym to shoot hoops. Later, he asked them to take him to Hippie Hollow, a clothing-optional parcel of land on Lake Travis. Two comely black girls in bikinis were on a raft and Tyrone decided to join them. Thinking the water was shallow enough for him to wade to the girls, he jumped off the small cliff. His 6'6" frame sank into the depths and when he surfaced, Woody and Mark learned something about Tyrone: he didn't know how to swim. His giant arms flailed as they swam to his rescue. Safely on shore, Tyrone was able to laugh at himself.

Another misjudgment happened on his first game at Gregory Gym, when Texas played tiny Centenary College. Tyrone spun around at the baseline to attempt his first shot as a Longhorn. At his full extension, he released the ball almost 10 feet above the ground, but the ball never left his hands—the defender blocked Tyrone's shot. "The Chief" later blocked over 2,300 shots in his NBA career, and won four championships: three with Larry Bird and the Boston Celtics, and another with Michael Jordan and the Chicago Bulls. Tyrone's initial rejection came at the hands of Robert Parish, a future inductee into the NBA Hall of Fame.

Tyrone helped Texas win the Southwest Conference crown in 1974, and Coach Leon Black said, "I never coached a better person than Tyrone."

Following graduation, Tyrone moved away to begin his coaching career and returned to Austin when he was chosen as the head coach at L.C. Anderson. The eastside campus closed after our senior year and re-opened in the fall of 1973 in the Northwest Hills area, which was largely white, and the mascot was changed: from the Yellow Jackets to the Trojans. Twice Tyrone took them to the State tournament, which had been moved, from Gregory Gym across campus to the Frank C. Erwin Center. More than 16,000 watched Anderson lose in the finals to Plainview 54-52 in 1994 and Port Arthur Lincoln 57-56 the next year.

Tyrone joked that he became a track coach for the stipend. In the spring of 1996, I went to Burger Center for a meet and saw him in a clump of coaches near the finish line. He saw me and shouted, "Tudey! What are you doing here?"

"My daughter runs track for Austin High."

"Is she fast?"

"Of course she is, Tyrone, she's white."

He chuckled and asked, "Where is she?"

Amy's skin is as melanin-challenged as mine is, and I pointed her out. "She's the albino in the infield." His fellow coaches did not know what to think of Tyrone's friend. We talked about basketball for a few moments, and he suggested, "With your skin, you should be in the shade."

"I was headed that way before I saw you." Seated in the shadows beneath the press box, I checked a suspicious-looking mole on my left forearm; two months later a surgeon removed the melanoma.

Coach Johnson plopped down next to me as the runners got in their blocks for the 400-meter race. Tyrone studied Amy quietly through the first curve, down the backstretch and into the final curve, and then he pointed at her and said, "There!" I do not remember how she placed; I was enthralled watching Tyrone gesticulate while I concentrated on his instructions. A quarter century after he advised me, he was helping my daughter.

To win a trophy, Amy's coach dropped the few talented varsity runners down to junior varsity for the district meet. On a steamy Saturday at the Pflugerville High track, Austin High won the junior varsity meet, and Amy ran her fastest race of the season. The varsity girls' district results in the paper the next day were revealing. If she had been allowed to run in that meet, she would have finished in fourth place—good enough to qualify for regionals.

In April of 2003, I was in Waco for the Cotton Palace Pageant weekend. A highlight was spending time with Judy and Jim Haller. Coach wanted updates on all the players, but most of our conversation was about Tyrone.

The Friday men's luncheon was held at the Texas Sports Hall of Fame next to the Baylor University campus. Touring the facility, I stopped in the high school area and read the familiar names and the year of their induction: Ira Terrell-1982, Rick Bullock-1985, and Eddie Owens-1991. Had he chosen a different high school, maybe Tyrone's name would have been listed next to those great players, but I did not torture myself wondering "Was it worth it?" because I already knew the answer.

On Saturday, October 27, 2001, Tyrone's cross-country team won the district title. That evening, he joined some buddies on a ranch east of Austin to hunt varmints. Sometime after midnight, Tyrone Johnson suffered a fatal heart attack. When Ken Campbell called Jack Nash to give him the sad news, Ken said, "Jack, he died 'coon hunting!"

His funeral was held in the Ebenezer Baptist Church at the corner of East 10th Street and San Marcos, directly behind the original site of the first all-black high school, Robertson Hill. Inside the packed church, it looked like someone had sprinkled the mourners out of salt and pepper shakers and mixed them together—a large and racially diverse group usually found at the service for a community leader. The term Ebenezer means "stone of help," which Tyrone had been to those in attendance. Listening to the eulogizers and surveying the audience, I received the answer to the question I never posed to Tyrone.

One of his tall daughters clutched a wisp of a woman with bright red hair and porcelain skin as they slowly made their way down the aisle. Woody Robinson saw the surprise in my face and asked, "You didn't know?" They had been married less than a year, and that union summed up Tyrone: he did not dole out his affections based on color.

When the service concluded, the mourners exited the church and I stood on the sidewalk visiting with friends. The white folks were in front of the church while the blacks congregated in the small parking lot on the other side the street. I crossed East 10th to greet my old classmates. "What's the matter, you all afraid of a bunch of white folks?" They laughed, nervously, and I motioned some white former classmates to come over. Ten minutes later, I walked to my car and glanced back at the gathering. The sun had slipped behind the tall downtown buildings, and in the fading light I saw blacks and whites crossing East 10th Street to greet each other, just like we had during the better days at Austin High. Our problems are not easily solved, but as Tyrone had shown us, race relations are like basketball: you show improvement only through practice.

Glory Road premiered in 2005. The movie detailed the 1966 Texas Western basketball team, the first NCAA championship squad with five black starters. Harry Flournoy was portrayed by Mehcad Brooks, who later joined the cast of **Desperate Housewives**. Mehcad had honed his basketball talent at Anderson under the tutelage of his head coach, Tyrone Johnson.

Tyrone's education had begun at all-black schools, then a multi-racial environment, and he achieved his greatest coaching accolades at the school named for a prominent black educator. A major part of the movie involved the title game between Texas Western and Kentucky: a seminal moment in collegiate sports—one that opened doors for Tyrone and other black athletes.

In October of 2006, Austin High will hold a super reunion on its 125th anniversary, marking its status as one of the oldest continually operated public high schools in Texas. A week later, our class will hold its 35-year reunion at Lucy's Boatyard, a restaurant built on the small patch of parkland where our houseboat used to pick up classmates and friends. In some ways, our basketball team shared qualities that built the houseboat. We had slogged through the muck of discrimination with a group largely comprised of neighborhood kids who had grown up together. Although we were missing an essential component, we did not steal Tyrone—it was his decision to join us. For one magical and glorious season, he had captained our ship through waters calm and rough to a destination the rest of us had only dreamed about.

That evening his basketball team will reminisce, trade jokes, and chide each other about lost hair and found weight, and we will note the irony of date: the fifth anniversary of Tyrone's death. At some point, the forgotten champions of 1971 will huddle together in a secluded corner. I'll recite the words I wrote after his funeral, thoughts shared by each of his teammates, as we raise our glasses to our absent friend. "Tyrone Johnson passed away on October 28th. Over the last half-century, Austin High produced no better basketball player or person; Tyrone was simply the best. The only things sweeter than his jump shot were his smile and disposition. I was fortunate he was my teammate. I was honored he was my friend."

THE ROAD LESS TRAVELED

Why We Fight/Why I Write

Part One: Adagio

When a father says he wants a better life for his child, the listener assumes he is talking about monetary wealth. What goes unsaid is the thing all fathers secretly wish for: that their children improve the human race by becoming a better person than dear old dad. In the quest to achieve that goal, all children encounter mishaps and commit numerous mistakes, and when their lives draw to a close many realize they have fallen short of those fatherly expectations. Some fail from lack of effort while others do not fixate on surpassing their dads, because that is an unattainable goal. For that second group of children, the final tally is less important than the series of separate journeys contained in the quest. I fall into the latter category because my father was the kindest, gentlest, and most decent man I have ever known.

This is about two vastly different sojourns: one my father took, which required physical and mental courage, and mine, which required neither. His was grandiose in scope; mine was miniscule by comparison. His was unusual, and the predicament that confronted him was unique; my journey was more mundane. Dad never witnessed mine; he passed away years before it started. Although this particular sojourn of his ended seven years before I was born, I can still see a portion of it. All I have to do is turn on the DVD player and watch parts of the HBO miniseries *Band of Brothers*.

In the tenth and last episode, the Americans were in a race with the French troops to be the first Allied soldiers to reach Berchtesgaden, the tiny Bavarian hamlet where Hitler and members of his hierarchy had summer homes. The American soldiers' progress on a cliffside road was stymied by the German SS troops who had dynamited the rocky hillside, completely blocking the highway. Major Winters sits patiently in his jeep and asked, "When are we expecting the engineers to arrive?"

Captain Nixon deadpans, "Half an hour ago," and I smile. One of the men they were talking about was my father. They were fortunate to have him.

He was working for Phillips Petroleum as a geologist when the war broke out and was given a deferment—finding oil was vital to the cause. As he drilled wells, one by one his friends peeled away from him, enlisted, and went off to war. Early in 1944, the 31-year old sat down with his wife, and they agreed he should give up his deferment.

In August of 1984, we sat together on the patio one night and he recounted his war experiences.

I asked him, "Why did you enlist?"

His initial explanation: he didn't want to be the only one of his friends who failed to serve. Then he mimicked what most of his friends had said, "To defeat Hitler." We sat quietly for 15 seconds as he debated whether to discuss those years in Europe and the real reason he gave up his deferment.

After clearing his throat, he mentioned a name. It was spoken only once and I have since forgotten it, but my father never did. Dad was born in Nebraska City, Nebraska, home of J. Sterling Morton, the man who gave us Arbor Day. When the Teten family moved to Lincoln, he met and befriended a man I will call Warren. The two went through elementary, junior, and senior high together and played football and baseball at Lincoln High School. Occasionally they combined to create mischief. Along with some junior classmates, they disrupted the senior prom—big time. The dance was going marvelously in the school when the younger boys sneaked into the basement, emptied their pockets, lit smoke bombs and ran away. Dozens of the little devils started spewing smoke that wafted up to the first floor and beyond. To a passerby, it appeared the school was on fire. Firemen flooded in as the prom participants poured out; it was a glorious success for Warren, Dad, and their co-conspirators.

My father remained in Lincoln to attend the University of Nebraska and kept in close contact with Warren. Following graduation, Dad moved away to begin his job with Phillips, but he corresponded often with his buddy, who had joined the Navy. In 1941, my parents became engaged. Warren was not able to share in the wedding on January 12, 1942, because on December 7, 1941, the Japanese attacked Pearl Harbor and the USS *Arizona* sank to the bottom of the harbor, killing 1,177 seaman, including Warren.

Dad stared at the ground and said, "He was my best friend."

Dad did not enter the military to avenge Warren's death; he did it to honor the memory of his best friend and for another, unstated reason. After the war, Robert Teten wanted to be able to stand as erect as the trees planted in Nebraska City, knowing he had done all that he could. In doing so, he would also get what every son wishes for: the admiration of his own father.

In the fall of 1944, he shipped out for Europe, almost halfway around the world from Pearl Harbor. Warren had died shortly after dawn on the first day of America's involvement in the war. The evening the Germans surrendered my father celebrated by drinking wine he had lifted from Hitler's personal cellar at Berchtesgaden, and at some point in the night he probably raised a glass to Warren. They were two boyhood chums from Middle America who had vastly different endings to their wartime experiences: one forever submerged in a ship in the Pacific Ocean and the other, days after leaving Berchtesgaden, accepted the surrender of thousands of German soldiers on a bridge at Salzburg, Austria, high in the Alps.

On a European vacation three decades later, he stood on that bridge with his wife. Days after they returned, a long rectangular package arrived at our house. Dad tore into the brown wrapping paper and opened the slender box. Mom groaned at the sight of the large oil painting, the quality of which was on par with those art shows that proclaim, "No painting over $100." He hung it at the end of the long entryway. Mom told anyone who would listen, "That's the ugliest thing I've ever seen." The amateurish brushstrokes depicted an Alpine scene. She hastily stitched a large needlepoint piece, had it framed, and sweetly told him, "I think my needlepoint is a better choice for this spot, don't you?" His contribution to their art collection was hidden in my old bedroom, out of sight.

A small watercolor had arrived in that same box, one mom displayed prominently. Beneath the gray sky in the background were snow-covered Alpine Mountains. In the middle section, steep hills on either side led to a valley and a large bridge that stood over a narrow river and in the foreground was a secluded chalet perched high on a hill surrounded by tall trees. Dad enjoyed the painting for the same reason he liked the larger one: the beauty of Bavaria reminded him of those first pleasant days after the war ended; a period of relief, jubilation, and excitement about returning home to a normal life.

To me, the scene depicted a cold, isolated locale far removed from civilization. Dad didn't view it that way; he had visited a much colder and more isolated place in the last days of the war and didn't need any reminders of it. Unlike my mother's experience, the ugliest thing he ever saw was real. No one knows how often those images skittered across the minds of the soldiers there that day, but I suspect all of them thought of that miserable spot hundreds of times more often than they uttered its name. The mental trip back was painful enough; rarely did they drag a listener along for company. They endured the knowledge of that day silently, not wanting to plaster the indelible memory on their friends and family like a dark ink stain on a white shirt. And they were right, as I found out on a warm August night a few years later. Some things stay with you forever: certain memories, like a conversation with your father when he decides to share the stain and you offer up your shirt, because it's the least you can do.

Around the time Dad and I sat down for that visit, my first attempt at writing was completed in 1980—a novel so dreadful that only a handful of unlucky friends ever saw it. Except for a few short stories written for my children, I did not pick up the pen again until 2001. The booster club co-chairs for the Austin High football team needed a parent to submit articles of the games to the *West Austin News*, and since my son was in the program, they picked me. Not the wisest of choices. In a state that bows before the altar of football, I was The Heretic, because I do not take the sport seriously. My goal was to expand the readership beyond the players and their parents. The first article was submitted on the day before September 11, 2001, and the events of that day did not keep me from adding a tincture of playful heresy to each game recap. Most articles had a theme that came to me as the contest unfolded, and they ranged from *The Scarlet Letter*, to *Custer's Last Stand*, a bullfight, and *A Tale of Two Cities*, to mention a few. My ploy proved successful; subscribers who did not have children at Austin High began following the Maroons and took an interest in their progress during the season, but amongst the football intelligentsia I had detractors.

One month after the season-ending playoff loss, I was at a Christmas party when one football father said, "Don't you ever write anything serious?" A smirk formed on my face, the same expression that had landed me in the principal's office on the last day of ninth grade at O. Henry Junior High.

The algebra teacher saw me sitting on the back row, sporting my infamous half-smile. That's when she lost it. Her long-sleeved silk, floral print dress began to ruffle as her body trembled in anger, and she spewed out, "Bill Teten! Wipe that *impish* grin off your face! I've *hated* that grin since the first day of school." The classroom was silent as we awaited the next explosive salvo. She had recently come back to work following a three-month sabbatical, and a particularly salacious and unsubstantiated rumor meandered through the school's hallways. It attributed her "absence" to a nervous breakdown, followed by a 90-day stint in the loony bin. Seeking to refute the rumor, she glared at me and said, "Apparently, there has been some discussion about why I was absent from school. I was gone because I had an operation." Pulling back her left sleeve to her bicep, she pointed at the oval-shaped skin graft in the crook of her elbow that was well-healed. Her eyes roamed over my classmates as she shouted, "See, there's the scar to prove it!" Many of them turned around and stared at me with mute expressions that seemed to say, "She was gone three months for that?"

While the students fidgeted in their seats, the teacher thrust her repaired arm in the direction of the door. "Bill Teten, out of my classroom. Go to the principal's office. Now!" I should have been embarrassed or felt like a condemned man walking to meet my deserved fate in the principal's office—a paddle whacking my backside—but I didn't. This was not the first time she had banished me from her class. I was just relieved that our year-long battle was finally over.

The principal groaned when he saw me at his door. "What did you do to her this time?"

"I smiled at her."

Motioning me to the couch, he slid a chair in front of me and sat down. "You don't like the woman, do you?"

"Not particularly, but she started into me on the first day of school and never let up."

"Did you ever talk with her and try to find out why?"

"No."

For five seconds he fidgeted in his chair, silently debating how much he wanted discuss. "She has had a very trying year; she has been through . . . a lot. More than most of us have to deal with in our daily lives. The last thing she needed was someone spreading rumors about her when she returned to school."

"I wasn't the one who started that rumor."

"But you didn't do anything to stop it, did you?"

"No, sir."

"You will learn in life that every person has their breaking point. Some deal with stress better than others, but all of us will snap if we are provoked enough. You spent a year goading that poor woman until she snapped."

He stood up and I asked, "So, you aren't going to paddle me?"

Forming a smile, he said, "No, that will be our secret." His eyes hardened. "Just remember, in the future if you cause someone to snap, the punishment may be worse than a trip to the principal's office."

The football dad studied my face and waited for a response. He was frustrated with The Heretic, or he was trying to goad me into writing more substantive stories. Either way, I understood what he meant: "It's time to give up your deferment on serious." I shrugged and walked away without uttering a word, yet I admired his intention and timing. It was December 11, 2001, the tenth anniversary of my father's death. The smirk lingered on my face for a few moments, because I knew something the football dad did not: the decision to tackle more serious fare had been made exactly six weeks before, on October 30, my father's birthday.

A re-run of the ninth episode of **Band of Brothers** was on that Tuesday evening, and it conjured thoughts of that warm August night Dad and I spent together on the patio. Like the altercation with my teacher, the words he spoke had not left my memory. He told me only a few people knew what really transpired on that tiny speck of Bavaria that day and he was right: the U. S. government did not release the secret report detailing the actions of a tiny number of American troops until 1991. I thought about my algebra teacher and what she had gone through; having never been in combat, I could not relate to it any other way. Whether that single day changed the life of Lt. Robert P. (Bob) Teten is unknown, but I suspect it did. Witnessing the three tenets of war—the good, the bad, and the ugly—all at once can do that to a person.

In Dante Alighieri's **The Inferno**, The Heretics inhabit The Sixth Circle. Dante's impressions of Hell were imaginings recounted in poetic verse. The level beneath The Heretics was real; my father had been there.

Part Two: The Seventh Circle

Around the midway point of episode nine of **Band of Brothers**, "Why We Fight," American transport vehicles that occupied both sides of the divided highway motored in one direction, while German soldiers who had surrendered marched the opposite way in the median of the road. As thousands of German troops gave up and trudged to the rear of the Americans' position, Hitler had others bombing bridges and fighting to the death to stall the advance of the Allied armies. Jaded from constant combat and watching their friends die beside them in battle, the Americans had become cynics of the war: they wanted the Germans to admit defeat and end the conflict. And they wanted to go home. One of them, Harvard-educated Corporal Webster sat in the back of an open truck and fumed, "Draggin' our asses halfway around the world, interrupting our lives. For what?" He stood and yelled at the German troops, "What the _ _ _ _ are we fighting for?"

On Saturday night, April 28, 1945, many Allied soldiers shared his anger and frustration, yet their thoughts were focused on tomorrow's mission: the battle for Munich. Occupation of the birthplace of Hitler's National Socialist Party would be a fitting death knell to the Third Reich. Portions of the American 42nd and 45th Infantries, the 101st Airborne Division's "Band of Brothers," and the 20th Armored Division were scattered to the west and north of Munich, preparing to bed down for the night.

A few miles up the road in Buchdorf, Lt. Bob Teten was just waking up. His 260th Engineer Combat Battalion was being reassigned again, which was nothing new. The previous Christmas Eve they had shipped out of Southampton and crossed the English Channel into France. During the next five months, they were attached to the 3rd, 7th, and 9th Armies, XV Corps, and 20th Armored Division, in addition to answering to the 1109th and 1101st Engineer Battalions. The 260th went where they were told and did not serve a particular master—one of the "bastard battalions." He said, "We were handed off more often than a church collection plate." On this night, the XV Corps was handing them off to the 20th Armored Division.

Dad preferred night assignments. Upon their arrival in France, his battalion had sped across the countryside just in time to join the XV Corps at the Battle of the Bulge. One of their duties was wiring explosives on bridges to halt the German Army in case an orderly retreat was necessary. Another involved snipping the dynamite wires on bridges where the Germans had placed explosives for the same reason. These missions were often performed under the duress of heavy machine-gun fire and incoming mortar bombardments. Dad said his sergeant saved Dad's life on many occasions, but never offered any examples.

317

The two acted as scouts numerous times after the Battle of the Bulge. Their job was to go in advance of the troops and check for tank traps—places Panzer tanks might lie in wait to ambush American troops—and pillboxes, where larger guns were trained on roadways. Of primary importance to the generals were the bridges. If the retreating Germans destroyed one, days could be lost. Dad didn't relish working in the frigid waters trying to fashion a pontoon bridge anymore than his superiors enjoyed waiting for the construction to be completed. The winter of 1944 was the coldest Western Europe had experienced in four decades: what some infantrymen did to keep their rifles from freezing was unorthodox, and unsanitary. Nighttime temperatures often dipped below zero, and barely reached the teens during the daylight, which seemed as fleeting as the warmth of precious moments spent in front of a log fire. Darkness came by 4:45 P.M. and lasted for 15 hours.

When asked if he ever killed any Germans, Dad responded, "No, but I could have. My sergeant and I would be driving along, and when they saw us coming they would run away or drop their guns and run away. I could have shot hundreds as they disappeared into the woods, but what would have been the point?" He paused, remembering how young they looked. "Most of them were kids . . . children."

Just before midnight on that chilly Saturday, with specific instructions not to venture too close to heavily-fortified Munich, the two traveled south from Buchdorf across the Danube River and reconnoitered the road for the large Allied troop movement scheduled for the morning. They made good time through the wooded area with the jeep's headlights off; the previous night a full moon had risen, and the bright orb faded only briefly when an errant cloud passed beneath it. Shortly after the vehicle rumbled by the hamlet of Petershausen, a cloudbank overshot them and dropped its precipitation: freezing rain. With the ground already saturated from earlier storms and visibility lowered from hundreds of yards to mere feet, the jeep sloshed through the muddy woods at what felt like a tortoise pace—five miles per hour—for hours. Eventually the system raced beyond them, and small cracks in the clouds released slivers of moon rays that acted like fractured flashlights, illuminating their way. Lt. Bob Teten shifted the jeep into the quieter second gear.

A large tufted cloud shrouded them in darkness minutes before the vehicle started to ascend a 45-degree embankment. Downshifting into first gear, he heard the jeep strain as it slogged up the muddy hill. The cloud broke apart, unveiling what lay above. The sergeant whispered, "Stop!" and they stared at the gates of Munich, yards away. Dad jammed into reverse gear and the jeep slid down the hill, spun around, and sped away with two men who were grateful the German sentries had not heard the vehicle's noise or their pounding hearts.

Retracing their route with headlights on, Dad and his sergeant meandered through the woods. Freezing rain came and went as they traveled northward. At intervals on that stormy night, the two scouts dipped into "The Third Circle of the torments," where "the frozen rain of Hell descends in torrents," (*Canto VI*) and passed within miles of the Seventh Circle of Dante's *Inferno*—Lower Hell—occupied by those who sinned against their neighbors, self, God, art, and nature: murderers.

> *We walked in silence then till we reached a rill*
> *That gushes from the wood; it ran so red*
> *The memory sends a shutter through me still.*
> — *Canto XIV*

Dad wasn't the only one driving around lost that frigid night. Another jeep attached to the 20th Armored was supposed to meet representatives from the 45th Infantry to coordinate artillery support for the assault on Munich later that day. By 12:30 A.M., the captain and his driver knew they had gone astray when the jeep crossed over the Würm River canal and its headlights shone on an iron gate with lettering. After opening it they found a light switch, turned it on, and stared into the spotlighted yard area. A few dead German soldiers were strewn across the enclosure, along with other corpses clothed in non-military attire. The glow from the strong bulbs gave out just as it reached a row of long, one-story buildings. In that scant space between fading light and pitch black, men wearing striped clothing looked out the windows of the nearest structure and stared back at the Americans who, unsure of what they had stumbled upon, lost and without military support, doused the lights, retreated, and drove off.

Hours afterwards, the American troops arrived and found a body dressed in striped clothes clinging to the electrified fence near the entrance; he had died chasing after the Americans as they departed. The captain and his driver heard nothing in the darkness and could not see the German soldier in the moat or the color of the water, but the next morning, others did.

Canto I: The Dark Wood of Error

When Dachau opened in 1933, it was the first "work camp" utilized by the Nazis. Factories dotted the 20-acre enclave, including one for munitions. The "workers" were German Communists, Social Democrats, and Jews, artists, intellectuals, gypsies, Catholics, and homosexuals. To oversee more than 30,000 workers detained against their will, the Nazis stationed a garrison of SS soldiers near the camps. At Dachau there were more than 1,400 of Hitler's revered troops. Heinrich Himmler oversaw the camps, and early on he used Dachau as a model for future sites. Rudolph Hess studied Himmler's system there, along with Adolf Eichmann, who devised and implemented Hitler's "Final Solution": the extermination of the Jews.

Hundreds, if not thousands, died at the hands of camp physicians responsible for performing experiments on prisoners. Questioned on liberation day about those gruesome tests, many SS soldiers shrugged, "They were all going to die anyway."

Shortly after the leaves fell from the trees in the fall of 1944, Dachau's role in the Third Reich changed. The Germans evacuated prisoners away from advancing Allied troops to more secluded camps; one of them was Dachau. Conditions worsened under the strain of thousands of additional people to house and feed, and a typhus epidemic erupted in the increasingly unsanitary environment.

By late April 1945, Polish Catholics comprised almost one-third of the 32,000+ held in the main Dachau compound; less than 10% were Jewish. On April 26, over 7,000 prisoners, mostly Jews, left Dachau headed south for Tergensee on what came to be known as the Dachau Death March. Many died en route from exposure, dehydration, or were shot when they were unable to keep up with the cortege. In freezing temperatures and rain, they walked silently through Gruenwald, Wolfratshausen, and Herbertshausen as locals peered at the procession through their windows. Rumors of such treatment and worse were not foreign to the townspeople, some of whom photographed the Death March. They knew places like Dachau existed, but they did nothing to stop the slaughter. As the Jews drifted past their eyes that day, some probably wished to, but they were outnumbered by those who felt the same as the SS soldiers: "They were all going to die anyway."

We came to the edge of the forest where one goes
From the second round to the third, and there we saw
What fearful arts the hand of Justice knows.
— Canto XIV

In the ninth episode of **Band of Brothers**, five men on patrol exit the edge of a forest. The camera focuses on their puzzled expressions, without revealing the object of their confusion. A bewildered soldier runs into town, finds Major Winters, and tells the officer they found something on patrol.

The Major asks, "Frank, Frank, what is it?"

The soldier shakes his head, "I don't know, sir. I don't know."

American troops descend on it, and a long scene of the human destruction plays out on the screen. Everyone there that day had a version of the events; some were more truthful than others. What the show did not chronicle were some of the things that haunted those eyewitnesses the rest of their lives: the hands of primal justice.

O you who come into this camp of woe
— Canto V

Members of the 45th Infantry "Thunderbird" Division were picked to liberate the Dachau concentration camp on the morning of April 29, 1945. Instead of entering from the main gate, the troops advanced along the railroad tracks and entered the SS garrison attached to the main camp. By the time the German SS troops surrendered, some members of the 45th were struggling to process the misery and carnage they had already seen. Officers from the 42nd Infantry Division later arrived at the southwest entrance of the complex. In Flint Whitlock's book *The Rock of Anzio*, he quotes Lt. William Walsh, "There's a big gate, and this German comes out of there. He must have been about six-four or six-five, and he's got beautiful blond hair. He's a handsome-looking bastard and he's got more goddam Red Cross shields on and white flags . . . My first reaction is, 'You son of a bitch, where in the hell were you five minutes ago before we got here? Taking care of all these people?'. . . Well, everybody was very upset. Every guy in that company, including myself, was very upset over this thing, and then seeing this big, handsome, son of a bitch coming out with all this Red Cross shit on him." The highest-ranking German officer, 2nd Lieutenant Heinrich Wicker, had recently returned from the Russian front and volunteered to surrender Dachau, so Commandant Weiss and the main SS force could escape under the cover of darkness the night before. Sometime after relinquishing the camp to the Americans, Wicker was escorted out of sight. His wife and children never saw him again.

American troops gathered a half-dozen or more German tower guards in front of the brick "B" tower and shot them dead. Near the southwest entrance of Dachau, Lt. Walsh ordered four surrendered SS members into a boxcar and emptied his pistol into the soldiers. An American private followed Lt. Walsh into the enclosure and ended the moans of the wounded men with his rifle.

Prisoners healthy enough to do so gathered by the thousands against the fenceline and cheered the arrival of their liberators and the frenzied attacks that followed. As some Nazi troops were rounded up, Americans turned away and allowed prisoners to savagely beat, dismember, and kill their former guards. Revenge was not limited to the SS troops. Dozens of prisoners judged to be "informers" met the same end.

A book written about that day claimed that all 560 Nazis on the grounds were killed, a charge refuted by eyewitnesses and the secret U. S. government report "Investigation of Alleged Mistreatment of German Guards at Dachau." The total number killed was closer to 50, approximately the number who were herded against a white wall near the camp hospital shortly following the Americans' arrival. Lt. Colonel Felix Sparks positioned a few of his men to watch the enemy and walked away. The unarmed Germans still held their hands above their heads when the machine gun began mowing them down. Lt. Sparks spun around, charged the gunner, and kicked him off the weapon. He picked the soldier up by his collar and yelled, "What the hell are you doing?" The 19-year-old private wept hysterically, "Colonel, they were trying to get away!"

All but 17 of the Germans survived. Americans walked among the SS troops looking for mortally wounded men, who expected to be relieved of their suffering by a shot to the neck—the coup de grâce, or stroke of mercy. Instead, one of them shielded his eyes as the pistol was lowered to his face. The gun blast blew away the top of his head.

Selecting the 45th Infantry to liberate Dachau was not the wisest choice. For more than 500 relentless days they had fought against the Italians and Germans from North Africa through Italy, then in France and Germany, with little respite. Another 19-year-old American soldier at Dachau explained the killings succinctly: the men had "gone berserk." They snapped. Perhaps the immaculately attired Wicker unwittingly goaded them when he greeted the liberators with the German salute and yelled, "Heil, Hitler!" But few Americans had found their breaking point during that first hour at Dachau; most were able to rein in their rage.

Some in the 45th thought what they saw in that first hour provided a plausible excuse for the vigilante soldiers' actions, but some high-ranking officers disagreed. Court-martial documents were given to General George Patton, who tore the papers apart and threw them in a wastebasket. The Germans at Dachau on April 29 were not SS-Totenkpfverbände, or Totenkopf, the "Death's Head" units responsible for controlling the concentration camps; Weiss had taken them with him the night before. Most of the Germans killed at Dachau were SS-Waffen. Even if Patton were privy to that nuance, it would not have mattered. Had he personally questioned the surviving Germans, they would have denied committing the atrocities later attributed to the "Death's Head" units. And his likely response would have been, "But you didn't do anything to stop it, did you?"

Some Americans snapped that morning, not from things they saw inside the camp, but from what lay beyond the barbed-wire fences along the railroad tracks—something the men of the 45th had walked past before entering Dachau.

Others told Lt. Bob Teten what to expect, so he grabbed his camera and made his way to the train. The first assault on his senses was invisible: a stench that made him stagger as it hit his nostrils and swirled around his mouth, before clinging to his tongue and nose hairs. There were no odors like this back in Nebraska.

As a little boy in Nebraska City, he sat in the grass and watched his father plant trees commemorating the birth of Dad's younger siblings, a German custom the family brought with them from the Fatherland. In the previous century, their ancestors had emigrated from the Friesland area in the northwest, as far removed from Dachau as a German region could be. And as he saw the first bodies lying on the gravel by the tracks Dad wondered how the birthplace of his great-grandparents could, in a few generations, spawn Germans capable of carrying out such an atrocity.

He halted at an open-air boxcar with wooden sides that rose four feet above its wheels. His shoulders were level with its floor as he leaned forward a few inches and peered inside the open door. Slowly, his eyes drifted over the contents of the car's left side, then returned to the center as his mind tried to register what he was seeing. The fingers of his right hand squeezed the camera tightly as he viewed the right side of the car before his eyes returned to the center. Dad stepped back and fixated on an object a few feet away: a face. Its two motionless eyes gazed back at him, the gaping mouth incapable of speech. But the death mask formed a question Bob heard over and over again. "Where *were* you when this was happening to us? Where *were* you. . . " And Lt. Teten wept.

The last train from Buchenwald

On June 2, three weeks following Germany's surrender and seven weeks after Buchenwald had been liberated, a passenger train departed the station near the concentration camp for Ecouis, in the Normandy region of France. Of the 427 Jewish survivors on board, some did not have suitable clothing for the six-day trip; they were forced to wear the only outfits available. On the initial stop in France, local townspeople became upset when they saw the attire. An official on board calmed the fears of the locals, then wrote on the side of the train:

KL Buchenwald
Waisen
Orphelins

KL was the German abbreviation for "Konzentrationslager," (concentration camp). The bottom two entries, respectively, were the German and French words for "orphans." The youngest boy was four, the oldest in his late teens. Only 30 were under the age of 13, but almost all of those wee ones were dressed in the uniforms of the Hitler Youth. A majority of them were Polish Jews separated from their parents, who had been sent to Auschwitz or other camps.

The rambunctious boys had been eager to flee Germany and regain their childhood and sense of humor. Before the train left Buchenwald, a playful survivor adorned the exterior of a passenger car with the words "Hitler Kapout [sic]" (Hitler is finished) in chalk. As the train traveled through Germany and France, other words chalked in a cursive hand by an older teenager puzzled most of the onlookers, because the question was in written in Yiddish. "Invo sind unsire elterin?" ("Where are our parents?")

The Dachau death train

On April 7, Allied troops were within four days of liberating Buchenwald when Germans marched thousands of prisoners to the train station where 39 boxcars lined the track (some reports stipulate as many as 50 were involved). Some of the open-air compartments had steel sides; most were fashioned from wood. The European-style cars were shorter than their American counterparts— capable of holding 40 German troops comfortably, but twice that number of prisoners were crammed into some containers, most of them Polish Jews. All were expected to die during the trip; they were being sent to Dachau to be cremated in the brick ovens.

The open, steel-sided coal cars allowed fresh air to wash over the men, but provided no protection against the snow, freezing rain, frigid nighttime temperatures, or American planes that were instructed to fire upon trains in the war zone. At least one strafed the Death Train with machine-gun fire, killing prisoners—the lucky ones, ending their misery.

Allied bombs had destroyed the tracks of the original route, so the train was forced to detour into Czechoslovakia and then wind its way back into Germany. The 200-mile trip, roughly the distance between Austin and Dallas, took three weeks.

Minimal light seeped through the wooden slats of the enclosed boxcars. The "displaced persons" were entombed in a locked space with no toilet, little water, and no food. Within days, urine and excrement were on the walls, floor, clothing, and thin blankets. Inside the cramped, dark space the number of dead mounted, many of whom weighed less than 70 pounds by the time they died. A thumb touching a middle finger would match the circumference of their forearms and biceps. The living lay in silence as the corpses emitted death gases, thankful for the darkness that prevented them from seeing what they smelled.

Those struggling in the open-air cars huddled next to the cadavers for warmth. Blankets covered their gaunt, sallow bodies as days turned into weeks; the dehydration, malnutrition, and freezing weather dried their mouths and sapped their withering bodies.

When the train arrived at Dachau on April 26 or 27, most were dead. German guards posted to watch them offered no succor to the living, the few men who had endured almost 21 days of starvation, filth, degradation, and death. Their triumph over insurmountable odds was short-lived. On the 28th, troops were ordered to kill the survivors. Hearing the gunfire, some prisoners managed to escape the enclosed boxcars. Others scaled the walls of the open cars and jumped down. All of those who made it to the gravel beside the tracks were shot.

The majority of the 2,300+ had passed away quietly during the trip, but a few did not. In an open-air boxcar, a dying man crawled over the stiff, putrefying bodies of his comrades and weakly worked his way across the car. In his delusional state, he probably thought Poland was just beyond the door. He succumbed a few inches before reaching it.

Lt. Teten turned away from the man's face, wiped his eyes, and continued along the tracks. After seeing all he could bear, he turned around and made his way to the compound. The Jorhaus, or gatehouse, was at the far end of the camp. Emblazoned on the gate were the words "Abreit Macht Frei" ("Work brings freedom.") Prisoners had passed through it on their way to the factories while a small orchestra played classical music. Dad chose the much closer southwest entrance that did not have words written above it, but he knew some appropriate ones. From *Canto I, The Vestibule of Hell*:

> *I AM THE WAY INTO THE CITY OF WOE.*
> *I AM THE WAY TO A FORSAKEN PEOPLE.*
> *I AM THE WAY INTO ETERNAL SORROW.*
> *ABANDON ALL HOPE YE WHO ENTER HERE.*

Walking through a small forest on the northwest portion of the grounds, he came to a secluded place. A ditch had been dug to catch the blood of the

5,000 Russian POWs and others who were shot at the firing range, their bodies were then dragged to the nearby building known as Baracke X. It had been constructed by prisoners whom the Germans had taught the building trade: Polish Catholic priests. Inside the crematorium were the brick ovens used to incinerate those Russians' bodies and tens of thousands of other victims of the Third Reich. A shortage of coal halted the process, but the dead continued to mount. Outside the building, an American soldier removed a tarp from a 5x20 foot stack and found the carcasses of hundreds of naked prisoners serried together, their bodies so intertwined it was impossible to distinguish one from the next. In the morgue room adjacent to the ovens, soldiers found another pile of skin and bones—corpses haphazardly tossed into the space. A few had toe tags, but most did not: the nameless dead.

> *The wood leaped with black bitches, swift as greyhounds*
> *escaping from their leash, and all the pack*
> *sprang on him; with their fangs they opened him*
> *and tore him savagely, and then withdrew*
> *— Canto XIII*

When the Americans advanced on Dachau, some of the German guards slipped into prisoners' clothing to escape detection, but they were rooted out by the "displaced persons," who mauled them. One guard was literally torn apart and his limbs were passed among the raised hands of a large congregation of prisoners standing near a fence line; they cheered his death with the same enthusiasm they showered on the Americans who came to liberate them.

Dad happened upon another guard's body. A prisoner had yanked barbed wire from a barrack window and ripped into the guard while an accomplice took a nail or crudely sharp object and did the same. They had pounded the German's face with a shovel repeatedly, until it was obliterated.

A hundred yards away, Lt. Teten halted at another lifeless figure. An American soldier turned to him and said, "They say this one was an inmate informer, sir." The striped clothing lay in tatters around the blood-drenched body. Much of the outer layers of skin on his arms, legs, and torso had been scraped off. "They used their fingernails." Dad stared at the mostly intact face; it reminded him of the Edvard Munch painting *The Scream*.

Death could scarce be more bitter than that place!
But since it came to good, I will recount
All that I found revealed there by God's grace.
— *Canto I*

Everywhere he looked there were dead—the number inside that five-acre tract neared 2,000. Other odors mingled with those of the decaying corpses: body waste, stench from the living who had gone weeks without bathing or changing clothes, and the breath of a thousand dying from typhus, which was spread by the pervasive body lice.

Dad approached a lone American private who was staring at the water tower. The soldier wiped his eyes and said, "Sir, have you heard? They said our planes bombed the water lines into the camp a few weeks ago."

"Is that water tower empty?"

"An interpreter asked one of the prisoners, and he answered, 'See for yourself.' One of our guys climbed up there and opened the hatch. He almost fell off; I guess the smell was pretty bad. He looked inside with a flashlight and didn't move for about ten seconds. Then he puked over the side, wiped his mouth with his sleeve, and yelled down, 'There're bodies in here!' Nobody said anything, so the guy kept yelling, "Did you hear me? There're goddam bodies in here!"'

The private's eyes moistened and he muttered, "I can't believe this place, sir. I, I just can't." Then the soldier quietly walked away, and Dad stared at the water tower.

Exiting one of the long barracks, he unzipped the lower pouch on the front of his uniform and dropped the camera in it, then zipped it closed. The last photo on the roll was of a dying man nestled between two cadavers. He checked his watch and knew the 260th would need to be leaving for Munich soon, so he started up the sidewalk.

Two buildings away, a man appeared at a barrack door and locked eyes with him. Hours before, the healthy prisoners had left their quarters to celebrate the liberation, and the Americans had been admonished, "Don't let them kiss you on the lips," for fear of contracting typhus. Still staring at Lt. Teten, the man began to move toward the main sidewalk. With each labored shuffle step his feet advanced six inches. The light and dark gray striped clothes, covered with grime and dirt, hid most of his 80-pound frame. Dad could have bypassed him by increasing his gait. Instead, he slowed his pace and still reached the spot where the paths intersected well before the feeble man did, and he waited.

Ashes, or earth that dry is excavated,
Of the same color were with his attire
— Dante Alighieri, *The Purgatorio, Canto IX*

"The angel is dressed in ashen-gray garments, the color (like that of earth) associated with penitence, humility." (Notes by Peter Bondanella and Julia Conaway Bondanella)

The man's facial bones looked like a pointy-backed chair draped with a sheet; the cheekbones jutting out against his sickly, bluish gray skin. His eyes were sunken, recessed, and black. The strain to reach the lieutenant had sapped the man's strength and he stopped. Dad approached him and the half-dead man tried to smile through the pain. Then he slowly raised his emaciated arms and held them out. Dad walked into them and the prisoner laid his head on the lieutenant's shoulder. Through the fabric, Dad could feel the man's bones as he gingerly placed his right hand on a protruding shoulder, while the fingers of his left hand feathered back and forth across exposed ribs. In a gravely voice, the man whispered softly, "Dziekuje. Dziekuje. Dziekuje." The Polish word for "Thank you."

Lt. Teten shed a tear for the skeletal man he held in his arms and the ones in the boxcars on the railroad tracks and the bodies dumped in the morgue of the crematorium. Then he glanced up in the sky and thought of Warren.

Part Three: Intermezzo

The hours spent at Dachau gave my father a deeper purpose of why he was fighting. Even though he did not say it, I knew that agonizing day had also affirmed what he had long wanted to believe—an observation he made after withdrawing from the arms of the Polish Catholic prisoner—that Lt. Bob Teten was an altruistic and virtuous person. A son who was worthy of the admiration of his father.

329

When the emaciated man hugged him, my father was filled with a profound sense of humility; he felt undeserving of the prisoner's gratitude. Hundreds of thousands of other soldiers merited thanks instead, especially his buddies who had died on the road to Dachau. In his mind, only a quirk of fate had placed him at that sidewalk inside the most infamous concentration camp ever constructed, on liberation day. From that bitter place, he accepted what he had been given, things he carried with him the rest of his life: humility and a commitment to charity, which had been revealed there by God's grace.

We sat on the patio listening to the cicadas. "I only wish I could have done more." Dad sipped his rum and coke to whet his mouth after the long monologue and continued, "I often wonder how many more lives would have been saved if we had gotten there a day, a week, or a month before. And then I think about people like Elie Wiesel, the writer. He was one of the Buchenwald orphans. That's what I try to concentrate on: the ones who made it and the impact they had on the lives of other people." He managed a faint smile and said, "Who knows, one of their children or grandchildren may help a Teten someday." The ripple effect.

Dad plucked the lime wedge from his glass, squeezed some juice into the drink and dropped the citrus back in the glass. His right index finger stirred the contents around a couple of times, then he clutched the cocktail napkin in one hand and set the highball glass on the wrought iron table with the other. We watched the whirlpool of sweet, sour, and potent concoction circle around until it was stilled. He took the napkin, wiped the fluid from his finger, and placed it next to the glass. Then he stood and walked in silence to the plate glass windows of the bedroom. After opening the sliding glass door, he stepped inside, brushed against the drawn curtains and turned around. Dad stared at me as he slowly pulled the door shut and flipped the lock. Then he disappeared behind the curtain and never mentioned Dachau again.

If I had rhymes as harsh and horrible
as the hard fact of that final dismal hole
which bears the weight of all the steeps of Hell
— The Inferno, Canto XXXII

After the war ended, members of the Nazi hierarchy were tried at Nuremberg. On October 16, 1946, Hitler's #2 man, Hermann Goëring cheated the executioner by swallowing cyanide two hours before his scheduled trip to the gallows. Ten other hangings went as planned that day, ending the lives of many of Hitler's most infamous minions: Keitel, von Ribbentrop, Kaltenbrunner, Frank, Jodl, and others. The bodies were photographed, and then, according to Anthony Read in his book *The Devil's Disciples* (W.W. Norton, 2004) they were "wrapped in mattress covers, sealed in coffins, then driven off in army trucks . . . to a crematorium in Munich, which had been told to expect the bodies of 14 American soldiers. The coffins were opened up for inspection . . . before being loaded into the cremation ovens. That same evening, a container holding all the ashes was driven away into the Bavarian countryside, in the rain. It stopped in a quiet lane about an hour later, and the ashes were poured into a muddy ditch." Another author states they were poured into a stream near Munich.

The final disposition of those ashes was less important to the Allies than how and where the bodies were actually destroyed, which was not a Munich crematorium. Instead, the vehicles that transported the bodies veered off and went to a place ten miles away. Under the cover of darkness, they went through the open Jorhaus gate where an orchestra had played while the "workers" filed by. The trucks rumbled past the barracks and the water tower, then crossed the bridge over the Würm River canal and entered a small forest. A hedge of tall poplars, manicured formal gardens, and birdbaths guided them to Baracke X.

At Dachau, the first concentration camp, the brick ovens that had incinerated tens of thousands of victims of the Third Reich were stoked. One by one, the 11 Nazis were laid on the two metal rods and inserted into the roaring furnaces. If the procedure went in alphabetical order, two of the last to burn would have been Fritz Sauckel, who oversaw the slave labor camps, and Julius Streicher, the most anti-Semitic of them all. And each time a steel door closed on that final dismal hole, one of Hitler's henchmen was reduced to smoldering ashes—in the ovens built by Polish Catholic priests.

Part Four: Symphony

The Munich photo lab technician was contrite with Lt. Teten when the American returned to pick up the pictures he had taken at Dachau. "Something happened; they didn't turn out. I apologize." My father knew why: the German was doing his part to erase any evidence of the Holocaust.

Anticipating that, General Maxwell Taylor ordered citizens of Dachau to show up on the morning after liberation day dressed in their Sunday best, and the locals were forced to bury some of the Dachau dead. General Eisenhower decreed the Death Train area off limits until reporters and photographers from the U.S. could fly over for a tour. In the meantime, members of the Hitler youth and high-ranking Nazis were paraded along the tracks and shown what their government had done.

On the United States Holocaust Memorial Museum website there are hundreds of photos depicting train scenes. Three show the Buchenwald orphans leaving for France. Many are of people boarding concentration camps transports or disembarking from them. At least 50 are graphic and heartbreaking shots of the Dachau Death Train. In one picture, a medic and infantryman are looking inside one of the enclosed boxcars. The camera's lens does not show any corpses, but it captures something else a few feet away, walking toward the car's open door: the kindest, gentlest, and most decent man I have ever known—Lt. Bob Teten.

After pledging to give up my deferment with regard to serious writing, it took a year for me to get "serious." The first two attempts were published in January 2003: "Changing Lives For Generations" and "Football's Lost Boys." That fall, I wrote "Death, Where Is Thy Sting?" the story of Randy McEachern's near-death experience during an anaphylactic reaction to wasp bites on a practice field at Austin High. His story and the football tale were submitted to the Texas Press Association's annual-contest: Randy's won nothing; the football saga came in fourth. I informed my wife of the snub and she asked, "So, is that why you started writing, to win awards?"

In early 2006, two of my friends died, and I wrote stories about them: "Brian Newberry: A Wonderful Life" and "Alec Beck: A Tribute." Soon after the second was published I called Randy, who had long ruminated on why he had been "thrown back," or allowed to live. He was not home, so I told his wife, Jenna, I knew of another reason. "Me. If Randy had not allowed me to do his story, I would not have had the confidence to do the ones on Brian and Alec. By helping me, Randy gave comfort to thousands of their friends who read the articles, many of whom Randy has never met." The ripple effect.

Brian and I sat down for an interview on December 14, 2005. For three months he had put me off, as the pancreatic cancer consumed his body, but he greeted me at the front door on that cold, gray morning with a warm smile.

He started a fire in the hearth and ambled over to a recliner. Easing himself into it, Brian leaned back and covered his body with a blanket that reached to his neck. For the next 75 minutes we discussed many subjects, including his extensive volunteer work and philanthropy. When that part of the chat concluded, Brian looked at me and echoed the words of my father, "I only wish I could have done more."

When it was time for me to leave, he followed me onto the front porch, and we talked a minute longer. The chilly air penetrated my heavy overcoat and Brian, dressed only in slacks and a dark sweater, trembled slightly.

I said, "Goodbye, Brian."

He smiled, and said, "Thank you." Then he raised his arms and hugged me, and as I returned the embrace, my left hand touched his ribs and my right rested on a shoulder.

During our talk, Brian had given me names of friends he wanted me to contact for the article. Tracking them down over the holidays was not easy; it took almost four weeks. On Tuesday, January 10, I called the managing editor of the *WEST AUSTIN NEWS,* and asked if she wanted the long article that week or the next?

"This week would be better."

I started it shortly after midnight, and when my head hit the pillow the bedside clock registered 4:00 A.M.

The next morning I e-mailed the story to the paper and dropped a copy off at the Newberry's. That evening I called the house to ask Brian's wife Gail if she had found it. Brian answered the phone and in a soft, strained voice, expressed his appreciation. We talked for a minute, and I said, "Well, Brian, I don't want you to waste your energy on me." I waited for him to say, "Goodbye," but during the moments that followed he was drawing the strength to say something else in a forceful voice.

"I love you."

I paused for a second and replied, "I love you, too, Brian."

Those were the last words we ever exchanged; he died the following Wednesday at 4:08 A.M., with his family at his side. Neal Newberry called that morning to let me know his brother had passed away and to tell me a few other things. When the family sat to discuss who would write the obituary and what it should include, Gail said, "What is there left to write?"

On Tuesday, the large, extended Newberry clan had gathered at the home; everyone knew the end was hours away. Each person spent time with Brian, saying goodbye. When it was Neal's turn, he sat beside his brother. They had been together for almost six decades and worked across the street from each other for 21 years. And in those dwindling moments they shared, Brian turned to his brother and asked, "Would you read me the article?"

Neal said it was not the first time Brian had made that request of a family member. Hearing those words, I think I experienced the same emotions my father felt when he hugged that prisoner on a sidewalk at Dachau: humility and a commitment to charity, and gifts of grace.

Three months after Brian's funeral, I returned to Tarrytown Methodist Church for Alec's service, and as I waited for it to begin, I thought about the similarities between the two men and others I had written about; common traits they shared with my father. All were altruistic and virtuous and possessed an abiding faith in a Higher Being, which manifested itself in their daily lives: each held fast to the belief that mankind is inherently good.

They were also extremely loyal to their friends, something I am reminded of whenever I look in my desk drawer and see the souvenir my father brought home from the war. He got it on the bridge at Salzburg, Austria, when the German soldiers were offering their surrender. An SS-Totenkopf officer, trained at Dachau, offered his weapon to dad. The soldier removed the metal clip from his belt loop. Attached to it were two metal bands that had the "SS" and "Death's Head" insignias on it, which were soldered to a metal sheath. Inside was a knife with writing etched on the blade: "Meine ehre heißt treue." (My honor is loyalty.)

I was not thinking about the knife on October 30, 2001, when I watched "Why We Fight." Earlier that afternoon, I had attended the funeral of a high school basketball teammate. Tyrone Johnson and I were not best friends like Warren and dad, but our relationship had been important to me. I knew I wanted to write stories about my father and "T," but my writing proficiency was not up to it. Instead, I added an "In Memoriam" paragraph about Tyrone onto the end of that week's football game recap.

Four years passed, and while I was selecting the previously penned columns that appear in this book, I wrote "What Mick Jagger Taught Me,"

"Capote and The Midnight Rambler," and "Death of a Bluebonnet," yet I knew the manuscript was not complete. Writing the two stories that nudged me into giving up my "deferment on serious" bring this journey to its conclusion, and the final words in Tyrone's tale, "The Black Swan," are the ones I typed on that October night.

So, why do I write? Archibald T. McAllister, in his introduction to *The Inferno* (Signet Classic edition) stated: "It treats of the most universal value—good and evil, man's responsibility, free will and pre-destination; yet it is intensely personal . . . ." That is also an apt review of this book. Dante and I share something in common with the passengers on the last train from Buchenwald: we were all orphaned. Dante's mother died when he was young and his father abandoned him. Those twin traumas affected how and what he wrote. I was lucky—my parents adopted me before I was three months old. Finding uplifting things to write about is much easier when you hold fast to the belief that mankind is inherently good.

When my father was working on that bridge in Germany, shells bombarded him. The mass media is constantly inundating us with negative news. Every time we turn on the television or read a newspaper, headlines highlight the problems in our cities, our country, and the world. A metaphor for my antidote comes from "Why We Fight," the ninth episode of *Band of Brothers*.

The first scene is set in the small, bombed out town of Thalem, Germany. A string quartet, similar to the one that serenaded the Dachau prisoners on their way to work, begins to play BEETHOVEN'S STRING QUARTET IN C-SHARP MINOR, OPUS 131. Dozens of townspeople rummage through the 20-foot mounds of rubble—bricks, mortar, and debris—searching for salvageable items: a two-legged table, rugs, a cane back chair, and whole bricks. The stucco side of a building overlooking the tiny square had crumbled during the shelling, and the Band of Brothers stand in an opening on the second floor. The last scene in the episode segues from Dachau back to Thalem, and the conclusion of Beethoven's piece. The musicians finish the opus and their elderly leader places his violin in its case, fastens the bow to the inside top, and closes it. In a close-up, the small black case resembles a coffin. The camera freezes on it for a few seconds, then the screen goes dark.

Most of us trudge through the grind of daily life; we are not attuned to that music. Like the Band of Brothers, I was fortunate to have heard them—

the stories that are in this book. Symphonies often begin and end with the same notes. Throughout the composition, there are adagios and intermezzos separating the grander movements. Some of the tales in this tome are majestic; others are intermezzos and adagios. A number of the people featured in them have been lowered into the ground, while others live on, but all of their stories deserve to be told. Because these stories affirm what we strive for every day of our lives: the opportunity to make our fathers proud, by improving the human condition.